THE DARK S

Roger Brook—Prime Minister Pitt's most daring and resourceful secret agent—had sailed for the West Indies with a party that included three beautiful women. His purpose: pleasure. But the Caribbean, blue seas, lush tropical islands, and palm-shaded beaches, was infested with pirates. The slaves of the 'Sugar Islands' were in revolt. All this Roger Brook encountered. But also he uncovered a mysterious episode in the early life of the Empress Josephine—a mystery that had its effect on the Parisian intrigue that led to Napoleon receiving his first great command: the Army of Italy. A mystery that tied together many strange scenes and unlikely events.

BY DENNIS WHEATLEY

NOVELS

The Launching of Roger Brook
The Shadow of Tyburn Tree
The Rising Storm
The Man Who Killed the King
The Dark Secret of Josephine
The Rape of Venice
The Sultan's Daughter
The Wanton Princess
Evil in a Mask

The Scarlet Impostor
Faked Passports
The Black Baroness
V for Vengeance
Come Into My Parlour
Traitors' Gate
They Used Dark Forces

The Prisoner in the Mask
The Second Seal
Vendetta in Spain
Three Inquisitive People
The Forbidden Territory
The Devil Rides Out
The Golden Spaniard
Strange Conflict
Codeword—Golden Fleece

Dangerous Inheritance
The Quest of Julian Day
The Sword of Fate
Bill for the Use of a Body

Black August
Contraband
The Island Where Time Stands Still
The White Witch of the South Seas

To the Devil—A Daughter
The Satanist

The Eunuch of Stamboul
The Secret War
The Fabulous Valley
Sixty Days to Live
Such Power is Dangerous
Uncharted Seas
The Man Who Missed the War
The Haunting of Toby Jugg
Star of Ill-Omen
They Found Atlantis
The Ka of Gifford Hillary
Curtain of Fear
Mayhem in Greece
Unholy Crusade

SHORT STORIES

Mediterranean Nights
Gunmen, Gallants and Ghosts

HISTORICAL

A private Life of Charles II
(*Illustrated by Frank C. Papé*)
Red Eagle
(*The Story of the Russian Revolution*)

AUTOBIOGRAPHICAL

Stranger than Fiction
(*War Papers for the Joint Planning Staff*)
Saturdays with Bricks

Dennis Wheatley

The Dark Secret of Josephine

ARROW BOOKS

ARROW BOOKS LTD
178–202 Great Portland Street, London W1

AN IMPRINT OF THE HUTCHINSON GROUP

London Melbourne Sydney
Auckland Johannesburg Cape Town
and agencies throughout the world

*

First published by
Hutchinson & Co (*Publishers*) Ltd 1955
Arrow edition 1961
Second impression 1965
Third impression 1966
This new edition 1970

*Made and printed in Great Britain
by The Anchor Press Ltd,
Tiptree, Essex*

ISBN 0 09 003680 8

DEDICATION

For

CECIL BLATCH

Whose wise counsel and friendship have meant so much to me since I came to live at Lymington, and for

CECILIA,

with my love to you both.

Contents

1

Now Robespierre is Dead?

The two men had breakfasted together off Dover soles, beefsteaks weighing a pound each, and cold-house peaches; then as it was a fine August morning, they had taken the decanter of port out into the garden.

The host was William Pitt the younger, Prime Minister to King George III; the place, his country home, Holwood House near Hayes in Kent; the guest, Mr. Roger Brook, his most successful secret agent; the year, 1794.

Although only thirty-five, Mr. Pitt had already guided the destinies of Britain for eleven years. During them he had spared himself nothing in a mighty effort which had brought the nation back from near-bankruptcy to a marvellous prosperity, and for the past eighteen months he had had the added responsibility of directing an unsought war, to wage which the country was hopelessly ill-prepared; so it was not to be wondered at that he looked far older than his age.

The fair hair that swept back from his high forehead was now turning grey, and below it his narrow face was deeply lined. The penetrating power of his glance alone indicated his swift mind, and his firm mouth his determination to continue shouldering the endless burdens of the high office which he arrogantly believed he had been born to occupy. A chronic shyness made him aloof in manner, and as with the years he had gone less and less into society he had become the more self-opinionated and dictatorial. He had the mental fastidiousness of a scholar and an aristocrat, but this did not extend to his clothes and the grey suit he was wearing gave him a drab appearance.

By contrast his companion, sheathed in a bright blue coat

with gilt buttons, a flowered waistcoat and impeccable fawn riding breeches, appeared an exquisite of the first order; but Roger Brook had always had a fondness for gay attire. At twenty-six he was a fine figure of a man, with slim hips and broad shoulders. His well-proportioned head, prominent nose and firm chin proclaimed his forceful personality. Yet at the moment, he looked as though he should have been in bed under the care of a doctor instead of discussing affairs of State with his master.

That he, too, even when in normal health, gave the impression of being older than his years was due to his having run away from home at the age of fifteen, rather than follow his father, Rear Admiral Brook, in the Navy, and the hazardous life he had since led. Danger, and the necessity for secrecy, had hardened his naturally sensitive mouth, although it still betrayed his love of laughter and good living; while his bright blue eyes, with their thick brown lashes that had been the envy of many a woman, showed shrewdness as well as mirth. But now those eyes were pouched, and his cheeks sunken, owing to innumerable sleepless nights; for he had only recently escaped from the horrors of the French Revolution, through which he had lived for many months, never knowing from one day to another when he might be betrayed, arrested and sent to the guillotine.

Although Roger reported to his master only at long intervals, he was regarded by him more as a friend than an employee, and had come to know his habits well. Being aware that the impecunious but incorruptible statesman could not afford a private secretary, and had such a strong aversion to writing letters that he left the greater part of his correspondence unanswered, he had sent no request for an interview. Instead he had risen early and ridden the sixteen miles across country, south of London from his home in Richmond Park; over Wimbledon Common, through orchards, market gardens and the pretty villages of Tooting, Streatham and Bromley. On previous visits to Holwood he had found that Mr. Pitt kept no secrets from such men as his cousin, Lord Grenville, who had the Foreign Office, his colleague, Harry Dundas, or William

Wilberforce, Bishop Tomline and the few other intimates whom he entertained in his country home; so he had felt sure that he would be invited to make his report over breakfast, but it had chanced that the great man was alone that morning, and Roger had had his ear without interruption.

Stretching out a long, bony arm Mr. Pitt lifted the decanter across the iron garden table towards his guest, and remarked: 'The nightmare scenes of which you tell me are scarce believable. Yet that four men should have been needed daily to clean the conduit from the guillotine to the sewer, lest the blood clot in and choke it, provides a practical yard-stick to the enormities committed by these fiends. Thanks be to God that at last they are overthrown, and France can look forward to a restoration of sane government.'

When Roger had filled his glass he shot an uneasy glance above its rim. This was not the first occasion on which he had felt it his duty to endeavour to check the Prime Minister's habitual but often ill-founded optimism, and he said with marked deliberation:

'It would be rash to count the Terror fully ended, Sir.'

'Oh come!' Mr. Pitt shrugged his narrow shoulders. 'You have just confirmed yourself what others had already told me, of the populace going wild with joy at the sight of Robespierre being carted to execution.'

' 'Tis true: and all but a handful of the French are now so sickened of the Revolution that they curse the day it started. The state of dread and misery to which all honest folk had been reduced before the recent crisis had to be witnessed to be believed. With everyone in Paris going in fear of their lives it's not to be wondered at that the fall of the principal tyrant led to an outburst of rejoicing. Yet, even so. . . .'

With an impatient gesture Roger's master cut him short. 'No government can suppress a whole people indefinitely, and it is evident that an explosion was due to take place. Now that the great majority have so clearly signified their antagonism to the excesses committed in the past, no new set of masters will be tolerated unless they conform to the general wish for a return to the protection of life, liberty and property by properly constituted courts of law.'

'I grant you that would be the case here, Sir; but, believe me, it does not apply in France. There the people have no means of removing power from the hands of those who have usurped it, except by a counter-revolution; and all the men capable of organising a *coup d'état* are now either dead, in exile or in prison.'

'You are wrong in that!' Mr. Pitt spoke cheerfully, and took a quick swig at his port. 'The events of Thermidor were in themselves a counter-revolution.'

Roger shook his head. 'If you think that, you have been misinformed. They were no moves against the political principles by which France has been misgoverned since the Jacobins got the upper hand. It was a purely domestic upheaval in which a group of unscrupulous demagogues succeeded in seizing the leadership from others of their own party. Those who are gone and those who remain have all subscribed to the extremist policy of the Mountain, and with others of the same kidney have been jockeying among themselves for power for many months past. It began with an intricate three-corner fight. The Hébertists were the first to succumb. They were the brains behind the *sans-culottes,* and with their fall the mob became a headless monster. One might have hoped then for better things, but the Terror continued unabated. In April the Dantonists followed them to the scaffold. That may have appeared a setback for more moderate councils, but I assure you that had they triumphed they would have continued to slaughter everyone who attempted to oppose their plundering the nation like a gang of robbers and turning Paris into one vast brothel. There remained the triumvirate of Robespierre, Couthon and St. Just. None of these so-called 'incorruptibles' was as venal as Danton or as vile as Hébert, yet they used the guillotine more ruthlessly than either. They had to, in order to keep themselves in power. Now they too are gone, but only to be replaced by others all of whom are steeped in innocent blood up to the elbows.'

For a moment Mr. Pitt continued to gaze placidly across the close-cropped sunlit lawn, then he said with an air of reasonableness: 'Mr. Brook, the extraordinary position you achieved for yourself enabled you to follow the inner workings of the Revolution so closely that I count you the first authority in England upon it. Yet I believe you to be wrong in your assessment of the future. The necessity you were under to escape from France via Switzerland, followed by your long journey home via the Rhine and the Low Countries, has placed you out of touch with events. You can know little of what has occurred in Paris since you left it towards the end of July, wheras I have had many more recent advices; among them that a strong reaction to the Terror has definitely set in, and that no less than ninety-five of Robespierre's associates have followed him to the scaffold.'

'That is excellent news.' Roger smiled; but added the caution: 'Yet its true import depends on who they were. Should they have been only the Incorruptibles' personal hangers-on it means little. If, on the other hand, Billaud-Varennes, Collot d'Herbois, Fouché, Barère, Vadier, Carrier, Fouquier-Tinville, Fréron and Tallien were among them, then there are real grounds for your optimism.'

'Fouquier-Tinville has been impeached; but in this connection I recall no other of the names you mention.'

'In that case, Sir, it would be wrong of me to encourage your hopes. When I left, Billaud and Collot had, by opposing Robespierre, retained their seats on the all-powerful Committee of Public Safety. The one superintended the massacres at the prisons in September '92, during which the Princess de Lamballe with scores of other ladies, priests, and nobles were brutally butchered; the other, jointly with Fouché, organised the *mitraillades* at Lyons, whereby many hundreds of Liberals were destroyed *en-masse* with grape-shot. Tallien, while proconsul at Bordeaux, decimated the upper and middle classes of that city; and last winter, after Admiral Lord Hood was forced to abandon Toulon, Fréron turned that port into a blood bath. Carrier, as you must know, has become forever infamous for his mass drownings of men, women and children in the Loire. It is said that during four months of his tyranny at Nantes he has slain not less than fifteen thousand people. While such monsters still have the direction of affairs, what possibility can there be of a return to the humanities?'

A frown creased the Prime Minister's lofty brow, and he said a shade petulantly: 'I find your assessment of the situation most disappointing, Mr. Brook; particularly as you played no small part yourself in bringing about the downfall of Robespierre. For that all praise is due to you; but you would have risked your head to better purpose had you chosen as your co-conspirators men whose qualities would have made them less likely to follow the policies of their predecessors after the blow had been struck.'

Roger would have been angry had he not known how little his great master understood the involved development of the Revolution. Having with one of his riding gloves, swatted a wasp that was displaying interest in his port, he replied with commendable patience: 'When I last waited upon you, Sir, at Walmer Castle, it was agreed that I should do what I could to weaken the regime in France by setting her rulers against one another. But this was no case of pitting a few game terriers against a pack of giant rats. I had to deal with a single hydra-headed monster, and all I could do was to induce its heads to attack each other.'

'Very well, then. Tell me now more of the men you picked on to serve your ends. What sort of a fellow is this Barras, who has suddenly become so prominent?'

'He is a *ci-devant* Count who has seen military service in India. Last winter as a general at the siege of Toulon he showed considerable ability, and it was there I met him. I chose him because he is ambitious, fearless and a good leader; but he is the most dissolute and unscrupulous man one could come upon in a long day's march.'

'And Dubois-Crancé?'

'Although a civilian, he too has played a prominent part in directing the revolutionary armies, and instilling some degree of discipline into them. It is to that he probably owes his life, as he is one of the few moderates with a first-class brain who has survived the Terror. His value lay in his ability to rouse the cowardly deputies of the Plain from their lethargy, so that they would support the attack that was to be made on Robespierre in the Convention.'

'He sounds a promising man; but need you have

approached an avowed terrorist, like Tallien?'

'It was essential to include one of the original mob-leaders. Only so could the base of the movement be made broad enough to insure against the *sans-culottes* rising in defence of the Robespierrists. I chose Tallien for the role because the beautiful aristocrat whom he is said to have married lay in prison under sentence of death, and in joining us lay his one hope of saving her.'

'What of the others who were later drawn in by the three of your own choice?'

'Unfortunately those who proved most valuable as allies in the plot were all men I would gladly have seen dead. Among them were the despicable Abbé Sieyès, the terrorist Fréron, and my own most dangerous enemy Joseph Fouché, who adds to his other crimes the role of the Revolution's high-priest of atheism. The only bond they had in common was the knowledge that if they did not swiftly strike at Robespierre he would have all their heads in the basket before they were a month older. But mutual fear spurred them to sink their differences and pull him down.'

'And you think this godless, blood-stained crew will be able to maintain themselves in power?'

'There being no opposition worthy of the name, I can see nothing to prevent a number of them doing so. They will, of course, fight among themselves, and some of their heads will fall; but between them they now control the two great *Comités*, the National Guard, the Army and the vast secret police organisation built up during the Terror; so those among them who survive will be able to rule in the same arbitrary fashion as their predecessors.'

'That they might be able to I will grant you, but that they intend to do so I regard as unlikely,' the Prime Minister remarked with a sudden display of his dictatorial manner. 'You are not up to date with the news, Mr. Brook, or you would realise that in the past month the French government has shown a definite change of heart. The iniquitous Law of the 22nd Prairial has been repealed, the Revolutionary Tribunal has been reorganised to give it some semblance of a court of justice, and hundreds of prisoners have been released from the Paris jails.'

With a disarming smile Roger replied: 'I am most pleased to learn of it, but not at all surprised. I felt confident that once the fanatics had been brought to book a marked decrease in senseless savagery would follow. The new masters are no set of fools, and one could count on their pandering to the reaction so far as they felt that they could win cheap popularity at no risk to themselves. But it would be a great mistake to regard these measures of clemency as a sign of weakness.'

'I said nothing of weakness. I spoke of a change of heart. I am informed that in Paris there is already wide-spread talk of a return to the Constitution of '91, and a restoration of the Monarchy.'

'I pray you, Sir, put no credence in such rumours.'

'Why?' Mr. Pitt refilled his glass and gave the decanter a quick push in Roger's direction. 'You say that these people are no fools. Now, then, is the chance for them to show real statemanship. With the temper of the nation so clearly known they might take the tide at flood and execute a complete volte-face. Did they call off the war and invite the armies of the Princes to enter Paris they would be rewarded with fortunes, honours and the gratitude of their fellow countrymen. Consider how much they have to gain by such a move.'

'On the contrary, Sir, they would have all to lose. Every one of them voted for the death of Louis XVI. To them more than most applies the saying "Put not thy trust in Princes". Were I in their shoes I would regard signing a pact with their Highnesses, his brothers, as putting my hand to my own death warrant.'

'Your travels have made you cynical, Mr. Brook.'

'Nay, Sir; but "a wee bit canny", as my dear mother would have said.'

'An excellent quality for one whose life has depended on his discretion, as yours must often have done. Yet it is a mistake to allow the caution you would exercise yourself to blind you to the possibility that others may take big risks to win great rewards.'

Distinctly nettled, Roger retorted with an angry flash in his blue eyes: 'There have, Sir, been many occasions when

I have done so in your interests. Nevertheless I would serve you ill did I not caution you now against succumbing to delusions that events in France will take the happy turn you so obviously expect.'

Having given vent to this outburst, he began to wonder if, in his anxiety to counter the Prime Minister's optimism, he had not somewhat over-stated his case. Before leaving Paris he had himself felt certain that the Terror had passed its peak, and it was possible that he had underestimated the strength and swiftness with which reaction would set in. Yet, as he recalled the many fierce, uncouth, suspicious, brutal men who had played so large a part in making the Revolution, and still occupied key posts in its administration, he remained convinced that they would go to any lengths rather than enter into a compromise with the *émigrés*.

After a moment Mr. Pitt had the grace to say: 'I intended no reflection on your courage. No one could have shown more audactiy than yourself in your numerous attempts to rescue members of the Royal Family; and it was hard indeed that misfortune should have dogged you to the very last, when you actually believed that you had secured the little King of France.'

Roger gave a bitter laugh. 'Fate can rarely have played a man a more scurvy trick than that, for I shall never now be able to collect the hundred thousand pounds you promised me for the safe delivery of his person.'

For a little they fell silent and the quiet of the garden was broke only by the drowsy hum of bees among the flowers in the nearby borders; then the Prime Minister said thoughtfully: 'You say that the child who is still in the Temple had been walled-up for six months, and that during that time his food was passed to him through a grill which prevented even his jailers seeing him. It is not to be wondered at that when you broke your way in you found him living like an animal, in an indescribable state of filth, scrofulous and ulcerated from neglect, and so ill that he could do no more than mutter a few almost incoherent words. Yet it seems to me that such conditions would have changed any child beyond normal recognition. Are you convinced beyond any shadow of doubt that he was not Marie Antoinette's son?'

'Certain of it, Sir. This child was at least two years old, and I had known the Dauphin well. Barras and Fouché saw him shortly after I did, and both were equally convinced that some other child had been substituted for the little Capet.'

'And you think the substitution was made by Simon on the orders of Chaumette or Hébert, at the time of the walling up, in January?'

'Yes; and since all three of them are dead there are no possible means of tracing the victim of their intrigue.'

'Victim, in its full sense, may not be the appropriate word. The poor child may still be a captive in some Parisian cellar, or hidden on a lonely farm.'

Roger had never previously lied to his master, but he did so now. He knew Louis XVII to be dead. How and where the boy had died was a secret that he had no intention of ever telling anyone, and the knowledge of it could be of no value to Mr. Pitt, so he said:

'Should that be so, and there is a counter-revolution in a few years' time, the people now acting as his jailers may pretend that they kept him hidden for his own safety, and produce him in the hope of receiving a great reward. But I greatly doubt it. When I last saw the boy his mind had been so brutalised and bemused by Simon that he had already almost forgotten that he was born a Prince; and it is most unlikely that whoever took him from the Temple would have disclosed his identity to his new guardians, for to do so would have been to risk their using him for their own ends. My own belief is that the sadist Hébert murdered him rather than allow Robespierre to get possession of so valuable a card. Otherwise, when he and Chaumette were brought to trial in March, why did not one or other of them offer to produce the priceless hostage they held in exchange for their own lives? In any case, the wretched child had been reduced to a state which made him hopelessly unfitted to succeed; so the wisest course would be to leave him out of all future calculations and account him dead.'

Mr. Pitt refilled his glass from the half-empty decanter, and murmured: 'Mayhap you're right; but 'tis a tragedy that bodes ill for the future of France.'

'Why so, Sir?'

'Because we must now regard his uncle, that pig-headed fool the Comte de Provence, as Louis XVIII. Had you succeeded in bringing the boy here we might have been able to make something of him, and sent him back well grounded in our democratic ideas to play the part of a good Constitutional Monarch. As things are now, when de Provence ascends the throne, so full is he of antiquated prejudices, he will endeavour to set the clock back a hundred years, and rob his people of the long overdue liberties they won for themselves in the early days of the Revolution. Then we shall be faced with the dilemma whether to continue our support of him as France's legitimate ruler, or stand by while the people revolt again, and perhaps once more become a menace to order and security throughout Europe.'

'It will be a long time before you are called on to add that problem to your other worries,' Roger said with a shrug.

'On the contrary,' came the swift reply. 'I foresee myself having to do so within a year from now.'

With a somewhat rueful smile, Roger enquired: 'Am I to take it then, that you still believe me wrong in my assessment of the way things will go in Paris?'

'No. Your appreciations have always been so well founded that you have sadly reduced the hopes I had of being able to make a peace with the new government. But there are other means by which the French nation may be brought to reason, and I had in mind the advance of the Allied armies.'

'Strap me!' exclaimed Roger, drawing up his long legs with a jerk. 'Do you then believe, Sir, that within a measurable time they are capable of achieving a conclusive victory?'

'I shall be much surprised if they do not. 'Tis true that we have suffered a considerable setback owing to the victory the French gained at Fleurus towards the end of June; but the daily increasing strength of the Coalition should soon do far more than make good that misfortune. In return for handsome subsidies, which owing to good management Britain can afford to pay, both Austria and Prussia are putting new contingents in the field, and our measures for raising many more troops in this country are at last taking effect.'

'When I saw you at Walmer in February you spoke of raising eight new regiments this autumn. Is it to them that you refer, Sir?'

'It is,' Mr. Pitt replied with a self-satisfied nod.

Mentally Roger groaned. Aloud he said: 'Then you must forgive me if I doubt the ability of such a reinforcement, plus some hired Germans, to turn the scale against the levies raised this year by the French. The indefatigable Carnot, whom I believe history will rank as the greatest War Minister France has ever had, set himself to raise fourteen armies, and he is well on the way to succeeding.'

'Fourteen rabbles, Mr. Brook! Fourteen rabbles! I'll warrant you that any of them would show their heels at the very sight of a battalion of His Majestys Foot Guards.'

'I'll not argue that. But I would be mightily interested to hear on what you base your hopes of a victorious campaign. In '92 and '93 the road to Paris was on numerous occasions left open, yet the Allies failed to take it. There is no particular reason to suppose that such opportunities will recur, and the Republican troops are in far better trim than they were then.'

The Prime Minister airily waved a long graceful hand. 'I agree that good opportunities were lost; but that was due to divided councils among the allied Generals, and now they are much more at one. As for the improvement in the French troops which you suggest has taken place, that will be more than offset by the handicap they are bound to suffer from incompetent leadership.'

'I fear I am at a loss in seeking grounds for your last statement, Sir.'

'Why, Danton at least had the sense to realise that armies cannot be handled by *sans-culottes*, and while he was War Minister continued to employ experienced commanders. Ask yourself what has become of them?'

'Lafayette and Dumouriez came over to the Allies. The Duc de Biron, Luckner, Custine, Houchard, and the Vicomte de Beauharnais were sent one after the other to the guillotine.'

'Precisely! The Robespierrists knew nothing whatever of military affairs. Any General who served them had only to suffer one reverse to be recalled, accused of treachery, and executed. The French had decapitated their own army. That is why its defeat should now prove easy, and Christmas see the Allies in Paris.'

With an uneasy glance, Roger said: 'You appear to have taken no account, Sir, of the ability which has been displayed by the young Generals who are products of the Revolution. Pichegru, Hoche and Jourdan, the present commanders of the armies on the Rhine, the Moselle and in Flanders, have all shown a natural flair for directing operations. The last, since his victory at Fleurus, has already wrested from us all the difficult country cut up by the Lys and the Scheldt.'

'What does that signify while we still hold the fortresses of Landrecies, Quesnoy and Velenciennes? By his rash advance he has thrust his head into a noose. Prince Coburg and His Highness of York will be monstrous unlucky should they fail to trap him there. Besides, France cannot much longer afford to support a war. Her finances are in chaos, her people starving and her coasts blockaded.'

''Tis true that the past five years of upheaval have entirely wrecked the former administrative machinery of the country; but, believe me, Sir, Cambon, Cambacérès, Dubois-Crancé and others have made good that handicap by brilliant improvisation.'

'Mr. Brook, an understanding of finance is not among your many talents. You may take it from me that the total destruction of a fiscal system that it took many centuries to build up must lead to bankruptcy. Wars cannot be fought without money, and a drying up of supplies must soon cripple the French armies to such a degree that they will fall an easy prey to the Allies.'

Roger forbore to comment further. His private opinion was that his master knew even less about military affairs than had the Robespierrists, and that while they had at least had the sense to give a free hand to the brilliant Carnot, he was becoming a menace to his own most cherished hopes by putting a distorted interpretation on facts whenever they did not fit in with his own opinions.

Having emptied his last glass of port, Mr. Pitt enquired casually: 'When do you plan to return to France?'

With equal casualness, Roger let fall the bomb-shell that he had come determined to deliver with his report that morning: 'I had not thought of doing so, Sir.'

'What say you?' exclaimed his master with a startled look.

'I was loath to return when I did in February, and now I am definitely set against it. In the past two years I have spent less than three months with my wife; and that is far too little for a couple who have some fondness for one another.'

No woman had ever played a part in the life of the austere Prime Minister, so it was difficult for him to appreciate how other men could allow the attractions of feminine society to distract them, even temporarily, from the nation's affairs. With marked coldness he spoke his mind.

'If I remember aright, you gave two of the best years of your life to honeymooning in Italy and afterwards idly dancing attendance on your wife; so even if your work has since taken you from her for long periods, she has no great grounds for complaint. Officers in our ships and more distant garrisons frequently do not see their families for six years at a stretch; so I pray you do not detract from my good opinion of you by allowing the calls of domesticity to ring louder in your ears than those of duty.'

''Tis not that alone, Sir; but also the strain I have been under these many months past. You can have little conception what life was like in Paris this spring and summer. The elimination of the nobility, the priests and the well-to-do had long since been achieved, and the Terror was turned against anyone and everyone who cherished the mildest belief in the liberties the Revolution had been initiated to bring. The Committee of Public Safety had its spies everywhere and acted with fanatical ruthlessness. Each night hundreds of surprise domiciliary visits were paid, and the discovery of a fire-arm or a letter from a relative who had fled abroad was enough to land a whole family in jail. Every morning the letter-box of the infamous Public Prosecutor, Fouquier-Tinville, was stuffed with scores of denunciations, and nine out of ten of those anonymous accusations became a death-warrant for the person named. For a single indiscreet expression, or open grumbling in the bread queues, people were seized upon and condemned to death. Even the *sans-culottes* had becomed cowed and no longer dared to question the will of the camarilla that held the whole nation enslaved. I was unable to prevent the death of one I dearly loved, and had to stand by while others died for whom I had considerable affection. Every hour of every day was like living through a nightmare, and I'll have no more of it.'

Mr. Pitt nodded, and his voice took on a more sympathetic tone: 'That is another matter. Such conditions would in time undermine the fortitude of any man, and when I first saw you this morning I thought you looking far from well. 'Tis clear you need a period of relaxation.'

To this belated recognition of his unhappy state, Roger replied with a bitter smile: 'Sir, I am sick in mind and body, and need far more than that to make me my own man again.'

'Oh come! 'Tis not too late in the year for you to take a holiday by the sea. The coast of Kent can be delightful in September. Allow me to give instructions for you and your wife to be installed at Walmer Castle. I know no better place for restoring a man's peace of mind. Then when you feel equal to it you could move on to Bath or Brighton and participate for a while in the gaieties of the autumn season. By November I vow you will be spoiling to take up once more the invaluable work you have been doing for me.'

'I thank you, Sir; but no. Whatever you may believe, I am convinced that for a long time to come Paris will remain a city ruled by fear, violence and arbitrary arrest. While serving you there I have made deadly enemies; and there are others there who know the double part I played. Were

I betrayed, my record is such that despite any lessening of the Terror I would lose my head, and I have a whim to keep it on my shoulders. That I should have lived through the worst and got away is not due to one, but a whole series of miracles. I would be made to tempt Providence further.'

'Mr. Brook, I appreciate all you say, yet I would still ask you to consider my side of the matter. I have many other agents in France who send me useful intelligence, but none like yourself. They can do no more than hover on the outskirts of events, whereas you have made your way into the councils of those who initiate them. God forbid that I should send any man to his death; but having, as you say yourself, lived through the worst, I have even greater confidence in your ability to er . . . keep that handsome head on your shoulders in the less dangerous circumstances now emerging. I will not ask you for a decision now. Let us postpone the issue. But I pray you reflect on what I have said, and come to see me again when you have recovered from the nervous exhaustion which at present afflicts you.'

'Nay, Sir. There would be no point in that. In '92 I agreed to go again to France because I was at that time in desperate need of money. Now, thank God, I am better found; so can afford to risk your displeasure. Until your own prognostications are fulfilled, and France once more becomes a country fitted for a human being to live in, I am resolved not to return to it.'

The corners of the Prime Minister's thin mouth drew down, and he asked sternly: 'Am I to understand that you refuse to continued to serve me?'

'By no means, Sir. My youth and good constitution should set me up again by Christmas. In the new year I hope you will find another mission for me.'

'Ah! Now you speak more in the vein to which I am accustomed from you. Should the autumn campaign go as I expect, by early spring the conditions you require may be fulfilled. You could be of inestimable value to me in Paris while I negotiate peace and a restoration.'

'No, no!' Roger exclaimed in exasperation. 'I thought I had made myself plain. I'll not set foot on French soil until the restoration is an accomplished fact. But there are other countries. In '86 you sent me to aid my Lord Malmesbury in Holland. In '87 I served you at the Courts of Denmark, Sweden and Russia. In '89 and '90 I carried out missions for Queen Marie Antoinette at the courts of Tuscany and Naples. In '91 you made me your envoy extraordinary to Madrid. I have useful acquaintances in all these places. Send me to any of them, to America, or to one of the German courts. I care not; but I have earned the right to ask that it should be to some city in which I can live like a civilised human being, and not a hunted, half-starved dog.'

Slowly shaking his head from side to side, Mr. Pitt replied: 'Now that Austria, Prussia, the Rhine Provinces, Holland, Spain, Sardinia and Naples are all joined with us in a grand alliance to crush the French, our diplomats furnish me with all the information I require of the happenings at their courts; and our relations with all the neutral countries are fully satisfactory. France is my problem, and among the minds that direct her policy you have made for yourself a niche that no other man can fill. 'Twould be a criminal waste to send you elsewhere.' Then, standing up, he added with a kindly smile: 'Think no more of this now. When you are restored to health I feel sure you will regard the matter differently. Near Christmas time I will get in touch with you; so be good enough to keep me informed of your whereabouts.'

Roger, too, had risen to his feet. His mouth set for a moment in a firm, hard line, then he said:

'It would be useless, Sir. Since you refuse me reasonable employment I have now made up my mind to accept an invitation I received but yesterday. By Christmas I'll be in the West Indies, and should I find the Sugar Islands as pleasant as they are portrayed I intend to stay there.'

2

The Silken Cord

As Roger rode away from Holwood House his feelings were very mixed. The nerve-racking existence he had led through the Terror would have satiated most men's zest for adventure for the rest of their lives; but it was the horror of it, together with the sordid conditions in which he had been compelled to live, more than the ever-present danger, that had so sickened him of his work in Paris. Previous to the rising crescendo of butchery that had taken place during his last mission to France, he had greatly enjoyed himself, both there and in the numerous other countries to which he had been sent. Meeting sovereigns, statesmen, generals and diplomats in court and camp, intriguing to secure information of value, and even at times succeeding in influencing events in favour of his country, had become the breath of life to him. He had, therefore, had no intention of severing his connection with Mr. Pitt, and would never have done so but for his master's uncompromising refusal to send him anywhere other than back to France.

On the other hand, the idea of dropping all cares for many months, while making a voyage to the West Indies, had been very tempting. The invitation had come quite unexpectedly and, as things had turned out, could not have done so at a more appropriate moment. He had been home only two nights, and the day before, his oldest friend, Georgina, now Countess of St. Ermins, had driven out to Richmond to pay a surprise visit to his wife, Amanda. The St. Ermins were in London in August only because the Earl had been suffering from such acute insomnia that Georgina had decided that he must consult a mental specialist. The doctor's recommendation had been a long sea voyage, and as St. Ermins had estates in Jamaica, it had been decided that they should go out there for the winter and later, perhaps, visit North America. Georgina had not known that Roger was back from France, and on finding him at home, but in such poor health, she had at once declared that he and Amanda must accompany her and her husband on their voyage.

As the four of them were such close friends no prospect could have been more delightful and Amanda had instantly pressed Roger to accept for them; but he had told her he feared that Mr. Pitt would have projects for his future which would put such a prolonged absence from Europe quite out of the question. Now, angry as he was with the Prime Minister for having forced his hand, he was glad of it for Amanda's sake; and, after he had ridden a mile, he decided that he was really glad for his own as well.

During the past two years Amanda had spent much of her time staying with relatives; so she had made no serious inroads into the payments for his services that the Foreign Office had remitted to his bank, and he had succeeded in getting out of France the bulk of the considerable sums he had received while acting as a high official of the Revolutionary Government. On a rough calculation he reckoned that he must now have at least £10,000 in investments lodged with Messrs. Hoare's, and although both he and Amanda were extravagant by nature, that was ample to keep them in comfort for a long time to come. When he returned from America it would be quite soon enough to look round for some remunerative employment.

At a fast trot he passed through Bromley and its adjacent village of Beckenham. Beyond it he left the main road by a lane that shortly brought him to the hamlet of Penge Green. Thence he rode through orchards towards Nor Wood, the three mile wide stretch of which now confronted him.

Ten minutes later, as he entered the wood, his thoughts had turned to Charles St. Ermins and his malady. Georgina had made no secret of its cause. Her husband was one of those gallant gentlemen who, under Sir Percy Blakeney, had formed a League to rescue French families from the Terror. At times, in order to carry out their plans for saving one set of people they had to stand by while appalling atrocities were inflicted on others. It was such sights which were now preying on the young nobleman's mind, and one in particular.

In Robespierre's native town of Arras, his friend Le Bon had shocked even hardened revolutionaries by his barbarities. On one occasion, having caught an *émigré* officer who had returned, he had had him strapped face upward to the plank of the guillotine; then, while the wretched man lay staring up at the heavily weighted triangular knife which was to come swishing down upon his throat, the terrorist had stood there for twenty minutes reading out to him from the latest news-sheet a long report of a Republican victory. To the victim, while waiting for the knife to fall, each moment must have seemed an hour, and St. Ermins, who had been present disguised as a National Guard, now dreamed each night that he was the victim; so that he woke hysterical with the agony the other must have suffered.

Roger, too, was afflicted by harrowing memories, but they plagued him mostly whenever his thoughts happened to drift in the day time. The death of the little King was one, and another a scene that he had not actually witnessed but which, as he had seen so many similar to it, frequently sprang unbidden to his imagination with sickening vividness. During one of his brief absences from Paris his first love, Athénaïs de Rochambeau, had been guillotined. In his mind's eye he could see the executioner's assistant performing his awful function of throwing her decapitated trunk into the cart, then thrusting her beautiful head between her legs.

Each time this horrifying vision arose he found it terribly hard to banish it, and he wondered now if he and St. Ermins had a softer streak in them than most other men; but he rather doubted it. Both of them had given ample evidence of normal courage; so it seemed that the sight of atrocities committed in cold blood were particularly liable later to play havoc with a man's nerves. That he and Charles were both seeking to escape from much the same thing now struck him as a fortunate coincidence, and he felt that the doctor who had advised the Earl must be a sound man. The peaceful routine of life aboard ship, followed by unmeasured time in which to laze in the sunshine of palm-fringed islands, was just the thing to banish the nightmares that beset them.

Emerging from the leafy glades of Nor Wood he passed Round Hod Hill, then rode a few hundred yards down a turning to the left until he came to the Horn Inn. There, he gave his horse half-an-hour's rest while drinking a couple of glasses of Malaga at a wooden table outside the inn, from which there was a lovely view over the gardens and country houses that lay in the valley to the west.

From the Horn he returned to the road leading down the south side of Streatham Common, but he still was on the high ground when, to his annoyance, just outside the gates to the Duke of Bedford's mansion, his horse cast a shoe. The occurrence necessitated his reducing his pace to a walk for the next mile, down to the main road and north along it up the hill into Streatham village; but on the apex of the fork roads there stood a forge, where he was able to order his mount to be re-shod.

As the smith and both his assistants were already busy he had to wait a while; so he sat down outside on the mounting block and idly watched the passing traffic. It was mainly composed of country carts taking farm produce into London, and the carriage of local gentry, but twice smart equipages clattered through, most probably on their way down to Brighthelmstone, or Brighton as the newly fashionable little watering-place was now beginning to be called.

Mentally he contrasted the busy, prosperous scene with the hopeless lethargy and squalid poverty which was now universal in villages of a similar size in France, and that set him thinking again of Athénaïs. He was roused from his gloomy thoughts by the smith calling to him that his horse was ready, but just at that moment a familiar figure caught his eye.

It was Mr. Pitt coming up the hill in his phaeton. Despite the slope its horses were being driven at a spanking trot, and the few other vehicles in sight quickly pulled aside to give it passage. On the back seat the Prime Minister sat, as was his wont, stiff as a ramrod and looking neither to right nor to left. He was utterly indifferent to either the applause or abuse of crowds, and of such a haughty disposition that even when taking his seat in the House he never deigned to glance at his closest supporters. Roger came to his feet and swept off his hat in a graceful bow, but his gesture received no acknowledgment. The beautifully-sprung carriage hardly slackened speed as it rounded the end of the smithy, then took the road past St. Leonards Church towards Tooting.

Clapping his hat back on his head Roger stared after it with an angry frown. He did not care a hoot about the attitude of god-like superiority that Mr. Pitt chose to assume in public; but he did intensely resent the treatment he had received that morning. Brooding now upon the lack of appreciation and generosity which he felt his old master had shown him, he paid the smith a shilling, mounted his horse and set off after the carriage.

Cantering across Tooting Common he came up to within a hundred yards of it, but on reaching the village it went on along Garrett Lane, from which Roger deduced that the Prime Minister was going, via Roehampton, to see the King at Kew, whereas his own way lay to the west through Wimbledon. Another hour's ride brought him to the Robin Hood Gate of Richmond Park, and by half-past three he reached his home, Thatched House Lodge.

It was a charming little mansion near the south end of the Park, with a lovely view of the Surrey Hills. An earlier building on the site had been used as a hunting-box by Charles I, and it was still a Crown property; but Mr. Pitt, in a more handsome mood than he had just displayed, had given Roger a life tenancy of it four years earlier for the special services he had rendered during the early stages of the Revolution.

Having handed his horse over to the faithful Dan, his black-bearded ex-smuggler servant, Roger went from the stables into the house by its back entrance. The kitchen door was open, and glancing through it as he passed he was much surprised to see that his wife was there directing the operations not only of the cook but also their two maids, and that every available space was occupied with meats in preparation, vegetables, pies and basins. As he paused in the doorway, Amanda looked up and exclaimed:

'Thank goodness you're back! There are a dozen things I want you to help with.'

He raised an eyebrow. 'What is all this to-do? 'Tis true that I need feeding up, but we'll not be able to eat a tithe of these things for dinner.'

Amanda was a tall girl with a fine figure, slightly frizzy auburn hair and the beautiful skin that often goes with it. She had good teeth and her mouth was so formed that it was always a little open, as though she was about to smile. Now it opened in a laugh, as she replied:

'We have guests coming, and to stay.'

Seeing his face darken she came over to him, pushed him firmly back and closed the kitchen door behind her.

'M'dear,' he expostulated, 'you must know that I am in no mood for company.'

'Now Roger,' she chided him gently, 'you must be sensible. Nearly all day yesterday you sat looking a picture of misery in the garden. You brightened a little while Georgina was here, and I know you did your best to respond each time I tried to cheer you; but drunkenness has never been a vice of yours and you punished the port after dinner so heavily that you spoilt our evening.'

He gave a rueful smile. 'I'm truly sorry for that, and for my general moroseness. 'Tis no fault of yours, and I beg you to be patient with me.'

'I will, my sweet; but to contend with your unhappy state is too much for me alone. I'd soon become as miserable as yourself and contemplate throwing myself out of a window. Help to make you your own cheerful self again I had to have; so soon after you left this morning I had Dan drive me in the gig to London. Georgina at once said yes to my appeal that she and Charles should come to stay for a while, and as they are lying in Bedford Square at her father's, I asked him to come out with them for dinner. Georgina, too, will try to collect dear Droopy Ned; so that this evening your best friends may begin the re-enlivening of your mind with a proper party.'

Leaning forward, he kissed her, and said: 'It was a sweet thought, my pet, and maybe you're right that the necessity to play host will take me out of myself. In any case I'm glad the St. Ermins are to stay, as it will give us ample opportunity to discuss going with them to Jamaica.'

'Roger!' Her eyes widened with delight. 'And you had led me to believe there was no hope of that! Oh, never again will I say aught against Mr. Pitt, after his generosity in releasing you for long enough to make this voyage.'

'Providing it be only to myself, you may now say what you will about him and I'll not contradict you; for he no longer is my master.'

'What! Do you mean that you have quarrelled with him?'

'Not that; but he treated me most scurvily. I have, of course, been paid for what I've done, but no more than I would have received had I been working in comfort and some degree of security. Even so, I asked him for nothing, except that in the new year he should give me a mission to some place where life would be endurable. I had a right to expect that, but he refused it, and did not even offer me a continuance of my salary until I recovered my health. I told him flatly that I'd go no more to France, and that has put an end to matters between us.'

'Then he has cut off his nose to spite his face,' said Amanda quickly. 'I've long felt his ruthless exploitation of others for his own selfish ends to be intolerable. He will never be able to replace you, and when he finds that out it should be just the lesson that he needs to make him a trifle more human in his dealings.'

Roger shrugged. 'Do not deceive yourself, m'dear. Were I the last servant he had, he would never admit to himself that he had been in error to dispense with me. But we must give him his due. He exploits people only from the highest motives; never for his own ends, but for the nation's, and 'tis that which has formed the basis of my attachment to him.'

Amanda's face showed concern, as she asked: 'Are you greatly distressed by this breach that has occurred?'

'I could be,' he admitted, 'but I have determined not to be. 'Tis a matter that I can put out of my mind more readily than some others, and while riding home I vowed I'd let the future take care of itself.'

She nodded, and then he added with a sudden smile: 'In fact I will go further. From now on I mean to do my utmost to think of nothing but your own dear self enjoying with me the sunshine of the Indies.'

'Oh Roger, how happy you make me!' she cried, throwing her arms round his neck. For a few moments they remained tightly embraced, then she went back into the kitchen and he hurried away to get wines up from the cellar.

An hour later their guests arrived: Georgina, whose dark rich beauty and tempestuous vitality made her an admirable foil for the magnolia-skinned, quiet-natured Amanda; Charles, a youngish brown-faced man of slight build, whose features, apart from his small Roman nose, had a distinct resemblance to those of his great great grandfather, Charles II; Colonel Thursby, Georgina's father, who by his fine brain had made a great fortune out of the beginnings of the Industrial Revolution, and whom Roger had regarded from boyhood almost as a second father to himself. Droopy Ned, too, was with them, as they had learned that he was staying at Sion House with the Northumberlands; so they had come by way of Isleworth to pick him up there. His proper style was Lord Edward Fitz-Deverel, and he owed his nickname to a chronic stoop brought about by his being short-sighted. He was a fop of the first order, but under his elegant posturing concealed an extremely shrewd mind which he devoted largely to antiquarian interests, and he had been Roger's close friend since their school-days.

Amanda delighted the St. Ermins by telling them at once of the decision to accompany them to Jamaica, then Roger took the whole party across the lawn to the summer-house, and there refreshed them after their journey with a Moselle Wine Cup that he had just made. As the ice tinkled in the tall glasses they plied him with a hail of questions about the state of things in France, and he replied by giving them a broad outline of what he had said to Mr. Pitt.

'You think then,' said Colonel Thursby, 'that despite the overthrow of Robespierre there is little hope of our making an accommodation with the French?'

'None whatever,' Roger declared. 'Even if the Thermidorians, who have newly seized the whip in Paris, wished for peace, they dare not make it. In France there are now a million men under arms. Peace would mean the disbandment of those serving on the frontiers and they would return to the cities as a vast armed rabble. No government could hope to prevent the excesses they would commit, soon reducing the whole country to a state of anarchy. Mr. Pitt's hopes of peace brought about by a change of heart are as chimerical as those he places in a speedy allied victory. Of that I am convinced.'

'Does he then visualise the Austrian and His Boneheadedness of York marching upon Paris this autumn?' Georgina enquired.

'He does; and that despite the hopeless incompetence they have so far displayed.'

' 'Tis not so much incompetence as neither the Austrians nor the Prussians having their hearts in the war,' Droopy Ned remarked. 'Both are looking over their shoulders on account of the projected partitioning of Poland, and holding back forces lest Catherine of Russia attempts to seize more than her agreed share.'

St. Ermins nodded. 'That is the rub; and 'tis aggravated by their divided councils. Each General is placing the interests of the allied cause second to the particular interests of his own government, and using his troops to besiege coveted cities instead of pooling them in one grand manœuvre to crush the French.'

'Both are contributory factors to our ill-success,' Roger agreed. 'But the root of the trouble lies in Mr. Pitt's mismanagement.'

'Hark at that now!' Georgina exclaimed with a laugh. 'Whoever would have thought to hear Roger make so disparaging a remark about his master. Time was when he never tired of preaching to us of Billy Pitt's greatness.'

Realising that his words had given an impression he was far from intending, Roger retorted swiftly: 'You misunderstand me. He is great. His obstinacy and conceit are at times infuriating, but he has qualities that make him the greatest man in England; and on occasion one catches a glimpse of his true nature, which is most lovable. I meant only that he knows nothing of military matters, and so is entirely at sea when considering the steps we should take to defeat our enemies.'

' 'Tis true.' Droopy nodded his forward-thrust head up and down. 'Billy Pitt's genius in the fields of finance, diplomacy and reform is indisputable; but he has an inborn hatred of war and lacks all understanding of it.'

Colonel Thursby smiled at Roger. 'Tell us what you would do, were you in the Prime Minister's shoes?'

'Since England pays the piper she has a right to call the tune, Sir. Mr. Pitt should bang our allies' heads together and make them concentrate their forces with us in a determined drive for Paris.'

'On that we are agreed, although it might prove more difficult than it sounds. What else?'

'Recall His Highness of York, and replace him with a more capable commander.'

'I doubt if His Majesty would consent to that. York is his favourite son, and of that boorish bunch the best. At least he is an honest man.'

' 'T'would be no precedent were the command of our army given to one who is not a Royal Prince; and this country does not lack for honest soldiers who are highly competent at their business.'

Roger had been about to add numerous other measures he would have taken, but at that moment Dan came out to announce that dinner was served; so they all trooped into the house. As was usual at that period, only two courses and a remove were served, but each course consisted of half-a-dozen different dishes and they helped themselves lavishly to fish, meat, poultry and game according to their fancy, and washed each item down with copious draughts of Vin de Grave, Rhenish, Claret or Florence Wine.

As the meal progressed, Georgina gaily outlined her plans. They were to sail in a West Indiaman from Bristol in the first week of October, and hoped to reach Jamaica early in December. The St. Ermins's plantations were on the north side of the island near St. Ann's Bay and they had a large house there which was occupied by a distant cousin who managed the estates. They intended to make it their headquarters, but would spend much of their time in Kingston where a considerable society made life most agreeable during the winter season.

Droopy Ned, who was a diehard Tory, took occasion to remark to Roger: 'At least you cannot complain of the conduct of the war in the West Indies. In the past year Admiral Sir John Jervis and General Sir Charles Grey have between them stripped the French of practically every possession they had there.'

'But I do!' Roger countered. ''Tis Mr. Pitt's dispersal of our forces that distresses me beyond all else. Could we but once overcome the French in their own country all else would follow from that. Had Sir Charles Grey's force been sent instead to Toulon, we might have held it. Had they been sent to Flanders so great a reinforcement could have turned the tide for us there. Still better, had they been thrown into Brittany while the Vendéean revolt was at its height, the Revolutionary Government must have collapsed from their inability to support yet another front.'

'My lord Moira's force was charged with that,' put in St. Ermins.

'So I gather. And that is another instance of gross mismanagement, for it remained sitting idle in the Channel Islands throughout the whole winter from lack of definite instructions. But I was speaking of the Indies, and 'tis there our best troops have been thrown away.'

'Oh come!' protested Colonel Thursby. 'The Sugar Islands are of immense value, and only by securing those lately belonging to the French could we hope to pay the cost of the war. Billy Pitt showed the sound sense that has made him what he is by seizing them while he had the chance.'

'I wonder whom he will make Governor of Martinique,' St. Ermins hazarded. 'Whoever gets that appointment will have a plum.'

Colonel Thursby nodded. 'Indeed he will. The work of such posts is mainly done by underlings trained in colonial administration, while the Governor takes all the perquisites. I'd estimate the governship of such a highly-cultivated island to be worth at least five thousand a year.'

'Is there not still fighting there, though?' Amanda asked. 'One hears that the French islands have been much affected by the Revolution, and that in most of them the slaves are in open revolt.'

'That is so in Saint-Domingue,' the Colonel agreed. 'There the French Royalists invited us in to save their lives and properties, and a full-scale campaign is in progress against the blacks incited by terrorists sent from France. In the other islands, our own included, there have been similar troubles, but on a much lesser scale, and no matter for serious concern.'

'By the time of our arrival there should be nought to worry about,' St. Ermins added. 'For now, since my lord Howe's victory on "the glorious 1st of June" the ocean is ours, and the French will no longer be able to send support to the revolted slaves.'

Roger looked across at him with a grim smile. 'I wonder, Charles, if you realise what that victory cost us. To my mind it was the equivalent of a major defeat.'

A chorus of excited protest greeted his pronouncement, but he silenced it with a gesture. 'Do not mistake me. I am well aware that his lordship's five-day chase and eventual bringing to battle of the French fleet were in the true tradition of British tenacity and courage. I am told, too, that although near seventy the grand old man scarcely left the deck of his flagship during all that time. It is the result of the action I presume to criticise, and my sojourn in France having enabled me to see the other side of the picture as well as ours, I feel I am better placed than yourself to form a judgment.'

Pausing, he took a drink of wine, then went on. 'This spring France was in a most desperate plight. Robespierre and his colleagues knew that unless they could feed starving Paris through the summer sheer desperation would drive the masses to revolt, murder them and call for immediate peace. In consequence they purchased a vast quantity of grain in the Americas and charted every available bottom they could lease to bring it over. Had it failed to arrive they would have been finished, and Admiral Villaret-Joyeuse was charged to get the convoy through whatever the cost to his fleet. My lord Howe was, of course, charged to intercept it and could have done so. With his superior forces he might have contained or even ignored Villaret-Joyeuse. Instead he allowed himself to be lured away from the French ports, and although in the battle he severely crippled the French fleet, his own was so crippled afterwards that his ships were incapable of getting back in time to intercept the grain convoy. It arrived intact and the corn it brought was sufficient to tide France over to the present harvest; thus the Terrorist government was given a new lease of life and our chance to end the war was lost.'

For a moment there was silence round the table, then Colonel Thursby said, 'Your account of this affair confirms my own impression that the war at sea is being ill-directed. Great sailor as my lord Howe may be, he is now too old to continue in active service, and too set in his ideas. It has always been his policy to spare his ships as much as possible, and preserve them from the wear and hazards inseparable from remaining at sea for long periods during winter. 'Tis that which has so far rendered our blockade of the French coast largely ineffective. As a commercial man I am very conscious of the great rewards that a full enforcement of the blockade might bring, but to reap them demands a new system of close patrols and unremitting watch.'

'The Navy is well enough,' Georgina chimed in after her father, 'but for the sleep-befuddled head upon its shoulders. What's needed is Mr. Pitt's removal of his brother, my lord Chatham, from the Admiralty. Daily a half-dozen of our finest sea-dogs are there at eight in the morning clamouring for orders, but his lordship declares it barbarous to be called on to leave his bed before nine, and comes to the Board at ten still yawning his empty head off.'

'Thou art right, my love,' St. Ermins supported her. 'And 'twas a thousand pities that when His Grace of Portland formed the new Coalition with Mr. Pitt, he did not insist upon someone more capable being given the Admiralty.'

Droopy Ned could not resist remarking with just a trace

of malice, 'Your leader, Charles, was so concerned with grabbing the lion's share of patronage for himself, that he could think of nought else.'

St. Ermins only laughed and retorted: 'We Whigs were overdue for some of the spoils of office, and those secured by His Grace are but a part of the monopoly enjoyed by Henry Dundas under the Tory administration.'

'Maybe, my lord; but Dundas is shrewd, immensely capable and has an insatiable appetite for work, whereas the Duke is a very mediocre man, and owes his new office entirely to the influence he wields as a political figure-head.'

Having so recently returned from France, Roger knew little about the changes in the Cabinet which had taken place in the preceding month, so at his request his friends enlightened him.

In the early years of the Revolution the sympathies of nearly everyone in Britain, and particularly the Whig party, had been with the French nobles and professional men of liberal views, who had endeavoured to force King Louis into granting a Constitution, and abolishing the many abuses to which the lower classes had been subject since the Middle Ages. But as the Revolution began to degenerate into class warfare, mob rule, and nation-wide attacks on religion, property and life, the upper and middle classes of England had gradually become more and more opposed to the new regime.

Charles Fox had, from the beginning, championed the revolutionaries and continued to do so even after war against France had been declared, using his brilliant oratory with complete unscrupulousness to embarrass the Government at every opportunity; but Edmund Burke, his friend and colleague of long standing in the Whig opposition, differed violently from him on that subject and had made known his views in 'Reflections on the Revolution'. This publication had had an enormous circulation and as it set forth very clearly how the triumph of the Jacobins would result in all Europe falling into a state of atheism and anarchy, it had not only convinced great numbers of waverers among the middle classes but deprived Fox of the support of the majority of his own party.

With the discrediting of Fox it had soon become apparent that all the sounder Whigs were as much in favour of a vigorous prosecution of the war as were the Tories; so Pitt, with a view to strengthening his administration, had agreed with their leader, Portland, to form a Coalition. Early in July the Duke had been given the Home Office, William Windham had been made Secretary of War, and the Earls Fitzwilliam and Spencer became Lord President and Lord Privy Seal. At the Admiralty Pitt had kept his elder brother, and at the Foreign Office his cousin, Lord Grenville, while his indefatigable man-of-all-work, Dundas, had been allowed to retain the India and Colonial Offices, and as compensation for giving up the Home Secretaryship had been made what amounted to Minister of Defence.

These changes had required the most delicate negotiations, as on the one hand Pitt was determined not to sacrifice the more valuable of his old colleagues and, on the other, the powerful Whig nobility was out to grab all it could get. The Viceroyalty of Ireland and several other valuable posts were still bones of contention, and as Roger listened to the accounts of the intrigues which had been taking place it was borne in upon him that his ex-master had been having an extremely worrying time; so after a while, he remarked:

'What you tell me may well account for the lack of consideration Mr. Pitt showed me this morning, in refusing me a new mission to my liking. 'Tis obvious that so many cares have temporarily blunted his sensibilities; but, with all due respect to you, Charles, I am inclined to wonder if this taking in of your Whig friends will make things any easier for him in the long run.'

'I think it will,' replied St. Ermins, 'for once these domestic matters are settled he will meet with little opposition in either House, and so be freed to give a much greater share of his mind to the war.'

Colonel Thursby nodded. 'There is something in that, but it will not free him from his worst embarrassment. I refer to the troubles that our English Jacobins have been stirring up in all the centres of industry. 'Tis true that they will now be able to voice their disloyal sentiments in Parliament only through Fox and a handful of irresponsible radicals, but such bodies as the London Corresponding Society and the Methodists are becoming a menace to the State. Had not those four days of burning, pillaging and murder while the mob wrought its evil will in London during the Gordon riots proved a danger signal to honest artisans, we might well have already had a revolution here. Yet, even so, the numbers of these malcontents increase daily, and they abuse the freedom we, in this country, enjoy both to preach sedition openly and publish pamphlets by the thousand advocating that Britain should become a republic. Their activities must be a matter of grave concern to government, yet short of instituting tyrannous methods of repression which would be obnoxious to us all, there seems no way to check them.'

Roger was now beginning to feel that he had been unfair in expecting Mr. Pitt to take a realistic view of the war when he evidently had so many matters on his mind that it must be near impossible for even the finest brain to see them in all their proper perspective. As he was about to say so, the clopping of horses' hoofs approaching at a swift trot caused a sudden silence round the table. A moment later they came to a halt outside the front gate. Roger glanced quickly at Amanda, but she shook her head to show that she had no idea whom their visitor might be. Then Dan came hurrying in. His dark eyes were bright with excitement as he exclaimed with his broad Hampshire accent:

'I could scarce believe me eyes, Master! But 'tis the great Billy Pitt himself be outside askin' for 'e.'

Quickly excusing himself, Roger hurried from the room and out of the house down the short garden path. There, sure enough, sitting bolt upright on the back seat of his carriage as though he had not moved a muscle since Roger had last seen him, was the Prime Minister. But now to Roger's bow he replied by a slight inclination of the head; then, holding out a large envelope towards him, he said briskly:

'Mr. Brook, I am come from Kew, where I spoke with His Majesty upon our affairs in the West Indies. Since you are set upon going there I suggested that you should carry this document with you. His Majesty desired me to express to you his hope that the voyage will restore you to health; and with that hope may I couple my own, that new interests in the tropics will soon erase from your mind the distressing experiences you met with while in France.'

Taking the envelope Roger bowed again, and replied: 'I am much indebted to you, Sir, for conveying to me His Majesty's most gracious message, and for your own good wishes. Naturally I shall be honoured to act as His Majesty's courier, and still more so if you will now step inside and join us in a glass of wine.'

The Prime Minister's lined face lit up in one of his rare smiles, but he shook his head. 'I thank you, no. I have urgent affairs requiring my attention at Holwood; so you must excuse me.' Then he pulled the string attached to the little finger of his coachman, and a moment later the carriage was bowling away down the road.

'It was just after seven o'clock, and in the deepening twilight the superscription on the big envelope had not stood out clearly enough for Roger to read it at the first glance. Now, as he held it up, he saw with some surprise that it was addressed to himself. Hurrying into the lighted hall, he tore it open and ran his eyes swiftly over the thick parchment it contained. When he had read only a few lines he gave a gasp of amazement. It was a Royal Commission appointing him Governor of the newly-won island of Martinique.

Running into the dining-room he held it high above his head and, with an excited shout, announced its contents. The girls embraced him; the men cheered, wrung his hand and slapped him on the back. While they were still crowding about him Dan produced champagne, and in the pink slightly effervescent wine of those times, they drained their crystal goblets to the health of His Excellency the Governor.

An hour or so later, when Amanda and Georgina had retired to the drawing-room, Roger went down to the cellar to get up more wine. In his absence his three men friends expressed their personal views on his appointment.

All of them agreed that, since this rich Governorship could have bought the support of some great landowner who controlled two or three seats in Parliament, and Roger was entirely without political influence, the gift of it to him was most generous.

Colonel Thursby added that, all the same, the Prime Minister's gesture showed his sound sense as well as generosity, as Roger was level-headed, firm, and high principled; and having lived in France for so long he was far better fitted than most men to bring tranquility to an island that had until a few months ago been a French colony.

But the shrewd Droopy Ned saw even further, and poking his narrow head forward, he said with a sly smile: 'I think you overlook one thing. Roger is the most gifted confidential agent who has served the Crown for many a long day, and Bill Pitt sets too high a value on him to lose him. This morning, having become temporarily sickened of his work, Roger freed himself from it, but tonight he is no longer free. By the gift of this Governorship he has been tied by a silken cord, and can be recalled at will. I will wager a thousand guineas that within a year Roger will once more be serving his master on the Continent.'

3

Westward Ho!

During the next few weeks Roger was very fully occupied. Having written to thank the Prime Minister he next wrote to Henry Dundas, as Minister for the Colonies, to ask for an interview at which he might receive specific instructions regarding his Governorship. The business-like Dandas replied by return, inviting him to dine at his house at Wimbledon on the following Thursday, and suggesting that he should come early so that they could discuss affairs before the meal.

Roger both liked Dundas and had a great respect for his ability. The minister was then in his early fifties, a big raw-boned red-faced man who still spoke with the broad Scottish accent he had acquired in boyhood. He was notoriously foul-mouthed and drank like a trooper, but his potations had no effect upon his splendid constitution, and he had an extraordinary capability for despatching mountains of work with swift efficiency. India was only one of his responsibilities but he knew more about it than any other man in Parliament, and the genial good-humour, that Mr. Pitt so sadly lacked, made him an invaluable manager of their party. By invariably giving every post that fell vacant within his patronage to fellow countrymen, he ensured all the members from north of the Tweed loyally following him into the lobby, and his influence had become so great there that he was known as Harry the Ninth of Scotland.

Within five minutes of Roger's arrival Dundas was pouring him a glass of shrub in his study, and saying with a jovial laugh: 'Ye've come ta see how much ye can get out o' me;

an' dina ye pretend otherwise.'

'I'll not,' Roger smiled. He knew that, Martinique being a new post, no salary would yet have been fixed for it, and added cheerfully: 'What say you to three thousand a year?'

Dundas sat back and roared with laughter. 'Strap me! The impudence of it! Dost take me for the Inca of Peru? Nay, five hundred is nearer the mark, though t'was eight I had in mind.'

Roger's face fell, and he protested: 'Damme Sir! I have been drawing twelve hundred from the Foreign Office.'

'Aye, an' ye've earnt every nickel of it,' Dundas nodded, suddenly serious; for he was as well informed as Mr. Pitt of the work that Roger had been doing. 'There'll not be any blood-soaked guillotine awaiting ye in Martinique, though; but a fine idle life with puncheons o' rum to drink an' a plenty o' coffee-coloured beauties ta tumble in th' cane brakes.'

'All the same, Sir, a thousand is nought but a pittance for the Governor of an Island.'

'Weel; on account o' yer past sairvices I'll try tae get tha Treasury tae gi' ye twelve hundred.'

'My expenses will be all of that,' said Roger glumly. 'Could you not ask for fifteen?'

'Nay.' Dundas shook his head. 'Twelve hundred I'll ask for, an' not a bawbee more. But listen lad. Were ye not half a Scot an' desairved the post into the bargain, I'd ha' found a way tae ha' excused meself from confirming the appointment. As things are I'm glad for ye an' will instruct your innocence. Ye ha' but ta use the shrewd sense your MacElfic mother gied ye, tae line those fine breeks o' yours wi' West Indian gold.'

'I had heard there were perks,' Roger admitted, 'but I can hardly suppose that they would amount to any really considerable sum.'

'Why mon, the patronage o' tha whole island will be yours! Ye'll need only a canny agent tae tip ye the wink wha' applicants for post can afford tae pay. Harbours, prisons, mails, barracks, customs; permits for this an' that; licences tae ships' victuallers, army sutlers an' privateers; all should bring grist tae your mill. Nair forget that many a mickle makes a muckle. Let not e'en the smallest fry get oot of ye something fer nothing an' ye'll return as rich as a nabob. Sie' practices are forbidden here, but providin' ye make no appointments that might prove detrimental tae th' ould country, they are winked at in tha islands; so ye've nought tae fret about.'

Somewhat reassured by this, Roger pressed the question of money no further, and for a while they discussed the policy to be adopted towards the French planters; then their talk became more general and turned to the new Coalition. Dundas was by no means happy about it, as he believed that the Duke of Portland had deliberately put a misconstruction on the Prime Minister's offer in an attempt to rob him of his entire patronage. This was no question of making money from the sale of posts, but he maintained that it was impossible to keep a political party together unless one had plenty of places in one's gift. So, rather than remain to watch Pitt's following fall to pieces, he had refused to take office in the new Cabinet. Pitt had been so distressed at the prospect of losing his old colleague that he had dealt sharply with the Duke, and gone to the length of getting the King to write Dundas a personal letter saying that his services were indispensable. But the affair had left an unpleasant taste and did not bode well for the Whigs and Tories settling down together contentedly.

At four o'clock a coach arrived bringing three other guests for dinner. All of them were intimates of the Small Pitt-Dundas circle and two of them, Pepper Arden, and George Rose, Roger had met before. The first was a rather bumptious hanger-on of mediocre talents whose ill-directed loyalty, coupled with an almost noseless face that gave him a most comical appearance, at times made him the butt of the House. The second, with able and industrious devotion, handled the spade-work at the Treasury of the Prime Minister's brilliant financial administration; and within a few minutes of his arrival Dundas had jollied him into agreeing that Roger's salary should be twelve hundred a year.

Henry Addington was the third in their party. He was a tall well-favoured man with charming manners and had been at Lincoln's Inn when Pitt was practising as a barrister there. It was Pitt who had drawn him into politics and had used his influence to get him elected as Speaker of the House in '89; but at this first meeting Roger thought him so modest and unambitious that he would have been greatly surprised had he been granted a glimpse of the future and from it learned that his new acquaintance was to become Prime Minister.

At dinner they ate and drank with the usual unrestrained gusto of the times, and as there were no ladies present Dundas kept them merry with an apparently inexhaustible fund of bawdy stories. Afterwards the talk became more serious, turning inevitably to politics and, in due course, to the progress of the French Revolution. To these close friends Dundas made no secret of Roger's activities in France and he was asked to give an account of Robespierre's fall and execution, then of other outstanding scenes that he had witnessed during the Terror. It was Addington who said:

'It is clear, Mr. Brook, that you must be a man of great courage to have continued with your mission in circumstances of acute danger for so long; so I mean no offence by suggesting that there must have been many occasions when you feared for your life. It would much interest me to hear of that of which your apprehensions were the gravest.'

Roger thought for a moment, then replied: 'The fear of betrayal was a constant anxiety, but I think, Sir, I felt more acutal terror on the field of battle than during any of my dealings with the revolutionaries. Last winter I was sent as one of the *Citizen Représentants en Mission* to the army besieging Toulon. Fort Mulgrave was the key point of the defence, and having learnt the date that a major attack was to be launched against it, I was most anxious to get warning to my Lord Hood of the intentions of the French. As it was impossible for me to leave Headquarters clandestinely, I decided that my best course would be to get myself captured. To the north of the Fort there was a small redoubt containing a masked battery. I suggested to General Dugommier that its destruction the night before the main assault would greatly faciliate the capture of the Fort, and offered to lead an attack upon it. He agreed, and my intention was, of course, to get separated from my men in the darkness, surrender to the first British soldier I met, get taken to my Lord Hood, then have him exchange me for a prisoner of equivalent rank; so that I could return and continue with my secret work without the French suspecting that it was I who had given away their plans. But my own plan went sadly awry.'

Having taken a swig of port, Roger went on: 'Most unfortunately for me, when the details of my project were discussed in Council, a scruffy little officer named Buonaparte intervened. He was Corsican, of about my own age; and although only a Captain of artillery who had recently been jumped up to temporary Lieutenant Colonel, he insisted on poking his finger into every pie. This moody down-at-heel follow maintained that although the capture of the redoubt was sound in principle, to attempt it the night before the main assault would result in setting the whole front ablaze prematurely. He persuaded his seniors that it must be carried out only a few hours before the assault, when it would be too late for the British to bring up reinforcements from the warships in the harbour. Of course it was impossible for me to back down; so owing to this interfering Corsican, I was compelled to lead an attack against the battery in full daylight and I don't think I've ever been so frightened in my life.'

The others laughed, and Rose enquired. 'Did you capture the battery?'

Roger gave a rueful smile. 'I don't even know, for no sooner had I reached it than a gunner stunned me with his ramrod. But if the little Buonaparte had deliberately planned my undoing he could not have done so better. Not only did I fail to get my information to Lord Hood; it transpired that the battery was manned by our Spanish allies. When I came to I found myself a prisoner in a Spanish man-of-war, and they took me to Majorca. As I could not reveal my true identity, I had the very devil of a job getting out of their clutches, and was unable to resume my proper work again for above two months.'

There was more friendly laughter, the port circulated

again and the talk went on. It was two in the morning before Roger mounted his horse and, swaying somewhat in the saddle, made his way home.

His next business was to kiss hands on appointment, and for this formality Dundas took him to a levee at St. James's Palace. King George was then fifty-six, a portly red-faced man of no great mental attainments, but a fund of sound common sense and dogged determination. Unlike his German forebears, he put what he believed to be the interests of Britain first in everything. He had a passionate conviction that the well-being of the State was bound up with the breaking of the stranglehold that the powerful Whig nobility had obtained over it, and for the first twenty-five years of his reign had fought them relentlessly. At last, by the bold step of nominating young Billy Pitt at the age of twenty-four to be his Prime Minister, he had succeeded in his aim, and together through many difficulties they had brought the nation to a great prosperity. Five years earlier he had for some months been out of his mind, and his recovery had been hailed throughout England with such heart-felt rejoicing that it was clear beyond doubt that his honesty, simple way of life, and delight in growing bigger turnips than any other farmer in his kingdom had, through the years, gradually made him an object of great affection to his people.

Roger, during his missions, had become quite well acquainted with several foreign sovereigns, but no occasion had previously arisen calling for his presentation to his own King: so he was pleasantly surprised when the Monarch said to him:

'You should have come to see us before, Mr. Brook; you should have come before. Seven years in our service we're told, and many a dangerous undertaking carried out with success. Our thanks are overdue. And now you go to Martinique, eh? What'll you plant there? Sugar cane of course. Not long ago we met on the road a rich equipage with six outriders, all most gorgeous clad. "Who's that?" we asked our gentleman-in-waiting. "Is it some foreign Prince or new Ambassador?" "Nay, Sire,' he told us. " 'Tis a merchant just returned from the Sugar Isles." "Why Bless me!" we said.

"Can there be all *that* sugar?" 'Twas true enough though But yams, now yams; or sweet potatoes as some call them. Could we but induce the planters to grow them in quantity, they would serve admirably to feed the slaves. Then we'd have no need to send out vast quantities of salted herrings each year for that purpose. Bear yams in mind, Mr. Brook; bear yams in mind.'

'I will indeed, Sire,' Roger promised; and having drawn a quick breath the King hurried on:

'When do you set out? With the first convoy of the season, no doubt. But that's not for some weeks yet; so you'll be seeing your father before you sail. Carry him our greeting, Mr. Brook. We hold him in high esteem. A good honest man. A fine sailor too. Yes, carry him our greeting and tell him what we said.'

Roger bowed. 'I should be most happy, Sire, to convey your gracious message to him; but it happens that he is at present on service in the Mediterranean.'

'Ha! Ha!' The King gave a high-pitched happy little laugh and, with his protuberant blue eyes suddenly merry, poked Roger sharply in the ribs. 'Beaten at your own game, Mr. Brook! Beaten at your own game. Our intelligence is better than yours. Your good father was at Windsor but two days back to tell us of the taking of Corsica. It was our pleasure to make him a Knight for his part in it: so now he is Admiral Sir Chris. Admiral Sir Chris. Admiral Sir Chris; that sounds well, does it not? Do you know Corsica? Your father says the island is near covered with chestnut trees, and the finest he has ever seen. The peasants make a flour from the nuts, which is most nutritious, thereby enjoying a staple food at little or no expense. Have you ever met with it?'

'I have never been to Corsica, Sire; but a similar flour is made in Tuscany, and there I found it very palatable.' Before the King could start off again, Roger added swiftly: 'And, Your Majesty, may I say how delighted I am to hear of this honour you have done my father. I shall lose not a moment in seeking him out to offer my congratulations.'

'Do that; do that.' The King nodded a little wistfully, thinking of his own boorish, ungrateful and neglectful sons.

'I count your father lucky in you, Mr. Brook; yes, very lucky. You are a young man of promise. Tell the settlers in Martinique that now they are our subjects we shall have their interests at heart. And forget not the yams, Mr. Brook; forget not the yams.'

The King then turned to speak to someone else and Roger bowed himself away. As his father must have passed through London, he was much surprised that he had not gone out to Richmond to see Amanda and enquire if there was any news of himself; but as soon as the levee was over he hurried to the Admiralty, and there learned the reason. Before Admiral Brook landed at Portsmouth, the crew of the ship which had brought him from Gibraltar had handed him a petition of grievances, and after he had submitted it to their Lordships they had requested him to investigate certain of the complaints before taking leave.

By the night coach Roger sent an express to Portsmouth congratulating his father and outlining his own plans. Two days later, he received a reply in which the Admiral said that he had completed his report to their Lordships and was about to start for home; he then asked that Roger and Amanda should manage at least a short visit to him before sailing for the Indies. In consequence, on the following Monday they set out for Lymington.

Roger's old home, Grove Place, lay only a quarter of a mile to the south of the High Street of the ancient Borough. It had originated as a farm house with red-tile walls, built about 1660; but that part of it had been turned into kitchen quarters when, a hundred years later, the main square block had been added, and in 1787 Rear Admiral Brook had spent a part of his prize money earned in the West Indies on adding two further rooms and a spacious central hall with a charming semi-circular staircase. It was now, therefore, no great mansion, but a very comfortable house with six lofty well-proportioned rooms and about twenty smaller ones. Behind it, on the slope up to the town, it had an acre of walled garden, and to its south front lay several acres of meadows, across which, from the tall windows of the house, there was a fine view of the Solent and the western end of the Isle of Wight.

The busy little harbour was only ten minutes' walk away; in the summer there was always sailing to be had, and in the autumn shooting on neighbouring estates. During spring the New Forest, which lay inland behind the town, offered a thousand lovely spots for picnics, and in winter the stag was hunted there. In such surroundings, other things being propitious, it was impossible not to be happy, and Roger had greatly enjoyed both his childhood there and the visits he had made since setting out into the world.

His father, a bulky, red-faced jovial man, welcomed them with his usual heartiness, and declared again and again how glad he was to see Roger safely out of France. The double celebration of the father's Knighthood and the son's Governorship called for the best wine in the cellar, and no one was more happy than old Ben, the house-man, to get it up for such an occasion.

The Admiral insisted upon hearing both about Roger's last months in Paris and their projected journey to the West Indies, before they could get a word out of him about his own affairs; but Amanda made the two men bring their port into the drawing-room after dinner; then she demanded to know how her father-in-law had earned his K.B.

'M'dear, I did not,' he responded gruffly. 'That is, unless you can count near forty years of readiness to do my duty on all occasions sufficient warrant for the honour. To be honest, it was a stroke of luck. The common practice is for despatches to be sent home by an officer of Captain's rank who has distinguished himself; but their Lordships' order had been received for me to transfer my flag to Harwich; so my Lord Hood would have it that I should carry them. That meant my conveying the latest news to His Majesty in person, and in honouring me his real intent was to express his gratification with the Service as a whole.'

'Come, Sir,' Roger laughed. 'He told me himself that you had played a part in capturing Corsica.'

''Tis quite untrue!' his father protested. 'The main fleet had no hand in that. Its business was to lie between the French ports and the island, in order to prevent interference with our operations against the latter. As Rear Admiral, my task was the unspectacular one of acting for

Lord Hood on the many occasions when *Victory* left us, so that he might run close in and by his inspiring presence lend fresh vigour to our men's attacks.'

'But tell us, please,' Amanda urged, 'how the island was taken.'

'At the outset it looked a simple enough undertaking. The patriot leader, Pasquale de Paoli, already controlled the greater part of the island, and the French held only three strong places in the north. But, in the event, it proved a hard nut to crack. We'd have had it sooner, though, had not the revolutionary troops put up an unexpectedly stout resistance, and our own army failed in a most lamentable manner to give us adequate support. At times the lack of spirit shown by the latter almost drove our sailor-men into a frenzy.

'The affair opened in mid-January by His Majesty's Commissioner, Sir Gilbert Elliot, and Lt. Colonel John Moore of the 51st being put ashore to formulate a plan with Paoli. The veteran patriot agreed to employ his partisans in keeping the French from reinforcing San Fiorenzo overland while we attacked it from the sea. Early in February troops were landed on a beach adjacent to the town, but they were slow about it, and it was our jack-tars who showed them how to man-handle guns brought off from the ships up on to the heights so that they could fire down into the fortress. 'Twas a gruelling business hoisting such weighty pieces with blocks and tackle up precipitous cliffs, but once the batteries were in position the game was as good as won. On the 16th an assault was made by moonlight on the principal redoubt, and I am told that Colonel Moore led it with commendable gallantry; but 'twas about the only episode creditable to the army until near the conclusion of the campaign.

'Next day the French abandoned San Fiorenzo and my Lord Hood at once urged the setting about of the reduction of Bastia. But General Dundas, who was the chief soldier there, acted in a most poltroon-like fashion. He pleaded that his numbers were insufficient for the task, and refused all further co-operation until he received reinforcements from Gibraltar. My lord was so angry that although he had no authority to do so, he used his great prestige to order the General home. By mid-March, feigning illness to save his face, he had gone, but his successor, General D'Aubant, proved no better, and would not move a man or gun across the mountainous ridge that separated San Fiorenzo from Bastia. Our great Admiral then declared that he'd take the place on his own.

'For the purpose he detached Captain Nelson in *Agamemnon* and two frigates. There followed one of the finest exploits in all our naval history. Horace, or Horatio, Nelson, as he now prefers to be called, although only thirty-five, and despite the loss of seven years between the wars spent on the beach, is become one of our finest Captains. He is quite a little fellow and of frail build, but for zeal, intelligence and courage he has no equal, unless it be my Lord Hood himself. In this affair he played the part of a Marine, landed his lower deck guns and inspired his men to Herculean efforts in dragging them up seemingly unscalable heights to bombard Bastia. Against him were pitted five thousands resolute French, but he acted as though his own thousand men were ten thousand, and for six weeks attacked the enemy with unflagging ardour. On May the 18th his efforts were rewarded by their asking for terms. That stirred the army to activity and to the chagrin of us all it arrived without having fired a shot on the 23rd just in time to accept the town's surrender.

'Calvi was then the only stronghold left to the French, and it justified the term, as its situation made it appear even more impregnable than Bastia. By then General D'Aubant had been replaced by General the Honourable Charles Stuart, who proved of a far finer mettle; but he was sadly handicapped by great numbers of his troops going down with fever; so once again it fell to Captain Nelson and his gallant men to haul the guns up the heights. It was there, too, that he had the great misfortune to be struck in the face by stones thrown up on the bursting of a shell, and 'tis feared he will lose the sight of an eye. Yet so fine a man is he that he refused to go sick even for a day, and saw the business through to the end. It was near two months of bitter conflict before the job was done, but on August the

10th the garrison marched out; and Sir Gilbert Elliot, who had given great help and encouragement in every operation, formally took possession of the island in the name of His Majesty.'

'It was Sir Gilbert's younger brother, Hugh, who played so fine a part in helping King Gustavus out of his difficulties while I was in Sweden,' Roger remarked; but Amanda forestalled the possibility of his beginning to reminisce by asking for further particulars about the Corsican campaign.

The Admiral responded, and before they collected their candles to go up to bed had drawn a fair picture for them of the patriot leader Paoli; of his barbarous Corsican partisans, who had been of little assistance but, like human vultures, had plundered the French and British dead indiscriminately; of what they termed the 'Lion' sun, which in summer made campaigning there more arduous than in Africa; of the fantastic crags, the great chestnut forests, and the off-shore marshes from which came the fevers that had decimated the British troops; and of the amazing devotion to duty displayed by the English jack-tars, although a high proportion of them had been brought in by the press-gangs.

He also spoke with considerable uneasiness of his recent enquiry into complaints from the lower deck, and felt there was good cause for them. Hardened as he was himself from many years of sea service to living in great discomfort, he regarded the conditions of the ordinary seamen as appalling, and the fact that men maimed in the King's service should be turned off without pensions to beg their bread for the rest of their lives angered him extremely. That their Lordships of the Admiralty should show little inclination to better matters he thought both reprehensible and short-sighted; for he feared, and as it transpired correctly, that unless reasonable reforms were soon instituted the seamen might be goaded into open mutiny.

The five days that Roger and Amanda spent at 'Grove' went all too quickly. It was the shortest visit they had ever paid, but the many arrangements they still had to make necessitated their hurrying back to Richmond. Dan, and

Amanda's personal maid, little sloe-eyed Nell, were going with them; but their cook's husband was a respectable man employed in a local livery stable, so it was decided that he should move in and the couple be left in charge.

As a Governor's wife, Amanda felt that she ought to take out some young woman who could help her with her social duties and act as her companion; and for this they had selected her young cousin, Clarissa Marsham. Clarissa was eighteen and an orphan. Since she lived in very straitened circumstances with a great aunt whose main preoccupation was the salvation of her soul, she had jumped at this chance to get out into the world as an unofficial lady-in-waiting, and was already at Richmond helping with the packing up of the more valuable contents of the house.

Previously Roger had met Clarissa only as a gawky, pop-eyed, high-nosed young bridesmaid at his wedding, to attend which she had temporarily been excused from attendance at an academy for young ladies; but on seeing her again he fully approved his wife's choice. In the past four years Clarissa's figure had filled out to perfection and her features had assumed most pleasing proportions. Her bright blue eyes no longer looked like pebbles and now held a merry glint, while the arch of her nose gave her face a provocative arrogance which was happily tempered by her anxiety to please. Pale gold hair and a milk-and-roses complexion added to her attractions; and Roger found himself parting quite cheerfully with a hundred guineas to provide her with clothes to take out although he had originally intended to give her only fifty.

During the latter part of September the whole household was in a turmoil, with dressmakers coming and going; plate, china, linen, books and the many other articles that might not be easy to procure being packed; boxes and bales being corded; insurance schedules being checked; and arrangements being made on behalf of the couple who were to caretake in the house for what was expected to prove a period of several years.

At last, on the 27th, the travellers set out; but only to London where they spent the night at the St. Ermins's town house in Berkeley Square. Then on the 28th the whole party, which in addition to Georgina and Charles included her maid Jenny, his man Tom, and their French Chef—who rejoiced in the name of Monsieur Pirouet—left London for Bristol in four heavily-loaded coaches. By evening they reached Newbury and lay that night at the White Hart Inn. Next day they covered a somewhat shorter stage, arriving in the afternoon at Normanrood in Wiltshire, the seat of Droopy Ned's father, the Marquis of Amesbury; as Droopy was in residence and had asked them to break their journey there.

The Lord Edward was considered a most eccentric fellow by the county; not so much on account of his hobbies, which were collecting antique jewellery, the study of ancient religions, and experimenting on himself with Eastern drugs, but because he abhorred blood sports. He was, however, a very keen fisherman and it was the reaches of the River Avon, which ran through his father's estate, that lured him to the country for a few weeks every spring, and a passion for eating mulberries fresh off the ancient trees that brought him to Normanrood again each September. Yet even there he continued to dress as fastidiously as ever; and when he minced out beneath the portico of the great mansion to receive his guests he was satin-clad, scented and curled as though about to attend a rout in the Pump Room at Bath.

After a merry evening, when they were all about to go to bed, Droopy kept Roger back and, telling him he wanted a private word with him, took him up to his own book-lined sanctum. From a cabinet he produced a flagon of one of the rare liqueurs made in a foreign monastery, that Justerini's imported specially for him, and having filled two tall slender glasses with the amber elixir, he said:

'You know, Roger, how glad I am for you in this fine appointment, and the last thing I would wish to do is to detract from your pleasurable anticipation of it; but I would not be your true friend did I not feel some concern at your going to the West Indies.'

Having now not a care in the world, and an admirable dinner inside him, Roger replied with lazy cheerfulness: 'Why so, Ned? The only thing to mar my joy of it is the thought that I am likely to see even less of you for some years to come than while undertaking missions to the Continent.'

Droopy shook his long forward-thrust, bird-like head. ' 'Tis not that I had in mind; but your health, and that of all who go with you.'

Roger shrugged. 'The very prospect of the change has made me feel like my old self already. As you make mention of the others though, perhaps you are thinking of the diseases that are said to afflict white people in those parts.'

'I was; and of the yellow fever in particular.'

'My father spoke of that. As you may remember, he was for most of the years we were at school together on the West India station; and he tells me that he lost quite a number of his ship's company by it.'

'In those days it was an occasional risk encountered only when ships were in port; but you will be living permanently ashore, and I am wondering if you realise what a terrible scourge it has become?'

'I have heard little about such distant places during my time in France, though I did hear a rumour recently that fever was handicapping our operations there, just as it did in Corsica.'

'Roger, this should go no further, as for obvious reasons the Government wishes it kept quiet; but during the past year we have lost upwards of ten thousand troops killed off by Yellow Jack in those accursed islands.'

'Ten thousand!' Roger exclaimed aghast. 'But 'tis an army; and those the very men who might have won the war for us had they been thrown into Brittany last spring, or sent to support Lord Hood while we still held Toulon. Are you quite sure of this?'

'Certain!' Droopy nodded his head vigorously. 'And they are still dying like flies. Therefore I urge you to take every possible precaution against contracting this deadly infection.'

'I will indeed, if you can but tell me what I should do.'

Droopy took a sip of his liqueur, then replied: 'Unfortunately little is yet known about this dreaded disease. The doctors say that it is borne on the miasmas that in the evenings rise from the swamps that lie along the low parts of the coasts; but I have a different theory. It is at least possible that it is carried by the mosquitoes which infest such places, and this is my own belief. In any case I would advise that on reaching Bristol you should buy a quantity of fine muslin to make nets under which to sleep. If it does nothing else it will protect you from the annoyance of their stings. Then as to treatment, a tea made from an infusion of the Cinchona bark has proved most efficacious; but prevention is better than cure, and if all of you will take a cup regularly each morning it may protect you from infection. I would like you to give me your promise, Roger, that you will do so.'

'That sounds most sensible. You have my promise and I will see to it that the others adopt a similar routine. Is there aught else that you can suggest?'

'I fear not; though I will give you a drug to take should you be seriously attacked. It will reduce anyone who takes it to unconsciousness for many hours, and you must exercise great care in the handling of it as an overdose would prove fatal; but it will give the body a better chance to fight the fever.'

'I'd be most grateful for it, and not let it out of my own charge.'

'There is one other thing. It is a known fact that the disease never strikes more than a mile away from land. It is that which makes me believe it due to insect stings rather than miasmas; for the latter can be blown far out by offshore winds, whereas the former are incapable of flying more than a short distance. Therefore, if on arriving in Martinique you find an epidemic raging, as I fear you may, use your overriding authority as Governor to clear the troops out of the barracks, and send them to cruise at sea in any ships available. Even those already sick may then recover through escaping a second infection.'

With the promised drug packed in his valise, and Droopy's valuable advice well in mind, Roger took his seat in the leading coach the following morning. Then the cavalcade drove away from the stately pile of Normanrood while their kind, short-sighted host waved after them for as long as his pale-blue eyes could discern the dust thrown up by their horses. That afternoon they reached Bristol and put up at the Negro's Head.

Bristol had for long been the second city in the kingdom, but it was on the point of losing its place to Liverpool. The latter had pioneered the wet dock system and could now afford better facilities for a quick turnround than any other port. The canal system, out of which Colonel Thursby had made a large part of his fortune, brought to it far more cheaply than could road transport the products of the now thriving industries of Lancashire and the Midlands; and, in addition, its shipowners had captured the great bulk of the enormously profitable slave trade. In consequence Bristol had now to rely mainly on its specialised trade with the West Indies, its great sugar refineries, and its long-established ship-building industry.

Like other great commercial centres, the revolution in France had had a most unsettling effect on its working population, and the propaganda of the so-called British Jacobins was making many converts to the doctrines of Communism. The landlord at the Negro's Head told Roger's party on their arrival that the yards were now at a standstill owing to a shipwrights' strike, but they were relieved to learn that this would not prevent their sailing.

Next morning, October the 1st, they made their final purchases, while the servants accompanied their baggage to the dock to see it safely stowed on board. After an early dinner at their inn they drove out to the Cumberland Basin, where their ship—the *Circe,* Captain Cummins—was awaiting only the arrival of her passengers to take advantage of a favourable wind, and sail.

With the evening tide, *Circe* dropped down the river. In the big after-cabin they drank with the Captain to a happy voyage; but long before they landed in the West Indies Roger would have given all he possessed to have exchanged the dangers that beset them, in this ill-fated ship, for another spell of risking his head in Paris during the height of the Terror.

4

Trouble Aboard

At that date there were over fourteen thousand merchantmen sailing the seas under the British flag. The majority of them were between three and five hundred tons burden. The East India Company alone owned a few giants ranging from a thousand to fourteen hundred.

But 'The Company' was a thing apart. Its monopoly of trade with India, Ceylon, Burma and China had made it fabulously rich, and its Board of Governors had used its resources wisely to build up a service worthy of their vast private Empire. Youths were enrolled as Cadets only after careful selection, and it was considered every bit as suitable for the younger sons of the nobility to enter the Company's service as to go into the Navy or study for the Bar. Its officers wore a handsome uniform; to achieve each step in promotion they had to have served for a specified number of voyages, which ensured a reasonable degree of efficiency to hold their ranks. All of them enjoyed the privilege of an agreed amount of cargo space, which enabled them to carry on highly profitable private trading, and the allocation of space to Captains was so considerable that it was not unusual for them to net ten thousand pounds, to split with their backers, out of a single voyage. Officers of the Royal Navy frequently transferred to the Company; its ships were well found in every particular, its seamen were efficient and by special decree immune from the unwelcome attentions of the press-gangs.

Very different was the status of all other ships of the mercantile marine. Strangely enough, to qualify for service as an A.B. in them a stiff examination in practical seamanship had to be passed; but the bulk of their crews was a rabble largely composed of ex-jailbirds or men fleeing the country to escape arrest; and their officers were almost invariably tough customers who had served for many years before the mast. No examination had to be passed to become a mate or master. It was sufficient for an ambitious A.B. to learn the three R's and a smattering of navigation, then a recommendation from his superiors to the owners was enough to get him a junior berth aft from which in time he might work up to become a Captain. In fact, it was a saying applicable to the retirement of most Merchant Captains that 'he had gone in at the hawse pipe and come out by the cabin window'. Yet, only too often when such men at last became masters, and answerable to no one during ocean voyages of many weeks, they took to the bottle and lost their ships, their crews and themselves owing to a combination of drunkenness and incompetence.

Captain Cummins of *Circe* was no better and no worse than many others of his type. He was a rough hard-bitten seaman of fifty odd, who could cope with log, lead and latitude, and for the rest trusted to his long experience of every type of weather. When seas were running high he conscientiously stayed on deck, sometimes for days on end; in periods of calm he often remained in his cabin, also for days on end, moody and half comatose from copious potations of neat rum. His breath was like a furnace, he packed the punch of a mule, his language could be more foul than that of any of his crew, and he maintained discipline among them with ferocious brutality.

Fortunately for his passengers they were called on to do no more than pass the time of day with him. In 'The Company's' ships *nouveau riche* merchants paid as much as a hundred pounds for the privilege of eating at the Captain's table throughout the voyage, but in West Indiamen the much more limited accommodation afforded space only for one large table in the after cabin, and the Captain fed in his own.

The *Circe* was a ship of four hundred and thirty tons, and like most of her class the one big cabin aft was, apart from the decks, the only place in which her passengers could congregate. Their possession of it was exclusive, but it had to be used for all purposes; so at each meal there were two sittings, the servants feeding at the earlier and the quality at the later so that they might linger over their wine if they so desired. Adjacent to the big cabin were twelve smaller ones, the majority of which had double berths, but St. Ermins had made a deal with the owners for the whole of the passenger accommodation; so there was ample room for their baggage in the spare cabins. The passengers' quarters were well equipped, having port-holes designed for protection from tropical heat. Below them, in the big after cabin, there was a long semi-circular sofa, and mirrors fitted into mahogany wainscoting adorned the walls. In one of the spare cabins a cask had been up-ended and secured to serve as a sea-water bath, and they had brought their own linen. So once they had accustomed themselves to habitual stooping, to avoid knocking their heads on the low beams of the ceilings, they were by no means uncomfortable.

There was, of course, no question of sailing direct to the West Indies. Even in peace time privateers of all nations, not by the score but by the hundred, swarmed in both Europe and American waters, and owing to the war with France they were now more numerous than ever. In consequence, except for specially fast ships, such as the Mail Packets, and other termed 'runners', a system of convoys had long been organised.

As the chances of a propitious passage were largely dependent on favourable winds the sailing of convoys was governed by the seasons, and the first winter departure habitually left home waters early in October. Owing to major war commitments the naval protection afforded was decidedly scanty; and usually consisted of no more than two eighteen-gun sloops, which were charged with shepherding anything from sixty to a hundred and twenty indifferently-handled and slow-moving merchantmen safely across the Atlantic.

Convoys for the West Indies assembled at Cork, and from first to last several weeks generally elapsed before they were fully mustered. Charles St. Ermins being aware of this had deliberately delayed the departure of his party until it was fairly certain that the bulk of the convoy would have put in an appearance, and that it would be waiting only a fair wind to sail. His timing proved good, as *Circe* dropped anchor off Cork on October the 3rd, and was delayed there no more than three days. During them the party went ashore and enjoyed the bounteous hospitality of Irish acquaintances who lived in the vicinity. Then on the 6th, with her crew lustily singing sea-shanties, the *Circe* weighed anchor, hoisted her sails and, in the company of some seventy-five ships, headed for the open ocean.

But, yet again, there was no question of sailing direct to the West Indies. Long experience had shown that, given normal conditions, the quickest passage could be made by a ship buffeting her way down to Madeira, then picking up the North East Trade Winds which ensured a swift and easy crossing of the Atlantic on a curve running from about 35° North to within 15° of the Equator.

On sailing from Cork the convoy set a course South by West, so as to clear Cape Finisterre by a hundred miles; and for the first four days out it enjoyed reasonably good weather. During that time, owing to the very limited area of the *Circe*'s decks, the passengers got to know most of her crew by sight and all her officers to nod to. She had a crew of forty-two, three mates, a purser, a supercargo and a doctor. Her cargo was mainly shoddy clothes and salt meat, as it was customary for the planters to make presents of these to their negro slaves at Christmas.

With a view to protecting British commerce from foreign competition, numerous laws had been passed, making it illegal for British goods to be exported, or Colonial produce shipped anywhere or re-imported from Britain, in any but British ships, and for a British ship to be manned by any but British subjects. But the breaking away of the North American Colonies, and the heavy demand caused by the war for trained seamen to man Naval vessels that had, in the years of peace, been laid up in dry dock, had brought about certain relaxations; notably that the Colonies might trade direct with the newly-independent States, and that the crews of merchant vessels might include a proportion of foreign seamen.

Owing to this comparatively recent departure, the First Mate of the *Circe* was a stolid Dutchman, and the Purser a lanky Swede, three of the crew were Balts and eight others who had been picked up at Porto Rico on a previous voyage were more or less of Spanish origin.

The Second and Third mates, Jennings and Baird, were ruffians hardly distinguishable from the crew; Wells, the Supercargo, who was carried only to act for the owners of cargo when the ship reached her destination, was a pimply youth suffering from tuberculosis who had undertaken the voyage for his health. Alone among them, the Doctor, a pleasant young Scot named Fergusson, had any pretence to more than a smattering of education.

With all sail set the convoy buffeted its way south. Few of the ships in it were as large as *Circe,* and although the majority were ship-rigged most of them were only two-masters, and there was a number of schooners and snows among them. On every side for miles around the October sun caught their white canvas against the blue-green of the ocean, making as fine a sea spectacle as one could wish for.

On their first Sunday at sea the Captain took Divine Service; Charles and Roger read the Lessons and all the passengers attended, but not all the ship's company. It was natural that the Porto Ricans, being Catholics, should absent themselves from a Church of England ceremony, but eight or ten British members of the crew refused to come aft for it and later held a prayer meeting of their own up on the fo'c's'le.

The meeting was led by one of the quartermasters, named Ephraim Bloggs. He was about thirty years of age and a splendidly built fellow with a shock of short curly black hair. It was obvious too that he was a man of strong personality and much superior to the average run of seamen.

As Roger watched the little group from the distance, he was somewhat perturbed by this schism, which in one sense divided the allegiance of the crew. It was not that he was a bigoted supporter of the Church of England, but because he knew that the so-called British Jacobins found their strongest adherents among Dissenters and often used their meetings to spread revolutionary doctrines.

When he mentioned this to Captain Cummins, the Captain said that he too regarded such meetings as most undesirable; but, as religious tolerance was always observed under the British flag, it was beyond his powers to put a stop to them. He added that Bloggs had been brought up as a blacksmith, and rumour had it that he had fled the country some years before on account of having half-murdered the squire of his village in a fit of ungovernable rage. He had already displayed the violence of his temper in a quarrel with the bos'n and been put in irons for insubordination; but, that apart, he was an excellent seaman, and no quartermaster could be more reliable when doing his trick at the wheel.

It was on the following day, and their fifth out of Cork, that a series of squalls forced the convoy to take in much of its canvas, and as the men hauled on the ropes their gay sea-shanties gave place to more doleful ones.

They were now in the latitude of the Bay of Biscay, and the weather worsened rapidly. By evening visibility was down to half-a-mile and they were running with naked masts before the storm. Georgina and Nell had retired with bouts of queasiness from the unaccustomed motion on the first evening out, but had soon recovered from it. Now both of them, and Amanda and Jenny as well, were prostrate from sea-sickness. Young Clarissa was the only one of the women who remained unaffected. Charles, too, proved a good sailor, but Roger had his work cut out not to succumb. He was not a particularly bad sailor, but lacked his usual confidence in himself when at sea, and from previous experience had a dread of bad weather.

During the night it blew great guns. Long before dawn Roger had given in and lay feebly cursing as he battled with nausea in his narrow cot. The awful rolling and pitching of the vessel apart, Monsieur Pirouet could have not cooked breakfast had he been offered a fortune, Tom was in no condition to serve it, or Charles to eat it; so Clarissa found herself the only candidate for the meal.

Dan, having spent so large a part of his life at sea, could stand up to any weather; so he knocked up a hearty breakfast for her in the passengers' galley, then stood by catching the various pieces of crockery before they could slide off the table, and watching her with admiration while she ate.

Afterwards she reeled from one cabin to another, doing what she could for the rest of the party, then insisted on going on deck; so Dan took her up to the poop and, from fear she might be swept overboard, belayed her to the mizzen mast with a rope's end. It was as well that he did, as the deck was heaving from one terrifying angle to another, and every few moments a sea washed over it. Drenched to the skin, her fair hair streaming in the wind, she remained there all the morning, and later told her friends that never in her life had she more enjoyed an experience.

For the three days that followed, the others lay prone in their cabins. Young Dr. Fergusson, Clarissa and Dan did what they could for them, but there was little that could be done. Each time the ship rushed up a mountain-side of water they held their breaths, then as it plunged into a seemingly bottomless valley they felt as though they were leaving their insides behind. Their groans were smothered by the thunder of the storm, the sheeting rain, and the ankle-deep water that slapped and hissed about the floors of their cabins. The wind screamed through the rigging, the timbers groaned; at times the ship, caught by a cross-wave, shuddered as though she was about to fall apart, while every hour or two there came a resounding crash as some spar snapped and fell, or a boat was stove in. They were in constant fear that each new crisis would prove the last, and their terrors were multiplied from the knowledge that, so exhausted were they from constant retching, should the ship begin to founder they would be incapable of making any effort to save themselves.

Although they did not know it, their apprehensions were well justified, as the tempest was driving the ship towards the coast of Portugal and had it continued unabated for a few more hours she must have been smashed to pieces on the rocks. On the fourth afternoon, by the grace of God, the weather eased, visibility became sufficient for the Captain to see the coast, and by setting the foresail they were able to veer away from it.

The convoy had been so completely dispersed that only one of *Circe*'s companions was now in sight; a brig that had lost both her top and top-gallant masts. *Circe* was in little better case as only her foremast remained intact; nearly all her upper yards were gone, and the decks were still a tangle of top hamper that had been hacked away in a series of emergencies. One of her crew had been swept overboard, another killed by a falling spar, and two more severely injured. Both captains decided to put into Lisbon, and their ships limped down to the port, arriving there to the relief of all on October the 15th.

Two other ships of the convoy were already there and three more made the port during the next twenty-four hours; but four of the five were so severely damaged that major repairs would prevent them from leaving for some time, and neither of the escort ships was among them. However, a Portuguese man-of-war was due to leave with a small convoy for Madeira on the 20th and Captain Cummins decided to make every effort to get *Circe* into condition to accompany it. Extra labour was engaged and from dawn to dusk for the next four days the ship was a pandemonium of hammering, sawing, clanking and shouting as new gear was rigged.

To escape the din, although hardly yet recovered, the passengers went ashore and the October sunshine soon revived their spirits. Forty years earlier Lisbon had suffered the worst earthquake of modern times. The greater part of the city had been thrown to the ground, the whole of the harbour and all the shipping in it had been totally engulfed and 40,000 people had perished in the space of a few hours. But the Portuguese had tackled this terrible calamity with great courage, and from the rubble a fine new capital had soon arisen which contained many beautiful buildings.

The travellers were filled with admiration as they strolled across Rolling-Stone Square, and on the third day they made an excursion to Cintra where they thoroughly enjoyed a meal eaten on a vine-covered terrace and washed down with new-made wine. Their joy in this brief respite from the confined quarters of the *Circe* was only marred by the news which kept coming in of other ships of their convoy which had been wrecked on the coast. At least nine had been pounded to pieces on the rocks and it was certain that others had foundered in the terrible storm; so they felt that they had been very lucky to escape with nothing worse than the considerable damage the sea water had done to their clothes and other belongings.

On the 20th the *Circe,* and one schooner that had arrived in the Tagus shortly after her, set sail with the Portuguese convoy. The weather was now fair, but the winds, as was to be expected at this season, were still contrary. Again the ships tacked in long sweeps from side to side, rarely making more than two miles an hour in the direction of their destination. Then, on the fourth day out from Lisbon, trouble started on board the *Circe*. A deputation of the crew led by Ephraim Bloggs came aft to protest about the badness of the food.

As Roger later found out, the complaint was fully justified; but the passengers knew nothing about it until they saw Bloggs strung up to a grating, and learned that he was about to be given fifty lashes with the cat. According to Captain Cummins, when the deputation had been told that nothing could be done Bloggs had had to be restrained by the older men from attacking him; so an example must be made by disciplining him severely.

Fifty with the cat meant four hundred and fifty cuts and such a flogging might cause death unless a man had a very fine physique. The women were appalled at the ferocity of the sentence, and Charles and Roger agreed that its severity would have been justified only if Bloggs had actually knocked the Captain down; but the latter's word was law on board his ship, and when he had refused to listen to their pleas that he should reduce the number of lashes there was nothing they could do to prevent matters going forward.

Amanda, Clarissa and the two maids hurried to their

cabins, but Georgina stood her ground. Charles touched her on the arm and said: 'M'dear, this is no place for you. I pray you join the others.'

She shook her head. 'Nay, Charles; I intend to remain, and have a reason for so doing.' Her knuckles showed white from the force with which she gripped the poop-rail and she turned her face away so that her glance was averted from the horrid scene below her; but otherwise she never moved a muscle, even when after the nineteenth stroke Bloggs began to scream and call on God to help him. At the thirty-fourth stroke he fainted, and Captain Cummins, evidently feeling that he had sufficiently exerted his authority, called to the bos'n to have him cut down.

As his lacerated body slumped on the deck, Georgina's voice rang out sharp and clear. 'Have that man carried to the empty cabin next that of my woman!'

The group of seamen about Bloggs looked up at her in astonishment, then towards the Captain for a confirmation of her order. He turned upon her, his coarse face reddening slightly, and exclaimed: 'My lady, 'tis not fitting that one of the hands should occupy an after cabin. He'll do well enough in the fo'c's'le, when the doctor's had a look at him.'

'You heard what I said!' she snapped. 'See to it that I am obeyed!'

'Madam!' he protested angrily. 'This is no affair of yours, and. . . .'

'Don't Madam me!' Her half gipsy blood was on fire and her black eyes blazing as she cut him short, then flung at him: 'I am set on this and mean to have my way. Cross me and when I return to England I'll see to it that your owners put you on the beach forthwith.'

It was a very awkward situation. Roger was in full sympathy with Georgina's generous impulse but, all the same, he thought it most regrettable that by this public quarrel she should risk humiliation or, if she won her point, undermine the Captain's authority. Fortunately Charles stepped into the breach and in his quiet good-humoured voice said to the irate Cummins:

'Her ladyship intends no criticism of your handling of the

ship's affairs, Sir; but her susceptibilities have naturally been much affected by this unhappy scene; and there is reason behind her contention. None of us questions your right to punish as seems fit to you; but you must agree that there is no warrant for withholding merciful ministrations from a sufferer after the punishment has been inflicted. Need I say more to ensure you acceding to her ladyship's wishes?'

Captain Cummins accepted the olive branch. The words that conveyed it were soft-spoken enough, but he had noted a certain hardness in the young Earl's brown eyes, and in those days an Earl was still a power to be reckoned with. Shrugging his broad shoulders he signed to the men to carry the unconscious Bloggs to the cabin next to Jenny's.

Without a glance at the Captain, Georgina went down to the cabin, had Jenny boil water, tucked up her own voluminous skirts, and washed the still seeping blood from Blogg's lacerated back with a very mild solution of salt, then made him as comfortable as possible there and left Jenny in charge. Two days later he was about again, apparently little the worse for his awful thrashing, and in the meantime Jenny had learnt quite a lot about him.

She said that he declared himself his own worst enemy from the violence of his temper; and that although it was true that he had been forced to run away to sea on account of having half-killed his squire, the gentleman had brought his beating on himself by turning a poor old invalid woman out of her cottage. He could both read and write, was a follower of the Methodist persuasion and, a rare thing in those days, had forsworn the liquor. His account of conditions before the mast was truly heartrending and, as a convinced disciple of Tom Paine, he had dedicated himself to the course of securing the 'rights of man' for the underdog, even if in the last event that meant resorting to force.

Georgina retailed this to the others with some misgivings; as although she and Charles regarded themselves as responsible for the well-being of their dependants they both held to the tradition that the lower orders should be content to remain in the station to which God had called them. Roger heard it with considerably more concern, as it bore out the forebodings he had felt about the Dissenters' meetings which Bloggs held on Sundays.

His uneasiness was increased by the fact that on the Sunday following Blogg's flogging, five more of the crew failed to attend the Church of England service but joined the Dissenters; and after prayers were over the dozen-odd men continued their meeting squatting on the deck, smoking their clay pipes and talking in low voices.

He had no grounds for supposing that Bloggs was preaching mutiny but he could make a very good guess at the kind of talk that went on at these discussions, and he had practical experience of the sort of horrors which might result from a general acceptance of Blogg's doctrines. Only too often he had seen well-intentioned men undermine authority among the illiterate masses, then be swept aside by unscrupulous ruffians who led frenzied mobs to commit the most brutal excesses; so he decided to take an early opportunity of having a talk with Bloggs.

It came that afternoon when the burly quartermaster did his next trick at the wheel. Sauntering up, Roger dropped into conversation with him and, after a few casual remarks, began to ask about the conditions of the crew.

The subject was one on which Bloggs had plenty to say. He described the year-old salt pork, bullet-hard peas, grey-coloured duff and weevily biscuits that they had to live on as 'enough to turn a man's stomach', and their quarters as 'scarce fit for animals'. Roger had already noticed that as soon as the ship reached a warmer latitude nearly all the men spent the nights on deck, and now Bloggs told him that they did so only to escape the bugs, fleas and rats that infested their airless foul-smelling den which had neither light nor warmth, or even space enough for all the off-duty watch to stretch out in comfort at one time. In the tropics it was customary for them to sleep near naked, but from the start of the voyage to its finish they never took off all their clothes, and their only facilities for washing were in a bucket of sea-water that had been hauled up from over the side.

In *Circe* and many ships like her, Bloggs said, the crew's lot was made still harder by unnecessarily harsh treatment, as some Captains allowed, and even encouraged, the mates and bos'n to belabour the men with ropes' ends when hauling on tackle, although in the long run it did not make them work any better. They were expected to take blows and abuse without protest, and the least sign of resentment was sufficient to get them clapped into irons. At times a man was picked on for some very minor slackness and given twenty-four hours in the hole just to ginger up his mates; and during the present voyage the only days on which there had not been one or more men in irons, for slight offences, were those of the tempest.

The wages of an ordinary seaman were three pounds a month, and with the object of preventing them from deserting they were not paid until their ship returned to her home port. Despite that, many of them preferred to forgo their earnings on the outward voyage rather than remain in a bad ship or under a tyrannous Captain; and there were so many of both that nearly a third of all the seamen who went out to the West Indies deserted ship when they got there. Some of them took a chance on signing on for a return passage in another vessel, but the great majority elected to join the lawless thousands already there, as beach-combers, smugglers of contraband to the Spanish mainland, or in privateers which were often little better than pirates.

Obviously matters were even worse than Roger had supposed and he made no attempt to defend the shipowners, who through meanness or neglect, were fundamentally responsible; but he did put it to Bloggs, as tactfully as he was able that, however strong the men's grounds for complaint might be, no good could come of encouraging them to hold meetings, at thich their natural tendency would be to exaggerate their grievances and in time become obsessed with them.

At this Bloggs, who had previously been most communicative, suddenly became abrupt and surly in his manner. Evidently he now suspected that Roger was acting as a stool-pigeon for the Captain, and endeavouring to trap him into admission that he was fomenting unrest among his shipmates. He muttered with a touch of truculence that the only meetings he knew of were those held on Sundays, that every man had a right to worship God in his own way, and that if a few poor mariners chose to join together in prayer that was no concern of their betters.

Hoping to restore the conversation to a friendly footing, Roger talked for a while about religion and his own tolerant attitude towards it, but either Bloggs was no theologian or thoroughly alarmed, as he refrained from comment, and replied to questions only by monosyllables; so Roger had to abandon the attempt to wean him from his potentially-dangerous activities.

On the evening of her tenth day out from Lisbon, the *Circe* reached Madeira. Captain Cummins had hoped to find there the bulk of the convoy with which they had left Cork, but in that he was disappointed. Between the 19th and the 27th both escorts and nearly sixty merchant vessels had come straggling in, but no more having arrived during the past two days the senior naval officer had assumed the remainder to be either lost or refitting in other ports; so, only that morning, he had given the order for the voyage to be resumed.

For any but fast ships to cross the Atlantic without escort was to run a grave risk of capture by a privateer on nearing the other side, but both *Circe* and the British schooner that had accompanied her from Lisbon had a fair turn of speed; so after consultation their Captains decided that as the convoy was only a day's sail ahead of them, rather than delay for a month awaiting the coming of the next, they would take a chance on being able to catch their own up. In consequence, the passengers had only a few hours ashore in the little port of Funchal on the morning of the 30th, while fresh water, vegetables, fruit and two pipes of Madeira wine were taken aboard; then anchor was weighed again and sail set for the long run to the Indies.

Now that they were down in the lower thirties conditions were very different. The weather was clement, the air balmly, and instead of progressing laboriously by cross-winds they bowled merrily along under full sail propelled by the North East Trades. The hot weather caused the girls to take to their muslins, and canvas awnings had to be rigged to shade the decks from the blazing sun. Any regrets the passengers had had earlier about making the voyage were now forgotten in the pleasure of long days spent in idle chatter, playing games, reading, and watching schools of porpoises and flying-fish or an occasional whale.

Captain Cummins now emerged from his cabin only at infrequent intervals. When he did he was always morose and often the worse for liquor; but that may to some degree had been excused by the fact that he had become a prey to considerable anxiety. *Circe* and the schooner should have overhauled the slow-moving convoy within three days of leaving Madeira, but they had failed to sight it. This meant that they and it were sailing on slightly divergent courses; so by the fourth, or fifth day at the latest, must have passed it, and now had very little chance at all of picking it up. In consequence the *Circe* would have to run the gauntlet through privateer-infested seas when she entered the Caribbean. As her armament consisted only of a nine pounder in the bow and a long eighteen pounder stern-chaser these would prove quite inadequate protection against a well-armed rover; so should she fall in with one she would not have much hope of escaping capture unless she could show a clean pair of heels.

In spite of the brutish Captain's rare appearances on deck the men were kept hard at it, the majority of the duty watch being slung over the ship's sides in cradles to give her fresh coats of black and yellow paint as she ran smoothly down the trades. There was no let up in punishments either—as unless there was always a man or two in irons the Captain cursed the mates, accusing them of failing to maintain a sufficiently rigorous discipline—and there were two more floggings.

Another member of the company who was far from happy was Monsieur Pirouet. As he cooked for the passengers in his stifling little galley he thought longingly of the spacious kitchens at Whiteknights Park, St. Ermins's noble seat in Northamptonshire, and at Stillwaters, Georgina's own great private mansion near Ripley, and even of his domain in Berkeley Square, where he had ruled over a pastry-cook, a vegetable chef and six kitchen-maids. But what troubled this culinary artist even more was the greatly curtailed menus he was compelled to submit to his mistress. Before leaving London he had despatched two wagons in advance loaded with meat, fish, game, poultry and many other things, all packed in crushed ice liberally sprinkled with freezing salt; and on arriving at Bristol he had seen to it that all these were stowed well away from the decks where they would not be affected by the heat. Yet, despite all his precautions, now that nearly two months had elapsed since they had left London, many of the items that remained started to go bad almost as soon as they were unpacked and exposed to the torrid heat. He still produced miracles of omelettes and soufflés from his crates of eggs and could always fall back on his hams and smoked salmon, but was nearly reduced to tears by the lack of variety in the dishes he could send to table, and Georgina had her work cut out to console him.

November the 13th was declared a gala, as on that day they crossed the Tropic of Cancer. West Indiamen did not go as far south as the Equator, where Neptune and his consort would have come on board; so instead it was customary for the traditional ceremonies of crossing the line to be carried out during a visit from Mr. and Mrs. Cancer.

All work was called off, a large spare sail was rigged to form a bath amidships and filled with water, then two of the crew were lowered over the side to reappear on deck in fancy dress representing the powers of the deep. Everyone aboard who had not previously crossed the tropic was mustered to be initiated into this seafarers' mystery, and a far from happy little crowd they looked, as they had good reason to expect rough handling. But the women were naturally exempted, as also were Roger and Charles, for in those days it was considered almost a crime to treat a person of quality with lack of respect, and to duck a noble Earl was quite unthinkable. Instead, they and their ladies were invited by the ship's cook, who was acting as Master of Ceremonies, to take seats on the dais erected to overlook the bath, at either side of the thrones which had been set up there for Mr. and Mrs. Cancer.

It was then they realised that none of them had seen Clarissa since breakfast, and Charles suggested that perhaps she had shut herself in her cabin rather than witness the rough horse-play that was expected. But that proved far from the case, as a moment later she emerged from beneath the poop, and at the sight of her they all gasped with astonishment.

As the coming gala had been a topic of conversation for some days past, young Clarissa had decided to enter into the spirit of the thing and give them a surprise. Swearing Nell and Jenny to secrecy, she had got the two maids to make for her a large fish's tail out of an old dress that was spangled with sequins. Her legs were now encased in it, and her bare shoulders cloaked only with her lovely fair-gold hair which had been brushed out to its fullest extent. To carry her two poles had been lashed to a chair so that it formed a sedan, and in this Tom and Dan bore her triumphantly up to the dais.

Amanda was extremely angry at this prank as, although there was nothing actually indecent about Clarissa's get-up, she thought it most unseemly that her young cousin should invite ribald comments from the seamen by appearing in such a garb. But to send her back to her cabin was clearly out of the question, for at the first sight of the lovely mermaid the whole ship rang with lusty cheers of appreciation from the crew, and she was at once invited to take the part of Mrs Cancer, as far surpassing the sailor who had been selected for that role.

While the ship's fiddler scraped away vigorously, and the men roared out the chorus of 'What shall we do with a drunken sailor?' the neophytes were 'baptised' by having a cross marked in ink on their foreheads, had their faces lathered with a huge brush, were shaved with a wooden razor two feet long, given a beating with ropes' ends and finally thrown into the canvas pool. The poor little Supercargo was given a terrible time and only rescued at the plea of the Mermaid Queen, but the initiation of Monsieur Pirouet proved the high-spot of the day. He showed such intense resentment at having to submit to the ceremony that he received a worse baiting than any of the others and his furious struggles to escape only provoked general mirth. At length Clarissa managed to get him off further indignities, but not before his beautifully waxed moustache had been ruined; and for several days afterwards even Georgina could not induce him to utter a word.

It was on November the 19th that another storm blew up and, by ill-luck, one the severity of which was quite exceptional in those latitudes for that time of year, as the hurricane season was in the summer. Again the *Circe*'s masts were stripped of canvas and her hatches battened down, while the wind tore at the rigging and heavy seas thudded on her decks. However, the ship's situation was at no time as critical as it had been during the two worst days of the tempest she had met with off the northern tip of Spain, and her passengers now having been for seven weeks at sea were far better conditioned to stand up to the violent motion. Georgina, Nell and Roger went down with short bouts of sickness, but the others suffered only discomfort, and Clarissa once more thoroughly enjoyed herself. The storm parted them from the schooner which had been their companion all the way from Madeira, and they now missed her familiar presence; but the most annoying thing about it was that for the best part of three days the *Circe* had to run before the storm, which drove her to the north-westward and over five hundred miles out of her course.

This was particularly infuriating for Roger, because had the wind continued fair for a further two days they should have sighted Martinique. On his appointment as Governor of the island, their original plan had been modified to the extent that his party was to be dropped off there while Charles's went on to Jamaica; and, if it proved practical, they would exchange visits after Christmas. This would have made no difference to *Circe*'s schedule, as the normal course for ships sailing to Jamaica was to pass between Martinique and St. Lucia. It was this which had caused the islands to the south and north of that Channel to be named the Windwards and the Leewards respectively; and after leaving them to left and right Jamaica-bound ships completed their voyages by a five-day cruise inside the semicircle that they formed.

But now *Circe* had been carried up to a point some distance north of the Virgin Islands; and Captain Cummins said that, since any attempt to thread a way between the innumerable rocky islets dotted about them would be fraught with grave danger, he must pass outside Porto Rico, then tack down the channel between that island and Santo Domingo. Roger therefore had no option now but to go on to Jamaica and take a ship back to Martinique from there, which would mean a delay of at least a fortnight before he could hope to assume his Governorship.

On the second day after the storm abated they made a landfall on Porto Rico, and all that afternoon ran along within sight of the big island's north coast. As its dense forests ran right up to the tops of its mountains it appeared to be uninhabited, but they were near enough to make out groups of tall palms dotted along its shores and the line of white surf creaming on its golden beaches. At this first glimpse of the green and azure playground they had come so far to enjoy the passengers were thrilled, but they were given something much less pleasant to think about early next morning.

As dawn broke Porto Rico was still in sight and *Circe* was about to round the western end of the island. The channel between it and the eastern end of Santo Domingo was some eighty miles in width but another ship lay almost directly in her path. The other was a three-masted barque painted from bulwarks to waterline a greenish-yellow colour that would have made her almost unnoticeable had she been lying up in a cover with her sails furled against one of the islands for background. It was this unusual colour which immediately aroused the suspicions of *Circe*'s First Mate. Having bawled an order to 'about ship', he ran down to fetch the Captain.

By the time Captain Cummins, bleary-eyed and clutching about him a revoltingly soiled chamber-robe, reached the poop, the barque was already crowding on more sail and standing out towards them. Within a matter of minutes all hands were on deck, anxiously staring astern, though the early morning haze prevented them from getting a very clear view of the craft which looked as though she was bent on pursuit.

Roused by the shouting, the passengers soon learned the disquieting news, and hurriedly pulling on their clothes came out to join the Captain on the poop. By then there could be no mistaking the strangely-coloured barque's intent to come up with them; but she was still some two miles distant and the *Circe,* now heading north-west to clear the invisible point of Santo Domingo, was scudding along on a good brisk breeze.

That morning, November the 24th, no breakfast was cooked or eaten, for everyone in the *Circe* too much depended on whether she could outdistance her pursuer for any other matter to be given a thought. Both ships set staysails, stunsails and flying jibs, and heeled far over in the water under every inch of canvas they could carry. As the morning advanced the sun blazed down from a cloudless sky, and with visibility now perfect it became evident that the gap between the two ships was slowly closing. For sailing powers they were fairly evenly matched but the *Circe* was heavy laden and the barque in ballast, which made all the difference.

At eleven o'clock the barque called on her quarry to halt by firing her forward gun. The shot fell a hundred yards short, but at intervals of ten minutes others followed, and the fourth crashed into the *Circe*'s stern.

Amanda was standing beside Roger. Her grip on his arm tightened a little as she asked anxiously: 'What is likely to happen if they capture us?'

'Nothing very terrible,' he replied; and while he wished to reassure her he believed that he was giving her a reasonable forecast, as he went on: 'It will be deucedly inconvenient and damnably expensive, but it is unlikely they will do us any injury. Should we have to surrender they will put a prize crew on board and sail *Circe* to their home port. If she's French that will almost certainly be in Guadeloupe, as the recapture of that island last spring again gave France a base in the West Indies. But she may be American, and if so we would be carried much further from our destination. In either case I fear it would be months before we reached Martinique, as privateers sell the ships they capture and demand ransoms for passengers and crew. But they operate on licence from their governments, so are under an obligation to treat their captives honourably as prisoners-of-war.'

On *Circe*'s being hit, Captain Cummins had ordered her ensign to be run up and the women to go below; then he had a round fired from her stern-chaser in reply. It failed to reach its mark, but now she had shown her intention to resist her attacker also showed her colours. To the astonishment of the little group on the *Circe*'s poop they proved to be a white flag embroidered with the golden Fleur-de-lys of Royalist France.

Charles lowered the spy-glass through which he had been looking, and remarked: 'How very strange. The French Monarchy has been dead these two years past. Should she catch us there is no port to which she could take us without being caught herself, and by her bitterest enemies, the Republicans.'

Roger's face had suddenly taken on a strained look, as he replied: 'Then she cannot be a privateer. Her Captain must be a free-lance—some Frenchman ruined by the revolution who has become a lawless rover, and is out to plunder, sink and kill. God help us if we fall into his hands. This means we have no option but to fight him to the last.'

5

'For Those in Peril on the Sea'

Very anxiously now Roger and Charles discussed the evil fate which, in the shape of a graceful white-winged ship, had come out of the morning to menace them.

As the barque tacked in pursuit it could be seen that she had eight guns on either side, in addition to the long-gun in her bow and two carronades mounted on her poop. She was still at extreme range, so could not yet use her main armament; but should she succeed in closing sufficiently to do so it was clear that the *Circe* would be hopelessly outgunned. Even if they fought on, the enemy's cannon would cause such havoc among their masts and sailing gear that they would be hove-to and become vulnerable to boarding. So unless some unexpected turn of events occurred, their chance of escaping seemed slender; and to be captured by a pirate was a terrifying thing to contemplate.

Half a century earlier buccaneers had still sailed the waters of the Spanish Main with comparative immunity, but the navies of England, France, Holland and Spain had since combined to put them down, or regularise their depredations by converting them into licensed privateers; so their numbers had greatly decreased and to have fallen in with one was a piece of exceptional ill-fortune.

To be taken by a privateer would have been bad enough, as that would have meant being robbed of all but the clothes they stood up in, then having to kick their heels, perhaps for months, in far from comfortable quarters while they arranged to buy their feedom with heavy drafts on London. But to fall into the hands of a sea-rover who owed allegiance to no government might prove infinitely worse.

Such pirate captains were, almost without exception, debased and illiterate men who treated their captives with ruthless savagery. The fact that they were outlaws debarred them from all communication with the civilised world; so they had no means of securing ransoms for their prisoners. Instead they either killed the men or marooned them on some desolate islet, and having raped their choice among the women gave them over to become the common property of the crew until death during some drunken scrimmage, or from disease, released them from their hideous bondage.

It was the thought of their wives, young Clarissa, and Jenny and Nell being handed on from one filthy ruffian to another which made the palms of Charles's hands go damp and Roger conscious of a horrid empty feeling in the pit of his stomach; although each endeavoured to reassure the other.

They argued that as the barque carried the flag of Royalist France the odds were all on her Captain being a man of gentle birth. If so, however criminal the life to which he had taken, his natural instinct would be to treat the women chivalrously; and, as one who had been brought up to put faith in the word of one gentleman given to another, he might be persuaded to put them all ashore on their promise to arrange for a large sum to be made available at some port where he could collect it without danger.

Yet these optimistic speculations were offset by grave misgivings, as they were aware that there were definite limits to the authority wielded by pirate captains. Their crews were the scum of the seven seas, desperate and vicious men, banded together in free association, and willing to obey their leaders only so long as doing so seemed likely to serve their own ends. Discipline could be maintained aboard such ships only by a captain shooting out of hand any man who challenged his authority, and provided the bulk of the crew thought the action for the common good that was the end of the matter; but if a majority got the idea that their captain was either falling off as a leader, or cheating them out of their full share of plunder, it was they who murdered him.

Governing the sharing out of plunder, and the enjoyment of captured women, they had rules well established by tradition, and the disturbing thought was the unlikelihood that they would be willing to forgo them. From that, it followed that even if this French Royalist sea-rover's instinct was to protect his prisoners, there seemed little chance that he would give his men just grounds for combining against him by doing so, if that entailed the risk of stirring up a mutiny which might prove beyond his powers to suppress.

Grimly, although they did not say so to one another, the two friends faced the fact that unless *Circe* could hold her lead until nightfall, then throw off her pursuer during the hours of darkness, both her passengers and crew would all be wishing that they had been quietly drowned some weeks back off the coast of Portugal.

Meanwhile both ships had exchanged another shot, neither of which scored a hit; but now the Frenchman fired a sixth. It landed plumb on the poop not a yard from the mizenmast before bouncing overboard, and was a clear enough indication that she was gradually creeping up on them.

Its arrival coincided with the striking of eight-bells; so although the whole crew was standing by, the watch was automatically changed. The Dutch First Mate took over from the Second, who had been on duty for the past four hours, and Ephraim Bloggs relieved the man at the wheel.

The north-east corner of Santo Domingo could now be made out distinctly as a dark irregular patch on the horizon, some twenty-five miles away. At the speed they were making Captain Cummins estimated that they should round it about three o'clock, and he said that when they did the wind, for a time at least, would be more favourable to him; but Roger now doubted if they could get that far before the Frenchman had come up close enough to fire a broadside and disable them.

Frantically he cast about in his mind for a means of saving the women. He was willing enough to play his part in fighting the ship, but no uncertainties troubled his well-balanced mind about where his first loyalty lay. As a passenger he was under no obligation to stand by Captain Cummins to the end, and he decided that he must abandon him if that would give a better chance to get his own party away. Taking Charles aside, he said to him in a low voice:

'Unless the Frenchman has the luck to shoot away one of our masts, we still have an hour or two in which to make preparations against the worst.'

Charles gave him a desperately worried look. 'I take it you have in mind the provisioning of some hiding place for our ladies and their maids. I greatly doubt though if they could remain undiscovered till a chance arises for them to get ashore. Any prize crew that is put aboard will ransack the ship from stem to stern in search of valuables.'

'That apart;' Roger replied, 'I fear that a number of our own crew are untrustworthy and may go over to the pirates. In any case some of them will give it away that there are women aboard, and under threats betray their hiding place. No; unless you have a better plan, mine is that we should remain aboard as long as there seems a chance that *Circe*'s resistance may prove successful; but should capture seem inevitable we will get the women into one of the boats and make off in it.'

'Anything would be better than surrender; but I doubt your idea being practical. To lower a boat full of people while the ship is still under weigh sounds a damnably difficult proceeding.'

'She won't be. Gunfire will have reduced her speed, and Cummins be on the point of surrender, or if he decides to fight it out they'll be about to board us. In either case we'll be as good as hove-to. The Frenchman may send off a boat to chase us, but there's a fair chance that he'll be too fully occupied. Anyway we should be able to secure a good lead. The sea is calm and in an hour's time we'll be within fifteen miles of the coast. It will be a stiff pull but with you and I, Dan, Tom, and Pirouet, we should be able to reach it.

Charles's brown face brightened. 'I believe you're right. What do you wish me to do?'

'Go down and warn the girls. Tell them to pack small cases. Nothing heavy. No more than each of them can carry —just their valuables and greatest necessities. I'll inform the men of our intentions. The gig is the lightest boat, so we'll take that. While everyone has their eyes fixed on the pirate, Dan will have no difficulty in giving her a quick look over without attracting attention. He'll see to it that there's water in her, and make sure that her gear is in running order so that we'll be able to get her out speedily.'

As they were about to turn towards the poop ladder they saw again the bright flash of the Frenchmen's bow gun. It was followed by a puff of white smoke and, a moment later, the dull boom of the charge. The report was still echoing across the water when the shot crashed into one of the *Circe*'s after cabins. A piercing scream came from below.

Scrambling down the ladder Roger and Charles ran aft along the passage under the poop fearful of what they would find. To their relief their wives were safe, but they were greatly distressed at the scene they came upon in the big after cabin. Poor little Nell lay with her head in Amanda's lap. The round shot had come through one of the cabin windows and had taken her arm off near the shoulder. For a yard around the place was spattered with her blood, and it was impossible to staunch the bleeding from so great a wound. Within five minutes she was dead.

Roger had already told them all that they must not use the big cabin because it would be dangerous; but it emerged that she had gone in there to fetch something and, by ill chance, the shot had crashed through the window just at that moment. Now, having covered her up, he hurried the others into the store-room amidships, where they would be protected on all sides by bulkheads. Leaving Charles to tell them of his plan, he went to his own cabin, hastily stuffed a few things into his pockets, collected his sword and pistols, and went in search of Dan.

When he came out on deck again the Frenchman was perceptibly nearer, and had landed another round, shattering one of the starboard mizen chains. Each time *Circe* came into the wind to alter tack she fired back, and now she scored her first hit. A cheer went up from the men who were manning the gun, and striding over to the bos'n who was acting as layer, Roger cried:

'Well done! If you can hit her often enough she may abandon the chase. I'll give five pounds for every shot that finds a mark, and a hundred if you can bring down one of her masts.'

With another cheer the gun crew set about reloading, and hurrying across to Cummins, Roger asked:

'What do you think of our prospects, Captain?'

The Captain glumly shook his head. 'They're none too good, Sir. Unless we can dismast her she'll come up with us before we make the point. Then a couple of broadsides will likely carry away enough of our gear to bring us to; so she'll be able to board us.'

'You mean to fight though?'

'There's naught else for it. Were she a privateer I'd surrender; but pirates are very different cattle. They'll not risk letting us go, so as we could later get a ship o' war sent from Jamaica to hunt them out. If we're taken, they'll hang you gentlemen an' me and my officers from the yard arm, or worse. Better by half to do our damnedest to drive them off, or die fighting if need be.'

Roger nodded agreement, and having satisfied himself that there would be no premature surrender, went in search of Dan. On finding his faithful henchman, he quickly outlined his idea for getting the women away in the gig during the height of the fight if the *Circe*'s crew looked like being worsted. The ex-smuggler agreed that it could be done and they settled the details. He was to look over the gig, then keep Tom and Pirouet near him, and once the *Circe* was boarded keep an eye on Roger. If Roger took out his handkerchief and waved it, they were all to run to the gig and set about lowering her while St. Ermins fetched up the women.

Another round shot coming over caused them to duck their heads, then jump for cover from the splinters as it smashed through a hatchway further forward. Exchanging a sheepish grin, they resumed their conversation and Roger gave Dan further instructions that he wished carried out should he be killed during the action, or if it proved impossible to get the gig away. Dan did not relish at all these but he had been in too many tight corners with Roger to question his judgment, so he reluctantly agreed to obey them.

It was now getting on for half-past-one. At every change of tack shots were being exchanged and both ships had scored further hits. The *Circe*'s after cabin had had four balls through it and part of her poop deck-house smashed in, but she had landed two rounds in the Frenchman's fo'c's'le and shot away the tip of her jib-boom, forcing her to haul in her flying jib. Yet, this loss of sailing power was so comparatively slight that she was still gaining upon them. Three bells had just struck when she suddenly turned into the wind and fired her first broadside.

The guns had obviously been aimed high, in the hope of bringing down one of *Circe*'s masts. With a whistling scream the eight balls hurtled overhead. Three of them passed harmlessly, three more tore rents in the sails, and two only cut pieces of rigging. No serious harm had been done and a little time must elapse before the enemy could get into position to fire another broadside; but that might have more serious results; so Captain Cummins decided that, rather than wait until wreckage might impede movement on the decks, arms should now be served out, and he gave the key of the armoury to the Second Mate.

A few minutes later, muskets, pistols, cutlasses and boarding-pikes were being passed from hand to hand until every man of the crew had a fire-arm and some other weapon. Those on the poop received their's last, and Bloggs was given a pistol and a cutlass. As he thrust the pistol into his belt his gaze travelled slowly over the little groups of men down on the deck, then he gave a swift glance at Captain Cummins, who was standing at the after rail with his back turned, and let go the wheel.

Instantly it and the ship swung round. Her sails emptied, billowed out and flapped with the noise of guns, then hung slack.

With a savage oath the Captain turned, strode towards him, and bellowed: 'The wheel, Quartermaster! The Wheel! What in thunder are you about?'

But Bloggs had turned his back to the wheel, and it was evident now that he had been waiting only for the moment when he and his fellow malcontents should be armed. Lifting his cutlass he shouted defiantly: 'Haul down your flag tyrant! Me an' my mates ain't going to be killed for the likes of you.'

At the sound of their raised voices all eyes were turned upon them. Down on the deck, as though at a pre-arranged signal, Blogg's friends drew their weapons and ran towards the Mates. Up on the poop, one of the gun-crew suddenly turned and whirling his ramrod on high struck down the Bos'n.

The Captain, his eyes suffused with rage, pulled out his pistol, but Bloggs was quicker. With a mighty swipe of his cutlass he clove Cummins from forehead to chin. His face pouring blood, the Captain slumped to the deck. The cutlass, stuck fast in the terrible wound, dragged Bloggs half down on top of him. Putting his foot on the dying man's chest he strove to drag it free.

Roger and Charles had been standing near the gun. Both whipped out their swords. Charles ran his through the man who had struck down the Bos'n; as the blade slid home below the mutineer's ribs his eyes bulged in their sockets, he gave an awful groan, doubled up and staggered away clasping his stomach.

Another of the gun-crew came at Roger with a boarding pike. It was the favourite weapon among seamen and very awkward to counter with a rapier. The man was small but very agile and jumping from side to side thrust with his pike at Roger's face. Roger managed to beat aside the strokes but one of them caught him in the forearm, ripping open the sleeve of his coat and drawing blood. The wound was not serious and he used it to carry out an old trick.

Pretending to have been disabled, he stepped back and let his sword arm drop. With a cry of triumph his attacker ran in on him. At the critical second he dropped on one knee and turned his sword upwards as though in a salute. The pike passed harmlessly over his shoulder, while the point of the sword pierced the sailor below the chin. With a violent thrust Roger forced the blade home. The man's scream was choked in his throat by a rush of blood. He dropped his pike, went over backwards and lay squirming on the deck.

Meanwhile, the First Mate had pulled out his pistol and fired at Bloggs. Just in time the Quartermaster caught sight of him and ducked. The bullet whistled through Bloggs's curly black hair. Giving his head a shake, he abandoned his efforts to free his cutlass from the Captain's skull, and sprang away. The Mate clubbed his pistol and ran at him to strike him down, but Bloggs seized his wrist and they closed in a desperate wrestle. The Dutchman weighed fourteen stone, and was a tough, powerfully built man, but the ex-blacksmith was as strong or stronger. Swaying this way and that, they strove for mastery.

Charles had been about to come to Roger's help, but as the man with the pike went down, he turned and took a step forward, intending to run to the assistance of the Mate. By ill luck he trod in a pool of blood, slipped, and measured his length on the deck. Quickly, he picked himself up, but it was then too late.

Bloggs had succeeded in breaking the Dutchman's hold. Stooping suddenly, he seized him under one knee and by the cravat, then heaving him up bodily, he staggered to the ship's side and threw him overboard.

Roger too had seen the Mate's desperate situation. As Bloggs swung the unfortunate man off his feet, he sprang over Charles's prostrate body and ran towards them. The boom of a second broadside sounded from the Frenchman, and at that moment it took effect. One of the shots struck the mizenmast full and true about twelve feet up. There was a frightful sound of rending timber. The upper part of the mast heeled over to port. Yards, spars, sails, rigging and blocks came crashing down smothering the poop and everyone on it beneath them. Roger was hit on the head by a piece of tackle and pitched forward unconscious.

6

Captured by Pirates

When Roger regained consciousness he found himself in the after-cabin. All sound of fighting had ceased and there were only the usual noises of the ship's gear straining against the wind as she ploughed her way smoothly through the sea. For a moment he wondered where he was, then the sight of the shattered mirrors and splashes of Nell's blood on the silk covering of the settee where he lay brought everything back to him.

Amanda was sitting beside him, and he took in the fact that she was crying. As he raised his bandaged head her sobs gave place to a sigh of relief, and quickly laying a gentle hand on his chest she urged him to lie still.

His head ached abominably, but he forced himself to keep his eyes open. By turning it slightly he saw that Georgina was sitting slumped over the table, her dark head resting on her arms, and that Jenny, also weeping, was endeavouring to comfort her with an arm thrown round her shoulders. Clarissa was not in his field of vision but moved into it shortly after Amanda spoke, to stare down at him. Her eyes were unnaturally bright and her small face drawn, but she smiled faintly.

'What happened?' Roger asked in a husky voice.

Putting her hand behind his head Amanda raised it a little and held a cup of wine to his lips so that he could take a few sips, then she said:

''Tis a mercy you were not killed, my love. You were struck on the head by a spar when the mizenmast came down. But you must not talk. It's bad for you. Close your eyes now and try to go to sleep.'

'I must know what happened,' he insisted.

It was Clarissa who answered. 'We know only what we have been told. 'Tis said that Bloggs killed Captain Cummins and led a mutiny. The ship ceased to go forward before the mast was shot away and it seems, thinking our case was hopeless, most of the crew had already decided to surrender rather than fight. When the pirates boarded us they met with no resistance, and we are now captives. After they had cleared the debris from the poop they brought you down here, but . . . but Charles. . . .' Her young voice faltered to a stop and she looked away.

Roger sat up with a jerk. A blinding pain shot through his head. With a groan, he shut his eyes, then gasped: 'You . . . you do not mean . . . ?'

Clarissa nodded. 'They say he was struck down by the mast and when found was already dead.'

Amanda rounded on her angrily. 'Need you have disclosed our loss while Roger is in so precarious a state? 'Tis wicked to disturb his mind when all above things it needs rest.'

'Reproach her not!' Roger exclaimed as he sank back. 'There are times when it is best to know the worst, and this is one of them. What else is there to tell?'

Feeling that he would demand an answer, Amanda took up the tale. 'The pirate is said to be a French nobleman named de Senlac. He has put a prize crew on board under a fearsome-looking individual—one João de Mondego. It seems that Bloggs's friends and the Porto Ricans all went over to the enemy. They have been left on board, while the four Balts and those of our own crew who remained loyal have been taken as prisoners to the barque. When they had hacked clear the fallen mast our remaining sails were trimmed again. We rounded the corner of Santo Domingo an hour back and are now proceeding along the island's noth coast. There! That is all we know. And now I pray you try not to think more than you can help of our predicament; for 'tis likely you are concussed, and may become subject to brain fever unless you can court successfully the soothing influence of sleep.'

'What of Dan?' Roger asked. 'And young Tom, and Monsieur Pirouet?'

'All three were taken aboard the Frenchman, with Doctor Fergusson, the Second Mate, and the loyal members of the crew.'

'Tom and Dan had a quarrel,' Clarissa put in. 'Tom told me about it before he was taken away. Our flag had fallen with the mizen gear, but caught high up so was still flying well above the deck. Dan climbed up, cut it down and threw it into the sea. Tom was taken with a great rage that Dan should perform so treacherous an act and fought with him, but got the worst of it.'

'Be silent, girl,' Amanda snapped. 'Have you not the sense to realise that this betrayal by our trusted servant will so distress Roger as to further excite his mind. Ill news will always keep, and additional woes the very last things that should be thrust upon him at this moment.'

Clarissa stuck out her small pointed chin aggressively. 'Your pardon, cousin, but I disagree. Wounded as Roger is, upon his leadership and ability to plan for us now rests our sole hope of preservation. 'Tis but proper that he should be made aware without delay of all particulars; so that he can formulate his policy accordingly.'

'She is right,' Roger murmured. 'My wound is painful but I doubt its being dangerous, and at least it has resulted in my being allowed to remain with you. Bad as things are we must not lose heart, but try to devise some means of either placating or tricking our captors.'

He strove to get into his voice a note of optimism, although his heart could not have been heavier. Clarissa's touching faith in his capabilities only added to his misery. He had not a notion that might even alleviate their situation, was still too hampered by pain to think clearly, and greatly doubted if he would be given any chance at all to influence such decisions as might be taken about their future.

Closing his eyes, so that Amanda might not see the tears that welled up into them, he thought of Charles. Young, handsome, rich, titled, debonair, no man could have seen more favoured by the gods, yet in one awful moment he had been snatched from those who loved him. His wit and kindness, quick perception and gentle nature had made him the most delightful of companions, and they would all miss him terribly. Roger's heart bled for Georgina. Her passionate half-gipsy blood had caused her to love many men, but for Charles she had had in addition something of a mother's fondness and had found with him a mental contentment that she had never known before, so his loss must prove for her a cruel affliction.

Every few moments a stab of pain shot through Roger's head, rendering all his efforts to concentrate abortive; so he was forced to give up, and lay for a while in a semi-stupor. He was roused from it by Amanda's uttering an exclamation. Opening his eyes, he saw that she was staring with a frightened expression towards the cabin door. Raising himself a little he saw that in it stood the fearsome figure of a Carib Indian whose hook-nosed face seemed to protrude from his chest.

A moment later he realised that the Indian was a hunch-back, and Amanda saw that her fears were groundless, for from his long ape-like arms there dangled a brush in one hand and a dustpan in the other. He had evidently been sent to tidy up the cabin and had found the things in Tom's closet. Having given them a not unfriendly grin he set about his task, swept up the broken glass, removed a wrecked chair and tied back the torn curtains. Then he signed to Jenny to pull Georgina away from the table.

As Jenny half lifted her mistress in her arms Roger saw that Georgina's lovely face had an unnaturally blank expression, and he feared that the shock of Charles's death had unhinged her mind. Without a murmur she allowed herself to be led away and made comfortable in a chair on the far side of the cabin.

The hunch-back left them for a few minutes to return carrying a big basket piled high with tropical fruits, then he went to investigate the larder. Fetching from it half a ham, a round of curried beef, a big wedge of cheese, a cake, biscuits and several bottles of wine, he set them out on the table, but did not bother to lay it with plates, cutlery or glasses, before going away again.

Five minutes later the pirate who had been put on board as the captain of the prize crew came in, accompanied by a woman. At the first glance Roger saw that Amanda's description of João de Mondego as a fearsome-looking individual was no exaggeration. He was very tall and at some time must have been severely burnt, as his face was almost fleshless and the scarred skin was drawn so tightly across the bones that it had the terrifying appearance of a living skull. He was dressed in buff breeches and a gold-laced coat that must have once belonged to a gentleman of the last generation. Two pistols and a knife was thrust through his broad leather, silver-studded belt, and in his hand he carried a naked cutlass.

The woman, on the other hand, was strikingly handsome. She was a splendidly-built mulatto with fine dark eyes, and an abundance of lustrous black hair that fell about her shoulders in carefully-curled ringlets. Her coffee-coloured skin was without a blemish, her nose was large but not flattened, and her partly negroid ancestry showed only in her full, ripe mouth.

She was wearing gold-tasselled, patent-leather Hessian boots, a knee-length mustard-coloured skirt, and a scarlet blouse which was so tight that it accentuated the shape of her full breasts almost to the point of indecency. In a black silk sash round her waist she carried a silver-mounted pistol and an ivory-handled riding switch. Roger judged her to be about thirty, but, having coloured blood, she might have been considerably younger.

Both of them surveyed the prisoners in silence for a moment, then the man said in guttural French: 'Come Lucette; let us eat.' Upon which they sat down at the table and set to. Using only their fingers and sheath knives they crammed the food into their mouths and washed it down with copious draughts of wine straight from the bottles.

For a quarter of an hour they gorged themselves without exchanging a word. At length João gave a great belch and sat back; then his companion got lazily to her feet and, fixing her big sloe-like eyes on Amanda, said in an educated voice, using the lisping French commonly spoken by Creoles:

'You are the tallest, so your clothes will fit me best. Where are they?'

Amanda told her the situation of her cabin, and with lithe grace she lounged out through the door. There was silence for a moment, then Clarissa, also using French, asked the pirate:

'What do you intend to do with us?'

A slow grin spread over João de Mondego's skull-like face and he replied with a heavy accent due to his Portuguese origin. 'You'll see in good time, my pretty. There's no call to be frightened, though. Provided you're a sensible wench no harm will come to you.'

His words were reassuring, but the implication that lay behind them was far from being so. Again a tense silence fell, while he continued to eye her speculatively between swigs at the bottle of claret that was before him.

He had just finished it when the mulatto he had called Lucette came in again. She was still wearing the same clothes but now had on over her scarlet shirt a brocade jacket of Amanda's. Showing her fine white teeth in a full-lipped smile she said:

'Your things fit me very well, Madame. I shall find a good use for them.' Then she asked: 'Which of you is the Countess?'

Georgina did not even look up, but Amanda waved a hand in her direction, and the mulatto walked over to her. For a moment Lucette stood looking down on the grief-stricken figure, then she said smoothly: 'I think your ear-rings would suit me, Lady. Be good enough to hand them over.'

It seemed as though Georgina had not even heard her, as she made no move to obey; her eyes remained blank and her face expressionless. Lucette's brows drew together in a frown and she exclaimed: 'You sulky bitch, you need a lesson.' Then, thrusting out a hand, she seized one of the diamond drops and tore it from Georgina's ear.

With a cry of pain Georgina suddenly came to life. Her eyes blazing, she threw up an arm, thrust the mulatto away and sprang to her feet. Roger, too, jerked himself erect. His head was swimming and his legs unsteady, but he lurched forward, crying in angry protest:

'Can you not see that the Countess is unwell! She is suffering from the shock of her husband's death. Have the decency to treat her grief with respect.'

For an answer Lucette turned, took a step towards him and struck him in the face with her clenched fist. The blow caught him on the left eye. A pall of blackness suddenly eclipsed his vision. Against it he saw stars and whirling circles, then his weak knees gave under him and he fell back in Amanda's arms.

Never had he felt so angry and humiliated. He could have sobbed with rage at the lack of strength which rendered him impotent to defend those he loved, even from a woman. As it was he could only let Amanda lower him back on to the settee, and sit there with his aching head buried in his hands.

It was another cry which brought his head swiftly up again, but this time it did not come from Georgina. Realising the futility of resistance, she had given up her other ear-ring, and the mulatto was standing opposite one of the cracked mirrors fixing the diamonds in her ears.

The short sharp scream had been uttered by Clarissa. Swaggering over to her, João had grasped her round the waist, and with one horny hand beneath her chin was forcing her head back so that he could kiss her. Amanda had jumped up and rushing at him seized his arm in an endeavour to drag him away from her young cousin; but lifting his heavy boot he gave her a kick on the thigh that sent her reeling.

Just as he did so, Clarissa seized the opportunity to jerk her head free. Next moment her teeth bit viciously into the pirate's wrist.

With an oath, he tore his hand away and lifted it to strike her, but help came to her from an unexpected quarter. At Clarissa's cry Lucette swung round from the mirror. Quietly drawing her silver-mounted pistol from her sash, she pointed it at João and shouted at him:

'Stop that! You know our customs, and I am here to see that all of you keep to them.'

With a shrug he let Clarissa go, and muttered surlily:

'Don't be a fool, Lucette. I meant only to buss the wench. There's no harm in that.'

'You'll buss no one without my permission,' she snapped back. 'You're mine as long as I have a use for you. Now get up on deck and relieve Pedro the Carib, so that he can have his victuals.'

'Who's Captain here?' he blustered.

'You are, by favour of my good standing with M. le Vicomte,' she retorted. 'But cross me and when we get ashore I'll have him fling you to his pet crocodiles.'

João's glance dropped before her angry stare. Sucking the blood from his bitten wrist he turned on Clarissa, and snarled: 'You shall pay for this, my beauty. Ah, and before you're a night older.' Then he gave a jaunty flip to his old-fashioned tricorne hat, picked up his cutlass and swaggered out of the cabin.

As soon as he had disappeared, Lucette said to Amanda: 'I've a mind to see on you some of the things I'll be wearing. Go to your cabin and put on your best ball-dress.'

Amanda was crying from the brutal kick that João had given her, and replied tearfully: 'I am in no state to dress up for you. I pray you excuse me.'

Lucette promptly pulled out her ivory-handled switch. Striking Amanda a vicious blow across the shoulders, she cried: 'Do as I bid you, woman. The sooner you learn that you are now a slave the better.'

With a burst of sobs Amanda stood up and limped across the cabin. Roger attempted to follow her, but his legs doubled under him again, and he fell back with a groan. Lucette gave him a contemptuous look, and said:

'They tell me you were on your way to become Governor of Martinique. A lovely island and I know it well, for I was born there. But you'll never reach it; M. le Vicomte has no friendship for Englishmen, and I do not doubt he'll send you to feed the fishes.'

At that moment Pedro the Carib came in. He was a swarthy half-caste with lank black hair. Perched at a jaunty angle on it was one of the broad-brimmed straw hats that many sailors favoured when in the tropics. His breeches were of leather and he was naked to the waist except for two heavy necklaces made of pieces of eight. They were not like ordinary coins, but simply an ounce weight of silver which had been poured molten on to an iron bench, then, when it had partially cooled, stamped with the arms of Spain, and an 8, signifying its value in pesetas. It was a common practice for seamen to bore holes in them and carry them in this manner round their necks, as it made their loss by robbery less likely, and it was easy to take off one or more in payment for liquor or a woman.

Pedro barely gave the captives a glance from the slits which half concealed his reddish evil eyes, but picked up a bottle, let a third of its contents gurgle down his throat, then grabbed the remains of the ham and began to knaw it like a dog.

While he ate, Lucette rifled the lockers round the cabin, showing a childish delight in anything she came upon that particularly interested her. Then Amanda rejoined them, now wearing a low-cut dress of peach-coloured brocade that had a drawn back overskirt of chiffon sprinkled with small gold stars. She had regained her composure and stood stony-faced in the middle of the cabin while Lucette sauntered lazily round her like a huge graceful coffee-coloured cat.

'The mode will flatter me,' was her comment. 'But go take it off now. I do not wish that it is spoiled, and when we celebrate our victory this evening it is certain that you will be the subject of some rough games, for one cannot deny the men their pleasure.'

Amanda closed her eyes, and half-fainting at the thoughts the mulatto's words had conjured up, staggered from the cabin.

When Pedro had finished his guzzling, Lucette said to him in a tone that brooked no reply: 'Now I intend to sleep for a while in the cabin of the Countess. Go up to the poop and remain there. Keep an eye on João. Should he make one sign to come down here, you are to wake me up; for I'll not have him cheat the rest of you in the matter of the women.'

He gave her a crooked grin, nodded and slouched away; then, after a final glance at the captives, she too left them.

Roger looked across at Georgina. For some time past she had been sobbing as though her heart would break; but he was glad of it, for it seemed a certain indication that Lucette's brutal treatment of her had brought her back to normal, and he had feared that her mind might have become deranged. The faithful Jenny, pale-faced but tight-lipped, was still beside her. Clarissa sat hunched in an elbow chair, her golden hair tumbled from her struggle with João, but dry-eyed and staring without expression through one of the cabin windows.

When Amanda came back she gave Roger a faint smile, and brought him some wine to drink before sitting down beside him. As he thanked her he thought that she looked ten years older than she had that morning, but there was nothing he could do and nothing that he could say to comfort her. His head still felt as though it were splitting, his eye had swollen up and was rapidly becoming black and blue, the place where the pike had laid open his right forearm now felt as though it were on fire, and the whole of his right side, with which he had hit the deck on being struck down, ached dully. He could only take one of her hands in his and put his other arm round her shoulders. Never before had he felt so utterly helpless and hopeless.

Gradually Georgina's weeping eased to a low sobbing and for a timeless interval they all sat silent in the depths of dejection. At length, as twilight began to fall, Amanda gently released herself from Roger's arms, stood up, and said:

'Come! Even if there is no longer anyone to summon us to supper we ought to eat something. In God is now our only hope; but I hold that He helps those who help themselves, and it would be flying in His face not to try to keep up our strength.'

'Well said, my sweet,' Roger murmured, and although he still felt groggy, he found that he could now walk to the table without assistance. Georgina stubbornly refused to join them, protesting that even a morsel of food would choke her; but she made Jenny take a place after helping Clarissa to fetch some plates, cutlery and glasses. In a grim, brooding silence they forced themselves to swallow some of the remains left by their captors and to drink a few mouthfuls of wine. Most of the fruits brought abroad by the pirates were strange to them, and in other circumstances they would have sampled them all with interest, but, robbed of appetite by their fearful apprehensions, they hardly noticed what they ate; and they were still seated round the table in the semi-darkness when the door was thrust open and the hunch-back came in.

He spoke in some uncouth jargon of mingled Spanish and Carib, but the significance of his gesture was plain. He had been sent to order them out on deck.

For a moment Roger contemplated rebellion, but he was still so feverish and weak that a child could have knocked him down. He had no doubts whatever that if he told the women to refuse to go they would be fetched, and it seemed better to go with them on the remote chance that by giving his life he might be able to save one of them in a crisis, rather than to remain behind and face the ghastly torture of not knowing what was happening to them. Rallying all his strength, he began to offer up frantic prayers for help, then led them from the cabin.

Out on the deck the scene was reminiscent of that—now seeming to the prisoners a whole lifetime away—which had taken place barely ten days earlier when *Circe* had crossed the Tropic of Cancer. There was no canvas bath and the dais was lower, but on it was the same pair of big chairs which had been used as thrones, and to either side of an open space before them the whole ship's company was congregated.

The thrones were occupied by João de Mondego and Lucette. In front of them was an upended cask of rum, the top of which had been stove in. Everyone present held a pannikin and most of the men were still avidly lapping down their first tot. As the captives appeared they were greeted with cheers, boos and cat-calls. The hunch-back led them up to the cask, pannikins were produced from somewhere and Pedro the Carib, who was doing the honours behind it, ladled out a portion equivalent to a fifth of a bottle for each of them; then ordered them to drink it.

Amanda and Jenny only sipped theirs; Clarissa took a

mouthful, then choked and spluttered; Georgina flung hers at Pedro's feet.

Instantly Lucette's voice rang out: 'Fill for her again Pedro. If the noble Countess abuses more of our good liquor we will make her lick it up off the deck.'

A shout of laughter greeted her threat. Pedro refilled the pannikin and again handed it to Georgina. Roger said in English loud enough for those with him to hear. 'For God's sake drink the stuff, and more if you can get it. 'Twill deaden your sensibilities.'

Obediently, between chokes and gasps, they swallowed the fiery liquor. Then the hunch-back led them to a wooden bench, placed opposite the dais but some distance from it, and signed to them to sit down. A moment later he seized Roger's arms from behind, thrust a cord between them and his back, then drew it tight and knotted it firmly. Instinctively Roger strove to free himself, but his struggles only provoked more raucous laughter from the spectators; and, having secured his arms, the hunch-back next firmly lashed his ankles, so that should he stand up with the intention of moving forward he would fall flat on his face.

His last hope was gone of grabbing a knife from someone and, perhaps, bringing this ghastly party to a premature end by stabbing João or Lucette; his left eye was now completely closed, but with the other he took stock of the assembly. Including João, Lucette, Pedro, and the hunch-back, the prize crew numbered only a dozen, with probably a man at the wheel and another on look-out duty. Bloggs was present with nine of his cronies, and all eight of the Porto Ricans.

The ship's fiddler had been one of Bloggs's following from the start; and now, seated on a chair in front of the rum barrel, he struck up a merry tune. Darkness had come with the swiftness usual in the tropics, but the bizarre scene was lighted by lanterns hung in the rigging. Some of the men began a rhythmic clapping, then four of them came out on to the circle of deck amidships that had been kept clear and danced a hornpipe.

After it the revellers lined up for another tot of rum. Then one of the pirates sang a soulful ballad in a deep baritone. The ship was moving almost silently over the deep waters, and in any other circumstances the captives would have been enraptured by his untutored talent; but, as things were, they could only listen with an awful apprehension of what might yet befall them as the night advanced.

Thunderous applause led to an encore, but after it the less musical among the men had had enough and called loudly for a country dance. Marshalled by Pedro the Carib, they formed two lines, and to the scraping of the fiddle began to tap their feet, bob awkwardly to one another, then utter loud shouts and leap about in a travesty of a gavotte.

The country dance was followed by more rum, then a succession of rollicking choruses in which the French-speaking pirates, the English mutineers and the Spanish-reared Porto Ricans at first were given a hearing in turn, but later endeavoured to out-shout one another; so that their combined voices merged into an ear-splitting babel of sound.

At length, when the din subsided, someone called for a pavan.

Most of them had asked others to be their partners, when one of the *Circe*'s men came up to Jenny and said: 'Please Missy, will 'e dance wi' me?'

Jenny cast an anxious glance round, but there seemed nothing for it but to accept. Reluctantly she stood up. The sailor put his arm round her and whirled her away. Others nearby saw them move off and swiftly followed his example. Half a dozen claimants squabbled over which of them should lead out Clarissa, Georgina and Amanda. Two free fights ensued, but those not involved seized upon the three girls and pulled them willy-nilly into the dance.

Roger now sat on the bench alone, suffering the worst torments that hell has to offer. He had fooled Catherine the Great of Russia, defied a Spanish Prime Minister, beaten the unscrupulous Fouché at his own game, tricked France's Minister of War, the shrewd Carnot, stood up to Robespierre, Danton, Hébert, and a legion of other evil, ruthless men. He had caused a Spanish hidalgo to be hung from a lamp-post, and had slain the finest swordsman in all

France in single combat; but now, against this filthy, villainous, verminous, brainless, besotted crew he was utterly helpless.

Staring with his single good eye at his wife in the close embrace of a bearded, broken-nosed ruffian, he cursed the day when he had opposed his old master's wish that he should return to France, and instead lightly declared his intention of going off to the West Indies. Better a thousand times Paris in the throes of Revolution, with all its horrors, squalor and dangers, for they were things with which, given courage and wits, one stood a fair chance of coping.

Yet, when the dance ended, to his unutterable relief, the partners of the four women brought them back to the bench. The night was hot and they were panting from the exertions to which they had been forced, but other wise showed no ill effects from their unwelcome experience.

Soon, the fiddler struck up again, and this time there was a wild scramble to secure the women as partners. Bloggs was in the forefront of the rush and buffeting two other applicants aside with his huge fists seized upon Jenny. Lucette had taken the deck with João. Pedro grabbed Georgina, a British seaman Amanda and one of the Porto Ricans Clarissa.

The moon had risen silvering the sea. Again Roger crouched on the bench, straining against his bonds in agony of mind while the nightmare dance went on; but once more all the women were brought decorously back when from temporary exhaustion the fiddler ceased his scraping.

Now that Pedro had abandoned his post at the rum barrel the men were helping themselves, and some were already reeling about the decks so drunk that they were barging into their fellows. It was then that one of the *Circe*'s men shouted: 'The Mermaid! Come Mermaid, show us your pretty tail!'

The cry was taken up by the rest of the mutineers, and some of them volubly explained to the pirates about the fancy-dress that Clarissa had worn at the crossing of the Tropic of Cancer. Soon a deputation was crowding round her, urging her to don her Mermaid's costume. Her face paper-white, she stubbornly refused, but one of Bloggs's friends, known as Marlinspike Joe, shouted at her:

'Go put it on wench, or we'll strip you and put it on for you.'

Stark fear in her blue eyes, Clarissa looked at Amanda. Feeling that worse might befall unless the raucous crew were humoured, Amanda nodded, and beckoned to Jenny. Together the three women stood up and walked towards the cabins beneath the poop, followed by Marlinspike Joe and a few of his companions.

While they were away the bulk of the crew began to sing again. They had reached the stage when bawdy songs claimed priority over all else, and for the next quarter of an hour obscenities in French, English and Spanish echoed out over the tranquil moonlit waters.

They died away in a triumphant shout from the starboard entrance to the after cabins. Marlinspike Joe and his friends emerged bearing shoulder high on a scantling Clarissa in her Mermaid's costume.

At the sight of her the men broke into a ragged drunken cheer, interspersed with shouted comments of indescribable indecency. Her bearers set her down in front of the two thrones and for a few minutes she was subjected to a hail of ribald comment. With a view to moderating her previous appearance in the role, she had not brushed out her hair, and wore a cloak draped over the upper part of her body, but when her bearers had lowered the scantling to the dais, Marlinspike Joe pulled the cloak from her, so that her naked shoulders gleamed white in the moonlight. There fell a sudden hush and one could almost hear the intake as breath of scores of eyes fastened upon her.

Lucette leant forward and shouted at the fiddler: 'Play man; play a dance.'

Bloggs was standing near her and asked her to partner him. She hesitated only a moment then agreed. The fiddler struck up and once again the deck was filled with a mass of lurching couples. But João did not rise from his chair and Marlinspike Joe remained standing just below him, his lecherous gaze riveted on Clarissa. Suddenly he leant forward, grasped Clarissa's tail and dragged it from her. Beneath it she had on only her shift and now her bare legs were displayed up to the knees for all to see.

With a drunken laugh João bent down, caught her in his arms and lifted her on to his knees. Her scream rang out above the fiddler's music. Everyone stopped dancing. Lucette thrust Bloggs from her and marched up to the dais.

'Enough!' she cried. 'Put down that wench, or it will be the worse for you when we reach our lair.'

'To hell with that!' he shouted back. 'I claim a Captain's privilege. Tonight this pretty baggage sleeps with me.'

7

Ordeal by Moonlight

The moon was now high in a cloudless sky. Its brilliant light eclipsed the stars and dimmed that of the lanterns hanging in the rigging. Flooding the scene it splashed the deck with jagged patches of silver between the stark black shadows of the groups of revellers, and threw their features into sharp relief.

But Clarissa's scream had brought an abrupt pause in their revelry. The fiddler stopped his scraping, feet no longer stamped and shuffled on the deck, all movement ceased; the whole company had become as rigid as though suddenly turned to stone by the baleful glare from a Medusa's head.

Every face was turned towards the dais. Upon it João still sat enthroned, one of his long arms tightly encircling Clarissa's waist. She lay where he had dragged her, half sprawled across his knees. Her face had flushed scarlet and, sobbing with shame, she buried it in her hands; but she could not hide her naked legs and shoulders. Lucette stood just below them, her arms akimbo, her fine head thrown back. All eyes were riveted upon the group. The tropic night was warm and still. Even the seamen who were drunk held their breath as they awaited the outcome of the quarrel. Lucette's voice rang out. It was loud and angry, but Roger detected a nervous tremor in it.

'You will sleep alone!' she shouted. 'Leave the little one be! I'll not permit that you should have your pleasure of her.'

'So you're jealous, eh?' João retorted with an ugly leer.

'Nay!' she brazenly flung back. ' 'Twas only your repertoire of strange blandishments that has reconciled me these past few weeks to waking each morning with your skulls-head next to mine. Now they are stale to me, and among the new men aboard there are others I have a mind to try as bedfellows. I care not for you, nor who is the first to rape her once we get ashore; but I am determined that you shall follow the rules of our fraternity.'

'Well; and what are those rules?' he cried mockingly. 'By ancient custom it is declared that a Captain should have first pick of any captured women. After that, lots are drawn by all and a roster made by which each watch of the night some man gets his turn with one or other, till all have spliced each of them. Then comes the daily auctions for further turns; the highest bidder securing first choice and the cash going into a common kitty. What could be fairer? I stand by it, and claim nought but a Captain's right to take this tender chicken's maidenhead—if so be she still has one to be taken.'

A guffaw of laughter greeted the sally with which he ended. It drowned the groan that Roger could not stifle. He could close his one good eye to the scene but not his ears, and João's brutal words confirmed his worst fears, bearing out all that he had heard of the customs of the pirates. His bound hands were clasped behind him, and in an attempt to alleviate his agony of mind by agony of body he dug his nails into his palms with all the strength he could muster.

A sudden rustle and heavy thump beside him caused him to open his eye. Amanda had slid from the bench on to the deck in a dead faint. Beyond the place she had occupied Georgina and Jenny sat, clinging to one another, their faces dead white, their eyes staring in horrified apprehension. But no one glanced at Amanda as she fell, for Lucette was speaking again.

'You are no Captain;' she declared, 'only a lieutenant given the task of bringing this prize back to our rendezvous. When M. le Vicomte decided to leave the women on board he charged me with their care. 'Tis he, and he alone, who has a Captain's rights over them, and I am answerable to him. I give not a jot what he does to you, but I've no mind to have him throw me to his crocodiles for having failed to protect his interests.'

Releasing his hold on Clarissa, so that she slid half fainting to his feet, João stood up, stepped over her prostrate form and down on to the deck. Thrusting his face forward into Lucette's he snarled:

'So I'm no Captain, eh? You spawn of hell, I'll soon teach you that I am, and one whose word is law aboard this ship.'

She gave back a pace, but cried defiantly: 'You besotted fool! Were you not drunk you would never have the courage to court M. le Vicomte's anger. You have but to wait a week at most to enjoy the wench in accordance with our rules, but do so this night and he'll have you flayed alive. Even a moron would have the sense to wait that long rather than pay such a price.'

'Nay, I'll not wait an hour,' he bellowed. 'M. le Vicomte may be harsh but he is just. Having made me Captain of the prize he'll not take umbrage that I should have exercised a Captain's right.'

'You fool yourself!' Lucette began hotly, but broke off short owing to an unexpected diversion. Unseen by Roger, who had again bowed his head in helpless misery, Georgina had risen from the bench and walked forward until she was confronting João. Her voice was low but clear as she said in French.

'Perhaps I can provide a solution to this difficulty. It seems to me that Madame Lucette is right, and that should you take this girl you may pay for it with your life. But there can be no rule against your taking a woman who offers herself freely. Besides she is of tender years and untutored; so would provide you only with poor sport. Since you are so set on having a bedfellow I volunteer to take her place.'

Her words filled Roger with mingled feelings of sickening revolt and admiration. All his life he had loved Georgina. She had meant more to him than even Athénaïs de Rochambeau or his dear Amanda, and the thought of her submitting herself to the embrace of this loathsome skull-headed creature filled him with horror. Yet he knew that she had slept with many men, some of whom she had not even cared for; so the ordeal would prove less ghastly for her than for a young virgin like Clarissa. Her bid to save the girl was but one more demonstration of her splendid courage, and on tenter-hooks between fear for her and dread for Clarissa, he listened for João de Mondego's answer.

Slowly the pirate surveyed Georgina from feet to head, taking in her fine figure, lovely heart-shaped face, big dark eyes and the abundant ringlets that fell about her shoulders, then he muttered:

'By the Holy Blood, you're a handsome enough piece to tempt any man. I'm mighty flattered Mam, to have made such a conquest.'

Her eyes were unnaturally bright and her voice had a slightly hysterical note as she replied: 'You may disabuse yourself of that belief. I offer myself only because, my husband having been killed this morning, I care not what becomes of me.'

'Since that is so, you'll keep a while;' he grinned, 'and I'll lose nothing by waiting my turn for you when we get ashore. But this chit here is a different kettle of fish. Do I not take her now, some other may forestall me.'

Turning away, he seized Clarissa by the arm and dragged her to her feet.

Lucette had been staring in amazement and with a new respect at Georgina. Now, grabbing at João's arm as he pulled Clarissa up, she exclaimed:

'Shrew me! But you must be fitted only for a mad-house. To persist in this rather than accept all that so well-endowed a woman as the Countess has to offer—and that of her free will—is nothing short of lunacy.'

'Enough of your interference!' he roared, and letting Clarissa go he swung round upon her. Next second his fist shot out. It caught Lucette squarely beneath the jaw. Her head snapped back, her body hovered for an instant, then she crashed full length upon the deck.

For a moment he stood cursing her still form obscenely. Then, grasping Clarissa's wrist, he cried: 'Now, my little beauty, we'll to your cabin and see all you have still to show under what's left of that mermaid's dress.'

'Hi there! Not so fast,' a deep voice boomed in English, and Bloggs shouldered his way out from among the spectators.

Being ignorant of the language, João gave him an expressionless stare, then turned to Georgina and asked: 'What says this fellow?'

With new hope that Clarissa might yet be saved Georgina threw a glance of appeal at Bloggs, and cried: 'If you can prevent this awful thing that is about to happen God will surely reward you. I implore you to speak out in that sense—even if it was not that you had in mind.'

Instinctively touching his forelock, Bloggs replied: 'May it please your Ladyship, one o' my mates 'ere, Jake Harris by name, speaks a bit o' the Creole lingo. 'E 'eard the skipper wot captured we say particular to Miss Lucette as 'ow she should 'ave a good care of the ladies. That bein' so, it seems to we that she's in the right of it, an' this skull-faced swab is actin' contry to orders about the young missy.'

'Bless you!' exclaimed Georgina, and gave João a swift translation; adding on her own account: 'So you'd best have a care. These men threaten to raise the whole crew in mutiny against you.'

'They would not dare,' snapped João. 'Do they but raise a finger and I'll have them both strung up to the yard arms within ten minutes. Tell them that; and that the decisions of a Captain in his ship are no man's business but his own.'

This time it was Jake who gave Bloggs a rough translation. Having done so, he added: 'I'll allow 'e's right in that, Ephraim. Anyways 'tis not our quarrel. Do 'e choose to have 'is will of the wench 'e'll not be answerable to we, but to 'is Frenchy master.'

Georgina's heart sank; but Bloggs still stood his ground, and muttered aggressively: 'Maybe; yet that's not all. Miss Lucette did no more than 'er plain duty. She be a foine woman an' I've taken a great fancy to she. I'll not stand by and see she handled so by any dago—be 'e or be 'e not captain o' the ship. Nay, do 'e now give 'im fair warning, Jake. Dost 'e bash 'er down again, I'll serve 'e as I served Cap'n Cummins.'

João's blow had knocked Lucette out. While the altercation was proceeding she had remained sprawled motionless upon her back; but now she groaned, half raised, looked dully round and put a hand to her aching jaw. As her eyes fell on João they suddenly lit with a return of consciousness. Scrambling to her knees, she made to draw her pistol from her sash.

The pirate had not understood a word of Bloggs's last utterance, neither had Jake yet had time to translate his warning. On catching sight of Lucette's movements, quite unaware of the possible results of his act, he gave her a vicious kick in the ribs which sent her over sideways. Then, turning to Pedro the Carib, who was standing nearby, he snapped:

'Have that coffee-coloured bitch disarmed and thrown into the chain locker.'

Bloggs took this new brutality as a deliberate challenge. His broad face suddenly became suffused with blood and his eyes flashed murder. Seized in the paroxysm of one of his ungovernable rages, he wrenched his cutlass from its sheath and rushed upon João.

Instantly, pandemonium broke out among the entire ship's company. Up to that moment the prize crew, Bloggs's fellow mutineers, and the Porto Ricans had all been mingled together, cheerfully fraternising. Now, every man in the crowd of thirty or so cast a swift, apprehensive glance at his neighbours, sprang away to get nearer others of his own people or plant his back against some solid object; and every man of them reached for a weapon.

For a moment it seemed certain that a most bloody affray way imminent. It was Jake who saved the situation. Raising his voice above the din of trampling feet, threats and curses, he cried in English:

'Steady mates! There's no sense in our all cutting each other's throats. What is the mulatto woman to us, or the young missy either? Hold on, I say. Stand back, and let these two bully-boys fight the matter out between them.'

Lucette had staggered to her feet and, knowing enough English to understand the tenor of Jake's shouts, promptly backed him up by yelling to the Creole-speaking pirate crew: 'Put up your weapons. This is no quarrel with the *Circe*'s men! João has brought a duel upon himself. Give them the deck to have at one another. Form a ring now, and let the best man win.'

João meanwhile lost no time in defending himself. By springing aside he evaded Bloggs's first murderous slash. Whipping out his own cutlass he parried Bloggs's second cut, and now they were at it hammer and tongs, the steel of their blades striking sparks from one another, as they clashed, clanged and slithered in swift give and take.

Recognising sound sense in the shouted appeals of Jake and Lucette the polyglot crowd of seamen took their hands from their knives and pistols and drew back, forming a wide ring to give ample space for the furious combat. For a few moments they watched it with bated breath, then some of them began to shout bets upon its outcome.

Bloggs was obviously the stronger and weightier of the two, but João was the taller by three inches and had the longer reach. He too was by far the better blade, as years of fighting had made him extremely proficient in the handling of a cutlass, whereas Bloggs was untutored in the art and could only hope to break down the other's guard by his great stength; yet he had one advantage, for he was sober while João was three-parts drunk.

At first they seemed so well matched that either might prove the victor, and their respective backers would give no more than evens. But as João skilfully parried cut after cut and Bloggs began to pant like a grampus, it became clear that if the pirate could tire his antagonist out he would have him at his mercy.

Stamping, whirling, lunging and slashing, they careered round and round, the bright light of the moon making their every movement as clear to the spectators as if the fight had been taking place in daytime. Both were now gasping from their exertions and rivulets of sweat were running down their faces. As the minutes passed and Bloggs still failed to get a blow home the betting began to go against him. Soon, three, four and five to one was being offered to João.

Roger could not see the fight, as a group of seamen blocked his view of it, and, as his ankles were still tied, he could not leave the bench; but from the beginning he had been praying with all his might that Bloggs would emerge victorious. So too had Georgina, yet her heart began to sink as she saw that Bloggs's blows were losing some of their former strength, and that he seemed near exhaustion.

Suddenly, it occured to her to run in and seize João's sword arm from behind. Next moment she darted forward, but Pedro the Carib grabbed a handful of her curls and jerked her back. As she fell in a tumbled heap at his feet the pain of the wrench on her hair caused her to give a piercing scream. It was at that moment the end came with unexpected suddenness.

João, well aware that he was carrying a load of liquor, had had the sense to keep to the centre of the deck, moving his feet only when compelled and letting Bloggs circle round him. Just as Georgina screamed Bloggs had reached the limit of his powers to continue battling without pause. Stepping back a couple of paces, he lowered his cutlass, hunched his great shoulders and drew a sobbing breath. João, his eyes glinting with ferocious triumph, sprang forward to administer the *coup de grâce*; but the rum had robbed him of his sense of balance. On landing he stumbled and lurched sideways. Before he could recover Bloggs brought up his cutlass in a swift horizontal stroke. It slashed the pirate to the bone through the muscle of his right arm.

With a scream of agony João dropped his weapon and staggered back. Bloggs promptly put his foot on the blade, but made no move to go in and finish João off. Seeing that he did not intend to do so, Lucette left the dais, on the edge of which she had been standing, and walked forward to confront the wounded man.

An evil smile played about the corners of her full mouth as she stood there gloating for a moment, then she said: 'Well, *Captain* Mondego, you cannot complain that you have not been given fair play. I could have shot you in the back any time within the past ten minutes; but I observed the rules and refrained. Now I am glad of that. Custom decrees that a defeated captain is fair game for anyone who has a score to settle with him, and it will give me special pleasure to obliterate your repulsive face.'

Stark terror showed in João's eyes. Blood was gushing from the terrible wound in his arm on to the deck, and he was already weakening from its loss. Lurching to one side, he made an effort to lug his pistol from his belt with his left hand. Before he could get it out, Lucette had drawn hers from her sash and pointed it at him. There came a flash and a loud report. The bullet struck him in the mouth. His face blackened by the powder and spurting blood he fell sprawling at her feet.

No one in the crowd made any protest, or even showed surprise at her callous deed. They simply stood round in silence while João lay there squirming; until, with a light shrug of her shoulders, she turned to Pedro and said:

'Have him flung over the side to feed the sharks.'

The Carib had her order carried out with alacrity and it now became apparent that with João's death she had become the dominant personality in the ship. Marching up to still panting Bloggs she publicly embraced him, kissed him heartily on both cheeks and thanked him in a mixture of French and broken English, then she pushed the pleased but embarrassed quartermaster before her up on to the dais. When Pedro had seen João's body overboard she beckoned him up to stand on her other side and, with an arm thrown casually round each of the men's necks, addressed the crew:

'As M. le Vicomte's trusted representative it is within my powers to appoint a successor to João de Mondego; but I want no jealousy or discontent aboard. Therefore I will give you a choice. Here are two good men both of proved courage. To him you choose I shall expect all to give implicit obedience.'

Pausing she turned to Jake and told him to translate what she had said into English; then, when he had done, she added: 'Now which will you have as your temporary Captain?'

The shouts for Bloggs and Pedro seemed about equal in number; so a count of hands had to be taken. As was to be expected the pirates were solid for Pedro and the *Circe*'s English mutineers for Bloggs, but the Porto Ricans were divided, and as they were closer by blood and language to the Carib most of them voted for him, so by a majority of five he was elected. Bloggs shook him by the hand, to show he harboured no ill feelings, and Lucette slapped him heartily on the back; then she announced that Bloggs would act as Lieutenant. Two minutes later the crowd began to break up. Pedro had the man at the wheel relieved and appointed look-outs for the night, while Bloggs had Roger untied and, having escorted the prisoners to their quarters, posted a guard on the entrance to the after cabins.

For the time being their terrible ordeal was over, but they were all too played out even to discuss it. Still fearful that Marlinspike Joe or some other drunken ruffian might attempt to break in on one of the women during the night, they decided that it would be safer for them all to sleep in the big saloon; so they dragged their mattresses and a few coverings there, and lay down in a row still fully dressed.

From soon after dawn they had been subject to acute anxiety and the strain of the past few hours had been almost beyond endurance. Nature took charge and within a few minutes everyone of them was deep in the sleep of complete exhaustion; yet their last waking thoughts had been as harrowing as the worst of nightmares. Lucette's loyalty to her French master, and Bloggs's rage at João's treatment of her, had gained them a respite from horrors even to think of which made them feel physically sick—but only a respite. They knew now that, short of a miracle, within the next few days they must suffer utter degradation.

8

A Midnight Marriage

When they woke it was near midday. Their fatigue had been so great that they had slept the clock round. As each of them slowly roused to consciousness they could hardly believe that they had not awakened from some appalling dream, but realisation that they were lying on the deck of the big after cabin brought home to them the awful truth. Georgina was stricken anew by the knowledge that her beloved Charles was dead, and burst into heart-rending sobs. It was the sound of her weeping that fully roused the others, and sitting up they gazed woefully about them.

As soon as Roger moved, his head began to pain him again, but now the wound ached only dully; and, apart from the fact that his mouth was as parched as a cinder pit, he felt moderately well. On getting up he found that he could walk quite steadily, and going to the table he took a swig of wine from one of the half-empty bottles that was standing on it. As he did so he noticed that the debris of the previous night's meal had been removed and that other items now littered it. Evidently Lucette and her officers had breakfasted there, but any noise they had made while doing so had been insufficient to arouse the prisoners from their sleep of exhaustion.

Jenny had left her mattress and was once more attempting to console Georgina. Amanda and Clarissa were both sitting up and staring before them, their faces pictures of misery. After one quick glance, Roger looked away from them. He ached to say something that would cheer them up but could not think of any possible opening which might do so. Never before had he wished himself dead, but now he felt that Charles had been luckier than himself. With an effort he said:

'Come, a wash would freshen us all up; and there's enough food here for us to make a scratch meal afterwards.'

Silently they accepted his suggestion. Goergina found evidence in her cabin that Lucette must have slept there; so with Jenny's help she moved her toilet things and some of her clothes into one of the spare cabins. By the time they returned to the saloon the others were all seated round the table. Their cabins had showed no traces of intruders; Roger had had a shave and Amanda looked considerably less haggard with her face made up. Clarissa's resilient youth had already obliterated all signs of her previous night's distress, and Jenny's robust health made her look better than she was feeling. Georgina's beautiful eyes were bleary and she had not attempted to remove from her face the ravages that grief had made upon it; but at least she had ceased weeping and again had full control of herself. Nevertheless, as they helped themselves to the food, and ate a little of it mechanically, depression weighted upon them so heavily that none of them felt capable of making conversation, until Clarissa electrified her companions by remarking:

'I'll not deny that I was near scared to death last night by that hideous fellow's designs upon me; yet all the same I incline to think that being raped is nothing near so terrible an experience as it is painted.'

'Clarissa!' exclaimed Amanda, in a shocked voice. 'How can you speak of such immodesty? And before Roger, too.'

Georgina gave a weary tight-lipped travesty of a smile, then observed cynically to Amanda, 'Is it not a little late, my'dear, to suppose that Roger has any illusions left about the nature of women. Nothing she can say is likely to make him think better or worse of the sex. Besides, as rape is the only subject upon which any of us have brought ourselves to utter this morning, surely it is better that we should discuss it rather than continue to sit here in dreary silence.' Then, turning to Clarissa, she added: 'Now, child, let us hear the reason for this belief of yours.'

' 'Tis based upon what a friend of mine once told me at

the young ladies' Academy which I attended, Clarissa replied. 'She was of French descent and her grandmother had the misfortune to be caught by the Prussians during the Seven Years' War. It so chanced that my friend was playing one day near a summer-house in which her mother and grandmother were talking of that campaign. She distinctly remembers having heard her mother say, "I cannot think, Mamma, how you survived that brutal assault. The first attentions of a husband are bad enough, but to be raped by a total stranger would drive most women into a madhouse." At that time my friend did not understand what was meant by the word rape, but when she learned it she recalled this conversation and her grandmother's reply.'

Clarissa's cheeks suddenly coloured up, and casting down her eyes she hesitated before going on, until Georgina asked: 'Well, what did the grandmother say?'

In a small voice, still looking down, Clarissa answered: 'She said: "My dear, you should realise that there is nothing unnatural about rape, and that until historical times it was normally every female's first experience of physical love. Therefore, providing she can save her face by appearing to have had no alternative but to submit, any sensible woman will shut her eyes, lie back and endeavour to imagine herself the bride of a cave-man lover".'

The story so amused Georgina that she was momentarily taken out of herself and cried with a laugh: 'Damme, the old woman was right!'

Roger laughed too, while casting a speculative glance at Clarissa. He wondered if nervous preoccupation with the subject had caused her to blurt out the story, or if she had told it with the deliberate intent of lessening the other women's dread of the role that capture would force upon them in a few days' time. At that moment she lifted her eyes and they met his. There was no trace of hysteria in them; so he decided that his latter assumption had been correct, and in silent admiration he marvelled that so young a woman should show so much courage.

Now that Clarissa had broken the ice, they talked for a while of the previous night, freely confessing the fears and emotions they had experienced, but by an unspoken agreement all speculations about their grim future remained barred.

They had been sitting round the table for the best part of an hour when the hunch-backed Indian came in. Walking across to Jenny, he tapped her on the shoulder and pointed to the door, obviously indicating that she was wanted outside. At first she violently shook her head, from fear of what might happen to her if she left the others; but the hunch-back then enunciated a word that was recognisable as 'Bloggs' and kept on saying it. Somewhat reassured by the agreement of the rest that 'Bloggs' really was the word he kept on saying, she followed him out into the passage.

She was absent for about twenty minutes and when she returned the excitement in her face told them at once that some new development had occurred. Resuming her place at the table, she said in a low voice:

'Bloggs says that we must not count upon it, but that he has the wish to save us if that be possible.'

Muted exclamations of relief and hope greeted her announcement, and she went on: 'He says that another mutiny would not be possible, because he and his friends are still in a sense on probation. They have been allowed to keep their pikes or cutlasses, but were deprived of their fire-arms. Thus the pirates, having pistols and muskets, could soon overcome them.'

'What, then, does he suggest?' Roger asked eagerly.

'He feels that if the pirates be skilfully approached it should prove possible to detach them from their loyalty to the French nobleman who is their master. But before he makes any move at all, he requires an honourable understanding with yourself about the future.'

'Honourable!' muttered Amanda in disgust. 'And he a mutineer and a murderer! How can one treat honourably with such?'

'It was to him we owe it that worse did not befall last night,' Georgina said quickly.

'Indirectly perhaps; but no more,' Amanda retorted. 'He intervened only because he has taken a fancy to that brazen-faced mulatto woman, and flew into one of his great rages on seeing her mishandled. Had he not killed Captain

Cummins in the first place and brought the ship to by abandoning her wheel, *Circe* might well have escaped. It was his treachery which has brought us to our present pass; and I'd wager this is some scheme he has hatched to get us into his own hands. I would not trust him an inch.'

'I think, Madame, you take too black a view of him,' Jenny remarked. 'Not that I would excuse his crimes; but he seems to me a man whose acts are dictated by two warring natures, so is not altogether responsible for the evil that he does. At least I can vouch for it that just now he referred with deep sensibility to the kindness shown him after his flogging; and spoke most earnestly of his desire to aid us.'

Roger nodded. 'I judge you right, Jenny. In any case, even if he is playing for his own ends, I cannot think we are likely to fare worse in his hands than those of this Vicomte de Senlac. Seeing our situation, it would be the height of folly not to clutch at any straw; so I will willingly hear what he has to say. Did he give you any idea of his proposals?'

'No, Sir. He only said that it would be dangerous for him to show special interest in the prisoners, but that he would be coming down to his dinner later than the others; and that if you would send the ladies and myself to our cabins, so that he should find you here alone, he should take that as meaning that you are agreeable to treat with him.'

For a moment there was no more to be said on the subject; so they whiled away the afternoon as best they could, until at four o'clock the hunch-back came in to set fresh food upon the table, and, shortly afterwards, Pedro and Lucette arrived to make their main meal of the day.

The Carib, as they had already noticed, was far from being a loquacious man, and he hardly opened his mouth except to cram food into it. Lucette, on the other hand, had plenty to say for herself, and after she had satisfied her first hunger she began to question the prisoners on a score of subjects, ranging from their ages and places of birth to the style of hats now being worn in London. In less than twenty minutes Pedro was replete and belched his way out;

but Lucette sat on, muching some candied fruits that had been found among the stores, and when Bloggs arrived on the scene she still showed no signs of leaving.

Roger now became worried that finding all the women captives in the saloon Bloggs would assume that his overture had met with rejection; but there seemed no way of hastening Lucette's departure and, short of inviting her dangerous anger, the others could not all walk out as long as she continued her lazy questioning of them.

By the time Bloggs had demolished a great plateful of meat and pickles Roger feared that the chance of talking to him alone that evening was as good as lost, and worse, that he might not risk a further rebuff by making another opportunity. But Georgina had sized up the situation and saved it by saying to Lucette:

'I am accounted something of an artist, Madame; and during our voyage from Madeira I amused myself for a part of the time by designing some clothes that I planned to have made. As they conform to the latest modes, and you are interested in such things, perchance you would care to accompany me to the spare cabin where I keep my trunks. I forget now in which I put them, but between us we should soon rout them out.'

Lucette at once accepted the invitation, and, as she stood up, Georgina said to Jenny: 'You had best come with us, to help us in our search.' That only left Amanda and Clarissa, and no sooner had the others disappeared than they made an excuse to go to their cabins.

After a moment Roger said in a low voice to Bloggs: 'I am well aware how desperate is the situation of the ladies and myself and Jenny has told me that you may be able to help us. I can only say that should you be able to do so, we shall owe you more than we can ever repay.'

Bloggs favoured him with a by no means friendly stare, and replied: 'Foine words my foine gentleman; but 'tis not fer the likes o' you that I be concerned. 'Tis fer Jenny, who did nurse me when I were near a corpse from the floggin' Cap'n Cummins ordered me; an' fer her ladyship, who showed a poor mariner kindly charity on that same occasion. 'Tis no wish of mine that they other ladies should suffer what's in store for 'em, either. Yet they'll all get a taste o' hell afore their time unless summat can be done within the next day or so.'

'I know it;' Roger agreed, 'and I ask no mercy for myself. If by giving my life I can aid them, count it as already given. Now, what have you in mind?'

'I've a notion that maybe I could talk round Pedro the Carib. 'E's a queer cuss, that one. 'E don't speak much, but 'e onarstans a bit o' English, an' Jake an' me got quite friendly with 'e up on the poop this forenoon. Seems like 'e got a 'ate agin this Frenchy skipper under who 'e's bin sailin'. I've got a mind to put to 'e that now 'e's cap'n o' the *Circe,* 'e should fly 'is own flag in she, an' make off on 'is own.'

'That would certainly create a new situation, but I don't quite see how it would save the ladies from the sort of thing we fear for them.'

'Ah, but it could; should you be willin' ter let bygones be bygones, an' gi' me an' my mates a clean ticket.'

'You mean forget that the mutiny ever occurred, and the fact that you killed Captain Cummins?'

Bloggs nodded his dark curly head. 'For the death o' that tyrant I'll answer to Almighty God; but meantime, should I be caught I've no wish to swing in chains fer it from a gallows in Kingston or on Execution Dock. I were figurin' that you bein' the new Governor of Martinique, you'd maybe 'ave the power to give I a pardon.'

As Roger had always placed the welfare of those he loved before any canon of morality, he replied without hesitation. 'I have, and I will. I take it, too, that as your companions are also liable to a hanging for mutiny you want pardons for them as well?'

'That's so, Mister Brook; an' there's yet another thing. Piracy be the resort only o' the most desperate characters, seein' that pirate ships be liable to attack by any naval vessel that may happen along, whatsoever be her nation. But privateerin's a very different kettle o' fish. 'Tis respectable as well as profitable; an' you bein' Governor of an island could, I make no doubt, give we a privateer's commission.'

'Yes, I could do that,' Roger agreed, much impressed with the good sense that Bloggs was showing. 'And I take it that in return you would arrange for us to be given our freedom?'

''Twas on them lines that I were thinkin'. O' course Pedro an' 'is mates would 'ave to be given a clean bill, clearing they from all counts likely ter arise out o' they's past. They'd not row in wi' we otherwise. But do 'e pledge me yer word about a privateer's commission an' free pardons for all, an' I've a good 'ope 'twill serve as a strong enough inducement fer Pedro an' the rest to agree that you an' the ladies should be put ashore.'

'What of Madame Lucette?' Roger asked a shade anxiously. 'Think you she can be persuaded to become a party to this deal—or at least prevented from wrecking it?'

Bloggs hesitated a moment, then he grinned. 'She be that unpredictable 'tis more 'an I would say as yet. But so happen she've taken a bit o' a fancy to me; an' me ter her fer that matter.'

'Then if Pedro definitely agrees to your proposals, there should be a good chance of your winning her over?'

'That's the rig o' it, Mister Brook. Jake an' me will make a cast at 'e durin' second dog watch, an' if all's well I'll broach it to Lucette arter I've boarded she agin this comin' night. Have I yer solemn promise as a gentleman ter abide by our onerstandin'?'

Roger smiled, partly at the thought that despite Blogg's enthusiasm for the doctrine of 'Equality' he should still place more faith in the word of a gentleman than in that of one of his own kind; but much more with relief, that above the black pit of terror in which the *Circe*'s passengers had been plunged these past twenty-four hours there should now have appeared a ray of light. Wisely, he decided that since their new hope was entirely dependent on Bloggs's goodwill there must be no half measures about burying the past; so standing up he held out his hand and said:

'You have more than my word, for we shall still remain your prisoners until you choose to release us; but I give it you willingly and here is my hand upon it.'

Bloggs crushed the extended fingers for a moment in an iron grip, grinned again, and left the cabin.

When he had gone Roger sat down quickly. For the past hour his head had been paining him severely, and after the effort needed for the interview reaction swiftly set in. The stalwart Bloggs had radiated confidence, but now he had gone Roger began to reckon up the odds against his being able to carry his scheme through successfully.

First, he might have read more than was intended into a few surly remarks about the Vicomte by the taciturn Pedro. Secondly, even if Pedro was game to double-cross his master, would his men agree to follow his lead? He was far from having the forceful personality of a João de Mondego and, Roger had gathered, owed his position as an officer only to the fact that having known the reefs and shoals of these coasts since boyhood he was an expert at piloting a ship through them. It seemed much more likely that the other pirates would follow whatever lead was given them by Lucette. And on the previous night she had braved João's wrath out of loyalty to the Vicomte.

From what Bloggs had said it was clear that she had become his mistress, so he was in a stronger position than anyone else to influence her; but Roger did not feel that any great weight could be attached to that. One look at the big healthy body of such a tawny tigress was enough to tell any man that she revelled in every form of sensuality. Seeing the life she was leading, it could hardly be doubted that in the past dozen years she had willingly allowed herself to be caressed by scores, if not hundreds, of men. That she should have taken the repulsive João for a lover showed that her appetite was now jaded to a point where it required constant new stimulants; so it was as good as certain that she looked on Bloggs as no more than just another dish to be tasted. In a week or two she would probably cast him off anyway, and a month later have forgotten his existence; so if his project did not appeal to her it was more than likely that she would rid herself of him overnight—quite possibly by sticking a knife between his ribs.

By the time the others rejoined Roger, he took a very

sober view of their chances; and, having given them an outline of his talk with Bloggs, warned them to set no great hopes on his succeeding in his plan. Georgina had relapsed into an apathy of grief, and Roger had a touch of fever, so after Amanda had bathed and re-bandaged his head, they decided to turn in.

Next morning, they were awake and up by the time Lucette and Pedro came in to breakfast, and when Pedro had done Bloggs took his place. As Lucette was still there he said nothing of his plan, but, unseen by her, he gave Roger a solemn wink, which seemed to indicate that things were going well, although Amanda inclined to the opinion that it was nothing but an impertinent familiarity.

During a good part of the day Jenny hung about the poop entrance to the after cabins, hoping that Bloggs would have a word with her about their prospects; but he did not do so and left them to spend the dragging hours in futile speculation. Neither did they become any wiser during the dinner hour. Lucette was unusually silent, which suggested that she had something on her mind, but she again remained at table after Pedro had gone back on deck, and did not rise from it until Bloggs had in turn finished his meal; upon which they left the cabin together.

It was over an hour later when Bloggs returned and, touching his forelock, said 'Ladies, I be come ter request the pleasure o' your company out on deck; and yourn too, Mister Brook.'

The civility of Bloggs's address raised Roger's hopes, and he shot him a questioning glance.

Bloggs nodded. 'Pedro be wi' us. 'E's sounded some o' 'is mates. Some's favourable, some's aginst. But I'll lay they'll all come over when you makes publicly they promises you made to I.'

'What of Lucette?' Roger asked anxiously.

'She be considerin' still. 'Tis fer she more than t'others I piped this 'ere meetin'. Love makin' wi' she be easy as kiss yer 'and; but our lingos bein' different makes talkin' 'eavy weather. Seein' that's the way o' things, it come to I that you bein' glib o' tongue could best do your own persuadin'.'

By no means sanguine about their prospects, but determined to do his utmost, Roger followed the others out on deck. It was still full daylight, though within an hour a brief twilight followed by night would come with tropical suddenness. In the meantime, the north coast of Santo Domingo, along which *Circe* had been running ever since her capture, could be plainly seen to port, and some three miles distant on her starboard beam, the barque of the Vicomte, presumably leading them towards some secluded bay in which he maintained a permanent base.

The deck was crowded with the whole ship's company. They were excitedly exchanging rumours concerning what they believed was about to take place. Bloggs made a way for the prisoners to the main sheet bollards. Lucette was there leaning negligently on one of them. Pedro called for silence then clambered up on to the midships capstan. First in Creole, then in Spanish, he addressed the men.

His words were few but to the point. He stigmatised the Vicomte as a man of mean, intolerable unpredictable nature, whom no one could trust; and asked why, now they had a ship of their own, they should submit to his tyranny any longer.

Lucette called out: 'For the reason that you have previously done so. Because in the past he has brought you much plunder. Because he is a cleverer man and a better leader than any of you will ever be.'

A murmur of agreement followed her counter-blast to Pedro's stilted speech; but Bloggs quickly took his place and drowned all opposition by a bull-like roar in which he put the situation to his mates and others who could understand English. The hearty ovation he received from his friends suggested that they had already secretly endorsed his plan, but the attitude of the Porto Ricans remained doubtful, and a number of the pirates were evidently averse to deserting their old master.

It was now Roger's turn, and one of the gifts which had proved most valuable to him in his career was an exceptional ability to express his thoughts, either in speech or writing, with telling clarity. Knowing how much depended on this now he spared no effort to convince his audience of the soundness of Bloggs's arguments.

Upon the English, since they had already been won over, he wasted little time, simply reiterating his promises to Bloggs, but he spoke at length in passable Spanish, and still longer in his impeccable French. In both he dwelt upon the hazardous life led by pirates; who were liable to be shot for the least disobedience by their own captains, could enjoy the pleasures offered in the larger ports of the Caribbean only at the risk of recognition by someone they had despoiled, and more often than not ended up on a gallows. By contrast he painted the life of a law-abiding privateersman in glowing colours, asserting that it was not only safer and happier but equally profitable. Finally, he boldly grasped the nettle by turning to Lucette and crying:

'Now Madame, let us hear you on this question. Do you prefer to continue as an outlaw, or will you encourage the crew of this fine ship to fight her worthily in future under the protection of my mandate?'

Her face was quite expressionless and she was toying with the butt of her silver mounted pistol. He was suddenly seized with the idea that she was about to whip it out in a swift attempt to shoot him. His eyes held hers, watching for the faintest flicker in them which might give him a second's warning; so that he could escape the ball by throwing himself off the capstan. But his fears were groundless.

Showing her splendid teeth in a broad smile, she replied: 'You have made a good case, M. le Gouverneur. But whether I sail with pirates or privateers I can take care of myself; so let the men choose. I will abide by the decision of the majority.'

A show of hands was called for. Lucette, three pirates, and two Porto Ricans refrained from voting. These apart, all the others put their hands up for abandoning the Vicomte. It was a clear triumph for Bloggs. But Roger was quick to grasp his chance of continuing to dominate the situation. Beckoning to Pedro, Bloggs and Lucette he said:

'Now we must make our plans; and for that it would be best to return to the cabin.'

They followed him obediently as he shepherded the women towards the poop, and when they were all gathered in the saloon a general conversation took place in a jargon of English, French and Spanish. It was opened by Roger saying briskly to Pedro:

'The ladies and myself are deeply grateful to you, Captain, and I shall do my utmost to ensure that you have no cause to regret the decision you have taken. I assume that your first move will be to turn the ship about as soon as night has fallen, so as to put as great a distance as possible between ourselves and M. le Vicomte before dawn informs him that we have made off on our own?'

Pedro nodded. 'That is what I intend. The next thing to decide is where I should put you ashore in exchange for the pardons and commission you have promised us.'

Roger raised his eyebrows. 'But that is already decided for us. It must be in Martinique.'

'No, no!' The Carib gave a violent shake to his lank, greasy locks. 'I am born in Cuba and know the coasts of the Great Antilles well; but I have never sailed to the far southward among the lesser islands.'

'That difficulty can be overcome. I understand enough of the rudiments of navigation to keep the ship in fair weather on any course we may set.'

'But Senor, it is a voyage of a thousand miles. The men would grumble at so great a delay in disposing of the loot we have taken with this ship, and having a fling with the money it fetches.'

'That cannot be helped,' Roger declared firmly. For over forty-eight hours circumstances had rendered him utterly helpless, but now that he was once more in a position to negotiate he was back on ground that gave such opponents no chance against him. Bloggs and Lucette joined their protests to Pedro's, but Roger produced arguments the logic of which there was no contesting.

First he put it to them that should they conduct their operations in the northern Caribbean they would sooner or later run into the Vicomte, which would at best mean a bloody battle to no profit and at worst the exacting of a terrible vengeance by their old master. Then, more telling still, he pointed out that his writing on a plain sheet of paper would be next to worthless. For the pardons and commission to be any real protection they must be properly drawn up with seals attached, and that could only be done after he had actually assumed his governorship of Martinique.

At that Bloggs and Pedro gave way, but Lucette called them a pair of numbskulls, and vowed that Roger was trying to lead them into a trap. It was certain, she said, that there would be one or more British warships lying in the harbour at Fort Royal; so what was to prevent him on their arriving there from having the *Circe* boarded and all of them hanged.

Roger countered her accusation that he meant to go back on his word by a proposal which would put it out of his power to do so; namely that instead of entering a port they should anchor in some secluded bay and that as a first move he alone should be put ashore. The womenfolk would remain on board as hostages until he had made his way to the capital and returned with the documents which were to be the price of their freedom.

To this Lucette could raise no objection; so he quickly passed to another matter, and asked: 'Now, what of our clothes and personal possessions? I take it you consider those as part of your loot?'

'Certainly,' Lucette replied promptly. 'You will be allowed to take only the things you stand up in, and we shall assure ourselves that you have no articles of value concealed about you.'

He smiled. 'I thought as much. But tell me now, how do you propose to fight this ship as a privateer while she is armed with only a bow gun and a stern chaser?'

In the hurried conspiracy which had led to the take-over this point had not occurred to any of them. Now in some consternation they discussed the matter, and the only suggestion forthcoming was that to start with they must confine their own operations to attacking ships with their own weight of metal until they could gradually accumulate cannon from such prizes.

Roger's smile broadened to a grin, as he said: 'I think I can do better for you than that. In the ports of Martinique there must be a number of spare cannon taken from captured ships that are no longer seaworthy. If I can provide you with two broadsides of eight guns, will you agree to give up to us all our personal property?'

Lucette met the offer with a sullen frown. She protested that securing an adequate armament was the men's business, and she did not see why she should pay for it by surrendering the fine clothes of the captives and her share of their jewels. But Pedro and Bloggs overruled her; and, as a concession to lessen her hostility to the deal, Georgina diplomatically suggested that Amanda, Clarissa and herself should each made her a present of a good gown apiece together with some silks and laces.

That being settled it was further agreed that the captives should again be allowed the liberty of the ship, so that they could take the air on deck, and that a better service of meals should be organised at which they would feed with their captors. By the time Lucette, Bloggs and Pedro left them Roger was again played out. He was also somewhat worried about one aspect of the deal he had made. Had the *Circe*'s legitimate Captain applied to him for a privateer's commission it would have been within his rights as a Governor to grant him one—but Pedro was not the *Circe*'s legitimate Captain. What would the *Circe*'s owners have to say when they learned of this unorthodox transaction? Of course it could be argued that they had already lost their ship by piracy, and normally they would be able to claim the amount for which she was insured. But should the underwriters maintain that the ship had been recaptured by Roger's coming to an arrangement with her repentant mutineers, they might refuse to pay; then quite possibly the owners would bring an action against him for the value of the vessel and its cargo.

It was a most unpleasant possibility, and one which in the long run might cost him the whole of his small fortune. But being philosophical by nature he realised that he had been envisaging a far more terrible outcome to the voyage only a few hours back, and decided that it would be quite time enough to face this new anxiety when they arrived in Martinique. Meanwhile he had every reason to be overwhelmingly thankful that Bloggs's scruples had led to a new situation, and pleased with himself for the way in which he had handled it.

While Amanda attended to his head, she praised him for his cleverness in inveigling their captors into carrying them to their original destination, and they all agreed that he had performed the next thing to a miracle in securing for them their personal belongings. That night, for the first time since the *Circe*'s capture, they felt a reasonable degree of safety, so decided to sleep in separate cabins. Their relief at the turn events had taken was so profound that all four women wept a little before going to sleep, and mingled their tears with thanksgiving to their Maker for His merciful preservation of them.

In the morning they once more took care with their toilets, and when they had gathered in the big cabin their faces showed fewer signs of strain. Breakfast was the usual casual spread by the hunch-back of the foods that came handy, and Lucette reminded Roger that he had suggested improving their cuisine. After a moment's thought he looked across at Georgina, and said:

'This is simply arranged. Madame la Comtesse shall cook for us.'

'I?' exclaimed Georgina, aghast.

He nodded. 'You have ever shown great interest in cooking, and are a very good cook yourself. The rest of us will help you with the meaner tasks, but I place the sceptre of the galley in your most capable hands.'

They had known each other for so long, and so intimately, that they were at times able to read one another's thoughts; and now his unspoken intention flashed upon her. He knew that she was grieving desperately for Charles and had decided that to give her a task requiring considerable thought would be the best thing possible for her.

An investigation into Monsieur Pirouet's remaining stores occupied them for most of the forenoon, then they went up on to the poop. At a glance they saw that the state of the ship had seriously deteriorated since the ending of Captain Cummins's regime. Instead of the white decks being spotless they were now littered with every kind of filth; and, apart from the man at the wheel and one look-out, the crew were idling the day away, either dozing or playing games of chance in the shade of the awning. However, the squalor of the once tidy ship was a matter of little moment compared to the fact that the coast of Santo Domingo lay on her starboard side; for, although she was tacking against the wind and making slow progress, every mile now carried her still further from the dreaded Vicomte de Senlac.

After a very welcome three-hour spell in the fresh air, they went below to prepare dinner, and under Georgina's directions the first really appetising meal they had seen for four days was cooked. Jake had been appointed second mate so that Bloggs could enjoy the hot food with the others. He sat down to table with them almost apologetically, and ate his food in embarrassed silence. Pedro, as usual, wolfed his, and disdaining the glass that had been set for him took swigs of wine from the bottle. But Lucette did real justice to each dish and was loud in her praises of Georgina's efforts.

Wishing to repay her compliments in some way, Georgina remarked: 'I should be interested to hear where you learned French, Madame, as you speak it when you wish with hardly a trace of the Creole accent, and most fluently.'

Lucette's white teeth flashed between her full red lips. 'Madame la Comtesse is most gracious; but French comes naturally to me, for I am a member of a noble French family. I am a Tascher de la Pagerie.'

Georgina, taking this to be a bare-faced lie, quickly lowered her eyes to conceal her disbelief at such a pretension; but Roger thought it quite probable that Lucette was speaking the truth.

For well over two hundred years colonies administered by French aristocrats had been established in Saint-Domingue—the western third of the otherwise Spanish owned island off which they were cruising—Martinique, Guadeloupe and several other islands. By the reign of Louis XV many of them owned vast estates, and on visits to Versailles had outshone their relatives who lived in France, owing to the immense wealth drawn from their plantations. Unlike the British they paid small regard to the colour bar, with the result that a high percentage of this Creole aristocracy now had a good dash of black blood. The Comte de Caylus, whom Roger had fought and killed seven years before, had been a product of just such a family history, for he had owned estates in Martinique as well as Brittany and had himself been a mulatto. Yet, while there seemed to Roger no particular reason to doubt Lucette's claim, it did strike him as strange that the daughter of a French nobleman should, even if captured or kidnapped in the first instance, have willingly adopted the sort of life she was leading. So he asked her:

'How comes it then, that we find you in your present situation?'

She replied without hesitation, and this time none of them felt doubt of her honesty. 'For having aided my young mistress in an intrigue I was punished by being sent to work in the cane fields; so I ran away.'

'Pardon my curiosity, Madame;' remarked Clarissa, 'but what you have just told us is difficult to reconcile with your being the daughter of a nobleman.'

'I did not say that I was,' Lucette retorted, quite unruffled. 'My white blood comes from the present M. de Tascher's grandfather. But I will tell you my story if you wish.'

A murmur of encouragement having greeted her offer, she went on: 'I was born on the de la Pagerie estate in Martinique and as my mother was a slave I, too, was technically a slave. But, as you must know, there are varying degress of slavery. My mother was a much beloved servant in the house, and it so happened that she gave birth to me in the same week as Madame de Tascher was delivered of her second daughter, Marie Rose Josephine. In consequence my mother was given Josephine to suckle as well as myself; so we became foster sisters.

'It is the custom on such estates for white children to be given coloured children of their own age as playmates from earliest infancy, on the principle that such a bond will lead to the slave child becoming a most devoted personal servant to the other later in life. For Josephine, I was the natural choice to fill this role; so we were brought up together, and treated in every way as though we were sisters by blood.

'Josephine had no brothers and only one elder sister, named Manette; but she was an insipid creature much given to introspection, so Josephine was much more drawn to myself. She was very pretty and of a very frolicsome disposition. Both of us loved to dance and sing, and as we grew older we encouraged one another in naughty escapades. Out here in the Caribbean white girls as well as coloured began to feel the urges of sex very young, and from the time Josephine and I entered our teens both our minds were filled with the thoughts natural to fully grown women. I let myself be seduced by the overseer's son; while she developed a passion for the son of one of our neighbours, who fell equally passionately in love with her.

'The name of her beau was William de Kay, and his family had been settled in Martinique only for some twenty-five years. Originally, I think, their name was MacKay, for they were of noble Scottish descent and related to many great Lords in their own country; but they had been deprived of their estates and exiled for having taken up arms in the cause of the Stuart pretender, during his attempt to gain the throne of England in 1745.

'Madame de Tascher and Madame de Kay had long been close friends, so from childhood little William was always in and out of the house, or we at his, and was our most cherished playmate. As he and Josephine grew older the two mothers smiled at the devotion they showed to one another, for at that time the parents of both children favoured the idea of a match between them. But later, on both sides events occured to alter their plans.

'I never fully understood the complications of the inheritance that devolved on William, but it seems that his father was heir to a Lord Lovell and that his own succession to the estates was dependent on his marrying this old nobleman's niece. Whatever the right of the matter, news arrived that Lord Lovell had died; it thus became necessary for Monsieur de Kay to present himself as the heir in London, and he decided to take William with him in order that the young man might complete his studies at the University of Oxford.

'At that time William was not aware that he would be called on to marry his cousin, and he considered himself irrevocably pledged to Josephine. Naturally, at the idea of a separation which might last for several years the two young lovers were distraught. Their parents had, some months before, consented to their regarding themselves as unofficially betrothed, but that no longer satisfied them. They craved some means of entering into a more indissoluble bond before a cruel fate tore them from each other's arms.

'Since both were of such tender years, no French priest would have married them without the consent of their parents; but, then being greatly devoted to my young mistress, I took it on myself to secure for them an opportunity to exchange the vows by which they set so much store.

'As you may know, there is nothing incompatible about being a Roman Catholic and a practitioner of Voodoo. In fact, all the best known Christian Saints are also gods and goddesses in the Voodoo pantheon; and a part of the training of the Houngans, as the Voodoo priests are called, is to fully familiarise themselves with all the rituals of the Roman Church. For some time past a local Houngan, who had recently graduated from the Roman Catholic Seminary for coloured men, had been casting eyes of desire upon me, so I had no great difficulty in persuading him to do as I wished. I then told the two lovers that I had found a priest who would marry them in secret, and two nights later the ceremony was duly performed beneath a giant cedar tree that grew not far from la Pagerie mansion.

'Some months after William arrived in England M. de Tascher learned from M. de Kay the conditions of the inheritance, but he was not particularly put out by these rendering a union between their families no longer practical, as by that time he had other plans for Josephine.

'His sister, a Madame Renaudin, who resided in France, was a rich and influential woman. Being a good aunt she was strongly set upon arranging an advantageous marriage for the eldest niece, and it had already been agreed that Manette should cross the ocean to live with her. But, just then, Manette was taken with a fever, and within a week she was dead.

'Monsieur and Madame Tascher decided that Josephine should take her place, but they did not tell her so at once, because she did nothing but dream and talk of William and they feared to disturb the balance of her mind. Instead, they suppressed his letters to her and hers to him, hoping that both would believe each had lost interest in the other.

'She became greatly worried by William's silence, but no wit less devoted to him; and at last the time came when her parents could no longer postpone breaking it to her that she must forget him, and that they were sending her to France where she was to make a splendid marriage.

'You can imagine their consternation when, instead of protesting and fainting, as they expected her to do, she told them she could not accede to their wishes because she was already married.

'An earthquake could hardly have created a greater upheaval in the household. By threats and abuse they had the whole story out of her that night. From her description of the man who she said had married her to William they recognised the Houngan, and sent for him. Threatened with being sent to the galleys, he confessed to having performed the ceremony, and disclosed that it was I who had persuaded him to unite them by the Catholic ritual.

'By morning the de Taschers had convinced themselves that I had led Josephine into the affair against her will, and that she was the innocent victim of my wicked wiles. That was not altogether true, as she had been overjoyed at the chance to marry William clandestinely; and I shall always hold it against her that she made no effort whatever to defend me when their wrath descended on me like a cyclone.

'They took from me all my pretty clothes and all the presents they had ever given me. They had me stripped naked, tied to the whipping post and flogged. Then they sent me out to labour in the cane-fields. To act so they were fools; for I told everyone the reason for my disgrace, and the story of Josephine's secret marriage went the round of the island. I did not remain in the cane-fields long, either. Knowing the house so well it was easy for me to burgle it. One night about a week later I took from it all the valuables I could lay my hands on and made off to the port. In return for part of my loot an old woman that I knew there had me smuggled aboard a ship that was sailing for St. Vincent in the morning, and ever since I have sailed the Caribbean seas.'

'You are lucky, Madame,' Amanda remarked, 'to have led so desperate a life for so long without being either killed or seriously injured.'

'I have a charmed life,' Lucette replied quite seriously. 'In Martinique there was an old coloured woman with some Irish blood whose gift for fortune-telling was infallible. She told me when a girl that I would live a life of wild adventure and witness many fights, but could not be killed by bullet, by steel or by rope; only by a fall from a high place. And you may be certain that nothing would induce me to go up into the rigging, or take any similar risk.'

Enthralled by her story, Roger asked: 'Did you ever learn what became of Josephine?'

Lucette shrugged. 'Some three years later I ran into my brother in Antigua. He told me that Josephine and the de Taschers had declared the story I had put about to be a malicious invention from start to finish; and that she had, after all, gone to France and made a fine marriage; but I know no more than that.'

For some while they talked on; then the party broke up, and the prisoners went on deck to enjoy the cool of the evening. Again they slept well, but on coming into the saloon for breakfast they found Bloggs and Lucette awaiting them with long faces.

The bad news was soon told. Some members of the crew were evidently opposed to making the long voyage down to Martinique, and had formed a secret league against them. When the pirate who acted as bo'sun had gone down to the hold that morning to supervise the drawing off of the day's water ration, he had found that the spigots of the last remaining full casks had been pulled out, so that the water in them had run to waste. And that was not all. Between two of the casks Pedro the Carib was lying dead with a knife through his back.

As none of them had the least reason to feel affection for Pedro, and his capabilities as a captain left much to be desired, they did not regard his death as a major calamity; but they were much concerned by the sinister manner of it. In addition, the loss of their water was a grave annoyance, as it meant that they could not now proceed to Martinique without first putting in somewhere along the coast at a place where the casks could be refilled.

Lucette and Bloggs agreed that the most likely suspects were the three pirates and two Porto Ricans who had refrained from voting on the question of making off with the *Circe* as opposed to continuing under the Vicomte. Since the voyage to Martinique was quite a different issue it was possible that others of the pirates were at the bottom of this attempt to keep the ship in the waters that they knew, but as a precaution it was decided to seize the five suspects and confine them in the lock-up.

When they came to the question of watering, Bloggs had to rely on Lucette's knowledge of the locality, and she advised that they should make for the island of Tortuga. That meant putting the ship about again, as this small island lay off the north coast of Saint-Domingue. But the wind being against them they had not travelled any great distance during the past thirty-six hours, and with it in their favour could hope to reach Tortuga in considerably less.

With some misgiving Roger pointed out that if they put about they might well run into the Vicomte; but Lucette said that by now he must be well on his way to his lair, which was far up a creek in the desolate coast of Great Inagua, a hundred miles north of the channel that separated Saint-Domingue from Cuba, and still ignorant of the fact that they were not following him to it. She then supported her argument for going to Tortuga by adding that whereas they might waste days lying in half a dozen anchorages along the coast they were passing without being able to locate a fresh water spring, she knew of three bays in Tortuga at any one of which they could refill the casks as soon as they were landed.

In consequence, the five protesting suspects were rounded up and the ship put about without further delay. All that day, on a fair breeze that was a most welcome offset to the broiling sunshine, they again sailed westward along the coast of Santo Domingo. When dinner time came round Bloggs and Lucette reported that despite their close questioning of the crew, they were no nearer discovering who had killed Pedro, and their investigation made them more inclined than ever to believe that the murderer was one of the men who was now under lock and key. This belief gave them good grounds to hope that there would be no further trouble; so, after an evening spent on deck under a myriad of stars, they turned in with minds that were reasonably tranquil.

Yet next day the passengers woke to find themselves in a situation which filled them with the gravest alarm. The galley was silent, the hunch-back nowhere to be seen. The table in the saloon had not been laid for breakfast, and both the doors leading from the after cabins to the deck were locked. They were prisoners again, and in vain they both beat upon the doors and tried to force them. No one answered their knocking and it soon became evident that the doors were being held to by heavy objects on their far sides.

The mystery of what had occurred during the night deepened when they went to Georgina's old cabin, which since the ship's capture had been occupied by Lucette and Bloggs. That too was locked, and apparently empty as no reply came to their shouts and knocking on its door.

It looked as if the unrest among the crew had been much more grave and general than they had supposed; and there was cause for fearing that in a new mutiny both Bloggs and Lucette had been murdered. Roger now roundly cursed himself for his over-cleverness in arguing them into agreeing to make the long voyage down to Martinique. Had he scrawled pardons and a commission for them on pieces of paper they would have accepted them readily enough, and put him and his party ashore two days ago. But it was too late to think of that now, and they could only wait events.

About ten o'clock, on glancing through the stern windows, he noticed that a new course had been set somewhat to starboard, and the ship was now heading away from the coast. By midday the skyline of the big island was becoming obscured by the heat haze. Shortly afterwards, only a few hundred yards away to port, a wooded promontory came into view; then another further off to starboard. Roger had little doubt that the two capes formed the entrance to a bay in the island of Tortuga; so whoever was now in control of the ship evidently intended to carry out Lucette's plan to water there.

A few minutes later they heard shouting, loud bumps and a rattling noise, as the ship's sails were lowered and her anchor let go. Slowly she swung with the tide, bringing into view the bight of the bay. On shore there was a long low house and a number of palm-thatched shacks. At anchor in the foreground lay a barque. As Roger recognised her his heart leapt to his throat, then sank, She was the Vicomte de Senlac's. For the past two days they had believed themselves saved. Now, either through evil chance or treachery, they were once more in dire peril.

9

The Harbour where Evil Reigned

Suppressing an exclamation of dismay, Roger turned away from the window; but the scene beyond it remained as clear in his mind as though he were still staring at a painting, although no oils could have conveyed such vivid colouring as did the blinding sunshine.

Wave after wave of rich green vegetation mounted to tree-covered heights that stood out in scimitar-sharp curves against a sky of cloudless blue. This seemingly impenetrable forest ran down over the two promontories that, like reaching arms, nearly encircled the land-locked bay. At their water-line no shore could be seen, only a belt of deep black shadow where the waves lapped gently at a natural palisade formed by an incredible tangle of mangrove roots. Towards the flattening of this great arc the barrier fell back, giving place to a deep beach of almost white sand that stretched for about a quarter of a mile along the centre of the bay.

A few hundred yards from the water lay the house. It was painted lemon yellow; only one small portion of it had an upper storey, and it appeared larger than it actually was owing to a wide veranda that ran the whole of its length. To one side of it palm-thatched slave quarters spread in higgledy-piggledy confusion and on the other were stockaded corrals containing cattle.

At one end of the beach a shooner lay high and dry almost on her side, evidently being careened, although no men were working on her during the blistering midday heat. Several boats were beached in front of the house, and one of them had just put off. Half a mile nearer to the

Circe, the Vicomte's sinister greenish-yellow barque lay with furled sails, yet another vividly contrasting patch of colour against the deep blue water of the lagoon.

Roger was still wondering how to break the news of their ill-fortune to his companions, when Clarissa broke it for him by crying out: 'Merciful God! That is the Vicomte's ship!'

The others ran to the window and her cry was followed by a chorus of woeful verification. Then, stunned into silence by this abrupt end to their newly-won security, they watched the boat approach.

Roger, having been unconscious when the *Circe* was captured, had never seen the Vicomte, but the others had caught glimpses of him on his own poop just before the prize crew had been put on board. Now, they recognised him as the thin, elegantly-dressed, smallish figure in the stern. As the boat came nearer they were seized with the wild hope that, all unsuspecting, he was being rowed into a trap. He could know nothing of what had occurred aboard the *Circe* since he had left her, so must suppose that João de Mondego was still in command and waiting to welcome him. If, despite the mystery of their having been locked up, Bloggs still had the upper hand aboard, he must resist the Vicomte or pay for it with his life, and one well-aimed shot from the long gun could sink the boat.

But no shot was fired and the boat disappeared from view beneath the *Circe*'s counter. They knew then that it was not an ill chance but treachery which had brought them to this lagoon and that it must be de Senlac's lair.

For a quarter of an hour they waited fearful, yet impatient, to learn what fate had in store for them. Then the cabin door was thrown open and the Vicomte walked in, followed by Lucette.

De Senlac was in his early forties, somewhat below middle height, spare of figure, and thin of face. His eyes were a cold hard blue with heavy lids, his prominent nose was pinched at the nostrils, and his mouth thin with almost bloodless lips. He was dressed in a fashion that had gone out six years before, with the coming of the Revolution: silk coat and stockings, a brocaded waistcoat, laced cravat and patent shoes with silver buckles. He still wore his hair powdered, and on his carefully tended hands there glittered half a dozen rings which must have been worth a small fortune.

Sweeping off his tricorne hat in a gallant bow to the ladies, he said in French to Lucette: 'I have not yet had the pleasure of meeting my prisoners; pray present me.'

As she made the introductions, he bowed to each of them again, then said with a thin-lipped smile:

'Madame la Comtesse, Mesdames; I learn to my distress that you have had cause for grave fears for your safety during the past few days. It may be, too, that having heard tales of the unenviable fate which generally overtakes females when they fall into the hands of sea-rovers, you are still a prey to anxiety. Let me hasten to reassure you. Were you persons of no consequence I could hardly be expected to put myself to considerable trouble on your account; but your birth makes me confident that either from your own resources or those of friends you will be able to reward me suitably for my protection. My followers, I am happy to say, have learned the wisdom of accepting my decisions without argument, and I shall compensate them for having to forgo any expectations they may have entertained regarding you by buying for their amusement a fresh batch of young women from one of the procurers in Santiago or Port Royal. While you are in Tortuga you have nought to fear, and I trust you will regard yourselves as my honoured guests.'

His courteous, if cynical, pronouncement filled them all with unutterable relief. Previously to the bargain Roger had made with Bloggs, to be allowed to go unharmed in exchange for a ransom was the very best they had hoped for, and after the sudden renewal of their worst fears so recently they could hardly believe their good fortune. Next moment they were thanking him as gratefully as if he had just made them a most handsome present, and it did not even cross their minds to resent his making free with their property, as he went on to say:

'Your jewels will form a pleasant addition to my collection, and Lucette, here, will decide which of your clothes it will be fitting for you to keep. You have, I am sure, many more than you need; and she deserves some small recompense for the skilful way in which she countered the designs of those who sought to deprive me of your company.'

Lucette, hands on hips, was standing beside him, her head turbaned in a colourful handkerchief, so tied that three of its corners stuck out in jaunty points. Tossing it, she said with a laugh that held a suggestion of a sneer:

'Monsieur le Vicomte is most generous; but it required no great skill to get the better of such simpletons. Not one of them showed the least suspicion that it was I who knifed Pedro, or let the last of their water run to waste to provide an excuse for putting the ship about. You should have seen the astonishment in the eyes of that fool Bloggs when he woke this morning to find that I had bound him while he slept, and was about to pull the cord with which I strangled him.'

De Senlac nodded vigorously and gave a hight-pitched chuckle. His obvious approval of her horrifying deeds suddenly brought home to them that he was neither more nor less than a gallows bird in fine plumage; but they swiftly concealed their revulsion, and soon after were again counting themselves lucky that avarice had decided him to protect them from his following of brutal desperadoes.

They were allowed to pack a portmanteau each to take ashore, and Lucette did not prove ungenerous in the things she allowed them to select. Then they followed their luggage into the boat that had brought the Vicomte off, and were rowed to a small jetty below the house. It was November the 28th, eight weeks and two days since they had sailed from Bristol; but as they at last set foot in the Americas it seemed to them as though the few days since the capture of the *Circe* had been longer than the whole of the rest of their voyage.

The sand of the beach was shimmering with heat, and the sun blazed down mercilessly; so, although they had been exposed to it in the open boat for little over a quarter of an hour, they were all perspiring freely and beginning to fear the effects of sunburn. When they reached the wide veranda of the house, the shade it provided was as welcome as a douche of cold water. On it there were a dozen or so lounge chairs of bamboo, and the Vicomte courteously bowed his prisoners to them. They had scarcely seated themselves when a Negro in livery appeared carrying a large jug, filled with what looked as if it might be lemon squash, and glasses. The drink proved delicious but quite unlike anything they had ever tasted, and Lucette told them that it was a concoction made from soursops and rum.

When their glasses were refilled, de Senlac said: 'While we finish our drinks let us dispose of the uncongenial subject of business, then we need refer to it no further. How much can you afford to pay me by way of ransom?'

Feeling that it would be futile to suggest too small a sum, Roger replied: 'There are five of us, so I suggest five thousand pounds.'

The Vicomte gave his high-pitched chuckle. 'Come, come, Monsieur le Gouverneur! You set too small a price upon yourself, and one which comes near an insult to the beauty of these ladies. You must do better than that.'

Roger spread out his hands and made a little grimace. It was a gesture which came quite naturally to him from having lived for so long in France. 'Perhaps you are unaware, Monsieur, that I have not yet taken up my Governorship. It is a reward for certain services I rendered to my government which were of a far from profitable nature; and neither my wife nor I have any private fortune. Mademoiselle Marsham had the misfortune to be left a penniless orphan, Jenny here is entirely dependent on her mistress and Lady St. Ermins's position is now most uncertain, owing to the death of her husband.'

'Monsieur, you bring tears to my eyes.' The Vicomte's voice was mocking, then suddenly became harsh as he added: 'Yet the tears will be in yours and theirs unless you can raise fifty thousand between you.'

'Fifty thousand!' Roger gasped. 'To find even a fifth of that sum would bring me near ruin. I beg you to show us a reasonable consideration.'

De Senlac shrugged. 'Persons of your birth must have connections who could raise it for you. If not, you know the alternative.'

'Oh Monsieur!' Amanda pleaded with clasped hands. 'I pray you believe my husband, for he speaks the truth; and we have no relatives to whom we could appeal for so huge a ransom.'

'Forgive me, Madame, if I suggest that your memory is at fault. Perhaps if for just one night I allow my men to follow their usual custom of drawing lots for the enjoyment of the favours of yourself and your friends, that would refresh your memory by tomorrow.'

They all paled at his abominable threat, but Georgina stepped into the breach and said in a low voice: 'My husband's estate apart, I have certain properties of my own, and if the sale of them proved insufficient I am confident that my father would make up the difference.'

'Ah!' exclaimed the Vicomte. 'Madame la Comtesse shows the most admirable sense, and relieves me from taking a step that I should have found most distasteful.'

Roger had far greater cause for relief; but, all the same, he wished that Georgina had made some attempt to get the amount reduced. He thought it quite probable that de Senlac would have settled for half the sum and the full fifty thousand was an appalling ransom to have to find. There would be no question of Georgina's selling Stillwaters as it was hers only for life, but although her rich father would certainly help her, this great inroad into her resources might make it impossible for her to continue living there; and the least he himself could now do would be to hand over to her as his contribution the bulk of his savings. However there could be no going back on her offer; so he said to de Senlac:

'May we take it then that if Lady St. Ermins writes to her father on the lines she suggests, you will prove means for us to continue our interrupted voyage as soon as possible?'

'No, no, *mon ami,*' the Vicomte cackled. 'That is too much to ask. Madame la Comtesse shall write her letter tomorrow, and I will give her to put in it the name of a Genoese banker who is a good friend of mine. It is to him that the money must be remitted; and when the full sum has been paid he will notify me to that effect. Only then can I permit you to depart.'

'But that will take months,' Amanda protested.

'Yes, four months at the least. Perhaps six or more. As we do not enjoy the amenity of a regular mail service here, my correspondence is subject to the additional delays consequent on being sent to and collected from certain of the larger Caribbean ports. However, we will do our best to make your stay in Tortuga a pleasant one.'

'You are very kind,' Roger forced himself to say. 'But should there be such long delay in my taking up my post, my Government may believe me dead and appoint some other in my place, so that I'll lose it altogether. Can you not possibly . . .'

'May I remind you, Monsieur,' the Vicomte cut him short, 'that you are very lucky not to be actually dead. You might well have lost your life at the same time as your friend, the Lord St. Ermins.'

'That is true,' agreed Roger. 'Yet since I am alive I am naturally anxious to secure my future. Will you not accept our word of honour to do nought which might invalidate the agreement at which we have arrived; and my promise to raise five thousand pounds to send you on account immediately we reach Martinique?'

De Senlac shook his head. 'I regret to disoblige you; but on this point my mind is made up. You must all remain here until I receive definite information that the money is lying to my order in Genoa.'

Roger had made his bid and could do no more. From the beginning he had felt that the chances were against the Vicomte's letting them go on the sole security of their word, but had hoped for a better bargain. Fifty thousand pounds and six months' detention on Tortuga was a heavy price to pay. Yet it was still cheap compared to the alternative; and there was always a possibility that they might be able to escape. The only thing to do was to try to look cheerful and hope that the future might bring better fortune.

Having finished his drink, the Vicomte went on: 'As a good half of the hottest hours of the day still lie before us I suggest that we should adjourn for the siesta. At sundown it is my intention to dispense justice to the *Circe*'s crew, and afterwards we will dine. The former may provide you with a spectacle of some interest; to the latter I shall look forward, as I rarely have the opportunity of entertaining persons of my own quality.'

Standing up, he made a leg to the ladies and, without waiting for a reply, strutted into the house. Lucette followed him and beckoned the prisoners after her. They entered a wide, airy hall with a broad staircase, up which the Vicomte was mounting to the floor above, but she took them through it and down a passage that ran along the back of the building. Throwing open a row of doors one after the other she said:

'Here are your rooms. They are not often occupied, but I think you will find them quite comfortable. At least you may count yourselves lucky to be in them instead of in the cells. But don't toy with any idea of escaping. You would only get lost in the forest, and we should be certain to catch you; then M. le Vicomte would have your toe-nails torn out, to prevent your running away again. I will send the slaves to you with your baggage. Ask them for anything you may require.'

As she stolled away, with her usual feline grace, they looked about them. The rooms were sparsely furnished and the plaster was peeling from the walls; but they were lofty, light and airy, and each had a pair of french windows opening on to the veranda.

Within a few minutes two negroes appeared with their portmanteaux; then a smiling negress who filled all their jugs with water, shook a variety of insects out of the bed curtains, and brought bowls of fruit which she set down on the bedside tables. While she was busy with these chores they stood about discussing in low voices their recent interview; but they were longing to get out of their heavier garments, so as soon as she had gone they pulled them off, had a quick wash and, exhausted by the heat, flung themselves on the beds to rest.

Roger was roused from an uneasy doze by a knocking on his door. Propping himself up on one elbow, he called '*entrez*' and a tall young man came in. He was a handsome, gaily dressed fellow, and his hair, which he wore long, was golden, but his features were slightly negroid, showing him to be a *sangmêlé,* as mulattoes having only a small proportion of black blood are termed.

With a bright toothed smile he said in lisping Creole-French: 'M. le Vicomte is about to hold his seigneurial court. He requests the presence of yourself and your ladies.' After a moment, he added: 'My name is Jean Herault. My father is M. le Vicomte's bailiff and I assist him in running the estate. We are likely to see a lot of one another; so I hope we shall get upon good terms.'

Scrambling off the bed Roger replied that he was happy to make Monsieur Herault's acquaintance, and would join M. le Vicomte as soon as possible. Then pulling on his clothes he went to rouse the others, and when all of them had dressed they walked through the main hall out on to the veranda.

The sun had already gone down behind the hills so the house was now in shadow; but a number of large, hanging lanterns had been lit along the veranda, and a trestle table carried out on to it. A paunchy, elderly man was arranging writing materials beside a ledger, at one end of the table, and nearby de Senlac stood talking to two of his pirates; a very thick-set dark-visaged sea-dog with at least five hundred pieces-of-eight forming a great collar of silver round his neck, and a taller fellow who had a great hook nose and diamond ear-drops dangling from his ears.

As the prisoners appeared the Vicomte introduced his companions as his two Lieutenants: the dark one as Philo the Greek and the other as Cyrano de la Mer, which was obviously a *nom de guerre*. He then presented the elderly man as his Bailiff, Hypolite Herault, and when they had made their bows he said:

'I will explain the proceedings that are about to take place. In a domain such as I have established here there are a great variety of duties, varying in their degree of hardship. Apart from our activities at sea, which are our main support, we have cane-fields and tobacco plantations further inland that must be cultivated. There is also the rearing and tending of our livestock, and the repairing and careening of our vessels.

'I own, of course, a number of permanent slaves, but after each voyage the conduct of my seamen during it is reviewed by me. Those who have shown initiative or special bravery are rewarded by periods of leave, so that they may go on the spree in our nearest ports. Others who have proved unsatisfactory are relegated to menial tasks, and those guilty of definite neglect of duty are sent for a time to labour with the slaves.

'When we take a prize, as on the present occasion, I have also to decide on the future of the captured crew. Fighting and sickness are a constant drain on our numbers; so good seamen who are willing to join us are welcomed as recruits. Those who show reluctance are enrolled among the slaves; while officers and others who might prove a focus for future trouble have to be disposed of. Our ways of disposing of them vary but it is always by some method which will provide good sport for my men.'

While he was speaking a motley crowd began to gather below the steps of the veranda. Twilight had now fallen, and as it swiftly deepened the full companies of the two ships assembled, including a score or more who were brought forward with their arms tied behind their backs. The majority of the captives were from the *Circe,* and among them Roger saw Tom, young Doctor Fergusson, the Second Mate, the Swedish purser, the consumptive Supercargo and Jake Harris, but with them were also four of the pirates who had formed part of the prize crew. Anxiously he searched among the rows of upturned faces for Dan's but beyond the semi-circles of light cast by the lanterns it was now difficult to make out individual features. For some moments he feared that the ex-smuggler must have fallen a victim to the pirates, then he caught sight of him on the fringe of the crowd and his heart felt lighter than it had for days at the knowledge that his old friend was safe and free.

Dan's apparent treachery had not been mentioned since Roger had come to after the taking of the *Circe,* and he had deliberately refrained from speaking of it to the others for his own good reasons. Fearing that the ship might be taken while they were still in her he had given Dan secret instructions that in such an event he was to go over to the enemy, with the idea that it would both save his life and, perhaps, later enable him to help them. To render such a step easier he had told Dan that, should all appear lost, he must bring himself to the enemy's notice by hauling down the *Circe*'s flag. Dan had done so, and the trick had worked. Evidently, with a number of others he had already been vetted by de Senlac and accepted as a useful member of the pirate fraternity.

The Vicomte now seated himself at the table between Philo the Greek and Cyrano de la Mer, while the elder Herault took one end of it and the younger the other. Georgina sat down in one of the basket chairs nearby, her companions followed her example and, as they did so, a brawny, bald-headed man came out of the crowd to the foot of the steps. Calling up a succession of men before the tribunal he praised some and blamed others. Most of them remained silent but certain of those accused of faults endeavoured to defend themselves, and at these he bellowed a stream of filthy abuse culled from a dozen tongues.

Apparently de Senlac was already well informed on the cases brought before him, as he dealt with all of them swiftly, only on two occasions troubling to consult with his Lieutenants; and in several he gave his verdict in less than a minute. Within half an hour the bald man had come to the end of his list and Lucette took his place.

She opened her part of the proceedings by describing how Pedro and Bloggs had conspired to make off with the *Circe,* and how she had tricked and murdered both in turn. It transpired that once Pedro was out of the way she had been able to release the members of the prize-crew who had shown reluctance to join him, and later been arrested on suspicion; then with their aid won back some of their companions and some of the *Circe*'s mutineers. She had undertaken to strangle Bloggs during the night, while the others either killed or overcame the men who they felt would remain loyal to Bloggs; and between them in the morning they had brought the ship safely into harbour.

According to how one looked at it the story was either one of high loyalty, brilliant planning, courage and daring, or of the basest treachery, despicable cunning, villainy and murder; but, from the tremendous ovation Lucette received, there could be no doubt about the view that the Vicomte and his followers took of it.

She then played the part of presenter, or accuser and witness, against her companions of the past few days. Those who had given her willing aid were suitably rewarded, those who had had to be won over were detailed for the gruelling work of careening, and four pirates of the prize-crew who had stood out against her till overcome were sentenced to slavery for life.

Finally the Vicomte dealt with those prisoners originally taken from the *Circe* who had refused to join his following. The seamen, and young Tom, were condemned to slavery; the rest to death.

Herault *père* had already entered all the decisions in his ledger, and on de Senlac's rising from the table the crowd began to disperse. Neither Georgina nor her friends had been able to find Monsieur Pirouet in it; so, stepping forward, she enquired what had become of him.

'In him, Madame la Comtesse,' the Vicomte informed her, 'I have to thank you for presenting me with a most admirable chef. He is at this moment cooking our dinner.'

'I am delighted to hear it,' Georgina replied, and added quickly: 'But why, then, do you throw away an equally excellent valet?'

'I fail to comprehend . . .'

'Tom Jordan was my husband's valet. Although he is quite young, he is highly proficient in his work; yet you have condemned him to slavery in the cane-fields.'

'I was not aware that he is a valuable servant; but in any case he is one of the recalcitrants who refused to accept me as his master.'

'Send for him, I beg, and offer to take him into your service. He would, I think, feel quite differently about that to becoming a pirate.'

With a smile, de Senlac told Jean Herault to fetch Tom to him; then Georgina went on:

'And Doctor Fergusson. During our voyage he proved himself to be both a surgeon and physician of considerable merit. You have told us that you lose many of your men from wounds and sickness; so surely . . .'

'Enough, Madame!' de Senlac cut short her plea harshly. 'He is of the very type most likely to attempt something against me; so better dead.' Yet when Jean brought Tom to him he spoke kindly to the young man, and on Georgina's expressing her wish that the valet should enter his service Tom replied at once:

'Since you advise it, m'lady, I'm agreeable to do so.'

At that moment one of the negro footmen announced dinner and the Vicomte offered her his arm. Her distress at the brutal sentences he had inflicted lightened a little by the thought that she had at least prevented one of them from being carried out, she took it and, followed by the others, they went into the house.

The dining-room lay on the opposite side of the hall to the row of bedrooms, and on entering it, Roger saw that the table had been laid with ten covers. A quick count of heads confirmed his impression that this was one short of their number, and it suddenly occurred to him that, although the Vicomte had said nothing of it, Jenny being a servant he would not expect her to dine with them. From a similar observation Jenny had reached the same conclusion, and, like the sensible girl she was, had backed away into the passage; but, not knowing where to go, now stood there looking decidedly embarrassed. Fortunately, Tom, having been left without orders, had followed them in and was standing just behind her; so Roger stepped over to them and said with a reassuring smile:

'Go to the kitchens and find Monsieur Pirouet. He will give you as good a dinner as we get, and later find somewhere for Tom to sleep.'

As Roger turned away from the door he saw that de Senlac had just finished seating the party, and thought his arrangement of it seemed very peculiar. He had taken the top of the table and placed all four women in a row on his left, with the two Heraults and his two Lieutenants opposite to them. Roger was evidently expected to take the bottom of the table, between Philo and Lucette, as that was the only place remaining unoccupied. Quietly he slipped into it, and it was not long before he was able to guess the reason for this unusual placing of the ladies all together.

If the Vicomte had separated them it would have appeared even more odd had he not placed one on either side of him; so he had evaded a deliberate rudeness to Amanda, who should have sat on his right, by seating the sexes on opposite sides of the table. That enabled him to have Jean Herault on his right; and, as the meal progressed, it became obvious that he had a special affection for the young *sangmêlé*.

Being a man of the world Roger observed it only with calculated interest. Ordinarily, his own instincts being entirely normal, it was only when unnatural relationships between others were particularly blatant that he even noticed them; but, when he saw de Senlac passing the blond Jean titbits off his plate, he hid a smile of cynical satisfaction. It explained why the Vicomte had refrained from claiming a 'Captain's privilege' with Amanda, Georgina or Clarissa, and was a reasonable guarantee that while they remained on Tortuga he was unlikely to force unwelcome attentions upon them.

For the prisoners it was the strangest dinner party they had ever attended, and at times seemed quite unreal. On the one hand the table appointments were elegant, the food excellent, the service of the negro footmen, under the supervision of a mulatto major-domo, everything that could be desired. In fact the setting could not have been more civilised and luxurious had they been in the house of a nobleman who owned great estates in one of the Sugar Islands. On the other the presence of Philo, Cyrano and Lucette was a constant reminder that they were sitting at table with men steeped in the blackest villainy and a woman who only that morning had strangled her lover.

Yet the Vicomte seemed quite unconscious of this anomaly and now gave the impression that he would not willingly have harmed a rabbit. He was telling Georgina something of the history of that part of the world, and how the French had first secured a foothold there.

Columbus, he said, had formed his first settlement in the great Carib island of Haiti, as Santo Domingo was then called. He had christened it Hispaniola, or Little Spain, and claimed for the Spanish crown all the islands in the Caribbean. But even after the Spaniards had subdued the fierce Caribs in Haiti they had not bothered to colonise its little neighbour, Tortuga. French outlaws and castaways had been the first to do so, and as in the island there were great herds of wild cattle and wild hogs, they had made a living by hunting them and selling the smoked meat to passing ships. It was from their daring handling of the wild bulls that they had got the name Buccaneers.

After some years the Spaniards had sent an expedition to turn them out; so they had taken refuge in the uninhabited parts of Santo Domingo, where as there were even greater herds, they had re-established themselves in their occupation. Later, learning that the Spaniards had vacated Tortuga, some of the Buccaneers returned there. Again the Spaniards despatched troops to dislodge them, but by then the French had greatly increased in numbers, and they proved the better men. Not only had they remained masters of Tortuga, but they wrested the most fertile third of Santo Domingo from their enemies.

Meanwhile, the number of pirates sailing the Spanish Main had increased exceedingly, and before proceeding on a voyage they had formed the habit of raiding the stockyards of the Buccaneers to provision their ships. This constant menace to the living of the Buccaneers caused many of those in Santo Domingo to become planters, which led to their descendants making great fortunes; but on Tortuga the area of cultivable land was negligible, so the Buccaneers there had abandoned their hunting and turned pirate, thus giving the latter their alternate name.

When the Vicomte had concluded this recital, Georgina asked him how it was that he had become a pirate himself. His thin face darkened as he replied:

'In '87 I inherited great estates in Martinique, so came out from France to inspect my property. I found that the climate suited me and that life in the island was delightful.

Every reasonable amenity was obtainable, and the nobility formed a cultured and charming society; so I decided to settle there. It was the accursed Revolution that deprived me, like so many others, of wealth and security.

'Soon after our foolish King gave way to his criminal advisers and summoned the States General, our troubles began. By 1790 agitators were arriving in the islands and preaching their iniquitous doctrine of liberty and equality to the slaves. Uprisings followed and on isolated estates the slaves murdered their white masters. For a time we succeeded in localising these revolts, but we were vilely betrayed by our government at home. The Convention passed a decree liberating the slaves, and sent a ruffian named Victor Hugues as their representative, to have the decree carried out. Civil war resulted. Later, with the help of the English, these revolts were suppressed; but I am speaking of the early days. In my part of the island we are hopelessly outnumbered. Several of my neighbours, with their wives and children, were massacred and those who survived fled for their lives.

'When I was younger I held a commission in the French Navy, and soon after settling in Martinique I had purchased a schooner which I kept in the harbour of Saint Pierre. By night I managed to get aboard her unseen with half a dozen mulattoes who had remained loyal to me. I had no money, few provisions and no refuge for which I could make; so I decided to continue the war as a free lance.

'Some nights later we surprised a larger vessel which I knew to be armed with cannon. I had planned the attack knowing most of her crew to be ashore; so we succeeded in overpowering the remainder, and forcing them to join us. For upwards of two months I then wrought much havoc among vessels trading with Revolutionary France. It was the English who caused me to abandon those waters, as some months earlier they had declared war on France, and their navy began to make it dangerous for French ships to leave port.

'My search for suitable quarry led me north to Saint-Domingue, but up here I found very similar conditions; so in order to maintain myself it became necessary to make prizes of any ships that offered, irrespective of their flags. My operations were ill regarded by one Bartholomew Redbeard, who had hitherto looked on these parts as his private preserve. By that time both my crew and the armament of my ship had been greatly strengthened; so one fine September morning I gave Monsieur Redbeard battle. By midday he was worsted, and as the sun went down I hanged him from his own yard-arm. Those of his followers who survived the conflct agreed to serve under me, and it was they who led me here. Since I acquired this property I have greatly improved it, and as I find the excitement of the life agreeable I shall probably continue in it for some years. However, I am amassing a pleasant fortune in Genoa, to which Madame la Comtesse is about to make a handsome contribution; so if I ever become bored I shall be able to retire to Italy in affluent circumstances.'

On the face of it the history he had related appeared to be one of calamitous ill-fortune overcome by audacity and high courage, but all his reluctant guests knew that if fully enquired into it would reveal him as cunning, unscrupulous, and a bloody-minded tyrant who, apart from one battle, had consistently preyed upon the weak. Roger hoped that long before he decided to retire on his ill-gotten gains he would be caught by a ship-of-war, and end his days kicking at empty air as he was hoisted to a gallows.

As the meal progressed conversation became more general, and Roger attempted to draw out his left-hand neighbour. But Philo the Greek had evidently been selected as one of the Vicomte's Lieutenants only on his qualities as a sea-rover. Although he had been born in Greece and had not come to the Spanish Main until well into his twenties he knew nothing of the history of his country. He was simply a rough diamond who in other circumstances might have made an excellent captain in a trading vessel. He was clearly not an evil man by nature, but accepted the merciless deeds, inseparable from piracy, as part of the way of life fate had decreed that he should lead. His ability to reply to questions was, moreover, considerably hampered by his having to concentrate on eating with some semblance of a propriety to which he was obviously unaccustomed.

Cyrano was much more forthcoming. He was a man of some education and the son of a Nantes ship owner. Romance had been the cause of his undoing; for he had seduced the daughter of a 'noble of the robe' as the legal nobility of France were termed, and been found out. To save him from prison his father had got him away in one of the family's ships; but she had been captured by pirates off the French island of St. Christopher, and the pirates had pressed him into their service. Finding a life of adventure, with easy money and plenty of women, much more to his taste than a bourgeois existence in France, he had made no attempt to escape but continued in it. Some years later he had joined Bartholomew Redbeard and, in due course, come under the banner of the Vicomte.

They had been talking for some time when he remarked to Roger: 'May I congratulate you on your French, Monsieur. You speak it with an accent and fluency quite exceptional in an Englishman.'

'Thank you,' Roger smiled. 'But that is readily accounted for by my having lived for a good part of my life in France.'

A momentary silence having fallen, the Vicomte caught the exchange and, looking down the table, said: 'I think, then, that we must have met before. When I first saw you this morning your face seemed familiar to me.'

'I had the same feeling,' Roger replied. 'But on your telling us a while back that you have been in the Indies since '87 I decided that I must have been mistaken.'

'Why so, if, as you say, you have spent a good part of your life in France?'

'That is true; for I ran away from home to France when I was not yet sixteen, and have since returned there many times, often for lengthy periods.'

'In what parts of France have you lived?'

'Mostly in Paris; but at one time or another I have stayed for a while in many of the great provincial cities. However, I spent my first few years in Brittany, and during them my circumstances were such that it is highly improbable that I should have made the acquaintaince of Monsieur le Vicomte. Indeed, had I done so I should certainly recall it.'

'Did you ever go to Versailles?' the Vicomte persisted.

'Yes; and lately I had the honour to be received on numerous occasions by their Majesties. But that would be after Monsieur le Vicomte had left for Martinique. My early visits to the palace were made only in the role of a young secretary carrying documents to a nobleman who had apartments there.'

'To whom do you refer?'

'I was at that time in the service of the Marquis de Rochambeau.'

There was a moment's silence. During it de Senlac's thin face paled and purple blotches appeared on it. Suddenly he sprang to his feet, thrust out a quivering jewelled hand, pointed to Roger and screamed:

'Murderer! Assassin! I know you now! 'Twas you who foully slew my beloved uncle, M. le Comte de Caylus.'

10

A Hand from the Grave

That recognition should have led to this caused Roger's heart to bound with swift, terrible misgivings. Rising more slowly he strove to conceal his emotion. With an effort he kept his voice level, as he replied:

'You are mistaken, Monsieur. I killed the Count, but fairly, in a duel.'

'Liar! Assassin!' stormed the Vicomte, trembling with rage. 'I know the truth! You waylaid his coach like a footpad in the forest of Melun, and did him to death.'

'That is not true!' Roger protested hotly. 'In the belief that I was not of noble blood, he refused my challenge. I had no alternative other than to force a fight upon him at a place of my own choosing. But it was a fair fight. In fact he was reputed the finest swordsman in all France while I was still a stripling novice; so the odds were all against me!'

'Lies! Lies! Lies! Without warning or witnesses you set upon and killed him.'

'Comte Lucein de Rochambeau was in his coach, and present throughout the whole affair. M. le Vicomte de la Tour d'Auvergne and the Abbé de Talleyrand-Périgord were also in the immediate neighbourhood. They were aware of all that took place at the encounter from start to finish. Both afterwards vouched for it that I did nothing unfitting in a man of honour.'

'You had no seconds; no doctor was present. You contravened every established rule of duelling. By the law of France that makes you an assassin.'

'So thought her Majesty Queen Marie Antoinette until

she learned the truth. She then secured me a pardon, and honoured me with her friendship.'

'Lies! More lies! You had abused your position in M. de Rochambeau's household to seduce his daughter. Then, when in ignorance of the fact, my good uncle was about to marry her, rather than lose your mistress you murdered him.'

'Athénaïs de Rochambeau was not my mistress,' shouted Roger, now almost as angry as de Senlac.

'I care not!' the Vicomte yelled back. 'The Comte was a father to me! The best man that ever lived! And it was you who took his life. Heaven be praised for having sent me this chance to revenge his death. *Mort de Dieu,* you shall suffer as few men have! Philo! Cyrano! Seize him!'

Springing aside from his place, Roger grasped the back of his chair and swung it aloft. As Philo ran in he brought its legs crashing down on the pirate's shoulders and their cross-bar struck his head. With a moan, he went down in a heap. But before Roger could raise the chair again the two negro footmen flung themselves on him from behind. As they grabbed his arms Cyrano seized the chair and wrenched it from him. He landed a violent kick on the Frenchman's knee, and received in return a blow beneath the jaw. It was not a knock-out but temporarily deprived him of his powers of resistance. A minute later, while Cyrano limped away cursing with pain, the two powerful negroes secured their grip and held Roger rigid between them.

Everyone had risen from the table and, thrusting his way between the women, de Senlac strode up to his now helpless prisoner. His slightly hooded eyes blazing with rage, he struck Roger across the mouth with the back of his open hand.

'For that,' cried Roger, 'unless you are prepared to disgrace your ancestry, you will give me satisfaction.'

Even as he uttered the words, he knew that his chances of goading the Vicomte into a duel were exceedingly slender; and he proved right, for de Senlac sneered: 'Are you half-witted? Is it likely that I would afford you a chance to kill me! No, you scum. I mean to stand by and watch you die horribly. Yes, and all shall witness the way in which I avenge my poor uncle. My crews, your women, the other prisoners, even the kitchen hands and slaves—everyone.' Turning away he shot a malevolent glance round the company and said: 'Come, let me have your suggestions for the most painful way in which we can send this assassin screaming down to hell.'

Now that they could get a word in, Amanda, Georgina, and Clarissa all began to plead or attempt to reason with him; but he silenced them all with a furious shout.

Cyrano was still cursing as he massaged his injured knee. With a malicious leer at Roger, he said: 'I'd like to see him keelhauled. He'd not be so handsome after the barnacles on the ship's bottom had scraped half the flesh off his face.'

The Vicomte shook his head. 'Nay, we can do better than that. You know how the rope that draws them under is apt to get fouled. He might even drown during the very first trip.'

'Why not have him flayed?' suggested the elder Herault laconically.

'No, no!' cried the younger. 'Have him die the death the Caribs used to inflict on their enemies. It was yourself who told me of it. I mean that where they stuck them full of thorns, each thorn having been slit to hold a piece of wadding soaked in oil; so that when these were lit the victim danced a death jig clothed in a garment of tiny torches.'

Nodding in turn to father and son, de Senlac muttered: 'Both ideas have possibilities; but I somewhat favour smearing his stomach with honey and setting the fire-ants to eat their way into him.'

Amanda's eye fluttered up and she fainted.

As Georgina caught and lowered her to a chair Clarissa shrilled at de Senlac: 'You cannot do such things! You cannot! Even the Fiend himself would baulk at inflicting such torment.'

'I can, Mademoiselle; and I will,' came the harsh retort. 'More; it now occurs to me to combine these punishments. I'll have my pet crocodiles snap off his feet, make thorn-stuck torches of his arms, flay his back and let the ants have his innards.'

Clarissa snatched up a glass from the table and flung it at de Senlac's face.

He dodged the glass but some drops of wine sprayed over his coat. As he flicked at them with his lace handkerchief, he snarled: 'The use to which you put that wine shall cost you dear. I'll make you weep a bucket of tears for every drop that splashed me. Aye, you shall slobber and gibber till the colour is washed from those blue eyes of yours.'

Facing about, he cried to Roger: 'You heard the sentence I impose. Tomorrow at sundown the first part of it shall be carried out. I'll have you swung out over the pool where I keep my caymens, and they shall battle for which of them gets your toes.'

Amanda raised her head from her lap, then flung herself forward, clasped the Vicomte round the knees, and sobbed: 'I implore you to have mercy. The affair that so distresses you is long past. Whatever the rights of it leave Our Father in Heaven, who is aware of all, to pass judgment. Oh I beg, I implore you, not to do this terrible thing.'

Still seething with almost apoplectic fury, de Senlac kicked her away from him, and shouted: 'God can do as He will, Madame; but I am master here. For the murder of my uncle there is nothing that I would not make your husband suffer—nothing! Aye, and as I think on it I've the power to make him squirm mentally as well as physically.'

Again he swung on Roger, and with dilated eyes screamed like one possessed. 'Since Madame la Comtesse could find fifty thousand pounds to ransom you all, she can find it to save herself. As you die by stages these next few days you may contemplate all that is in store for Madame your wife, and her young spitfire of a cousin. On the night of your death I'll have them stripped of their clothes and flung to my men to make what sport they will with in the moonlight.'

Roger, goaded beyond endurance, hurled back insults, imprecations and defiance; but he might just as well have held his tongue. At an abrupt order from de Senlac the negro footmen dragged him from the room and through the hall to the back quarters of the premises. Herault *père* had accompanied them and produced a big key. With it he unlocked a massive door studded with iron nails. Through it, Roger was thrust into pitch darkness. He stumbled down a few steps then fell heavily, measuring his length on a stoneflagged floor. A moment later the heavy door clanged to behind him.

The breath driven from his body, distraught with rage, misery and the bitter knowledge of his helplessness, he would have remained where he lay, had not there come a quick mutter of voices and groping hands that raised him until he was sitting up.

During the past two days the wound in his head had been mending nicely and he had not suffered greatly from it; but now, with every beat of his pulse, pain seared through it again. Temporarily, shock, agony, and the almost unbelievable change in his circumstances which had occurred in less than ten minutes bemused his mind.

After a brief respite he managed to pull himself together sufficiently to reply, in stammered sentences, to the questions with which his fellow prisoners were eagerly bombarding him. They were, he found, young Doctor Fergusson, Jennings, the *Circe*'s Second Mate, and Wells the Supercargo, all of whom had been condemned to death.

In halting phrases he told them what had happened to himself but without raising false hopes could find no word to comfort them in their equally desperate situation. They had already explored the dungeon and found escape from it impossible; but none of them was bound, so for a while they speculated on the chances of a breakout next time the door was opened. Yet even as they discussed it they knew that with so many armed men at call, they would be overcome before they could get out of the house. Despair reduced them temporarily to silence; then, at Fergusson's suggestion, they prayed together earnestly for deliverance. Afterwards fatigue dulled their distraught minds and they lay face down on the hard stone, their heads pillowed on their arms, in an attempt to get some sleep.

The swift succession of questions and answers which had landed Roger in his present sorry pass ran again and again through his mind. He wondered now if by denying that he was the man who had killed de Caylus he could have saved himself, but doubted it. De Senlac had probably seen him a dozen times when he was working in the bureau of the Marquis at the Hotel de Rochambeau in Paris. In any case he would certainly have been one of the guests at the great ball given there for the King and Queen, at which they had sponsored the betrothal of Athénaïs to his uncle. A denial could have only postponed the evil hour when some chance phrase, or trick of movement, struck a spark in the Vicomte's brain and illuminated in it the vivid memory of a past meeting.

As Roger mused upon the matter it struck him as peculiarly grim that for a second time de Caylus should have stretched up a hand out of the grave to drag him down into it. In '89 Roger had put down to ill-chance his arrest for the unorthodox duel he had fought two years earlier, but this seemed more in the nature of a lingering malignity exercised by the restless spirit of the dead Count. In that first case Roger had narrowly escaped execution but powerful friends and his own wits had saved him. He doubted if anything could save him now.

His one hope lay in Dan. He knew that Dan would willingly risk his own life in an attempt, if he thought it had the least possibility of succeeding; but there would be no chance of that unless he could get help and he could not be expected to make a martyr of himself to no purpose. His prospects of securing adequate aid seemed far from good, for as a new recruit among the pirates he had probably been accepted only on probation and was being watched. Even should he be unhampered by restrictions on his movements those whom he could risk asking to join him in a forlorn attempt were lamentably few. Tom was now free as also was Monsieur Pirouet; but apart from them there could be no more than half a dozen of the *Circe*'s crew who had joined the pirates with some reluctance whom he dare approach. Any of them might well betray him before the attempt could be made, and even if he succeeded in getting together a little band of stalwarts what hope could such a handful have against de Senlac's men, who must number well over fifty?

In spite of all the obstacles with which Dan would be faced Roger had great confidence in the courage and resource of his henchman. In consequence he clung to this one ray of hope, and as he turned miserably from side to side on the hard stone, he kept listening for cautious footsteps outside which might herald his delivery.

Gradually the dark hours passed, but no sounds broke the stillness. High up in the wall on the opposite side of the dungeon to the door two patches of greyness appeared. Within ten minutes they had taken on the sharp outlines of small heavily-barred windows. Dawn had come and with it Roger's last hopes vanished. If Dan had found the odds too high against pulling off a *coup* during the night, it was a certainty that nothing he could attempt would succeed in daylight.

Although the floor of the dungeon was below ground, as Roger could now see, it was a lofty place and roomy enough to hold a score of prisoners without undue crowding; but its only furnishings were a crock of water and a big earthenware vessel half full of fruit. There were no sanitary arrangements and the place stank abominably.

The windows were closed, and except where one small pane had been knocked out, were encrusted with the grime of ages; so they let in little light and he could still see only imperfectly. To quench his thirst he stretched out a hand to take a paw-paw. As he did so something moved on the pile of fruit. Leaning nearer he saw that, half obscured by the rim of the vessel, a huge black spider was lurking there. Its body was as big as a duck's egg, and its hairy legs as long as those of a good-sized crab. From its face protruded what appeared to be four large teeth, set like those of a rabbit.

At Roger's quick movement of retreat the others roused, and saw the venomous-looking brute at which he was staring. Unbuckling his belt Jennings made a swipe at the spider but missed, and as it scuttled away into a dark corner, he said:

'They're not poisonous, but can give a chap a nasty bite. Lucky the fruit was there fer 'im ter feed on, else 'e might ha' tried ter make a meal orf one of us.'

'Oh, what's a spider's bite when we shall so soon have

to face death,' exclaimed the young Supercargo desperately, and burst into a flood of tears.

They did what they could to comfort him, but his nerve had gone and he quietened down only after a fit of hysterics had reduced him to exhaustion. Then for a long time they sat in silence, being unwilling to talk of what lay in store for them yet unable to think of anything else.

At an hour they judged to be about half-past eight, there came a trampling of footsteps in the passage, the key rasped in the lock and the door was flung open. Followed by five other men Cyrano came down the stone steps.

Roger noticed that his left knee was bandaged and that he grimaced with pain every time he put any weight on the leg. But that was small compensation for what followed.

With evident enjoyment he gave an appraising look at Jennings, Wells and Fergusson in turn, then said in a silky voice: 'M. le Vicomte has now settled his programme. For the next three days one of you will provide an overture each morning for a vocal concert by the noble Governor of Martinique towards the latter part of the afternoon; and on the fourth day he will give us his final solo. As inducements to you to give full play to your lungs the first of you is to be keelhauled, the second rent apart from being tied by the hands and feet between two downward bent young palm trees, and the third fed to M. le Vicomte's crocodiles.'

Neither Jennings nor the Supercargo knew enough French to understand fully what Cyrano had said, but Fergusson did and after a moment he gulped: 'Which of us is to die today?'

Cyrano pointed at Jennings. 'He goes first. As a mate of the *Circe* he knows well the feel of her deck beneath his feet, and now we mean to make him kiss her bottom.' With a glance at his men he added: 'Come! What are you waiting for. Get hold of him.'

Jenning had grasped enough to realise that when they got him outside they meant to kill him. His eyes staring from their sockets he backed against the wall. Then, mouthing a stream of profanity, he suddenly hurled himself upon the nearest pirate. The man went down under the attack but the others grabbed the mate and dragged him towards the steps. Cursing and kicking he was lugged up them. For minutes afterwards his shouts echoed down he passage, until they gradually died away in the distance.

Meanwhile one of the men had refilled the water jug and tipped a basket full of fresh fruit on to the remains of the old supply. Cyrano made a gesture towards his injured knee, bared his teeth at Roger, and said: 'I shall take a special pleasure in watching you dance for M. le Vicomte's crocodiles later in the day.' Then he limped up the steps, the door was locked behind him and the three remaining prisoners were left to their terrifying reflections.

During the rest of the morning, except for short intervals of violent coughing caused by his tubercular lung, Wells lay semi-comatose, but the other two could not free their minds from a series of mental pictures in which the unfortunate Jennings was the central figure. They saw him stripped to the waist, and round his body the knotted bight of a long rope, one end of which had already been passed beneath the *Circe* amidships. They saw him, fighting and yelling, thrown over the side to splash with whirling arms and legs into the water. They saw the rope now taut and being hauled upon by a mob of running men, so that Jennings should be dragged under the hull and up the far side of the ship before he could drown. They saw him again on deck, dripping, gasping and bleeding from a score of lacerations to his flesh, while with brutal jests his tormentors revived him with neat rum to undergo the second scraping —and the third, the fourth, the fifth, until they could revive him no more.

Roger knew that there must be sharks in the bay and that they would be attracted by Jennings's blood. He prayed that one of them might get him during the first plunge, and so put an end to his agony swiftly. Yet the thought conjured up sickening visions of the ordeal to which the vengeance-crazed Vicomte intended to inflict upon him later that very day. There seemed little to choose between having one's feet gnawed off by sharks or crocodiles; and for him that would not be followed by a swift if painful end. Tomorrow that fiend in human form meant to burn his arms away, and the next to have the skin stripped from his back. Lastly there would come the excruciating agony of lying pegged out on an ant heap while the fire-ants ate away his vitals.

If his torn legs were given prompt attention it seemed certain that he would survive the first day's unholy sport, but there was a chance that the shock of the burns on the second day would kill him. After the third, at least, he might die from the loss of blood and nervous exhaustion, or have become a raving lunatic no longer capable of registering physical suffering with full consciousness. He could only pray that it would be so.

During the heat of the day the atmosphere became stifling and the stench almost unbearable. Mosquitoes plagued them and the itch of the bites drove them to a frenzy. But gradually the afternoon dragged through its awful length. At last the door was thrown open again.

Cyrano limped down the steps with his gang of butchers. They were carrying cords with which to tie the prisoners' hands behind their backs. The Supercargo, now nearly off his head with fear, screamed and fought but was seized with a desperate fit of coughing and soon overcome. Fergusson was white to the lips but had the fortitude to allow his wrists to be tied without a struggle. So did Roger. He knew that to resist or attempt to get away in this confined space, was utterly hopeless. It could lead only to exhausting himself quite fruitlessly. He must husband every ounce of strength he had, just in case a chance offered for him to break away when he was in the open.

But his hands were bound and he would be one against fifty, or more probably a hundred, as the Vicomte meant the slaves also to witness his ruthless revenge. Even if he could drag the end of the cord that now bit into his wrists from the man who held it, what chance would he have? Before he had covered ten yards recapture was certain.

This was his third round with de Caylus. When he had set out upon the first he had expected to meet his death by a sword thrust. Bitterly, he wished now that he had. After all these years de Caylus had caught up with him. As he walked up the stone steps he faced the fact that this must be the end; but a lingering end, from which he could escape only after countless hours of torture.

11

The Crocodile Pool

As Roger was led across the main hall of the house the bright sunshine was still streaming through its rear windows, and he judged that there must be a good hour to go before brief twilight heralded the tropic night. Out on the veranda Amanda sat hunched in a chair, her head bowed in her hands. The other women were grouped round her and behind them stood four pirates who had evidently been set to keep watch on them. The sound of feet caused Amanda to lift her head. Immediately she saw Roger she jumped up to run to him but one of the men roughly pulled her back. The three prisoners were pushed past the women and down the steps; then each of the pirates took one of the women by the arm and fell in with them behind Cyrano.

The foreshore presented an animated scene. Boatloads of men from the two ships were landing on the beach; others, and with them a score of slatternly looking women of mixed nationality, were emerging from the long low building which formed the south wing of the house, and little groups of slaves, ranging in colour from coal black to tanned whites, were leaving the lean-to's roofed with banana palm. The pirates and their molls were gaily dressed in looted silks and cottons; whereas the slaves had on only scanty, ragged garments; but nearly all had coloured handkerchiefs knotted about their heads, and a festive atmosphere prevailed. All were making their way across the front of the house towards the northern arm of the bay and laughing and joking as though they were setting out on a bean-feast.

Cyrano now had water on the knee, but was evidently determined not to miss the fun. Muttering curses with every step he took, he led his seven captives and their escort along the strand to a path that wound up into the forest.

As they entered it they passed into a new, fantastic, twilight world. Trees of enormous girth reared up two hundred feet in height, but their upper boughs could not be seen because they became lost in a smother of other vegetation. Out of their hollows and every cranny in them sprang ferns, many themselves as large as medium-sized trees. From their branches tangles of lianas and creepers cascaded down like green waterfalls. Some of their stems were as thick as a man's arm, and snaked upwards like green pythons, while countless others looped in all directions or hung down as straight as a weighted string. Between the giant acomas, candlewoods and palms, a vast variety of other trees struggled for room, their branches interlacing. Many were loaded with fruit: golden mangoes, green avocados, clusters of yellow paw-paws, prickly soursops looking like huge pears, custard apples, wild apricots, limes and citrons. Below them rioted bushes and big tufts of coarse grasses half submerged under more tangles of creeper with here and there the fallen limb of a great tree that, even as it rotted, was giving birth to ferns, mosses, and other forms of the teeming life that sprouted everywhere with almost incredible abundance.

The path wound upwards, and after ten minutes' hard trudging they emerged into an open space floored with an outcrop of rock, in the crevices of which only mosses and small plants could find enough soil to maintain a foothold. On the inland side of this clearing a tangle of great boulders sloped up to a twelve-feet high cliff, overlapped with verdure where the forest began again; at its far end the cliff continued, curving and rising to a sheer wall over fifty feet in height. Below this high cliff lay the pool, on the edge of which had been erected a long-armed gibbet. To the seaward side of the open ground trees again towered skyward and between them the dense jungle cut off any view of the bay below.

Several score of people had already congregated to see

the sport, and the prisoners were led through them to the pool's edge. It was roughly oval and lay in a deep hollow so that the water was some eight feet below the rocky floor of the clearing. Near the place where the boulders stopped a small waterfall tumbled down from the cliff to feed it, and the overflow was carried off, after passing through an iron grille by another that fell into a gully leading down to the sea. From the clearing the only exit, other than that by which they had entered it, was across the gully by a plank bridge beyond which another track opened leading further up into the forest.

Men and women were still crowding into the clearing and jostling one another for the best places to sit up on the boulders, where they could get a good view of the proceedings. Some of the slaves had already secured good positions there, but were being roughly dispossessed by the pirates and their molls and herded with their fellow slaves on the opposite side of the clearing. It was to that side, too, that the prisoners had been brought; and, with the exception of Roger, they were all thrust back by their escorts towards the gap in the rim of the pool where its water poured off down the deep gully. Hoping for a word with Amanda, Roger tried to follow them, but, on a harsh order from Cyrano, he was pulled up short by the man who held the cord tying his wrists. In the wide circle that had now been cleared about the gibbet, he stood between them with every eye in the eager, murmuring throng upon him.

Staring back, he searched the great ring of cruel or indifferent faces for Dan's, still hoping again all reason that his old friend might yet make a last minute attempt at rescue, but he could not see him. That was hardly surprising as in some places the crowd was four deep. Neither could he see Tom, but he caught sight of Monsieur Pirouet. The plump Frenchman was standing a few feet behind Dr. Fergusson; but on meeting Roger's desperate glance, he looked quickly away..

Roger was already suffering a minor torment from the bites mosquitoes had inflicted on him during his many hours in the dungeon, and never in his life had he cut so poor a figure. Gone was all semblance to the debonair Mr.

Brook of Whites Club or the elegant M. le Chevalier de Breuc who in other days had supped and danced at the courts of half a dozen continental monarchs. His clothes were torn and stained, his stockings laddered; his hair was matted under a dirty bandage, his face mottled by stings and his eyes dull from sleeplessness. Even when he had played the part of a *sans-culotte,* for all the filth of his apparel, his bearing singled him out as a man of vigour and determination; whereas now he stood with slack limbs and hunched shoulders, so that the pirates, fearing he would show them only poor sport, began to jeer at him for cowardice.

Actually he was now endeavouring to close his mind against coherent thought, so that terror might not drive him to some desperate futile act which could only cause even greater distress to Amanda and the others than they were already suffering. For their sakes, too, he wanted to conserve every atom of mental resistance he could muster; so that when the ordeal came, even if he could not manage to remain silent, at least he would not wring their hearts by screaming.

A murmur of excitement and a few cheers heralded the approach of the Vicomte. The crowd parted, forming a ragged lane through which he advanced, a tall malacca cane in one hand, the other resting lightly on the arm of his blond *mignon,* who in the sunlight looked more than ever like a slightly negroid young Viking. As they came up beside Roger, de Senlac pointed to the long-armed gibbet and said:

'You need fear no mishap, Monsieur, for you are not the first to afford us this type of entertainment, and practice has enabled us to perfect our arrangements. The harness dangling from the arm of the gibbet will be strapped about your shoulders, and the main post turns upon a pivot so that you may be swung out over the pool. Then we shall lower you by inches until your feet are near enough to the water for my pets to snap off your toes.'

For the first time Roger forced himself to look at the water rippling eight feet below him. The sun had now gone down behind the hill and no reflected light flickered from it, but the splashing of the little waterfall kept it in perpetual motion so that he could not see beneath its surface. But on the far side of the pool a narrow sickle-shaped beach shelved up to the cliff-face and, half submerged in the water close to it, there floated several long shapes whose rough texture gave them the appearance of rotting tree trunks.

De Senlac pointed with his cane. 'There are a few of my beauties. Although we talk of them as crocodiles they are, more strictly speaking, a type of alligator and in these parts called caymen. Let us rouse them up for the treat they are about to be given.'

Turning, he beckoned to the elder Herault, who was standing a few yards off with two negroes beside him, both of whom carried big wicker baskets on their heads. When the baskets were set down Roger saw that they contained pigs' trotters, cows' hocks and other offal. Selecting half a calf's head Herault *père* threw it into the middle of the pool. It had scarcely touched the surface when the water was broken in a score of places. Snouts with knobbly ends were thrust up, long lean jaws gaped open showing rows of strong fang-like teeth, little eyes gleamed evilly, and scaly tails that could have knocked a man off his feet, threshed the water into foam. In a moment the leaping and plunging of the ferocious creatures had churned the pool into a seething cauldron.

Herault continued to throw lumps of offal to them until he had half emptied one of the baskets, then the Vicomte checked him by crying: 'Enough! We must not take the edge off their appetites. You can give them the rest of their meal afterwards.'

But now they had been excited by the food the great reptiles did not settle down. Eager for more they splashed and wallowed, snapping their jaws, lashing their tails, and in their disappointment turning on one another. As Roger watched them with horrified fascination he wished for the twentieth time since the capture of the *Circe* that he had been caught six months earlier with Athénaïs, and suffered with her the clean swift death of the guillotine.

De Senlac gave Jean Herault's arm a gentle pat, nodded

towards the gibbet and said with the smile of an elderly roué giving a present to a young woman he wished to please: 'For you, dear boy, I have reserved the pleasure of fastening the harness upon him. But take care that the straps beneath his arms are tight; otherwise he might slip out of it, and deprive me of my full revenge by making a quick end of himself.'

As the tall youth walked past the Vicomte to the gibbet, the man behind Roger untied the cord that bound his wrists. It had been tied so tightly that for a moment his hands hung numb and useless. Flexing his fingers, he glanced wildly round. Amanda and Jenny were on their knees praying for him. Clarissa stood with bowed head and one arm thrown across her face. Georgina, white as a sheet under her tan, was staring at him, all the love that she had borne him through her life in her big eyes. Neither Tom nor Dan was anywhere to be seen.

Jean Herault turned the pivot of the gibbet so that its long arm swung towards the pool's edge. At Roger's side the Vicomte stood watching the graceful movements of the young *sangmêlé* with a doting leer. As he reached for the harness Roger acted.

Taking one pace back he brought his right knee up with all his force. It struck de Senlac a violent blow on the bottom. With eyes starting from their sockets and mouth agape he lurched forward. For a second he tottered, his arms flailing wildly, on the very edge of the pool. Then unable to recover his balance, he pitched head-foremost into it.

His terrified yell was cut short as he hit the water. With the speed and strength exceeding that of tigers the caymens leapt upon him, tearing him limb from limb, until his blood made a great red streak across the heaving surface of the pool.

Roger did not see his enemy's ghastly end. His desperate stroke had given him an outside chance to break away through the ring of spectators and plunge into the forest. If he could succeed in that the dense vegetation would swallow him up. Even a penetration of a dozen yards might be enough to enable him to escape recapture; but it was now or never.

The instant de Senlac jerked forward on to his toes Roger swung about. He had deliberately refrained from using his hands, in order that he might have his fists already clenched. One stride brought him within a yard of the man who had just untied him. His right fist caught the man beneath the jaw and sent him sprawling. He was flat on his back even before the sound of the splash made by the Vicomte's body cut short his yell.

Roger's actions had been so swift that only the nearer members of the crowd had yet grasped the full significance of them. While they remained motionless and gaping in astonished silence he seized the opportunity to shout with all the power of his lungs:

'Dan! Tom! Old *Circe* men! Help!' Then he yelled in French: 'Slaves! Free yourselves! The Tyrant is dead! Take courage! Rally to me!'

His last words were drowned in a pandemonium of shouting, yells and curses. As though the tension had been released by a spring, every figure in the clearing leapt into motion. The younger Herault whipped out a knife and ran at him from one side, the elder from the other. Catching the *sangmêlé*'s wrist he gave it a violent twist. He let out a screech of pain; but his father had seized Roger round the waist in a trained wrestler's grip and, with surprising strength for a man of his age, threw him off his balance.

As he went down he caught a glimpse of the women. Amanda and Jenny were on their feet again. The former was clawing the eyes out of her guard and his cheeks were scored with bloody furrows, where her nails had gashed them. The latter was still struggling with hers and beating at his face with her clenched fists. Clarissa had broken free and was running towards him. Georgina had snatched a knife from her guard's belt and was stabbing with it at his stomach.

Roger hit the ground with a thump. Next moment, despite the gallant diversions created by the women, he thought the game was up. Both the Heraults were about to throw themselves upon him and out of the corner of his eyes he caught sight of Cyrano brandishing a cavalry sabre.

When the mêlée started de Senlac's Lieutenant had been

talking to some men half way along the ridge of boulders. As his back was turned he had not seen Roger knee the Vicomte into the pool, and owing to the agony he was suffering from his knee he had made poor speed in recrossing the clearing. Yet now he was only a few yards off, his long curved sword held high ready to deliver a deadly stroke. Roger, prone on his back, could do nothing to evade the flashing blade. His bid for freedom had started so well, but it seemed he had made it in vain.

Help came from an unexpected quarter. The report of a musket rang out above the shouting of the crowd. Cyrano's eyes started in his head, his jaw went slack. Shot through the back, he crashed forward on to this face, his right arm still outstretched so that the tip of his sabre struck a spark from the rock only six inches short of Roger's head.

It was Dan who had saved him. The ex-smuggler and Tom were lying hidden in the undergrowth on the edge of the low cliff above the boulders. Thinking it certain that Roger's hands would be untied before he was bound up afresh in the harness attached to the gibbet, Dan had been waiting for that moment intending, as soon as Roger once more had the use of his fists, to shoot the Vicomte. But Roger had forestalled him with de Senlac so he had to hold his fire until he could aim at a worthwhile target without risk of hitting his master.

Again the element of surprise stood Roger in good stead. As Cyrano fell within a few yards of them, both the Heraults took their eyes from him to stare around in swift apprehension, wondering whence the shot had come, and fearing to be the next target.

Rolling over, Roger jumped to his feet, struck Jean a glancing blow with his fist and kicked the older man in the groin. With a screech *père* Herault doubled up and staggered back clutching at his genitals. His son landed a kick on Roger's thigh which again sent him sprawling.

Two more pirates were running to the young man's assistance but once more Roger was saved by a new diversion. A bang like that of a small cannon sounded above the din. Tom had discharged a blunderbuss loaded with old nails and scraps of iron into a tightly packed group of pirates and their molls on a flat-topped boulder just below him.

At such close range every fragment from the terrible weapon found a lodgment in human flesh. Screams, curses, groans rent the air. Next moment Dan and Tom, cutlasses in hand, leapt down on to the ledge and were laying about them among the survivors. Those up on the boulder offered no resistance and, scrambling down on to the flat floor of the clearing, the two stalwarts began to hack their way towards Roger.

But the fight was far from over. Seizing Jean by the ankle Roger lugged at it and brought him down. Shooting out a hand he grabbed Roger by the hair. Next moment they were grappling wildly. One of the pirates who had run up held a pistol. Aiming at Roger's head he fired; but at that second Roger gave a violent jerk to free his hair. The bullet missed him and smashed the *sangmêlé*'s elbow. In an instant Roger had struck him in the face and he rolled away now *hors de combat*.

Their struggle had brought them to the edge of the pool. As Roger scrambled to his knees, both pirates came at him together; and a third was now close on their heels. The nearest aimed a heavy kick at his face, with the intention of sending him over the edge. Roger jerked his head aside so that the man's foot went over his shoulder. Throwing himself forward, he flung his arms round the leg upon which the man was still standing. With a terrific heave he lifted the weighty body straddled above him, then let go. For a moment it was suspended on his back head down and feet in the air. He gave another heave and the man slithered off behind him, with his arms threshing the empty air three feet out from the pool's rim.

The second pirate had clubbed his pistol, but seeing his comrade's desperate situation flung it at Roger's head, then seized the first man's foot in an endeavour to save him. Roger dodged the pistol, scrambled up and as the third man rushed upon him was just in time to trip this new adversary.

He was gasping as though his lungs would burst; but now, after days of helpless despair, he was his old self again.

None of these lumbering brutes was his match for quick wits and agility and he felt that only numbers could overcome him.

The last of the three to go down was a mulatto, and in his hand he still held a short sword. He had hardly hit the ground before Roger brought a heel down on his wrist with such force that both of them heard the bone crunch. Stooping, Roger tore the sword from the nerveless fingers. Of all weapons it was the one he would have chosen for such a fight. He plunged it into the side of the pirate who was trying to drag his comrade back from the pool's edge. The wounded man gave a horrible gurgle, flung back his head, and let go; the other flopped into the pool with a resounding splash, came up to give one howl that echoed through the clearing, and was dragged under by the caymens.

The mulatto with the broken wrist scuffled off as swiftly as he could. Jean Herault was some way away moaning over his shattered elbow. His father had collapsed and lay writhing on the ground. Cyrano, paralysed from the waist down by a smashed spine, could now only curse feebly between bouts of vomiting blood. But the man whom Roger had knocked unconscious with a right to the jaw was coming round. Stepping forward, he kicked him hard on the side of the head and put him out again.

Now, for the first time since the murderous affray had started, Roger had a chance to get a full look round. The whole of the open space had become a scene of wild confusion and desperate fighting. Several major mêlées and a score of individual combats were in progress. Whites and blacks, slaves and pirates, men and women, were all embroiled in life or death struggles. Some were slashing or stabbing at one another, others locked chest to chest strove grimly to strangle or trip their antagonists; a group of negresses had attacked two of the coffee-coloured molls, and were dragging them by the hair towards the pool. Feet stamped, steel clanged on steel, and every moment a pistol shot rang out or a woman gave a piercing scream.

Roger had been facing slightly towards the boulders, and in that direction he saw Dan and Tom. They had half a dozen pirates against them, but were fighting gamely, and had been joined by two of the *Circe*'s men. Looking quickly to his other side he saw Fergusson slicing with a razor-edged machete at a big negro.

Monsieur Pirouet and Jake had been in the plot with Dan. Their part had been to free the other prisoners. The chef had brought concealed under his jacket a weighty meat chopper. He had been waiting for Dan's shot as the signal to act, but on seeing Roger deal with the Vicomte he had waited no longer. With two swift strokes of his chopper he had cleaved the necks and the jugular veins of the two guards behind whom he had stationed himself. As they fell Jake had dived forward knife in hand and cut the cords that bound the hands of the Doctor and the Supercargo. Fergusson had grabbed the cane-cutting machete from a nearby slave, and was still making good use of it; but young Wells lay dead with a knife through his chest.

Amanda too had gone down, but a man named Catamole from the *Circe* was standing over her with a pike and beating off two of the Porto Ricans, who had evidently decided for the second time to throw in their lot with the pirates. Georgina must have been stunned or wounded, as Monsieur Pirouet was carrying her towards the plank bridge over the deep gully while Jake and Jenny protected his back. For a moment Roger could not see Clarissa, then he caught sight of her some way from the others. Marlinspike Joe had her by the wrist and was dragging her off into the bushes.

In less than a minute Roger had taken in the whole ghastly tangle of slaughter. Racing towards the group fighting above Amanda he drove his sword into the small of the nearest Porto Rican's back. As he intended it pierced the kidney, from which a blade can be withdrawn with ease instead of becoming muscle-bound. Whipping it out, he left Catamole to deal with the other, and dashed after Clarissa.

Marlinspike Joe had pulled her into the dense vegetation but her cries told Roger whereabouts they were. Crashing his way through the undergrowth and forcing the low branches aside with his free hand, he plunged deeper in until he came upon them. On catching sight of Roger the ruffian let go of Clarissa and attempted to draw his cutlass, but she gamely hung on to his sword arm. That made him easy meat, and without the faintest scruple Roger delivered a lunge that pierced him through the windpipe.

Choked by the rush of his own blood, the lecherous mutineer made a sound like a premature death rattle, slipped to his knees and, still gurgling, fell from sight through a screen of creepers. Wrenching his point free, Roger took Clarissa by the hand, drew her back into the open and, pointing at the plank bridge, cried:

'Quick! Make for the bridge. Look! They're carrying Georgina across it. Tell them to take her further up the path into the forest. I'll join you as soon as I am able.'

As she set off at a run, he gave another swift look round. Amanda was on her feet. She was swaying dizzily, but Fergusson was supporting her and leading her towards the bridge, while Catamole still battled with the remaining Porto Rican. Roger had hoped that after being deprived of their leaders, and with the slaves raised against them, the pirates would lose heart, panic and scatter. But things did not seem to be going at all that way. Surprise had enabled him and his allies to inflict a dozen casualties on them in the first few minutes of the struggle, but now that they had recovered from the unexpectedness of the attack they were putting up a stout resistance. They were better armed, more used to handling weapons, and of tougher fibre, than most of their opponents. Moreover, as far as he could judge, only five or six of the *Circe*'s men and less than half of the slaves had responded to his shouts to turn against the pirates.

Many of the slaves were now fleeing down the path towards the bay. All the other molls had come to the rescue of the two the negresses had attacked and it was now the black women who were being dragged screaming towards the pool. At least forty pirates were still unscathed, and a dozen of them had driven Dan's party back to the boulders. One of the *Circe*'s men who had joined up with him had been cut down; the other, a big fair fellow named Kilick, was on his right, and Tom was on his left. But Tom had received a nasty cut across his forehead and blood was streaming down from it over his face.

Charging across the open space Roger flung himself into the fray. Now, he had the chance to use the short sword with maximum effect. It was much thicker than a rapier, so strong enough to parry a stroke from a cutlass without risk of snapping off; yet it enabled him to use the tricks of fencing of which he was a pastmaster.

Hearing the pounding of his feet behind them, three of the pirates turned to face him. Leaping from side to side, he feinted—lunged, feinted—lunged, feinted—lunged with incredible rapidity, his point darting hither and thither like lightning. It ripped through the fore arm of one man, tore open the cheek of another and pinked the stomach of the third, while the frantic slashes they made at him with their heavier weapons met only empty air and threw them off their balance.

None of the wounds was serious, but quite nasty enough to make all three men hastily draw back, thus breaking the semi-cricle that had enclosed Dan and his two companions. Roger shouted to them:

'Come on! Now's your chance! Have a care for your backs and make for the bridge.'

There was a moment of wild, confused fighting, then they were through. But Tom, faint from loss of blood and half blinded by it, tripped and fell. Kilick smashed the hilt of his cutlass into the face of the nearest pirate, stooped, seized Tom by the arm with his free hand and dragged him to his feet. Staggering but still game Tom lurched along beside him while Roger and Dan laid about them furiously to cover the retreat.

Twilight had began to fall, and as they backed towards the bridge Roger prayed that night might come quickly; for the pirates now had the upper hand and as long as the light lasted it would give them a better chance to pursue into the forest a party hampered by wounded.

There followed three more minutes of savage cut and thrust, then a new peril threatened the retreating party. Monsieur Pirouet and Jake had got all the women safely across the bridge, while Fergusson and Catamole remained on its near side defending it from a group of pirates who sought to cross it and recapture them. Now three of this group abandoned the attempt, to turn and attack Roger and his companions in the rear.

Their progress towards the bridge was checked no more than a dozen yards from it; but they could get no further, and with the half-fainting Tom in their midst were compelled to fight back to back. Surrounded and outnumbered as they were, it seemed certain that they must be overwhelmed. Kilick's long reach enabled him to keep his attackers at bay. Dan fought like a demon, Roger's blade snaked in and out constantly menacing the eyes and throats of those who assailed him. But their exertions had already been terrific, and all of them were now near spent.

Help came only just in time. Their friends had seen their plight and were doing their utmost to come to their assistance. Pirouet, Jake, Jenny and Clarissa had run back across the bridge. The two men joined Fergusson, Catamole and a ragged dark-haired stranger who had just emerged from the forest to fight beside them. Led by Fergusson, they all fell upon two pirates who were still trying to force the bridge, killed one and drove the other off with a great gash in his sword arm.

Jenny had found a pistol somewhere and Clarissa a knife. Wide eyed but determined they remained to guard the crossing against the pirates' molls who, close by, had just thrown the negresses into the pool; while Fergusson and his companions ran towards Roger. Another frightful mêlée ensued; Catamole was cut down by a stroke that half severed his head from his neck, but the others succeeded in reaching the bridge.

One by one they backed across the plank. Roger went last and a great bearded swashbuckler attempted to follow him, slashing at his head with a cutlass at each backward step he took. But, using both hands, Jenny let off her pistol at him, and, by good luck, the bullet tore away part of his left ear. The shock caused him to lower his guard for a second and Roger promptly ran him through. With a loud groan he heeled over sideways and fell into the foaming water twenty feet below. Next moment Roger was safely on the far bank of the gully. Before any of the other pirates could attempt to cross, Dan had wrenched the plank from its lodgment and drawn it in.

Roger was streaming with sweat and so breathless that he could hardly utter, but he managed to gasp: 'Get up the path all of you. Some of them have fire-arms. Now they are no longer mixed up with us they will not hesitate to use them.'

At that moment a shot rang out. Missing his neck only by a finger's-breadth, it snicked away a fragment from the collar of his coat. Needing no further warning they all ran up the path until a bend in it hid them from their enemies' view. Panting and moaning as a result of their terrible exertions, they flung themselves down on the ground to rest their aching limbs and get their breath back.

Georgina and Amanda had already been carried up there, and as soon as Roger had recovered a little he went over to them. Amanda was sitting up, but with her head hanging down and nursing an injured arm. It had been badly wrenched by a pirate who had twisted it and thrown her to the ground. He had then kicked her in the stomach, causing her acute pain and vomiting, but her case gave no cause for immediate alarm. Georgina had fared worse. A pirate had slashed at her head with a cutlass, and only the fact that she had at that instant spung forward to strike him in the face had saved her life. Her movement had resulted in her being struck down by the hilt of the weapon instead of its blade but she was still unconscious.

Doctor Fergusson came over to them and, after examining her head, relieved their fears by saying that her thick hair had saved her from the worst effects of the blow. He could find only a slight fracture under it and thought that although she might suffer from concussion she was in no great danger.

Going over to Dan, Roger thanked him and the others for all they had done, then said he thought it would be best for the party to move further up the path. There was still a risk that the pirates might find a way to cross the gully, and should they do so the more warning the party had of their approach the more time it would have to get well hidden in the undergrowth.

It was therefore decided that they should proceed until they came upon another clearing, or should they fail to find one within half a mile, halt there while Roger remained behind to watch for any attempt that might be made to follow them.

Meanwhile Fergusson was doing the best he could for the injured. Shirt tails were torn off to serve as bandages, a sling made for Amanda's arm, and a rough stretcher constructed from branches on which to carry Georgina. When these first aid measures were completed Roger watched them set off slowly up the hill, then walked down it back to the entrance of the path.

The twilight had now almost faded into night. He could see enough to be certain that the pirates had withdrawn from the far side of the gully, and just to make out that there were still people moving about further off, in the clearing. Sitting down he thought over the frightful fight.

Less than half an hour had passed since he had sent the Vicomte to a well deserved death in the pool. During that time at least a score of other people must have died and as many more been seriously injured. The pirates, having been taken by surprise, had suffered much more heavily than their opponents, and they had also lost a number of their slaves who had seized the chance to run off into the forest; but they were still a formidable body, whereas of the *Circe*'s men only Jake and Kilick had succeeded in getting away with the escapers. Several others had attempted to but had been struck down before they could join either of the parties led by Dan or Fergusson. Considering the odds against them Roger thought it little short of a miracle that any of them should have got away, and it still seemed to him almost unbelievable that he should be alive and free himself.

For a good two hours he sat keeping watch. By then it was a long time since the last of the wounded had been carried away, and no sound, save the croaking of the tree-frogs, broke the silence of the dark, deserted clearing. Feeling that no attempt to cross the gully was now likely to take place while the darkness lasted, he got to his feet and began to make his way up the path.

It was no easy matter, as although his eyes had become accustomed to the darkness he could hardly see a yard in front of him and every few paces blundered into the undergrowth. But at length he heard the murmur of voices a little way ahead and emerged from the tunnel of foliage into a small open space faintly lit by starlight.

The party had been getting anxious about him so were much relieved by his appearance. They had, too, been waiting for him to rejoin them before discussing how they might best keep their new-won liberty, and as soon as he had sat down among them they proceeded to do so.

It seemed fairly certain that they would be able to evade recapture by remaining in the forest. To do so presented no problem of hunger or thirst, as there was an abundance of fruit to be had for the picking. There were also any number of wild pigs and game that could be trapped, and an inexhaustible supply of fuel for fires on which to cook them. But to remain there could be only a temporary expedient, and the real question was how could they get back to civilisation?

The man who had joined Fergusson towards the end of the affray proved to be an American trader named Wilson. Nine months before, while on this way from Boston to Jamaica, he had been captured by de Senlac and, with three other passengers who had since died, forced into slavery. On learning this, Roger said to him:

'You must know more of the island than ourselves, Mr. Wilson. What is the name of the nearest town; and how far distant is it?'

'There is only one, Sir,' replied Wilson, 'and that a miserable place; although it has quite a good harbour. It is called Cayona, and was for many years a very minor post for a French Governor. The force he controlled was so insignificant that he could do no more than protect the handful of planters established nearby on the south coast of the island; so generations of buccaneers had always been the masters of nine-tenths of it, and Cayona a port where they met to enter into every sort of villainy.'

'Still, think you we could get a ship there?'

'Not one with an honest master. Soon after France declared herself a Republic, the slaves revolted. They murdered the Governor and the more prosperous of the planters. Since then Cayona has been entirely lawless. It would mean a gruelling march through the forest to reach it, and when we did we should stand a great risk of falling victims of another gang of freebooters; so I certainly do not advise going there.'

Dan suggested that they should make for the north coast and camp upon some prominent headland; so that from it they could fly distress signals to attract some passing ship which might pick them up. But the American poured cold water on that idea too, by saying:

'The north coast is so precipitous and rocky that ships do not put in there even when in need of water. We might scan the horizon from it for months without sighting a sail; and when we did it would like as not be that of another pirate.'

At that their hearts, which so recently had been filled with fresh hope, sank again. It looked now as if there were no alternative to remaining in the forest, and that they were condemned to live there the hard life of savages, perhaps for months, perhaps for years, before some unforeseeable turn of events enabled them to get away from this accursed island.

12

Night in the Forest

At the thought a gloomy silence settled on the conference, but Roger was not the man to accept such a miserable existence as long as there was any possible alternative. After a few minutes he sighed and said thoughtfully:

'God knows, I've had my fill of fighting for today, but it seems there's only one thing for it. We must attempt to recapture the *Circe*.'

The starlight penetrated to the glade in which they were sitting only just enough for each of them to make out the vague forms of the companions to whom they were nearest, so Roger could not see the faces of the others; but he heard a murmur of astonishment and dismay run round the circle.

'Why should we not?' he asked, 'With Dan, Tom, Jake, Kilick, Monsieur Pirouet, the Doctor, Mr. Wilson, and myself, we are eight, not counting such help as the ladies may be able to give us. That is fully sufficient to handle a ship in fair weather for so short a voyage as the ten or twelve miles which are all that separate us from Saint-Domingue.'

'Aye, Cap'n; it could be done!' cried Dan. 'An' it rejoices me old heart ter hear ye propoundin' sich schemes agin'. Let we set out upon it here an' now afore we fall asleep an' the night be lost.'

'To make the attempt tonight is out of the question,' Fergusson put in quickly. 'At least half of us have been wounded to a greater or lesser degree, and her ladyship is still unconscious.'

'Even with that handicap, I feel that we should be ill-advised to delay the venture,' Roger argued. 'Down at the house everything must be in confusion. A score or more of the slaves ran off. It is quite possible that they started to loot or burn it before the pirates got back; so our enemies may have been hard put to it to suppress a mutiny. In any case, all their leaders having been killed or rendered *hors de combat,* it is certain they are at sixes and sevens. I saw Lucette perched up on a high boulder, and she had the sense to keep out of the fight; but, able and unscrupulous as she is, I greatly doubt if many of them would be willing to serve under a woman. Both the Heraults are crippled, and neither is of the stuff from which leaders are made. Philo the Greek can hardly be sufficiently recovered from the bash over the head I gave him to take charge. The odds are that they are at this moment squabbling about whom to appoint as the new chief, and they may not finally settle the matter till tomorrow. In the meantime, everyone being his own master, no watch will be kept or guards set. We should be able to secure a boat with ease, and with luck we may find the *Circe* deserted. Such a chance is most unlikely ever to occur again.'

The sound sense of what he said impressed them all so strongly that, weary as they were, they agreed that this favourable opportunity to reach a safe port within the next few days must not be lost. In consequence, stretcher bearers were nominated to carry Georgina, and others among them made specially responsible for the protection of the three other women. It was then that Clarissa was discovered to be missing.

Thinking that she had left them only for a moment and must be near at hand, they called to her. But no reply came from the surrounding darkness. Greatly puzzled, Roger and Dan made their way several hundred yards further up the track, still calling her name. Only the echoes of their voices came back to them; so they decided that she must have gone a little way down hill towards the clearing.

By that time the party was ready to set off; so they all proceeded down the track in single file, continuing to call to Clarissa as they went. It was not until they were within fifty yards of the gully that they caught a faint reply. Halting, they anxiously discussed what they should do. The scared note in Clarissa's voice as she now shouted to them made it clear that for some reason she had blundered off the track and got hopelessly lost in the pitch dark forest. But the faintness of her cries also made it clear that she was some way off, and for any of them to plunge in after her was to risk getting lost too.

Fergusson suggested that several of them should go in ten yards apart, but the denseness of the vegetation was such that even in formation they must soon have lost touch with one another; so Roger would not hear of it. After a moment's thought he said:

'The safest course would be to guide her back by continuing to call her; but that may prove a long and weary business, as she will probably blunder about all over the place before she gets near enough to be certain of the direction the calls are coming from. But there is no point in us all remaining here; so you had best continue on your way while I remain to do the shouting. We still have most of the night before us, and our chance of getting away in a boat unseen will be all the greater if we wait until our enemies are asleep. You might even snatch an hour or two's badly needed sleep yourselves; but see to it that you take it in turns, and that two or more of you are constantly on watch against surprise. The best place to spend the time of waiting would be on the edge of the forest where the track comes out on to the beach. I shall be able to find you there without difficulty, and I'll join you as soon as I can.'

Again the others agreed that his proposals were sound, and the thought of a few hours' sleep was more than welcome to all of them; so they resumed their weary trudging and left him there.

At intervals he kept on calling to Clarissa and gradually her replies grew louder. After twenty minutes she was near enough for him to encourage her. Soon afterwards there came a loud rustling of the leaves close by him in the darkness. He could just make out her form as she came towards him. Next moment she gave a gasp, flung her arms round his neck and sobbed:

'Oh Roger! Thank God you're safe!'

For the first time in days he laughed. 'Safe, m'dear. But

it is you whose safety sent us near distraction some half hour back. What crazy notion impelled you to separate yourself from us and get lost in this nightmarish jungle?'

'I came to seek you,' she murmured. 'You remained behind down by the gully for so long. I feared that some ill had befallen you. But I blundered in among the trees and could not find my way out again.'

'Poor child,' he soothed her. 'It must have been terrible for you.'

'I am no child,' she exclaimed with sudden anger. 'And I sought you because I love you.'

Dumbfounded by this declaration he could find no words to reply, as she hurried on: 'There! I've said it now. But I don't give a rap! If you'd had half an eye you'd have seen it long ago. You're all that a man should be, and I've loved you since the first moment I set eyes on you.'

'Clarissa!' he protested sharply. 'You must not say such things.'

'Do you not think I know it!' she cried bitterly. 'I owe Amanda a debt I never can repay for rescuing me from that dreary life with my Aunt Jane. Oh, I am ashamed as never a woman was; yet I can't help it!'

Roger knew only too well that in such matters most men and most women too, are the playthings of their own passions, so he reproved her only by saying gently: 'Even so you had no right to speak of it, knowing me to be happily married to your cousin.'

'Ah, that's the tragedy!' There were now tears in her voice. 'I know that you're not. Not happily married, I mean. I'll vow you've been unfaithful to Amanda more than once, and I know for a fact that you recently had a hectic love affair when you were in France. More, 'tis common knowledge that while you were away Amanda was unfaithful to you, so that you were near separating from her on your return.'

'Who told you these things?'

'No matter, but I know them.'

Roger pulled her arms from about his neck and his tone suddenly became harsh. 'Do you think then, that by setting your cap at me, you can seduce me from Amanda?'

'I would I could,' came the quick retort. 'But even if you'd have me I'd be bound out of common decency to say you nay. Amanda is my friend and benefactress. I'd rather die than bear the shame of having betrayed her trust in me. Yet I know you to be a lonely man at heart, and were matters otherwise I'd stop at nothing to have you for my own.'

Again he was at a loss for adequate words to chill this desperate youthful passion; but he did his best, by saying: 'Believe me, you'd regret it soon enough. 'Tis clear that you have heard tales of my doings while abroad, and invested me with a glamour for which there is no warrant. I am no braver or better than the average man and, as you have found out for yourself, considerably worse as a husband.'

'That I will not believe. But for your courage and resource today I'd have been forced to the life of an unpaid whore in a brothel. To see you fight is a thing to marvel at, and that it was even in small part for myself made my love for you ten times stronger. As for your frailties, who in this world is without them? And did you but love any woman with all your heart she would wean you from them.'

'Listen, Clarissa,' he said a trifle hoarsely. ''Tis understandable that you may have formed a wrong impression. But Amanda and I would never have drifted apart had I not been so long abroad. Now that we are reunited I love her as much as I am capable of loving any woman.'

'Since you protest it, I'll not argue that. In any case, I have already told you that my last thought would be to endeavour to take you from her.'

'Then I beg you to be advised by me. Do your utmost to free your mind from this infatuation, which can but be embarrassing to us both. These early loves are rarely lasting, and you are still so young . . .'

'Young!' she broke in impatiently. 'There are no more than eight years between us. I am eighteen, and at that age many of my friends are not only married but about to bear their second child.'

Roger knew that she was right, but persisted. 'I meant only that you have ample years ahead of you before you need give your heart to the love of a lifetime.'

G

'I have already given it to you.'

He sadly shook his head. 'In that case I can only say how deeply I regret that you should have fastened your affections on such an unsatisfactory and unworthy object.' His tone grew firmer, as he added: 'And now, it is only right that I should let you know that I feel in honour bound to terminate, as soon as possible, the situation that your declaration has brought about. It would be indelicate both to Amanda and yourself for me to keep you with us.'

'D'you mean that you intend to send me home?' she cried in dismay.

He felt a sudden impulse to laugh, but swiftly suppressed it and replied: 'At the moment I am in no position to send anyone anywhere; but should we succeed in getting away I am sure that for your own sake it would be the best thing to do.'

'Oh Roger, I beg you not to,' she pleaded. 'I never meant to say anything. And if I hadn't you wouldn't have known. All this came out only because I was overwrought. You see, until I got near enough to realise it was you calling me I feared you dead and . . . and, my relief at finding you alive proved too much for me.'

Moved by her distress, he said with mental reservations: 'Very well then, we'll not pursue the subject further. The others must have reached the beach ere this, and the sooner we join them the better. Then you can snatch a couple of hours sleep before we make the attempt we have planned to get away in the *Circe*.'

'Must we?' she asked. 'Go yet, I mean; if there's no immediate hurry. I could drop with fatigue from having staggered about for so long among those awful bushes. Can we not rest here a while before making this new effort. I would so much rather.'

Roger considered for a moment, then he shrugged. 'As you wish, but we must not remain here above an hour, otherwise our friends will become anxious about us.'

'Oh thank you,' she sighed. Then backing away she added: 'There's a fallen tree trunk here. I stumbled into it just now. It will serve to rest our backs against.'

They fumbled about in the dark until they found the

tree trunk, and sat down side by side. After a few minutes she said: 'Roger, are you angry with me because I told you that I love you?'

'No,' he replied. 'I would that you had refrained; but no man could be insensible to such a compliment, or so churlish as to think less of anyone because they had admitted that they held him dear.'

'Some would, I think; but not you, dear Roger, for you are kind as well as brave.'

To that he made no reply. Silence and the deep night then engulfed them. It was over thirty-six hours since, aboard the *Circe,* Roger had woken from his last proper sleep, and during them his vitality had been drained both mentally and physically. Before he was aware of it he was fast asleep.

He was woken by soft fingers stroking his stubbly cheek, and roused to find himself in a woman's arms with his head pillowed on her breast. As he started up memory flooded back to him, and he realised that he was in the forest with Clarissa.

The darkness hid her smile as she murmured: 'Never in all my life have I been so reluctant to do a thing as when I bought myself to wake you; but the night moves on.'

'How long have you let me sleep?' he cried apprehensively.

'Two hours; three at the most,' she replied with a shrug.

'Thank God it was not more!' he exclaimed, scrambling to his feet. 'Are you certain? Did you not also sleep?'

She stood up beside him. 'No. I remained awake to wake you should you sleep too long. But don't grudge me those hours, Roger. They are my treasure, and no one can now ever take them from me.'

Touched, angry, embarrassed, he could find nothing to say but 'Come, we must get down to the others. We had better tell them that I went into the forest to find you and got lost as well.'

She laughed. 'Tell any fib you please. 'Twill form another secret bond between us. But I vow that I'll give you no cause to blush for it.'

Somewhat reassured by this evidence of her intention to refrain from further demonstrations of her feelings for him, he took her by the arm and they walked as fast as they could down to the gully.

While Roger slept the moon had come up and they found the clearing now flooded with silvery light. By it, as they crossed the plank, they could see the still bodies of the men who had died that evening, and were even able to identify some of them. Roger could not repress a shudder as he glanced at the dark pit of the now silent pool, then he hurried Clarissa across the open space to the black tunnel where the path entered it on its far side. Plunging into the gloom again, they made their way down the slope until they were met by a cautious challenge.

The voice was Fergusson's, and as soon as he was certain who they were he uttered an exclamation of thankfulness at seeing them again. Most of the party were asleep, but Kilick was also on watch a little further off where the path opened out on to the beach, and he now joined them.

Roger quickly said his piece about having got lost himself while searching for Clarissa, then asked how the prospects looked for getting away, and they gave him their report. The pirates had spent the early part of the night carousing in the house, but evidently they suspected that the escaped prisoners might attempt to get away by sea, as a sentry, who had been relieved every hour, had been posted on the boats.

That was bad news, yet Roger felt that the attempt must be made all the same. When he asked the time they told him that they judged it to be past two in the morning; which meant that there was less than three hours of darkness left. Rousing Dan he held a quick consultation with him, and they decided that to delay much longer might lessen their chances of success. Georgina, Roger learned, was still unconscious but for the moment showed no alarming symptoms. Fergusson woke the others and warned them to get ready, while Roger and Dan debated how best to tackle the sentry.

Owing to the bright moonlight they thought it unlikely that either of them could creep up behind him and take him completely by surprise; so they concerted measures by which they hoped to overcome him between them. Dan was to do the creeping up to him, as near as he thought he could get undetected. Roger was to approach as though coming from the house, and engage the man's attention. Then Dan was to rush him from behind.

Roger watched Dan squirm away across the sand. Then, having given him ten minutes' start, he set off himself. Keeping in the deep shadow of the trees that fringed the beach, he headed for the house; but when he was half way along the hutments that formed the slaves' quarters he altered course, and calmly walked down the beach towards the sentry. The man halted, turned until he was within twenty feet, then asked a shade uncertainly: *'Qui êtes vous?'*

'Je suis Henri,' replied Roger, that being the commonest French name he could think of.

'Henri?' repeated the man in a puzzled tone, and lowered the musket he was carrying from his shoulder to the ready. *'Henri qui?'*

By that time Roger was only ten feet from him, and did not reply. There came a sudden scuffling in the sand behind the sentry. He half turned, but thought better of it, and aimed his musket at Roger. As Dan ran in Roger dropped flat. The sentry went down without a sound under a swipe from Dan's sabre, but not before he had fired his musket.

They had failed to prevent the alarm being given, so now everything hung on speed. As the report echoed round the bay Roger sprang to his feet unhurt and ran to the nearest boat. Dan was already on her other side. Seizing its gunwale, they strove to drag it over the few yards of sand that separated it from the water; but it was a heavy whaler and its weight proved too much for them.

Within a minute their friends came racing up to their assistance. Three great heaves and the boat was afloat. Some of them scrambled in while others lifted the make-shift stretcher aboard on which Georgina lay. Seizing the oars they began to row frantically towards the *Circe*.

Lights were already appearing in the house. Shouts soon came from it. There were four other boats on the beach and any or all of them might be used for pursuit. Success or failure now depended on how quickly they could get aboard the *Circe*, haul up her anchor and set a few sails.

Ten minutes' hard rowing brought them below her counter. No lights had appeared in her so they had good hopes that she was deserted. Dan was already standing up in the bow of the whaler holding her painter, ready to make her fast before they clambered aboard. Suddenly there came a crash of musketry from out of her broken stern windows. Kilick gave a shout and Roger a loud groan. The one had been hit in the shoulder and the other in the thigh.

In the stillness that followed the crash there came the rich laugh of a woman, then Lucette's voice cried from the dark windows above: 'You fools! Had you not the sense to credit me with expecting you to have a try for the *Circe*? Pull back to shore and surrender, or come aboard to be slaughtered. The choice is yours.'

Fearful that as soon as the muskets could be reloaded another burst of fire would rake the boat, the men in her who held the oars were backing water hard. Roger was at her tiller and, although half fainting with pain, retained the presence of mind to turn her bow. With all their strength the rowers then pulled away from the ship. When the second fusillade came they were far enough off for the ill-aimed bullets to fall short and splash harmless into the water.

As soon as they were out of danger the rowers ceased their frantic exertions and lay, panting, on their oars. There followed a hurried council to decide what their next move should be. An anxious scanning of the beach showed that only a handful of pirates had come down on to it. The rest, presumably, were still sunk in a drunken slumber, and those who had turned out appeared to be engaged in a heated argument. It looked as if, owing to their small numbers, some of them were averse to manning a boat for immediate pursuit. Nevertheless, should the escapers attempt to land it was certain that they would be attacked, and at any time the pirates might receive reinforcements from the house. To take the *Circe* by assault was out of the question; and lights now appearing in the pirates' barque showed that Lucette had had the forethought to man her also with a skeleton crew.

It seemed their only course was to struggle ashore among the mangroves that fringed the water along the outer arms of the bay, and again take to the forest, until Wilson said: 'Anyhow, we've gotten the boat. Why shouldn't we make for Saint-Domingue in her? It's no much more than ten miles across the strait.'

As no one had any better suggestion to offer, the American's proposal was agreed to, and they began to pull steadily towards the entrance to the lagoon. Meanwhile Fergusson did what he could for the wounded. Kilick's injury was not serious, as the ball had only scored a shallow furrow through the flesh above his shoulder. But that which had hit Roger had embedded itself in his thigh; so he had to submit to the agonising operation of having it extracted. Fergusson did not think that the thigh-bone had been fractured but, as Roger could bear his weight on it only with great pain, that it had probably been severely bruised. In any case it looked as if the wound would render him *hors de combat* for some time to come, and they gloomily made him as comfortable as they could beside Georgina on the bottom boards in the sternsheets of the boat.

After half an hour's rowing they rounded the western point of the bay. As they passed out of it there were still no signs that their enemies meant to follow them; but on reaching the open sea they were confronted with an unexpected cause for dismay. A strong current was running dead against them and, pull as hard as they would, they could make only heartbreakingly slow progress towards Saint-Domingue.

When dawn came a little over an hour later it revealed them to one another as a haggard and miserable party. They had found that there was no water in the boat and no provisions. Most of them were suffering from injuries of one kind or another, and two of them lay in the stern seriously wounded. Soon the sun would be blazing down on them without respite, burning and blistering them with its terrible heat. And, now that day had come, should the pirates choose to set sail either in the *Circe* or their barque in pursuit of them, nothing could save them from recapture.

13

Out of the Frying-pan into the Fire

Jake Harris and Will Kilick had both made previous voyages to the West Indies but the American, Benjamin Wilson, was the only member of the boat's company who had lived in them for any considerable time; so he was the first to realise the new ordeals of sun-scorch and thirst which they must now face owing to having adopted his own suggestion of making for Saint-Domingue.

While darkness lasted they could have landed unseen on the west point of the bay, hidden the boat among the mangroves and concealed themselves in the jungle, slept all day and then had a full night before them in which to make the crossing. But they were a good mile from land. To turn back now meant exposing themselves to a still greater risk of recapture, and even if they could get safely ashore they would have to abandon the boat from fear that they were under observation by a look-out on the point who would swiftly bring the pirates to the spot where they had landed.

Silently the American cursed himself for his misjudgment; although in fact he was little to blame, as he had known nothing of the adverse current which made every yard they gained a struggle, and in the urgency of the moment anyone might have overestimated the pulling powers of his eleven companions.

As it was Dan, Jake, the Doctor and himself were the only members of the party capable of putting in an effective spell at an oar, and even they were already nearly played out owing to their previous night's exertions. Roger, now in great pain, lay helpless on the stern boards. The wound in Kilick's shoulder, although only flesh deep, made rowing an agony for him. Pirouet and Tom had both proved broken reeds; the one because he had a weak heart, and the other because the blood he had lost after receiving a cut across the head had resulted in his becoming weak and feverish.

That left only the women. Georgina was still unconscious, and Amanda had a wrenched arm. But soon after dawn Clarissa and Jenny volunteered to relieve in turn for a spell two of the four men who were rowing. Neither of the girls had ever before handled a heavy oar; so at first their erratic efforts proved far from helpful, but after a while they got into the rhythm of pulling and gamely stuck it for an hour.

By then the boat had gained another hard-won mile to seaward, and there were still no signs of pursuit; so most of them felt an increasing optimism about their chances of escape. But the seafaring members of the party, while keeping their thoughts to themselves, were much less inclined to think they were nearly out of the wood. They rightly assumed that they had been allowed to get so far unpursued only because the early morning calm would have made it futile for the pirates to hoist the sails on either of the ships, and that as soon as a breeze sprang up they might expect to see their enemies coming after them. With this in mind, when Fergusson suggested that they should take it easy for a while, Dan would not hear of it, and insisted that they must not relax their efforts as long as they had an ounce of strength left in them.

The next hour was a grim one. The arms of the rowers ached to breaking point and the sun was mounting with an ever-increasing glare. As some consolation the strength of the current gradually lessened until they had passed right out of it; so they were able to maintain the boat's pace with less exertion, and the mangrove-tangled shore of Tortuga dropped below their horizon. But Dan, knowing that the boat could still easily be picked up by a look-out from a ship's mast, continued to urge them to stick it for a while longer.

Soon after eight o'clock both Fergusson and Wilson were

so worn out that every few minutes one or other of them caught a crab, and it became obvious that they had become more of a hindrance than a help; so Jenny and Clarissa again relieved them. By nine the hands of the two girls were badly blistered from the unaccustomed work and they were hard put to it to suppress tears, while Dan and Jake had also reached the limit of their strength. There was then nothing for it but to ship oars and let the boat drift, praying that a now favourable current they had struck would continue to carry it further from Tortuga.

The rest of the day was one long nightmare that seemed never ending. The pursuit which would certainly have meant their recapture never matured, because it proved one of those days which occasionally occur in the tropics when a calm continues almost unbroken from dawn till dusk; yet at times they would have almost welcomed the sight of their enemies' topmasts as the price of a refreshing breeze.

Hour after hour the glassy sea for miles around reflected the cloudless blue sky, and a brazen sun blazed down upon them unmercifully. In vain they cowered in the bottom of the boat seeking to take advantage of every vestige of shadow thrown by thwarts and the oars laid along them. Their clothes were their only protection from the scorching rays, and adjust them as they would it was next to impossible to keep heads, necks, ears, faces, hands, wrists and ankles covered at one time; yet the exposure of any area of skin for more than a few moments had to be paid for later by most painful burning. Had the *Circe*'s late passengers not become to some degree immunised to tropical sunshine during the last weeks of her voyage, they must all have been driven insane; even as it was they suffered acutely.

They were in no urgent need of food but by midday thirst began to worry them. At first it took the form only of parched throats but as the seemingly interminable hours of the afternoon wore on their tongues began to swell and they no longer had enough saliva in their mouths to moisten their cracking lips. Tom added greatly to their distress, for he became delirious, and their hearts were wrung by his cries for water, which they could not satisfy.

Meanwhile, the current had carried the boat out into mid channel and some miles to westward of the course they had set early that morning. From time to time two of the men got out oars and again impelled the boat towards the shore that meant safety and succour, but short spells were all that they could manage. To southward, for as far as they could see on either hand, stretched the shores of Saint-Domingue. From them the western end of the island rose in fold after fold of forest-covered slopes to a great range of peaks eastward in its distant centre, which had caused its aborigines to call it Haiti, meaning 'Mountainous'. Its lack of all signs of human habitation gave it a mysterious, slightly sinister, look, yet with aching eyes they gazed towards it as to a Promised Land.

At about three o'clock Georgina at last came round but, mercifully, almost at once fell again into a torpor. By then the pain of Roger's wound had dulled to an ache which was supportable as long as he remained quite still; and since he had been lying almost motionless all day with his coat rigged like a tent over his face he was not plagued by thirst to the same degree as the others.

Some of them, crouching between the thwarts with their heads similarly buried, managed to doze fitfully for short periods but their physical distress was too acute for them to free their minds from it for more than a few minutes at a time. They were, too, constantly a prey to the terrifying thought that as they lacked the strength to propel the boat it might be carried by adverse currents out into the open ocean, where they must die in circumstances too horrible to contemplate.

At last the fiery sun began to lose a little of its terrible potency and when it had sunk to within some twenty degrees of the western horizon Dan roused those of his companions who were capable of rowing, urging them to man the oars in a new effort.

In voices made hoarse by thirst they argued against undertaking any fresh exertion before the sun had set, but he pointed out that the injured were in urgent need of proper attention. Within the past hour they had picked out a tiny white patch high up on a headland which jutted out from the coast some distance to the west. There could now be little doubt that it was a large house, and if they could beach the boat below it they could hope to find ready aid there; but if they waited until darkness to make the attempt they might miss the point by miles. As a final incentive he added that if with sundown the sky became overcast, veiling the stars, they might lose their direction altogether, and so fail to get ashore at all.

They needed no telling that if dawn found them still several miles from the coast another day like that which was all too slowly ending would be the finish of them; so they agreed to the sound sense of Dan's reasoning and set to rowing with renewed determination.

When the sun at last went down they were still a long way from the promontory, yet near enough to see that the house upon it was a big building in the French Colonial style and so, presumably, the residence of a wealthy planter. With straining muscles, aching backs and rasping throats the rowers doggedly continued their pulling, but half an hour later they had to give up from sheer exhaustion. Lights had now appeared in the house; so with a single oar thrust out from the stern of the boat Dan was just able to keep her nosing at tortoise pace towards the beacon it now formed, although a slow current from the east threatened to carry them beam on past the cape while they were still a mile or more from it.

Dan could do no more, and it was Clarissa who stepped into the breach. Impelled by the desperate need for getting Roger ashore she insisted that even the weakest of them must now play their part by double banking the men who had so far done the rowing. Then she appealed to Kilick and Monsieur Pirouet, urging that even if the one lost a lot of blood from the wound in his shoulder and the other collapsed, they should risk that for the common good in a final bid to save the whole party.

Both men willingly agreed, and while they double banked Jake and Fergusson, Jenny and Clarissa shared oars with Wilson and Dan. It proved a grim struggle but the leeway the boat was making was promptly checked and soon it was moving slowly forward through the darkness. About nine o'clock, to their unutterable relief, it grounded on a beach no more than half a mile west of the cape for which they had been making.

For a time they simply sat slumped over their oars, gasping, aching, and incapable even of savouring the fruits of their hard-won victory by landing on Saint-Domingue. But as soon as they had had a chance to recover a little Amanda took charge of the situation. Her wrenched arm had made it impossible for her to help at an oar, but during the final phase she had captained the boat by taking the tiller. Now, as the others were still so done up that they hardly knew what they were doing, she called on each by name and directed them how best to lend a hand in getting the wounded ashore.

Within a quarter of an hour the operation was safely completed; then they all sank down utterly wearied-out on the sandy shore some dozen yards above the tide level. But there could be no real rest for them yet. From the jolting Roger had received he was again in great pain, Kilick had not spared himself once he had taken an oar so his shoulder was now causing him to utter half sobbing curses, Georgina had again become semi-conscious and was moaning pitifully, while Tom, whom they feared had developed brain fever, was rolling from side to side in the throes of delirium.

Although the lights of the house were no longer visible, they knew that it could not be any great distance away along the crest of the tree-covered slope that ran steeply up from the fore-shore; but such was the state of weakness to which they had been reduced that they could not possibly have carried the injured up there. So, after a brief respite, it was decided that Fergusson and Dan should act as an advance party with the object of getting help.

Fortunately the trees, which they had seen only as a distant screen of green by daylight, turned out to be palms growing in a sandy soil; so their fears that they might have to fight their way through dense undergrowth proved unfounded. But some forty minutes after they had set out the main party were much concerned to hear the faint barking of several dogs, followed by the sound of shots.

Twenty minutes later Dan and the Doctor reappeared a little way along the beach, staggered towards them and flung themselves down in the last stages of fatigue. When they could get enough breath back they gasped out that about fifty yards from the house they had been set upon by three fierce mastiffs, then someone had come out and fired both barrels of a shotgun blind in their direction. The pellets, evidently aimed high to avoid harming the dogs, had rattled harmlessly through the foliage overhead, but the warning had been too dangerous to ignore, and they had been much too fully occupied in saving themselves from being savaged to attempt a parley; so there had been nothing for it but to beat an ignominious retreat.

Bitterly disappointing as was the abortive outcome of their mission, they could not be blamed for having failed to stand their ground until they could satisfy the man who had fired the gun that he had nothing to fear from them; for in their sadly weakened state it had required great fortitude to climb the hill at all. But the fact remained that the party had now no alternative other than to spend the night where it was.

At least they were lucky in the type of beach on which they had landed, as they were able to scoop out troughs in the soft sand and so lie down without discomfort; but in other ways they were very far from being at ease. With the going down of the sun they had ceased to suffer from raging thirsts, but they were still subject to intermittent cravings, during which they would have given a great deal for a cup of water, and in one or more places nearly all of them were now being tortured by that ceaseless agonising scorching of the skin which results from severe sunburn.

Yet there was nothing the uninjured could do to alleviate the sufferings of the injured or themselves; so they settled down as well as they were able to wrestle with their miseries while the hours of darkness lasted.

At first light Dan and the Doctor, this time accompanied by Wilson and Jake, and all armed with thick staves to drive off the dogs, again started for the house. Again the others heard the distant baying of hounds but no shots followed, and somewhat over an hour after the reconnaissance party had set out it returned with a richly-dressed white man and a score of cotton-clad negroes and Negresses.

The leader of the newcomers was introduced by Fergusson as the Seigneur de Bouçicault. He was a big fair-haired florid man aged about fifty, and the owner of the house. Bowing to the ladies he apologised profusely for the misunderstanding which had prevented him from coming to their aid the previous night, and explained that on the dogs giving the alarm he had thought an attack was about to be made upon the house by a band of marauders.

His slaves had brought down fruit, wine, a medicine chest, and hammocks in which to carry up the injured; so within a short time the worst distress of the castaways had been alleviated. Yet it was a sorry crew that made its way up to the house about an hour later. In addition to Roger and Tom all four women had to be carried, and the others had to be helped at the steeper places. Dirty, bedraggled, their hair matted, their faces peeling and puffy from insect bites, their hands blistered, their eyes feverish and sunken, they at last came to shelter and safety in the cool lofty rooms of the gracious colonial mansion.

De Bouçicault made them all drink a strong infusion of Cinçhona bark to ward of Yellow Jack, and Fergusson, although in a worse state than some of the other men, insisted on seeing all the injured put to bed; then he too allowed himself to be helped to undress and, like the rest, fell into a sleep of utter exhaustion.

Roger slept the clock nearly twice round then lay dozing for a long while; so it was not until the following afternoon that he was urged by returning appetite to ring the handbell that had been placed beside his bed. The summons was answered by a negro houseman who in due course brought him a tray on which was a cup of bouillon, boiled chicken and fruit.

He was just finishing the meal when Fergusson came in, and Roger asked him anxiously for news of the others. The young doctor replied that Georgina was suffering from shock and concussion, but in a better state than might have been expected and, owing to her youth and vitality, in no serious danger. Tom was now giving him more concern as he had undoubtedly developed brain fever and it yet remained to be seen if he would survive the crisis. Amanda too was in poor shape. Her strained arm was nothing to worry about; but although she had bravely refrained from complaining during their ordeal of the previous day she must have been in great pain, as her stomach was black and blue from a vicious kick one of the pirates had given her, and it was possible that she had sustained internal injuries. Kilick's shoulder was badly inflamed from his having manned an oar during their last bid to reach the beach, but should yield to treatment. The rest of them had met for a midday meal and were the worse for their adventures only by cuts, bruises and inflammation. Then he said that, having heard that Roger was awake, he had come up to re-examine his wound.

Roger submitted to some painful prodding, after which Fergusson declared himself satisfied that his first diagnosis had been correct. The bone of the thigh had not been smashed; and, as within a very short time of the wound being received it had been thoroughly cleansed with salt water, it showed no signs of festering. Providing Roger remained in bed the healthy flesh should soon heal and he might hope to be about on crutches in a week or so.

Having anointed his mosquito bites with a soothing ointment and promised to convey his loving messages to Amanda the doctor left him; but returned in the evening bringing a sedative to ensure him a good night.

With his breakfast tray next morning the negro servant brought an enquiry from M. de Bouçicault, who wished to know if Roger felt well enough to receive a visit from him; and he sent back a reply that he would be happy to do so.

An hour or so later the burly French nobleman arrived. Having congratulated Roger on his wound being less serious than had been feared he sat down beside his bed, and said:

'I had heard something from the doctor of the terrible trials to which you and your party have been subjected during the past week, but he was kept busy with his patients most of yesterday; none of the ladies have so far left their rooms, and the others lack the education to speak of their adventures with much coherence; so I pray you, Monsieur le Gouverneur, if you feel well enough, to give me an account of these most distressing happenings.'

Roger raised a smile as he repeated: 'The past week! It seems more like a year since the pirate barque attacked our ship off the coast of Porto Rico. But now that I have slept my fill I should thoroughly enjoy talking for a while; so, Monsieur, I will willingly oblige you.' He then proceeded to give a graphic description of the perils he and his party had survived.

When he had done de Bouçicault said: 'That you should be alive to tell this tale thanks must be rendered to *le Bon Dieu,* but it is due in part at least to the courage displayed by yourself and your companions, and I am honoured to make your acquaintance. I need hardly say that you are all welcome to remain here for as long as you wish; but without intending any discourtesy I should be glad if the ladies could be transferred to Mole St. Nicholas as soon as they are sufficiently recovered to travel.'

'I am sorry that you should find it inconvenient to let them stay here until my wound is healed and we can all leave together,' Roger replied in some surprise.

'No, no! You must understand me,' de Bouçicault rejoined hastily. 'Surely you know that war, revolution and civil war are all now tearing this island apart; so that no white persons, particularly defenceless women, are really safe anywhere in it except in the towns held by British troops. It is the certain knowledge of the ghastly fate which would overtake your ladies did they fall into the hands of the revolted negroes that causes me to urge their removal as speedily as may be possible.'

14

The Terror-ridden Island

Roger's face fell, then he admitted a shade apologetically to his host: 'I fear I am but sadly ill-informed about West Indian affairs, my appointment came as a surprise and I had little time to study them before I left England. I knew, of course, that as a result of the Revolution in France there had been revolts among the slaves in all the islands, and that here they were said to have been particularly serious; but I imagined that they would have been put down ere this seeing that, as in Martinique, the planters had called in the English to aid them against the Terrorists.'

'Far from it,' de Bouçicault sadly shook his head. 'There are British garrisons in the capital, Port-au-Prince, at Mole St. Nicholas, which is only about thirty miles away, and in most of the coastal towns; but they can do little more than aid our army of colonists and loyal mulattoes to hold its own. The greater part of the interior of the country is still at the mercy of the negroes and infested by marauding bands of slaves turned brigand.'

Having condoned with his host on this unhappy state of things, Roger said: 'Pray enlighten me if you can, Monsieur, as to why matters should have gone so much worse here than in the other islands.'

'Perhaps because it was the largest, richest and most progressive of all the French possessions in the Indies, and therefore more closely *en rapport* with popular feeling in the mother country. Possibly, too, because we had here a higher proportion of slaves than in any other colony. In '89 there were half a million negroes and sixty thousand mulattoes to only forty thousand whites. Although, as a matter of fact, it was not the blacks but the mulattoes who initiated our long chain of troubles.'

'How so, Monsieur?'

'Looking back I am inclined to think that we colonists were largely to blame, for having stubbornly refused to advise our government in France to rectify the anomalous situation of these half-castes. Had we confined ourselves to taking their women as concubines, as you English do, that would have been regarded as a normal privilege of the ruling caste, but many of us married them; yet we still refused to receive their families or grant them any political rights. A high proportion of them were free men who between them owned about ten per cent of the land and some 50,000 slaves. Naturally they bitterly resented such contemptuous treatment. A group of the more intelligent among them began, as early as '88, an agitation in Paris for equal rights; and coupled with it there started a movement for the abolition of both the slave trade and slavery.

'While the monarchy remained absolute these agitations for reform made no headway, but soon after King Louis summoned the States General and it had formed itself into a National Assembly, it issued its famous Declaration of the Rights of Man. Mulattoes and negroes alike instantly seized on that as their Charter, and unrest here became widespread. In March 1790, alarmed by the urgent representations of our Governor, the Assembly passed a resolution to the effect that the Declaration applied only to France and not to her colonies. On that, a mulatto delegate named Vincent Ogé, who arrived back here in the following autumn, called on his fellows to secure their rights by force of arms. It was thus there started the appalling bloodshed which has since drenched this country.'

'You interest me greatly. Do please continue.'

Acceding to the request, de Bouçicault went on: 'Ogé was soon defeated and took refuge in the Spanish part of the island. But he afterwards surrendered and was executed by being broken on the wheel. By then the revolution in Paris was gaining momentum, and the news of Ogé's martyrdom, as it was termed, provoked a great outcry. In consequence, in May '91, the law was amended giving coloured people born of free parents in the French colonies equal civil rights, including that of sitting in our Assemblies.

'For the white minority to submit to a decree which might later lead to their being governed by negroes was unthinkable. We decided to ignore it; but the news of it soon got about and set the whole island in a ferment, which culminated on the unforgettable night of August the 23rd.

'A Jamaican negro named Boukman assembled a large number of slaves in the forest. He was a giant in size and a Houngan, as the priests of Voodoo are termed. After sacrificing a pig and drinking its blood the mob he had collected set out to slay and burn. The movement spread like a prairie fire through the north and west, and for a week or more there ensued the most appalling butchery of the white planters and their families. Not content with killing the men and raping the women, the blood-maddened negroes put their victims to the most excruciating tortures—such as binding them between two planks and sawing them in half. In their senseless fury they also attacked inanimate objects, setting fire to houses, barns, crops and forest, until the blaze was such that the inhabitants of distant Bermuda were puzzled and alarmed by the red glow in the sky.

'In the second week troops arrived from the south, the surviving whites formed themselves into armed bands, and with our superior brains and weapons we began to stamp out the revolt. On hearing of the massacres the Governor of Jamaica also sent a contingent of British troops to help us restore order.

'As France and England were then at peace he did so on humanitarian grounds and without any ulterior motive; but his generous gesture showed us that whereas our own government in Paris had callously thrown us to the black horde, his government considered it their duty to protect the lives and properties of white colonists. It was this which led that autumn to our repudiating the rule of France and sending delegates to London to offer our country to Britain.

'Unfortunately, at that time, your Mr. Pitt was maintaining a policy of strict neutrality with regard to matters connected with the Revolution in France; so on those grounds he rejected our offer. In the meantime, fearing to lose France's richest colony, the National Assembly had rescinded its decree of the previous May; but its action came too late to put a stop to the bloody vendetta that the decree had started. Its only effect was to divide the colonists on the question of severing their relations with the mother country or remaining loyal to her.

'That question was finally decided for them in the spring of '92. By then the extremists in Paris were gaining the upper hand and they forced a new decree through the Assembly. It gave absolute equality of rights with whites to both half-castes and blacks, and Commissioners were sent out with full powers to see the decree enforced. Our Governor refused to place the white population politically at the mercy of the blacks, so the Commissioners called on the revolted slaves to support them. In addition a high proportion of the French troops had become imbued with revolutionary ideas, so sided with the fire-brands from Paris. Thus a civil war within the civil war began, in which whites, mulattoes and blacks were fighting on both sides.

'That we survived the desperate year of '93 is nothing short of a miracle, but somehow we managed to keep the republicans and blacks from overwhelming us. At times though there were happenings of such horror that they beggar description. At midsummer the negroes succeeded in breaking into the fine city of Cap Français, slaughtered the entire white population of four thousand, then burnt it to the ground.

'Repeatedly we had appealed again to Britain to take the colony over, and as by then she had entered on war with France an agreement was reached that she should do so. But she had heavy commitments in other theatres and for many months could not spare forces to send to our assistance. That autumn, in despair, we begged further aid of the Governor of Jamaica and he nobly answered our appeal. In September the British reinforced our great stronghold at Mole St. Nicholas and they have since sent large numbers of troops who are now acting as garrisons in our principal towns. But the war continues and, alas, I see no end to it.'

Having concluded his account de Bouçicault fell silent, and after a moment Roger said: 'As it is now over a year since British forces landed here in some strength it surprises me that they have been able to do no more than protect a few ports. After all, in Jamaica they have a base that is no more than two days' sail distant; so they should have no difficulty in securing ample arms and stores for the waging of an offensive, whereas the negroes must be ill-armed and their supplies from revolutionary France have long since been cut off. If well directed, a few battalions of our troops ought to have made mincemeat of such a rabble.'

The big Frenchman shook his blond head. 'My friend, if you think that, you are sadly ignorant of conditions here. It is true that we have been greatly disappointed in the lack of initiative shown by your countrymen; but they are by no means altogether to blame for that. Yellow fever has killed ten British soldiers for every one that has fallen a victim to the blacks. Hundreds of them have died of it, and when I was last at Mole St. Nicholas, a fortnight ago, I learned that the garrison had been reduced to a mere three hundred and seventy-eight, of whom one hundred and sixty-six were sick.

'Again you are quite wrong in your assumption that the negroes are lacking in a source of supplies with which to continue the war. Although Spain is the ally of Britain in her war against France, here she is secretly stabbing your country in the back. As you must know, this whole island was for the first two hundred years after its discovery a Spanish possession. The western, and by far the most valuable, third of it was ceded to France only under the Treaty of Ryswick in 1697, and then became known as Saint-Domingue to distinguish it from the part retained by Spain known as Santo Domingo. The Spaniards have never given up hope of regaining the lost third with its richer plantations, and in this terrible civil war of ours they see their opportunity.

'One of the boldest, and by far the most intelligent, of the negro Generals is a man named Toussaint l'Ouverture; and he has had the good sense to make a pact with the Spaniards. They treat their slaves comparatively well,

they react swiftly to every primitive impulse of the moment, and are easily led by stronger personalities for either good or ill. Normally, they respond to kindness as readily as those of us who have been blessed with white skins; and during the terrible week of the initial revolt. I and my family owed our lives to the fact that we had always treated our slaves as human beings. They protected us and refused to allow the revolted slaves from neighbouring plantations to set fire to the house.

'Yet the crux of the matter is that they took that stand only because we were present, and could exert a stronger influence on them than could comparative strangers whom they had no reason to regard as in any way superior to themselves. Had we been absent they would almost certainly have joined the insurgents and gleefully participated in the atrocities committed by others of their race.

' 'Tis, of course, because I was little more than a cipher to the majority of my estate slaves that most of them were suborned by tales of easy plunder and ran away believing that the country was about to become a black man's paradise. The house slaves, on the other hand, considered themselves to be well off where they were, and I was in a position to counter any idea that by becoming outlaws they would enter into a Utopia. Nevertheless, did I depart, their minds would become fluid and subject to the first plausible rogue who sought to induce them to abandon their trust.

'Probably they would at first refrain from plundering my belongings; but were they confident that I did not intend to return until the disturbances were over they would not prevent their relatives from doing so, and soon they would persuade themselves that they were behaving stupidly in letting others get away with all the loot. Within a few weeks the house would be as bare as if it were a mule's carcass that had been picked clean by vultures, yet would be crammed to capacity with negroes of both sexes and all ages.

'That is what has happened to all the big houses in the interior. They have been stripped even to the door knobs, and become reeking tenements which are best described by the term human ant-heaps. Banisters, cupboards and everything burnable in them is used to light fires because the inmates are too lazy to go out and collect more wood than they have to in the forests. The roofs may leak, the plaster crack, the paint peel from the walls and the floors become charred from the several cooking fires that are lit by different families daily in every room. It is no one's responsibility to maintain or repair the structures, and if their owners ever regain these places they will find that the gracious homes they left have become smoke-begrimed barren shells. That is what would happen here if I went to live in Mole St. Nicholas.'

'I see your point.' Roger smiled. 'All the same I marvel that during all these years of strife you have not been driven out.'

'I should have been on several occasions had I not taken precautions against being caught off my guard.'

'Such as?' prompted Roger.

'In half a dozen places along a semi-circle, from coast to coast, running roughly five miles distant, I have negroes living who would give me warning of the approach of any hostile body. In this case it is no question of counting on their loyalty but on their greed. I pay each of them a monthly wage for doing nothing, which of course would cease if I were driven out, and any of them who brings me a timely warning knows that he will receive enough money to keep him in idleness for five years.'

'That sounds an excellent system, but no warning could prevent an ill-intentioned rabble advancing on the house.'

'On receiving one I let loose the dogs.'

Roger raised his eyebrows. 'Your three dogs might drive off a few unarmed men, as was the case with Doctor Fergusson and my man Dan Izzard two nights ago; but they could do little against a mob bent on plunder.'

With a hearty laugh de Bouçicault replied: 'You are right in that, but I was referring to my pack. It consists of well over a hundred wild dogs: fierce mastiffs each capable of savaging a man to death. Many of the revolted slaves have shown great courage in battle, but experience has proved that these bands of marauders have no stomach for a conflict with my four-legged troops.'

'If they are wild I should have thought they would have bolted when released, instead of remaining to attack your enemies.'

'They are wild by breed but tamed to the extent that I have trained them for their work. I keep them in a big courtyard beyond the stables and no one other than myself ever enters it. As you no doubt know, the negro has a distinctive smell quite unlike that of a white man. I keep the dogs somewhat underfed and from time to time I wrap a chunk of the pig meat on which I feed them in an old garment that a negro has saturated with his sweat. In that way they have come to associate food with the negro smell. One of my slaves once ignored my order and entered the yard behind me. Before I could lift a hand to help him the poor devil was torn to pieces.'

'You have certainly evolved a most ingenious means of defence,' Roger commented. 'But how did you manage to collect so many wild dogs in the first place?'

'That was not difficult. The forests of the island are infested with them. During the first century after its discovery the Spaniards endeavoured to force the Indians they found here into slavery, but they proved a difficult people. Neither good treatment nor the infliction of the most cruel punishments would induce those they captured to work; while those who continued free waged a bitter unrelenting war against the white settlers.

''Tis said that when Columbus first arrived here there were at the very least a million of them; but even after they had been defeated many times in battle and countless thousands of them slain they would not give in. From forest lairs and caves in the mountains they sallied forth to harass the invaders, neither giving nor expecting quarter. In consequence the Spaniards decided to import negroes to do their menial tasks and totally exterminate the aborigines.

'To assist in doing so they sent to Spain for large numbers of hunting dogs, and with them systematically searched the forests, putting every Indian the dogs routed out—man, woman or child—to the sword.

'When this terrible business was over they found that they had many more dogs than they could conveniently feed; so they drove the majority of them away from their settlements. Left to fend for themselves the dogs soon became wild, and so fierce that even a small pack of them will not hesitate to attack a wild boar. Later many attempts were made to put them down, but they breed with great rapidity so there are still very large numbers of them. The actual securing of them was a somewhat dangerous business, but by digging pits in their runs it was easy for me to trap as many as I required.'

'It was certainly an excellent idea,' said Roger with a smile. 'I only hope that you will have no cause to let them loose while I and my friends are here—or for that matter ever again before order is restored and you can drive them back to the forest. About the departure of the ladies, though —I doubt if Lady St. Ermins will be fit to leave her bed much before myself; her maid is far too devoted to her to leave without her, and I think we should find great difficulty in persuading my wife to leave without me. Moreover I am much opposed to giving them cause for alarm unless you consider the danger really pressing.'

De Bouçicault hesitated for a moment. 'I would not say that. Toussaint's army being reported as at no great distance along the coast is the only thing that causes me some uneasiness. I am confident that my dogs would drive off any band of casual marauders, but should this house chance to lie in the path of Toussaint's advance, we could not possibly put up any serious resistance. 'Tis that I fear, although admittedly without any special grounds for doing so. However, from what you tell me there seems small hope of getting the ladies away until you are at least sufficiently recovered to stand a thirty-mile journey over rough roads in my coach; so there is little point in our discussing the matter further for the moment.'

During the week that followed the sadly battered party gradually recovered from the worst effects of its ordeals. Having once turned the corner Georgina made excellent progress. Amanda was still subject to a shooting pain inside her whenever she coughed, but Fergusson was now satisfied that it would wear off, and that she had not sustained any serious injury. The wounds of both Kilick and Roger were healing well, while of the burns, stings, and blisters that had afflicted the others few traces remained.

Tom alone continued to give them anxiety. He had weathered the crisis but it had left him so weak that Fergusson feared that he might yet be carried off by a relapse, and declared that in any case it would be out of the question to move him for another week at the very least. Owing to Georgina's already having become convalescent and Roger's good prospects of soon being able to get about again, de Bouçicault reopened with him the question of their leaving, suggesting that with the exception of Tom, whom he undertook to have well cared for, they should all set out for Mole St. Nicholas in a few days' time. Roger put the matter to Amanda, who in turn spoke to Georgina, but she would not consider even temporarily abandoning her servant until he was definitely pronounced out of danger; so there the matter rested.

From Roger's first long talk with de Bouçicault onward, except during the rest hours that Fergusson insisted that he should observe, he had an almost constant stream of visitors. Clarissa slipped into his room shortly after de Bouçicault had left him and laughingly pooh-poohed his no more than half serious reprimand that she was outraging convention by remaining there without a chaperon. Dan's bronzed, black-bearded face peeped in at the door that evening and he was gladly bidden to enter. Roger's host came to have a talk with him every morning, Jenny brought him news of Georgina every evening, and from the third day Amanda was well enough to sit with him for long periods. Monsieur Pirouet had invaded the kitchen to cook special dishes for the invalids and when Roger sent for him to thank him he learned that the French chef was greatly enjoying himself taking lessons in Creole cooking from de Bouçicault's hugely fat and jolly old negress cook. The other three men in turn asked permission to come and pay their respects, and he learned that they had all voluntarily taken up some form of work about the place, finding it a pleasant change from their normal activities. So the days in the big comfortable house passed quickly and happily.

On the eighth day after their arrival, as Fergusson had predicted, Roger was able to try out a pair of crutches that had been knocked up for him, and on the ninth Georgina made her first appearance downstairs. The following day being a Sunday—the second in December—the whole party with the one exception of Tom, gathered in the chapel of the house to give thanks for their merciful deliverance. Tom's appetite having been revived by the tempting delicacies Monsieur Pirouet thought up for him, he was now getting back a little of his strength, but no further news of Toussaint's movements had been received, and it was clear that their coming had made such a pleasant break in de Bouçicault's lonely life that he would now be most loath to see them go. Moreover, they could hardly have found better quarters in which to convalesce, as at the back of the house there was a terrace with a splendid view over the rocks to the blue bay, and up there on the point they reaped the full benefit of the light sea breezes. So still no definite date had been fixed for their departure.

It was during the night of December the 13th-14th that de Bouçicault's first fears were suddenly and alarmingly confirmed. Shortly before two o'clock a panting negro roused the house by beating frantically on its heavy front door. Eloi, the old grey-haired butler, aided by his two footmen, Zabeth and Thoédule, were reviving the man with neat rum when de Bouçicault came hurrying downstairs.

The negro proved to be one of de Bouçicault's outposts, and directly he saw his paymaster he gasped out the news that a column of General Toussaint's men with a number of wagons were advancing along the coast road. He would have known nothing of it had he not been roused owing to the still night, to which he was accustomed, being broken by the dull rumble of many wheels.

When questioned further he said that he did not think there were more than thirty marchers, but they must be a part of Toussaint's army because the transport of brigand bands rarely consisted of more than a few donkeys, whereas these men were escorting something between twelve and twenty wagons. Having made it plain that, although he had run all the way to get as far ahead of them as possible, they could not now be much more than three miles off, he begged urgently that he might be given his reward so that he could make himself scarce well before their arrival.

De Bouçicault paid him off and at once sent Dan up to fetch Roger; then, while Dan was assisting Roger to dress, he assembled all the male inmates of the house in the big salon. There, he put the situation to them.

He meant to remain in the house himself, but there was still time for any or all of them to leave it and hide in the woods. Anyone who elected to do that could be practically certain of evading Toussaint's men, but they would have to take the risk of being attacked by his dogs, because they were the only means he had of protecting his property; so he could not afford to refrain from turning them loose. On the other hand the coast road ran over half a mile inland from the house, and it was quite possible that this transport column would pass by without even knowing of its existence. Lastly, in the worst event, it seemed unlikely that including drivers the column was much more than fifty strong, while they totalled sixteen who would be well armed behind stout defences; so if all of them remained, with the assistance of the dogs they should stand a very good chance of beating off an attack.

Led by old Eloi, the eight negro house slaves said that, as in previous emergencies, they were willing to stay with their master. The others all looked towards Roger for guidance, and he found himself in a very difficult position.

Had he had only to think of himself he would at once have declared his intention of staying, as he felt under an obligation to help de Bouçicault defend his property should the need arise; but he had also to think of the women, and their best interests must be placed before all other considerations. Although a night in the woods would be far from good for the still convalescent Georgina, and if they took Tom with them might cause him a serious setback, that was not a very high price to pay for an almost certain prospect of escaping Toussaint's men. But there remained the very unpleasant thought that the hungry pack, once loose, might attack white humans as well as blacks; so the crux of the matter was—could they get far enough from the house to be out of danger from the dogs in the limited time before de Bouçicault would consider it imperative to release them? It was a very nasty decision to have to take and, after moistening his lips, he asked his host:

'At what time do you intend to let out your wild dogs, Monsieur?'

De Bouçicault glanced at the Louis Seize clock on the mantelpiece, and replied: 'It is twenty-five minutes past two. By now this column must have advanced to between one and two miles of us. I have good hopes that they are not making for the house, but should they be they may arrive here any time after a quarter to three. I dare not leave the freeing of the pack later than twenty to; so if it is your intention to leave us, Monsieur le Gouverneur, you must hurry.'

'Nay,' Roger shook his head. To get the women out and with himself only able to hobble, a quarter of an hour was too slender a margin. With a glance round the men of his own party, he added: 'The ladies and myself will remain here, and I recommend you to do so also.'

'Aye, aye, Cap'n,' muttered Dan, and the others nodded in agreement.

Quickly now they set about preparring to defend the house. Fergusson went upstairs to warn the women what was afoot, while de Bouçicault unlocked a big cupboard under the main staircase and began to hand out weapons. There were more than enough muskets and pistols for all, with a plentiful supply of powder shot and side arms. Every window on the ground floor had stout shutters and they already had loopholes bored through them. Old Eloi and his companion took up the positions they had been allotted in similar emergencies, while de Bouçicault posted the others to the best advantage, and impressed upon them that they were not to fire until he gave the word.

As it was still bad for Roger to stand for any length of time without support, he had a small table, on which he could sit, placed for himself opposite one of the shuttered slit windows on either side of the front door. He had hardly done so when Tom, pale and shaky but resolute, came downstairs and insisted that he was strong enough to lend a hand. He was followed by the women, who declared their intention of acting as loaders for the men. The next ten minutes passed in giving them a demonstration of how to handle the weapons swiftly and safely. Then de Bouçicault went out to release the pack.

Five minutes later Roger was endeavouring to reassure the girls, when their host came running back and burst in upon them, his ruddy face a picture of consternation.

'We are betrayed!' he cried, striking his fist in furious anger against the jamb of the open doorway in which he stood panting. 'Many of the dogs are dead; the rest are vomiting and useless. Earlier tonight someone must have thrown poisoned meat in to them over the courtyard wall.'

'That settles it, then,' said Roger grimly. 'An attack is definitely intended. But how could this column while still several miles distant have known aught of your pack?'

'Everyone in the district knows of it,' came the prompt reply, 'and Toussaint has spies everywhere. As I have told you he far surpasses in intelligence the other negro Generals. While planning his advance he would have learned about my dogs, and he must have sent some men ahead to ensure their destruction.'

It was too late to take to the woods, as they now had reason to suppose that the house was under observation, and the column might arrive on the scene within the next ten minutes; so to leave the house would have been to risk running right up against trouble in the open.

All they could do was to make a final check up on their defences and pray that after a first assault so small a force might decide that the house was too tough a nut to crack. After barring the big door and loading every available fire-arm, they put out most of the candles and masked others, so that the rooms should appear to be in darkness; then stood at their posts anxiously awaiting the appearance of the enemy.

The moon was up and brightly lit the wide sweep of the drive in front of the house, so they had a good field of fire on that side and there was an even better one at its back across a balustraded terrace to the garden; but they thought it unlikely that the attack would come from that direction as the depth of the garden was a bare hundred feet, ending in another balustrade, beyond which the ground dropped almost sheer to the sea. There remained the sides of the house, both of which were flanked by outbuildings; but Dan and Jake were up on the roof with two negroes named Chrysostome and Clovis, and from their greater height could shoot down on anyone who clambered up to the lower roofs on either side of them.

Three o'clock came without sound or sign disturbing the moonlit vistas that the inmates of the house were watching with ever-growing tension. But at five past they caught the rustle and snap of broken bushes, and a moment later a body of men emerged from between the tall palms that fringed the long drive.

They halted about a hundred yards from the house, but one of them continued to walk forward. De Bouçicault, who had stationed himself near Roger behind the shuttered window on the other side of the front door, quickly passed the word that everyone should pick his man but refrain from firing until he did. The negro who was approaching was clad in a gaudy uniform with a tricolour sash draped across it, so was obviously an officer. Halting when he reached the foot of the steps, he cried in a high-pitched voice:

'Open up! There are chinks of light showing from some of your windows, so I can see you must be expecting us. I have wagons with me full of wounded, and require this house to shelter them. Open up now, or it will be the worse for you!'

De Bouçicault's only reply was to fire his musket. Shot at point blank range through the chest the officer fell dead at the foot of the steps. A second later a volley crashed out from the defenders of the house. Several of the negroes in the main body sank to the ground killed or wounded. Screams and curses suddenly made the night hideous. Those unhit replied with a ragged volley, then dashed for cover in the nearby bushes. The glass of broken windows crashed and tinkled, and bullets thudded into the shutters. There followed a brief silence while both sides reloaded and sought fresh targets.

During it Roger said to de Bouçicault: 'Was not your act a rash one? As he wanted the house for a hospital he would certainly not have destroyed it; and we might have made a pact with him to surrender it peaceably if he allowed us to leave it with the honours of war.'

The Frenchman grunted. 'You do not understand these people. Pact or no pact our lives would not be worth a moment's purchase if we fell into their clutches. Besides, such a chance to kill their leader might not have occurred again. Now that he is dead they will all be at sixes and sevens and act without proper direction; so our chances of driving them off are increased tenfold.'

That he was right became evident during the next half hour. A small group of the braver negroes attempted to rush one of the windows, and were driven off with severe losses. But apart from that no concerted action was taken; the others kept up only a desultory fire at the faint blurs of light that indicated the loopholes in the shutters.

The garrison, intently watching the black shadows that contrasted so strongly with the silver moonlight, fired at every movement they saw, or thought they saw, among the oleanders, bougainvillaeas and hibiscus. Occasionally a sharp cry told them that they had scored a hit, but another hour dragged by without the besiegers losing heart and abandoning the confict, as it was still hoped they would.

Just after half-past four one of the snipers sent a well-aimed shot through one of the loopholes. It laid open Théodule's cheek and smashed some of his back teeth. Amanda left Roger's side to do what she could for the wounded negro footman, and by the time she returned to her post the moon had gone down behind the palms.

Starlight still lit the drive, although more faintly, and the attackers took advantage of the dimness to creep up closer to the house. Ten minutes later a dozen of them made a dash for the front door. Roger dropped one but de Bouçicault's musket misfired, and once the group had reached the porch it was too close to the house for fire to be brought upon it from any of the windows. With heavy staves, an axe and musket butts the negroes beat frantically on the door, striving to break it in. They might have succeeded had it not been for Dan and his little party up on the roof. At the sounds of the commotion they ran to the front parapet and, leaning over, began to fire down on the attackers. Two of them were hit and the remainder panicked, flung away most of the things they were wielding and bolted for the bushes.

Again there was a long spell of relative quiet, until Eloi came from the back of the house to tell his master that he felt sure he smelt smoke, and thought that some of the outbuildings had been set on fire.

With an anxious glance at Roger, de Bouçicault muttered: 'Although I made no mention of it, that they might try to smoke us out is the one thing I feared.' Then he hurried off to investigate.

It transpired that the maize store was ablaze, but between it and the house was sandwiched the laundry, and de Bouçicault felt that if they could well douse the roof and walls of the latter with water there would be a good chance of preventing the fire from spreading to the main building. Swiftly, he set about organising two fire fighting squads.

The task of the party on the roof was an easy one, for they had only to carry buckets of water from the big cisterns up there and throw their contents down on to the lower level of the laundry; but to reach the walls of its interior the party below had to get out of the end window looking on to the terrace and either pass buckets, or run with them, the half-dozen yards to its entrance. Short as the distance was, it meant temporary exposure to the bullets of any of the attackers who might have posted themselves in positions from which they could enfilade the terrace; so de Bouçicault transferred four of the defenders to first-floor windows at the back of the house to form a covering party, then led the ground floor fire fighting squad in person.

There ensued a short, sharp battle. Twice de Bouçicault, Kilick and two negro grooms succeeded in getting buckets into the laundry. Shots spattered round them, and others in reply from the first floor windows whistled over their heads. Then, at the third sortie, one of the grooms went down, shot through the leg. Dropping their buckets, the others picked him up and got him back into the house, but while helping to do so de Bouçicault was hit in the side.

A few minutes later, sweat pouring down his face he staggered into the main hall and gasped to Roger: 'Come with me, please. I want a words with you in private.'

Obediently Roger followed him into a small room in which he had been used to deal with the business of the estate. Slumping into a chair, he said jerkily: 'We'll have to give up. They hit two of us. If we don't they'll pick us off piecemeal. I fear I'm done for.'

'Don't say that!' exclaimed Roger, turning towards the door. 'I'll get Doctor Fergusson.'

De Bouçicault stayed him with an impatient gesture. 'No good! One of those black devils got me through the innards. Listen, Monsieur. I have little time left. Tell my wife—if you ever get to Mole St. Nicholas—how I died. But that's the rub. They've got the better of us. Your chances of getting there now are not worth ten sous.'

His face suddenly worked convulsively, then he was seized with a violent fit of coughing. After spewing up some blood into his handkerchief, he made a great effort, leaned forward, took from a drawer in his desk a small bottle filled with a pinkish liquid, and went on:

'Unless the wind changes the fire will spread to the house. You will be tempted to surrender. Put the thought from you. I am thinking of the women. These fiends will not only violate them; they will mutilate them most horribly afterwards. I know; I have seen what they have done to others.'

Again a fit of coughing choked him. Then he handed the bottle to Roger and gasped: 'There is wine in the dining-room. Put this in it. Use any pretext to make them drink. In your place I would take some myself. It is a quick poison. By it you can save them from . . . from . . . Should things become hopeless, do not hesitate, I beg. This . . . this is a duty you owe to those you love.'

15

The Choice of Evils

De Bouçicault had barely finished laying this terrible charge upon Roger when he was gripped by another convulsion. A hideous rattling noise issued from his throat and a few moments later he slumped forward dead.

No one could accuse Roger of lack of courage, but for once he had gone white to the lips, and could feel himself trembling. Reason told him that de Bouçicault was right, but his every instinct made him cringe from the thought and he doubted if he could possibly bring himself to do this awful thing. With shaking hands he propped the dead man up in the chair, drew an antimacassar over his distorted face, and limped slowly from the room.

It was now nearly half-past five and dawn not far off. As usual at that hour the wind had dropped, but a light breeze from the sea still fanned the flames of the burning maize store; and there was good reason to assume that the negroes had deliberately chosen that building to start a fire in because it was on the seaward side of the house. With the abandoning of the attempt to get buckets of water along to the laundry the shooting had ceased; so in the early morning stillness Roger could now actually hear the crackling of the flames as they ate into the old rafters.

As soon as the others learned of de Bouçicault's death, by an unspoken but unanimous consent they looked to Roger as their new leader, and the responsibility weighed with crushing heaviness upon him. Had he been strong and well he could as a last resort have led a desperate sortie, hoping that some of them might break through with the women, then turn and make a stand while they ran on to hide themselves in the woods; but, crippled as he was, that was out of the question. He put the idea to Fergusson, suggesting that he or Dan should act as leader, but immediately Amanda and Georgina heard of it they refused to leave without him.

All he could do then was to send more men up to the roof to aid the fire-fighting party there, in the hope that if enough water was poured down on to the laundry that might yet check the advance of the fire. But the flames from the maize store were now leaping high and casting a new lurid light upon the scene. By it the attackers were able to see and snipe at the fire-fighters. Kilick was again wounded, this time in the hand, and shortly afterwards Ovid, de Bouçicault's mulatto valet, was shot through the head; so these casualties, and the caution the others now had to exercise, nullified the extra help that had been sent up to them.

Soon after Kilick came down to have his hand bound up, flames burst through the laundry roof as if it had been a lid clamped down upon a seething volcano. In a matter of moments the main building caught fire and smoke began to drift through the house.

Sick with distress, Roger made his way to the dining-room. Taking a large jug he poured two bottles of wine into it, then the poison. Setting the jug on the table he placed nearby it a glass apiece for each of the survivors. But when he got back to the hall he could not yet bring himself to tell any of the others what he had done.

Unnoticed by him while he had been preparing the deadly brew, dawn had come. As he peered out through one of the loopholes at the side of the front door his heart sank afresh. Some way down the drive a body of at least a hundred negro soldiers stood casually leaning on their muskets and evidently awaiting orders. Reinforcements had arrived, so the last hope had gone of persuading the others to try a breakout instead of taking the terrible alternative.

As he watched, a tall negro in a plumed cocked hat signed to one of the soldiers to go forward. The man held something white. Next moment as he walked towards the house he raised it above his head, and Roger saw that it was a flag of truce. With trembling fingers he set about unbarring the door.

'In Heaven's name, what are you about?' exclaimed Amanda.

'They are offering us a parley,' he replied, 'and I am going out to meet them.'

'Have you become crazed?' she cried. 'They will tear you limb from limb. Monsieur de Bouçicault knew these wretches well. He told me that he would sooner take the risk of sporting with a hungry shark than place his trust in them.'

'No matter,' replied Roger curtly. 'It is a risk which I must run.'

As he resumed the unbarring of the door Amanda stepped forward to fling her arms about him. Dan, sweating and smoke begrimed, had just come down the wide staircase to report. Roger, with his bright blue eyes hard as agates, called to him.

'Quick, Dan! Hold your mistress. It is imperative that she should not be permitted to thwart me at his moment.'

After a second's hesitation Dan ran forward, gripped Amanda by the shoulders and drew her back. The other women were acting as loaders in other rooms. Old Eloi was getting a fresh supply of powder from under the stairs and Fergusson was guarding a door at the extreme back of the hall, which gave on to the terrace. Taking up his crutches Roger swung himself swiftly along to the doctor and in a low voice told him about the poisoned wine. As he returned, swirls of smoke were curling like the tentacles of a giant octopus across the lofty hall. Pausing before Amanda he said in a now gentle voice:

'My love. You may be right; but what I am about to do offers the only chance for all of us. Should your fears for me prove justified I beg you to promise me one thing. It is that you should do your utmost to persuade the others to drink the wine that I have left prepared in the dining-room, and to drink of it yourself.'

The sudden distension of her eyes showed her realisation that it was no ordinary glass of wine to which he referred. Slowly she nodded, then murmured: 'You are right, my sweet. It is the easier way. May God protect you and bring you back to me.'

Old Eloi had seen that it was Roger's intention to go out; so now he completed the unfastening of the door, drew a deep breath, and opened it.

With his home-made crutches tapping sharply on the stone steps Roger swung himself down them. The soldier with the flag of truce had by now approached to within twenty yards of the house. Halting he called out in a rich voice: 'General Toussaint l'Ouverture would speak with you.'

'Lead on,' replied Roger, and as the man turned he followed him down the drive.

On seeing him approach, the negro officer with the plumed hat left his men and came to meet him. When they were within two yards of one another both came to a standstill. Roger eyed the General with anxious speculation, striving to learn something of his character from his face. It was long and thin with a sensitive mouth, high forehead, and deep-set intelligent eyes. He was tall, bony and his gaudy uniform with its enormous gold epaulettes hung loosely upon him. After a moment he asked in the lisping Créole French that all the negroes used:

'Are you the owner of this house?'

'No,' replied Roger. 'I have been here only as a guest for the past two weeks, after having escaped from pirates, by whom I had the misfortune to be captured.'

'What is your name, and when you were captured upon what were you engaged?'

'I am an Englishman named Brook, and I was on my way to take up the Governorship of Martinique.'

The negro's eyes narrowed slightly. 'Then you are a person of importance?'

Roger had swiftly seized upon the opening given him, and added quickly: 'Apart from those permanently resident in the house, all the inmates are British; and among them is the Countess of St. Ermins, a lady who has far greater influence and wealth then myself.'

The General nodded. 'I had heard that there were women here. That is one reason why I offered you a parley. I am averse to making war on women, whatever their nationality.'

'Do you mean that you are willing to grant them a safe conduct to Mole St. Nicholas?' asked Roger with a sudden surge of hope.

'To that I cannot agree. But I am anxious to have the house so that I may lodge my wounded in it, and that will be out of the question if it is allowed to burn down. If you will at once vacate it I will give you reasonable terms.'

'What are they?' Roger enquired, striving to keep his anxiety out of his voice.

'With one exception, I am willing to grant you your lives. The exception is the man who shot my officer when you were first called on to surrender. For his callous act it is just that he should die.'

'It was Monsieur de Bouçicault, and he is already dead. What are your intentions with regard to the rest of us?'

'I mean to hold you as hostages. In view of your quality it may be possible for me to arrange to exchange you for some of my people whom the British have taken prisoner; but I can make no promise about that.'

'Does your promise of protection apply to the coloured servants in the house as well as to my own party?'

'Theirs is a mistaken loyalty, but I admire honest devotion to any cause. They may go free. I will give orders that they are not to be molested, and shall hope that in due course they will realise where lie the true interests of their race.'

'Should you fail to arrange an exchange, what is to happen to us?'

The deep-set eyes of the tall negro smouldered with a sudden glow that betrayed his fanaticism. 'You will remain in captivity until I have driven every white man out of this island, then I will send you anywhere you wish.'

Roger took mental note that the French terrorists had caught a tartar in making such a powerful personality as this negro General their ally, and that by secretly supportting him the Spaniards in the eastern end of the island were paving the way for the cutting of their own throats. But at the moment he was far more concerned with the fate of himself and his friends. To become the prisoners of a horde of bloody-thirsty negroes, perhaps for an indefinite period, was a prospect that would have filled anyone with dismay. Yet it meant life—if General Toussaint's word could be relied upon.

De Bouçicault, Roger felt sure, would have maintained that the offer was a trap, simply designed to get them out of the house before it was burnt down, and that remained a terrible possibility. But during their conversation he had formed the impression that the General was an honest man, so decided that if he could get him to commit himself as deeply as possible, he would take that risk. Holding out his hand, he said:

'Will you give me your solemn pledge to carry out the terms you offer, and give me your hand upon it?'

A sudden smile lit the lean dark face of the negro, as he replied: 'Monsieur, it is a rare thing for a white man to offer his hand to a black. I am very glad now that news of the trouble here caused me to leave the main body of my troops during the night with a small reinforcement. I take your hand gladly and you may rely upon my word.' Then his long bony fingers closed upon Roger's in a powerful grip.

Greatly relieved by this firm reassurance, Roger returned to the house, while General Toussaint set about organising his men to fight the fire. As Roger and his party had arrived entirely destitute of belongings, de Bouçicault had made their lack good as far as he could from the wardrobe of his wife and daughters and himself; so now those of them who were in a condition to do so ran upstairs and hastily packed small portmanteaux with a variety of things which might make their captivity slightly more endurable. Roger, meanwhile, threw away the poisoned wine; then, choking from the smoke, he and his party went out to the General, who sent its white members under guard down to the small lodge at the entrance of the long palm-lined drive.

There, the wife of the old lodge-keeper knocked up a scratch meal for them; after which they sat about grouped round the porch of the lodge wearied out by the night's fears and activities, yet with minds too harassed by the uncertainties of their future to escape for more than short periods into fitful sleep.

At about ten o'clock the General rode up accompanied by a solitary A.D.C. Reining in, he called to Roger. 'The fire has been got under, and I must now rejoin the main body of my troops. I have made Lieutenant Charlemange responsible for your safety. Obey his orders and no harm will come to you.'

Somewhat over an hour later a heavy travelling coach lumbered down the drive which, together with the horses that drew it, had evidently been taken from de Bouçicault's stable. Out of it clambered a young negro officer who had only one arm, and half a dozen soldiers. The officer gave the group outside the lodge an unfriendly stare, and announced sharply:

'I am Lieutenant Charlemange. The women and wounded will ride in the coach. The rest of you will walk.'

The girls, Tom and Roger entered the roomy vehicle, the other men fell in behind it with the squad of soldiers bringing up the rear, Lieutenant Charlemange clambered up on to the box and they set off.

It was a nightmare journey which lasted two days and two nights. Charlemange and his men made it clear that they neither understood nor approved the order they had received to keep the prisoners alive. In consequence, nothing whatever was done to make their slow progress over appalling by-roads under the torrid sun more easily supportable. On the contrary, morning and evening their food was flung to them, they were frequently denied water for many hours at a stretch, and the women were at times placed in such embarrassing situations that but for a certain stoicism that their previous unhappy experiences had developed in them, they must almost have died of shame.

At last this grim progress came to an end. Of the name of the locality they had reached they had no idea. They knew only that they must have travelled some fifty miles in a south-easterly direction and had come to a big rambling mansion that stood in a forest clearing among the foothills of a range of mountains.

This once noble property was in just the state de Bouçicault had described as the fate of large houses taken over by the negroes. Evidence of neglect was everywhere and the building swarmed with negroes, negresses and piccaninnies, all living together in an indescribable state of squalor. Several hundred of them inhabited the house and every corner of its outbuildings. On seeing the coach draw up they poured forth in a swarm and surging round the white prisoners screamed abuse and insults at them. No one seemed to have any authority over this dangerous rabble, so Roger feared that they were all about to be massacred upon the spot. But Charlemange stood up on the box of the coach and shouted to them that General Toussaint had ordered him to shoot anyone who attempted to lay a hand on the prisoners, upon which the crowd sullenly gave back.

The question of quarters for the newcomers was settled arbitrarily by Charlemange's ordering his men to eject half a dozen protesting families from three attics at the top of the house. The women were given one, the men another, while the Lieutenant took the largest of the three for himself and their guard.

The low-ceilinged rooms were filthy and bug infested. As the ejected negroes had taken their scant belongings with them they were also now bare of furniture, and appeals to Charlemange to procure even mattresses proved unavailing. With a callous shrug he said that there were none to be had. Asked what he meant to do about himself and his men, he replied that he would commandeer their requirements but had no intention of depriving honest coloured folks to provide comforts for the type of people who for generations had treated them like animals. His orders went no further than to protect his prisoners from harm; so for a change they could live like animals themselves.

That was indeed the miserable state to which they were very near reduced. They had at least been allowed to retain the small portmanteaux they had brought, so were able to use these for pillows, and the contents of them provided minor ameliorations of their hard lot. But the food they were given was hardly better than pig swill, and they had to eat it out of one big crock with their fingers; the sanitary arrangements were degrading and the smell of the place disgusting; no water was allowed them to wash with and for many hours each day the atmosphere of the attics was stifling from the strong sun beating down on the roof.

Soon they were all scratching themselves from scores of insect bites, and had not Fergusson had the forethought to bring with him a bottle of de Bouçicault's essence of Cinchona bark, a little of which he gave each of them in water every morning, some of them would, almost certainly, have gone down with Yellow Fever. In spite of the appalling conditions in which they lived their health remained good; and as they were not called upon to exert themselves in any way both Tom and Roger regained some of their former strength.

As a means of combating melancholia they divided the day into sections with a variety of activities which would occupy their minds. First thing every morning they held a competition while delousing themselves, the winner being given the choice of what games should be played up till midday. During the heat of the afternoon they endeavoured to sleep, then later took turns in telling stories or describing events in their own lives. Dan's yarns of his years as a smuggler proved particularly popular, and Wilson kept them interested for many hours telling them about the War of Independence and life in the new United States. Then in the evening they held a sing-song.

Yet by the end of the week the lack of new items to introduce into this routine and, by then, the certainty that their jailers had no intention of ever taking any step to lessen the utter wretchedness of their existence, began to make these sessions more like work than play.

For most of the day the negro community below lazed about, but with the coming of night they roused up and threw all their latent energy into Voodoo ceremonies. The chanting, drumming and dancing at these took the place for them of all other recreations, with the exception of watching cock fights. By midnight they had hypnotised themselves into such a frenzy of abandonment that the house shook from the stamping of their feet on the floors of the lower rooms, and frequently it was not until the early hours of the morning that the sound of their orgies gradually ceased.

Night after night, as Roger lay turning restlessly on the hard boards listening to the maddening rhythm of the drums, he tried to plan some means of escape. But the problem proved beyond him.

By now he no longer needed his crutches; so had he been alone, or his party consisted only of men, an escape might have been effected by night through one of the skylights and over the roof. Although, even had it been successful, it was very doubtful if the many miles of hostile country that separated them from British troops could have been traversed without recapture. But such an attempt hampered by four women was out of the question. A breakout was equally unthinkable, as, although they might possibly have overpowered their slack and somnolent guards, they could not have done so without the alarm being raised, and their chances of fighting their way through the horde of negroes who lived in the house were about as good as trying to swim the Atlantic. In fact, ill-disposed to them as Charlemange was, he and his men were their only shield. They had already proved their loyalty to their General by standing their ground in the face of several hostile demonstrations against the prisoners; so to have deliberately rendered them *hors de combat* while the murderous mob below had still to be encountered would have been sheer madness.

The thought of indefinite captivity in their present surroundings appalled them all, and in vain they endeavoured to reconcile themselves to the fact that even months away there was no deadline beyond which they could be certain of release. Clarissa, perhaps because she was the youngest, was the most seriously affected by this demoralising uncertainty. In every crisis of action she had so far kept her head and shown as much courage as the older women; but now, with ultra pessimism, she declared that they would be there for years, that if ever she did get free again it would only be with a haggard face and scrawny body, and that the cruel Fates clearly intended to rob her of her youth in this way. Each night she sobbed herself to sleep and, in fact, her looks did begin to deteriorate with alarming rapidity.

Her high-bridged nose became a bony beak, her cheeks lost their bloom and her golden hair its lustre. Yet there was nothing they could say to cheer her or do to check the draining away of her vitality.

Christmas Day came and passed like any other, as to attempt any form of rejoicing would have been too bitter a mockery. But on the afternoon of Boxing Day they were aroused from their torpor by an order which brought them scrambling to their feet breathless with excitement. From the passage-way Charlemange had shouted:

'Get your things together. We are leaving here.'

Instantly their hearts bounded with the hope that General Toussaint had succeeded in arranging an exchange for them; but the one-armed Lieutenant would neither confirm or deny that. After spitting on the floor he just shrugged and muttered surlily:

'I have received an order to take you to another place. That is all you need to know. Hurry now!'

They needed no urging. Their quarters and treatment at the place to which they were to be taken could hardly be worse than the conditions under which they had lived for the past ten days. Within a few minutes they had packed their meagre belongings and were again being protected by their guards, as they made their way downstairs, from the menaces of scores of yelling blacks of both sexes.

The coach stood before the house. They noticed at once that its window curtains had disappeared and that the fine leather harness had been replaced with pieces of old rope. Then they saw that its well-sprung seats and back cushions had all been ripped out, leaving its interior a bare wooden box. Nevertheless, those of them who had come there in it were glad enough to take places on its floor in the hope that it would carry them to better times.

Actually, owing to the removal of the seats, the continued infliction of needless hard usage by their guards, and their journey being somewhat longer than the previous one, they suffered even more severely. Yet, hope now strengthened by the knowledge that they were being taken towards the coast, enabled them to bear it with a greater degree of fortitude.

On the fourth evening the coach was halted at a cross-roads and its occupants told to get out. With the others they were marched some distance along a track and then, just as the sun set, into a wood. After another half-hour's walk they came to a ruin, which they judged to be the remains of a monastery erected in the days of the Spanish occupation.

Some negro soldiers emerged from among the piles of great stones, and their officer held a brief consultation with Charlemange, at the conclusion of which the one-armed Lieutenant marched his men away without so much as a glance at his late prisoners. They knew that they probably owed their lives to his conscientious obedience to the orders he had been given, yet none of them could feel sorry to see him go.

The other officer gruffly told them to follow him, but refused to answer any questions; so surrounded by a new and larger escort they proceeded deeper into the forest until they reached a wide clearing. On its eastern edge they waited for over an hour, so pent up with excitement that they could hardly contain themselves. At length a single shot rang out somewhere to the west of them. The officer gave an order and two of his men fired their muskets into the air; so it was evident that the first shot had been a pre-arranged signal.

A few minutes later, in the faint starlight, several groups of men could be seen emerging from the trees on the far side of the clearing. Led by their officer a number of the negro soldiers went forward to meet them. There was an exchange of passwords, then Roger heard a voice speaking in such bad French that it could only have belonged to an Englishman. Several of his companions had realised that too, and with unutterable relief they kissed, embraced and with tears of joy running down their cheeks, wrung each other's hands.

After that everything seemed to happen very swiftly. Laughing and chattering the negro troops disappeared with the prisoners that the British had handed over to them, while Roger and his party found themselves surrounded by grinning red-coats and shaking hands with a plump young man who introduced himself as Captain Mansfield of the 41st.

As in a dream they walked another mile to a road where carriages were waiting. During a long drive they hardly spoke but soon after dawn they entered Mole St. Nicholas.

It had well been termed the Gibraltar of the Indies, as it possessed a fine natural harbour and the great fortress out on the promontory dominated the strait between Saint-Domingue and Cuba. But Captain Mansfield did not take them up to it. He explained that it was already overcrowded with refugees; so accommodation had been taken for them at the Hotel de France, which was situated in the central square of the little town that lay in the shelter of the Mole.

At the hotel they were welcomed by its proprietor, Monsieur Ducas. The plump Captain said that he would wait upon them later in the day, and they managed to murmur their thanks to him. Then they were led to their rooms and, pulling off their filthy clothes, flopped into bed.

When they awoke they could hardly credit that they were free again, but were soon reassured that they were not dreaming by the tangible comfort of their beds and solid appointments of the well-furnished rooms. The dinner hour had long since passed but Mansfield had foreseen that they would sleep through most of the day, so had called only to leave the Garrison Commander's compliments with a purse of twenty-five guineas for their immediate necessities, and orders that trays were to be sent up to them as soon as they roused from their slumbers. Having eaten and, although still almost speechless from relief, paid brief visits to one another in their rooms they slept once more.

Next morning the hotel servants were kept busy for an hour carrying up many copper cans of hot water, so that the new arrivals could thoroughly cleanse themselves in hip baths. Two barbers were sent for and a mercer who brought with him a selection of ready-made garments. By midday the gentry of the party, if not fashionably dressed, were at least presentable, and the others had substituted clean tropical attire for their flea-infested clothes.

At two o'clock Mansfield arrived to carry Roger, Wilson,

Fergusson and the three ladies up to the fortress to dine with its Commandant, Colonel Seaton. He proved to be a dour, elderly Scot, who had made his way in the Army by conscientious, if not enlightened, endeavour. It was at once clear to them that he was no courtier, but shrewd enough to realise that the goodwill of such influential people as the Governor designate of Martinique and the Countess of St. Ermins might one day stand him in good stead. Having commiserated with them on their misfortunes he expressed his willingness to help them in any way he could.

They thanked him in no measured terms for having rescued them by agreeing to an exchange of prisoners, and for his other courtesies; after which Roger reimbursed him for his loan with a draft on Hoare's Bank, and said that they would all like to go to Jamaica as soon as a passage could be arranged. He told them that as his communications with Kingston were frequent he thought there should be nothing to prevent their leaving in the next few days. They then went in to dinner.

It proved an indifferent and far from cheerful meal. Although the Colonel spoke guardedly, it was clear that he felt a bitter resentment against the powers at home who showed a most lamentable lack of understanding about the problems and needs of troops campaigning in the West Indies, and that he was greatly depressed by the heavy toll that death from Yellow Fever was taking of his men.

Recalling Droopy Ned's advice, Roger suggested that he should send the greater part of them to sea for a short voyage; but he seemed pessimistic about such a step having results of permanent value, and said that in any case his numbers were so reduced that he could not possibly do so without risking the security of the Fortress.

They finished dinner about seven, upon which the ladies retired to the drawing-room while the men sat over their port. An hour later they joined the ladies and soon afterwards Georgina initiated the polite movements for making their adieux. At this the Colonel expressed unfeigned surprise, reminding them that it was New Year's Eve, and saying that his officers were greatly looking forward to welcoming them in the mess to celebrate seeing the old year out.

In their complete absorption with their freedom they had completely forgotten the date, and although they would rather had once more savoured the joy of getting between clean sheets at the hotel, politeness demanded that they should now stay on where they were. As none of them had any acquaintances in common with the Colonel, and he did not know enough about Saint-Domingue to be interesting on that subject, the conversation was kept up only by gallant efforts on the part of the visitors. But at last it struck ten o'clock and he led them through several chilly stone passages to the Officers' Mess.

As British women were as rare at Mole St. Nicholas as flies in December at home, the thirty-odd officers assembled there greeted Georgina, Amanda and Clarissa with a tremendous ovation. But they had been through too much too recently to meet it with a genuine response. They did their best to show their appreciation of the many gallant toasts drunk to them, and did their utmost to disguise the accumulated weariness from which they were still suffering, but they, and Roger, Fergusson and Wilson too, were heartily glad when the New Year of 1795 had been ushered in with the singing of Auld Lang Syne, and they were at last free to take their departure.

Next day, after sleeping late and the luxury of another bath, Roger felt much more like his old self and, having found out where Madame de Bouçicault was living, he performed the sad duty of waiting upon her with the news of her husband's death. Then, on returning to the hotel, as he had nothing to do, he decided that it would be interesting to learn the views of a rich bourgeois on possible developments in Saint-Domingue. Accordingly, he sought out Monsieur Ducas and suggested that the landlord should join him in a bottle of wine.

Murmuring his appreciation of the honour '*Son Excellence le Gouverneur*' proposed to do him, the hotelier led Roger to his private sanctum and sent for a bottle of his best Chateauneuf-du-Pape. Soon, as Roger's French was so perfect, he kept forgetting that he was talking to an Englishman and in response to skilful leading questions began to give free rein of his beliefs.

He was a loyal Frenchman. In Saint-Domingue, just as in France, the nobility had been stupid, greedy and overbearing; so to begin with he had been all in favour of the Revolution which promised to pull them down a peg or two. But somehow everything had gone wrong. In Paris the demagogues had abandoned God and murdered their King. Then they had seized upon the discord in the colonies to further their criminal designs against all owners of property. To save themselves from wholesale massacres the colonists had been forced to call in the English. What else could they do? Yet France would in time become sane again, and Saint-Domingue was almost as much a part of her as Provence. So in due course it must be restored to the mother country. There would be difficulties of course. But it was to be hoped that the British would see the obvious necessity for this.

The great tragedy was, he added, that there a moderate Revolution could quite well have been effected without bloodshed. That it had been otherwise was due to the mulattoes. It was they who had first taken up arms, and had they not done so the negroes would never have followed their example.

'I thought,' remarked Roger, 'that tne mulattoes had played only for their own hand, because they realised that while liberal sentiment in pre-revolutionary France might gain for them equal rights with the whites, there could be no question of such rights being granted to the negroes.'

'That is true, *Monseigneur*. And, of course, many of the wealthier mulattoes were slave owners themselves. But once a country becomes divided against itself in civil war, who can say where the conflagration will stop? It was seeing the white planters murdered and their houses plundered that inflamed the minds of the negroes. But for that, the windy orations of the Terrorists sent out from Paris would in most cases have fallen on deaf ears. The slaves did not then understand what freedom meant, or want it. They were in the main quite contented with their lot.'

'You surprise me. Are you really convinced of that?'

'Indeed I am. When in France you must have seen how the peasants toil in the fields from dawn to dusk, and turn their women too into beasts of burden. It is the same in Italy and most other European countries; yet these people are free. The negroes were no worse off while working here in the cane-brakes.'

It was a new point of view to Roger. He remembered an occasion when he had breakfasted with Mr. Pitt. The Prime Minister's great friend William Wilberforce had been present, and had talked at considerable length on the horrors of the slave trade. Now, he repeated some of the statements Wilberforce had made to Monsieur Ducas.

The Frenchman shrugged. 'I do not deny that the conditions under which fresh cargoes of slaves are brought over from Africa are often appalling, and that many of them die from sickness or ill-treatment on the voyage. For that, *Monsiegneur,* I fear that your countrymen are mostly to blame, since "blackbirding", as it is called, has long been one of the most profitable fields of British enterprise. I spoke only of the condition of the slaves either born here or once they have been purchased by our colonists.

'I spoke, too, only of those who are put to the hardest manual labour. A high proportion of them were employed in shops, cafés, bars; as boatmen, coachmen, grooms, gardeners and house slaves. In most cases those so employed were much better off than people in similar occupations in Europe.'

'On what do you base that contention, Monsieur?'

'Because they had security. And that applied also to those who laboured in the fields. In Europe a workman is paid only as long as he is useful to his master. Should he fall sick he is dismissed and must live on charity. Should he be in no position to obtain it he starves. The situation of the slaves was very different. A good one cost up to 4,000 *livres* —in your money £160. They were therefore valuable properties. When they became ill their owners naturally took good care of them in order that they might soon become fit to work again. Moreover, food is very cheap here; so when they grew old and could work no more there was no question of turning them adrift, as happens in Europe. They were put on to light tasks suited to old people, then allowed to just sit about taking care of the piccaninnies, without being a burden to their relatives, until they died.'

Again Roger recalled previous conversations he had had bearing on the subject. For many generations the peasantry in England had been much better off than those on the continent, but in recent years great numbers of them had been forced to leave the land. The enclosures of the commons had in many cases deprived them of the free grazing, free fuel and other amenities they had long enjoyed. Then the spinning jenny and other inventions had sadly depleted the amounts they could earn by their cottage industries; so by the thousands they had migrated to the towns.

As long as they had remained cottagers, in bad times, or cases of personal misfortune, they had been able to turn to their landlords or the village parson for assistance; but once they became workers under the smoke clouds belched out from the chimneys of the new factories, no one any longer felt responsible for them as individuals.

In association with Sir Richard Arkwright, the Duke of Bridgewater, Josiah Wedgwood and other such industrial pioneers, Georgina's father, Colonel Thursby, had made his great fortune from the new canals and mechanical inventions. It was he who had told Roger that, too late in life, he now realised the misery that investors like himself were bringing to the people of the Midlands and the North. He had then described the desperate struggle for employment during periods when trade fell off; the starvation wages paid which necessitated women and children as well as men toiling in the mines for such long hours that only in summer did they see the light of day; the drunkenness in the filthy gin-shops on Saturday nights, which had become the only outlet for once decent men who when youths had taken their recreation in the gay gatherings at the hiring fairs, and such annual jollifications as beating the bounds, jumping St. John's bonfires, welcoming Jack-in-the-Green, and dancing round the village Maypole.

As Roger thought of these things he felt that Ducas had made a good case, and after a moment he said: 'You paint a very different picture, Monsieur, from what I had imagined slavery to be. But now that things here have come to such a pass, it seems to me that there is little hope of pacifying the country unless it is agreed once and for all that the slaves should be given their freedom.'

'But that is impossible!' exclaimed the Frenchman. '*Monseigneur* cannot have realised that our slaves form a large part of our fortunes. To suggest that we should surrender our right to their labour is much the same as proposing that we should give away our houses or land. Besides, unless the planters got back the capital invested in their slaves few of them could finance the payment of wages to them for many months, until paid for the produce they had raised. No; all we French loyalists are agreed that the slaves must continue to be slaves, otherwise this island will fall into final destitution and ruin.'

Roger thought that Ducas and his kind were displaying typical traits in the French mentality. They wanted the British to fight the negroes for them but keep the colony for France; and after the negroes had been defeated set the clock back four years by reinforcing slavery on those who had already freed themselves. He was tempted to remark that to cling to such ideas amounted to a refusal to face facts, but decided that to do so would not impinge on the Frenchman's narrow vision, so instead he said thoughtfully:

'All people of sensibility are now agreed that the slave trade is abhorrent; so perhaps a solution could be reached by first abolishing that, then entering into an understanding with the negroes here to the effect that all children born to them in future, instead of automatically also becoming slaves, should be free. Such a measure would protect the interests of present slave owners, yet lead in time to the complete abolition of slavery; so it is possible that if and when the negroes are defeated they might accept such terms.'

'No, no!' Ducas stubbornly shook his head. 'That would never do. In a generation or two there would be no slaves left. Without them we colonists would become terribly impoverished. The piccaninnies are our slave labour of tomorrow. To give them freedom at their birth would be to rob our own children of their just inheritance.'

There the conversation ended, as a messenger was announced from Colonel Seaton, who sent to say that a sloop of war would be sailing for Kingston next morning; so Roger finished his wine, excused himself and went upstairs to tell the others.

At eleven o'clock next day the Colonel escorted them on board. The accommodation in the little ship was very limited, but everything possible had been done for the comfort of the ladies, and after their recent experiences they were happily conscious of the safety on which they could count in sailing under the White Ensign. As soon as they had taken leave of the Colonel the ship cast off, made two short tacks, then with a good breeze behind her set course for Jamaica.

Early two mornings later they sighted Morant Point and a few hours afterwards came opposite Port Royal. They gazed at the now semi-derelict port with fascinated interest, as it had once been the most infamous town of the whole Spanish Main. In the days when Sir Henry Morgan had been Governor of Jamaica, and carried out his exploits against the Spaniards, freebooters of every nation had made it their favourite haunt after successful piracies. Thousands of pigs of silver and ingots of gold had changed hands there, jewelled crucifixes, necklaces of pearls and girdles flashing with inset diamonds, emeralds and rubies, had been bartered for a night's lechery, and millions of pieces-of-eight, doubloons and moidores been squandered in its scores of gaming-hells and brothels. But, like another judgment on Sodom and Gomorrah, in 1692, when at the peak of its riotous prosperity, it had been almost totally destroyed by a terrible earthquake.

Tacking again, the sloop nosed her way past the palisades up to Kingston harbour, and as soon as she docked the Lieutenant who commanded her sent a runner off to the Governor, Major General Williamson, to inform him about the passengers on board. Three-quarters of an hour later a young A.D.C. arrived with the General's compliments and a request that they would accompany him to Government House.

There, the Governor and his wife received them most kindly, insisting that they must stay at the Residence until they had settled their plans. Wilson alone courteously declined, as he had old friends in Kingston with whom he wished to stay. Monsieur Pirouet, Dan, Tom and the two sailors who had survived from the *Circe* were placed in charge of the steward with instructions that they were to have their every need supplied; then the others were taken by their host and hostess up to comfortable rooms gay with flowered muslins, leading on to a wide veranda. It was thus, after the hazards and discomforts of an eight-week ocean voyage, followed by six weeks of acute fears, sickness and distress, that they were once more able to savour to the full the pleasures of gracious living.

For some days they gave themselves up to it entirely while recuperating; lazing away the days in the richly furnished salons of the Residence or under the shade of palm trees on the lawns of its lovely garden. On two nights the Williamsons had already arranged dinner parties; on the others Roger and his host sat long over their port, as they had taken a great liking to one another.

General Williamson was a man of imagination and vigour, and it was he who, unasked, had sent the first help to the colonists in Saint-Domingue. He had also, the preceding summer, inspired the brilliant dash by British troops on Port-au-Prince, the splendid capital which, with its fine squares and beautiful buildings, rivalled any provincial city in France, and so had saved it from a similar fate to that which at the hands of the rum-maddened negroes had overtaken Cap Français. From these long conversations with him, Roger eagerly absorbed much invaluable counsel as to how best to conduct affairs when he too took up his duties as the Governor of a West Indian island.

By January the 8th, Roger's twenty-seventh birthday, the girls were well on their way to getting back their looks and, except for Georgina who still grieved for Charles, had recovered their spirits. Meanwhile, General Williamson had arranged credit facilities for Roger, which enabled them all to order new wardrobes, and by the end of the week, when the clothes began to arrive, they felt the time had come to settle plans for the future.

It was Fergusson who first actually raised the matter by saying that he could no longer afford to remain idle, and must set about trying to find a ship requiring a doctor, that would take him back to England. The capability, good sense and courage that he had displayed throughout had greatly impressed Roger; so he told the young doctor that, if he wished, he would find for him a much more remunerative post in Martinique, and Fergusson gladly accepted.

Georgina then said that Jake and Kilick deserved better for the loyalty they had shown than to be allowed to return to their hard life at sea, and that she would willingly find them some congenial employment with cottages to live in on her estate at Stillwaters, her lovely home in Surrey. But both men proved overjoyed at the prospect of future security from hardship and want in her service.

Later that day she told her friends that as she and Charles had talked so much of the happy time they hoped to have with his relations on the golden shores of St. Ann's Bay, now that she had been robbed of him she could no longer support the thought of going there; so she intended to return to England as soon as possible.

Amanda and Roger pressed her to spend the rest of the winter with them in Martinique, but she said that blue seas, palm trees and tropical sunshine were a constant reminder of her loss; so it was better that she should bury herself for a while among the friendly woods and green fields of England. When she consulted General Williamson about sailings he would not hear of her making the voyage in a trader, but said that a ship-of-the-line would be leaving within the next ten days, and that he would arrange with her Captain to carry home her ladyship and her servants.

Roger had not forgotten Clarissa's outbursts on the night she had lost herself in the forest on Tortuga; so next morning he took an opportunity to have a word with her alone. He told her that having thought matters over he had decided that it would be better for all concerned if she did not accompany Amanda and himself to Martinique, and that

Georgina's decision to return to England now offered an excellent opportunity for having her pleasantly chaperoned; so he wished her to make some suitable excuse to Amanda for going home.

For a few minutes Clarissa panicked, pleading wildly to be allowed to stay with them, and urging that it would be cruel in the extreme for him to send her back to a regime of prayers and near poverty with her Aunt Jane. Then, as she saw his jaw set stubbornly, she calmed down and said in a deceptively meek voice:

'Knowing the circumstances from which she rescued me, I think Amanda will be much surprised. What excuse do you suggest that I should make for leaving her?'

'You could say that all that you have suffered in the Indies has given you a nausea of them; and that like Georgina you'll know no tranquillity of mind until you can get away from the sight of negroes and sun-scorched beaches.'

Suddenly she laughed. 'I could, Roger, but I won't. If you are determined to get rid of me, you must think of some way yourself to make Amanda send me home.'

For a moment he was silent, then his eyes began to twinkle. He knew that she had got him, and by just the sort of subtle trick that he admired. 'You wicked baggage,' he admonished her with a grin. 'You know as well as I do that I would never disclose to Amanda my real reason for wishing you to leave us; and there is no other I can give her. So be it then. Let's hope that I can find you a promising young soldier in Martinique, to give your mind a new occupation.'

In consequence Clarissa, after all, accompanied Roger, Amanda, Dan and Fergusson, when they too left Jamaica in a warship. General Williamson had insisted that the least he could do for a fellow Governor was to send him on his way in a frigate, and as there was nothing to delay their departure, they sailed five days earlier than Georgina. After fond farewells, and most heartfelt thanks to the Williamsons for all their kindness, they were waved away from Kingston's quay on January the 18th, and after a fair passage docked at Fort Royal, Martinique, early on the morning of the 24th.

While the passengers were dressing the Captain sent

ashore to inform the acting Governor of the new Governor's arrival, so that an official welcome could be prepared for him. Soon the harbour front became crowded with coloured folk who heard the news and were eager to witness the proceedings. Next a regiment of British red-coats and a squadron of Hanoverian cavalry appeared to form a guard of honour. By then the Captain of the frigate had dressed ship, and had all his tars and marines on parade. Two A.D.C.'s came aboard, saluted Roger and were duly presented to the smiling ladies. A minute gun began to fire a salute from the fortress. The band struck up 'The British Grenadiers'. The senior A.D.C. murmured to Roger that the time had come for 'His Excellency' to land.

Dressed in his best new suit, and fully conscious both that this was a great moment in his life and that he cut a fine figure, Roger walked with a firm step down the gangway. A warm smile lit his handsome face as he glanced from side to side at the people to whom by his Sovereign's will his word would henceforth be law.

Suddenly, the smile was wiped from his lips. A stalwart, square shouldered, red-faced man dressed in a Colonel's uniform was advancing to meet him. Obviously this must be the acting Governor. It was also the man who as a boy had bullied Roger fiendishly at their public school; a pig-headed brute whom he hated and despised, named George Gunston. There was no one in the world whom he would not rather have had to collaborate with him in his new duties.

16

His Excellency the Governor

With every eye upon them there was no escape from shaking hands. As they did so Gunston gave a slightly derisive smile and murmured: 'At your service, Mr. Brook. You will find a pretty kettle of fish here; but as your talents are evidently considered superior to my own I wish you joy in handling it.'

Gunston had once wooed Amanda so, although Roger had won her, she still regarded the freckled, red-headed soldier as an old friend, and when the ladies came down the gangway she exclaimed:

'Why George! How lovely to find you here.'

'The pleasure is all mine, M'am,' he replied with a grin. 'This is the most God-forsaken station I've ever been on so the society of some English ladies will prove a rare blessing.'

As he spoke his eyes switched to Clarissa, taking in her young loveliness with evident appreciation, and Amanda presented him to her.

Roger next inspected the guard of honour, then the party moved off to a row of open carriages that had been drawn up behind the troops. According to protocol Roger and Gunston got into the first, while Amanda and Clarissa were escorted to the second by the two A.D.C.'s. The band struck up again and they drove off.

At an order the troops raised their shakoes and gave three cheers. Some of the coloured folk joined in the cheering, but most of the whites and mulattoes in the crowd remained silent.

'Sullen lot, these lousy Frogs,' remarked Gunston. 'But I

stand no nonsense, and have been keeping them well under my thumb.'

'Would it not have been a better policy to endeavour to win them over by conciliation?' replied Roger quietly.

The young Colonel gave a sneering laugh. 'There speaks 'Bookworm Brook', the little toady that I used to lick at Sherborne. You can't have changed much to advocate a policy of toadying to the French. But I suppose it was toadying to Mr. Pitt that got you your Governorship.'

'Listen, Gunston,' Roger said with an edge on his voice. 'I could call you out for that. But we have already fought one duel with pistols, and rather than expose you to the possibility of being cashiered for fighting another, I gave you satisfaction a second time before an audience of both sexes with buttons on the foils. In that I proved by far the better swordsman, and I could kill you tomorrow morning if the choice of weapons lay with me.'

'I'm in better practice now,' Gunston retorted, 'and I'm game to take you on with the buttons off any time you like.'

'I have never doubted your courage, but you have not heard me out. I have no intention of either giving or accepting a challenge in your case. I have been sent here for a purpose which I mean to do my best to fulfil. You, too, are in the King's service. Having been thrown together in this way is most unfortunate, seeing that we have a natural antipathy for one another. But as your superior I shall expect from you a prompt obedience to my orders, and a reasonable politeness. Should you fail in either, I warn you here and now, I shall have you placed under arrest for insubordination.'

Gunston shrugged. 'You need have no fears about my doing my duty; and you are right in that for the sake of the Service it would be a bad thing for us to be at cross purposes. But there is still much antagonism to the British here; so this is a soldier's job, and you will be well advised to be guided by me in all measures for keeping the population under.'

'I shall certainly consult you, but form my own judgment in due course,' replied Roger quietly. And that closed the conversation.

Meanwhile the carriage had carried them through streets which had some fine examples of Louis XIV and Louis XV architecture and up a steep winding road to the Governor's Residence. It was a large chateau and still contained many handsome pieces of furniture, carpets, tapestries and pictures which had been collected there by a long line of noble governors during the *ancien régime*. Its tropical garden was gay with flowers and from its situation high up on the hill there was a lovely view over the five mile wide bay to a famous beauty spot called Trois Ilets on the opposite shore.

As they got out at its entrance and the A.D.C.'s handed the ladies down from their carriage, Gunston looked towards them and remarked: 'That's a fine little filly that Amanda's brought with her. I must put her through her paces.'

'You will treat Miss Marsham with every respect!' snapped Roger. 'Or find yourself accountable to me.'

'Indeed!' A mocking smile appeared on Gunston's ruddy countenance. 'Does your Excellency's authority then extend to prohibiting your staff from polite attentions to young ladies?'

With an angry frown Roger turned away. Gunston had him there, and as he was a fine dashing figure of a man many women found him attractive. After a time, Clarissa might well yield to his experienced wooing, and while Roger had persuaded himself that he would be glad for her to have an *affaire* with someone like one of the young A.D.C's, the thought of her in Gunston's arms made him seethe with impotent rage.

Having acknowledged the greetings of a staff of some thirty coloured servants who had been assembled to welcome their new master and mistress, Roger said to Gunston: 'Please take me to the room in which you transact your business.'

'Damn!' the Colonel muttered in a low voice. 'After getting us all up at an ungodly hour by your early arrival this morning, surely you do not mean to start work now the hottest part of the day is approaching? You won't last long here if you play those sort of games.'

'I am anxious to have the latest news out of Europe,' Roger replied coldly; so with just the suggestion of a merry wink at Clarissa, Gunston led him away to a pleasant room at the back of the house overlooking the bay. There, Gunston rang a handbell, which brought a negro footman hurrying in with the ingredients for a 'planter's punch' and while mixing the drink the Colonel began to comply with Roger's request.

''Tis said that my Lady Southwell gave birth to a child covered with hair, and that it matched in colour the beard of the Netherlands Envoy, who has long pursued her. So the wits have made a rhyme on it that runs:

> The Dutchman, bearded like a goat,
> has at last had his Southwell.
> But it cost him a fur coat.'

Had anyone else told Roger this silly story he would have laughed. Instead he said impatiently: 'I am not interested in scandal. I want the latest particulars you have of our war against the French.' Yet even as he said it he felt that he was being horribly pompous, and acting like a man twenty years older than Gunston rather than one two years his junior; although as far as their mentalities were concerned the former was the case.

'Ah well!' The Colonel shrugged his broad shoulders. 'You shall have it, then, though there's little enough to tell. Some three months ago the French sent an expedition to recapture Corsica, but it was driven off. In all other theatres they are still getting the best of it. General Jourdan has had several successes on the Rhine and Pichegru has invaded the Low Countries.'

'I learned that from General Williamson whilst in Jamaica. Is there no later news?'

'Not of the war; but from the news-sheets carried by a packet that arrived here three days ago I gather that in Paris more members of the old Terrorist gang are meeting with their just deserts at the hands of the Reactionaries.

You may have heard of a brute named Carrier, who drowned hundreds of poor wretches at Nantes. An honest fellow named Fouché brought tears to the eyes of his fellow deputies when describing this monster's vile crimes, and so secured his death.'

Suddenly Roger laughed. 'Honest fellow! My God, Gunston; if you only knew! Fouché was responsible for the murder of near as many people in Lyons as Carrier was in Nantes. Yet such an act is typical of him. His capacity for hypocrisy is bottomless; although I would have scarce thought, considering all those other rogues know of him, that he could have succeeded in staging such a volte-face. Still, it only goes to show that power remains in the hands of the extremists, and they are still at their old game of cutting one another's throats.'

'You know this man Fouché, then?'

Roger forebore to say that the mutual hatred between Fouché and himself was even deeper than that he bore Gunston, and nodded. 'Yes; as Mr. Pitt's agent in France I have had to have dealings with most of these cannibals at one time or another.'

'I fear I should have found your late occupation, to say the least, repugnant.'

Ignoring the covert sneer, Roger asked: 'What else?'

'There was one item of local interest in the despatch which arrived with the packet. It seems that although the Spaniards are our allies, their people in Santo Domingo are assisting the negro army against us by furnishing it with supplies and weapons; so my Lord Grenville has instructed our Ambassador in Madrid to demand that Don Garcia, the Governor of the Colony, should be recalled.'

'I am glad to hear it; for I have recently been in that island, and had intended to inform Whitehall of the perfidy of the Spaniards.'

Gunston began to mix them another drink, and while doing so said: 'In the confidential news circular that accompanied the despatch there was much about the situation in Poland; but I don't suppose you would be interested in that.'

'On the contrary. The ill success of the allied armies on

the Scheldt and Rhine has been almost entirely due to the Prussians and Austrians both holding a large part of their forces in reserve, lest Catherine of Russia seize the whole of Poland whilst their backs are turned. So I am very interested indeed. Pray tell me of it.'

'Strap me! I had no idea of that.' The Colonel raised his ginger eyebrows. 'Well, apparently, last spring, the Russians, who were exercising a sort of protective custody in a large part of Poland, feared a rising aimed at driving them out; so they decided to disarm the Polish troops. Their attempts to do so put the fat in the fire. There was a lot of fighting in Cracow, Warsaw and other Polish cities, which ended in the Russians getting pushed out. Then a Polish patriot named Kosciusko got an army together with the idea of liberating the whole of Poland; but he had the Prussians, who were occupying another sector of the country, on his hands as well as the Russians. They inflicted a severe defeat upon him and proceeded to invest Warsaw. But Polish partisans played the very devil with their lines of supply; so in September they were forced to raise the siege.'

Roger already knew all this, but he waited patiently for his informant to go on. Gunston poured the fresh drinks and continued.

'The Poles weren't given the chance to remain cock-a-hoop for very long. An Austrian army had started to invade their country from the south, the Prussians were still to the west of them, and a new Russian army under a General Suvóroff was advancing upon them from the north. Early in October Kosciusko went out to try to prevent two Russian forces joining up and his army was utterly routed. He was taken prisoner and in the first week of November, after a frightful slaughter, Suvóroff captured Warsaw. That put an end to the last hope the wretched Poles had of regaining their independence.'

'Then we may assume that Russia, Prussia and Austria are now squabbling over the bones of Poland's carcass. This explains why the French have been able to invade the Low Countries. Last spring my Lord Malmesbury negotiated a pact with King Frederick William of Prussia to send

62,000 troops there in return for further subsidies from us and the Dutch. He will have taken the money and by now have gone back on his word.'

Gunston gave Roger a puzzled glance. 'You are right there. I recall now that in the confidential summary there was a passage to the effect that towards the end of October, on some trumped up excuse, the Prussians had denounced a treaty with the Maritime Powers by which more troops were to be sent against the French. But how did you know of it?'

'I did not know it; but it is my business to judge what repercussions events in one place are likely to have in others. And now, if you will produce the most recent despatches from London, I will look through them for myself.'

Having unlocked a cabinet, Gunston handed Roger its key and a bundle of papers; then he said: 'I gave orders this morning for the removal of my personal belongings to a house nearer the town. If you have done with me for the present I will go and see that my instructions have been carried out.'

'By all means.' Roger made him a semi-formal bow, then added: 'But I should be glad if you would make arrangements for me to inspect both the fortress and its outlying batteries tomorrow morning. May I count upon you calling for me at eight o'clock?'

'By all means.' Gunston grinned at him again. 'As a civilian you can know little of such matters; but, providing you keep your mouth shut, the inspection you suggest may favourably impress the men.' With this parting shot, and his sabre-tache banging on his thigh, the stalwart Colonel swaggered from the room.

He little knew the surprise that was in store for him. Less then a year previously Carnot, the greatest Minister of War that France had ever known, had sent Roger to inspect the fortifications of Brest and then Boulogne, and had complimented him on his reports. During his inspection next morning he kept up a running commentary of pertinent questions and picked upon every weakness of the defences with an eagle's eye that a senior General might have envied. Gunston was left amazed and breathless.

The inspection satisfied Roger that from a purely military point of view Gunston knew his business. The discipline was good, the troops were being kept up to the mark with frequent drills, exercises and practice in taking stations at an alarm; and, as far as the capital was concerned, the disposition of its garrison was sound. But he was appalled when he learned the number of men who had died since Admiral Sir John Jervis had captured the island and left Gunston there as its Garrison Commander, with two regiments of Foot and some auxiliary troops. He was, too, greatly concerned by the sick lists that he had demanded to see, and the fate of the several hundred men who now lay in hospital; the more so as on his ordering that they should all be dosed daily with an infusion of Cinchona bark, he learned that the plant was not grown in the island, and that the drug itself could be obtained only in small quantities.

Another matter that worried him was the hostile attitude of the island's inhabitants. As the garrison was small and much weakened by sickness, he felt that, as a temporary measure, Gunston's policy of repression might possibly be justified; but to maintain it permanently could lead nowhere. Henry Dundas, with his sound common sense, had said that if the captured islands were to prove real assets, rather than a drain on British resources, their peoples must be weaned from their old allegiance, and brought to realise that under the British flag they would enjoy more individual liberty, together with a greater security and prosperity, than they had done under the flag of France. Roger was fully in sympathy with the Minister's policy, and determined to carry it out.

As a first step in the one matter he instructed Fergusson to investigate and make a full report to him on the state of things in the hospitals; on the other, from lack of more promising counsel, he consulted Gunston, inquiring how best he could get a message to the people.

The Colonel said that his own method had been to have what he wanted to say translated into French, printed off and posted up in the principal towns of the island. Then if such fresh regulations as he had issued were ignored, he had a few people who had infringed them arrested and flung into prison, thus ensuring his orders a much wider publicity.

When Roger told him that this practice was anything but suitable for the object he had in mind, Gunston said: 'Well, you can always try your luck with the Assembly. It is a collection of notables who in the old days used to make recommendations to the Governor. When Sir John Jervis took over it was decided that it should not be abolished, but remain quiescent, so that it could be summoned as required for any special purpose. On the few occasions that I've had its members called together I've found them noisy and truculent. But it's just possible that they might give you a hearing.'

On this, Roger asked that they should be assembled in three days' time; then he gave considerable thought to composing an address, the keystone of which was the verbal message the King had given him when he kissed hands, expressing his intention to have a good care for the interests of his new subjects in Martinique.

When the day came Roger had no reason to complain of Gunston's arrangements. A troop of Hanoverian cavalry had been detailed to escort his coach and British red-coats lined the approaches to the Assembly Hall. Gunston, the senior Naval officer in the port, the Mayor and numerous other French officials were gathered on its steps to receive him. Having acknowledged their greetings, he drew himself up to his full six feet, and, followed by them, marched into the building. He was directed to a curtained archway which led on to a dais at one end of the hall. Two footmen drew aside the curtains. Flushing with mortification and rage he halted between them. Every bench in the hall was empty.

For a moment he was utterly at a loss, then he turned about and marched straight back to his coach. As he got in, he beckoned Gunston to accompany him. He felt that he had been made a complete fool of, and that his *bête noire* was responsible. Now, white to the lips with fury, he snapped:

'What's the meaning of this?'

'Don't ask me,' the Colonel replied quite calmly. 'I had the notices sent out as you directed. But I did warn you that they are an unruly lot of bastards. I suppose they got together beforehand and decided to ignore the summons to attend you.'

'You must have known that the hall was empty.'

'How could I? It's not my business to act as usher to a crowd of Frogs and see them into their seats. I never went inside the building until I entered it behind you.'

There seemed no reply to that; yet Roger remained convinced that Gunston must have known, or at least suspected, that he was about to be made the laughing stock of Fort Royal. He was, moreover, intensely annoyed by the thought that such an affront to himself, as the representative of his Sovereign, could not be allowed to pass without his taking some appropriate action.

Gunston suggested that the obvious course was to arrest some of the leading deputies and send them to cool their heels in prison until they learned better manners; but Roger was most loath to antagonise them still further. After some thought that evening he penned a circular letter to be sent to each of them, which read as follows:

His Excellency the Governor appreciates that in every occupation a new hand is expected to pay his footing, and should not resent jokes played upon him. But the repetition of a joke deprives it of its humour.

His Excellency had intended to convey to the Assembly a message of goodwill from His Majesty the King, and also to announce the relaxation of certain restrictions. He therefore counts upon a full attendance of deputies when they are next summoned, for the betterment of relations between the Government and people of Martinique.

This, Roger felt, would not only save his face but evoke considerable surprise and discussion; and, in order that his good intentions might have ample time to become generally known, he decided not to summon the Assembly again until another week or ten days had elapsed.

Meanwhile he thought it would be a good plan to spend a few nights in St. Pierre, the oldest settlement in the island, which had since become a fine city and the centre of its commerce. It was only some fifteen miles away along the coast, but there was another Governor's Residence there; so he sent orders for rooms in it to be prepared for him, and despatched Dan and his new negro body-servant by coach in advance.

Gunston's two A.D.C's had automatically been transferred to him on his arrival. To one of them, a tall fair-haired youth named Colin Cowdray, he at once took a liking, but the other was a boorish Captain whose sole conversation consisted of grumbles that he was missing the fox hunting in England; so after a few days Roger had returned him to Gunston, saying that he would, in due course, replace him with another officer more to his taste. Accompanied therefore only by Colin Cowdray and a groom Roger set out on horseback late one afternoon for St. Pierre.

A Colonel Penruddock, who commanded the garrison there, received him with due honours and entertained him to an excellent dinner. Penruddock, a man in his late thirties, came of an old Cornish family which had fought for Charles I during the Great Rebellion, and Roger found him both efficient and congenial. The following day they made a round of the fortifications, and the next an excursion through ever steepening jungle-fringed paths to the summit of Monte Pelée, the great volcano five miles inland from St. Pierre, which one hundred and seven years later was fated totally to destroy the city.

On the third afternoon, pleased by all that he had seen, but much worried at having learned that the 57th Regiment of Foot, stationed in St. Pierre, was as severely stricken by Yellow Fever as the troops in Fort Royal, he took the road back. They had not gone far when Colin Cowdray's mare cast a shoe; so Roger told him to return and have her shod, while he rode on with the groom.

Presently he came abreast of a small but charming property; and, reining in, asked an elderly negro engaged on clearing out a ditch at the side of the road who lived there.

To his surprise the old fellow replied that the house belonged to a Madame de Kay.

Dismounting, Roger gave the bridle of his horse to his groom and walked up the short drive. On a veranda before the house a coloured maid was laying a small table; so he told her who he was and asked her to request her mistress to allow him to pay his respects to her.

The maid went in but returned with the reply that her mistress begged to be excused, as she was averse to receiving the Governor in her house.

Roger frowned at this new evidence of the dislike with which the British were regarded, but sent the girl back with another message to say that he would much like to talk to her mistress about her son William's early marriage to a Mademoiselle Tascher de la Pagerie.

A few minutes later a grey haired lady wearing a lawn mob cap, a tight bodice, voluminous black skirts, and carrying an ebony cane, came out of the house.

When Roger had made a leg to her curtsy, she said: 'I am much surprised, Monsieur, that you should know aught of my son's marriage—if indeed it can be termed so, for it has long been regarded as invalid.'

'That, Madame,' Roger smiled, 'I gathered from a handsome mulatto woman called Lucette; and it was she who recently told me of it.'

'Then that limb of Satan is still alive?'

'Yes. And I was so intrigued by the youthful romance she related, in which she said she had played a part, that on learning that you lived here I felt I must find out how much, if any of it, was true. On second thoughts, though, I fear you must regard my curiosity as an impertinence, and the means I used to overcome your reluctance to receive me an aggravation of it.'

Making a slight inclination of the head, she said: 'You were announced to me as the Governor; so I thought you to be the brutish young Colonel who lords it in Fort Royal and rides rough-shod over all our susceptibilities.'

He gave a rueful smile. 'Alas, Madame, from what I have gathered there are good grounds for the antipathy you display towards him. I am the new Governor, and landed but ten days ago. As I have lived long in France and am accustomed to French ways, I hope before long to give people here cause to form a better opinion of myself.'

Her face softened then, and she gestured with her long cane towards the table. 'In that case, as I was about to partake of a dish of tea, perhaps you would care to join me?'

'Indeed I would; and for me it will be a treat, as tea is so hard to come by in these coffee islands.'

As they enjoyed the brew he described how the *Circe* had been captured and how Lucette's duplicity, after she had made Bloggs second-in-command of the ship, had nearly cost him and his party their lives.

In turn she told him that she had lost her husband during a hurricane that had swept the island in '91; but that William was still alive and well, although he now lived for long periods in England. He had continued to be in love with Josephine, and she with him; but after she had sacrificed her feelings for her duty to her parents, and married according to their wish, he had been persuaded to secure the family fortunes by marrying Lord Lovell's niece. Josephine's aunt had fulfilled her promise to the de Taschers by finding a rich *parti* for her; and in '79 she had been wed to the Vicomte Alexandre de Beauharnais.

'Surely that would have been the General who was sent to the guillotine by the Terrorists in '94?' Roger put in.

Madame de Kay nodded. 'Yes; and poor Josephine also came within an ace of losing her head. I still frequently see her parents, and when they learned that she had been thrown into prison they were greatly worried for her. Mercifully, like many other innocent people, she was saved by the fall of Robespierre, and through the good offices of a Monsieur Tallien restored to her distracted children.'

With a boyish grin, Roger took the last scone from a plate that Madame de Kay had been offering him, and said:

'I pray you forgive my greed; but it is years since I have tasted scones the equal of those my dear mother used to make.'

'She must, then,' his hostess smiled, 'like myself, have been born north of the Tweed.'

'Yes, she was a MacElfic.'

Madame de Kay nearly dropped the plate. 'Mercy be! But I was born a MacElfic too. And did you not say your name was Brook? It was an English naval officer of that name that pretty Marie ran away with. You must be their son.'

'I am indeed. My mother, alas, died three years ago; but my father is still alive and is now Admiral Sir Christopher Brook. It seems, then, that you knew my mother?'

'Knew her, dear boy!' There were tears in Madame de Kay's eyes, and she laid her hand gently on Roger's. 'Why, we were cousins, and in girlhood the closest friends.'

For a moment Roger was thunderstruck; then he said; 'I recall hearing my mother speak of a cousin named Margaret whom she would fain have seen again. But after her elopement with my father he severely wounded her brother in a duel; so from a double cause the two families remained permanently at daggers drawn.'

Madame de Kay nodded. 'There was also the original cause for illwill, in that we had a passionate devotion to the Stuarts, while your father was hot in favour of the Hanoverian line. But it is overtime that old quarrels on that score should be forgotten.'

While two hours passed like twenty minutes, Roger talked with his new-found kinswoman, telling her of his life, and of his hopes of bringing tranquillity to Martinique. She gladly promised to aid him in that, with the many friends she had made among the leading families of the island during her long residence on it. Then as dusk fell he kissed her, promised soon to bring Amanda to see her, and walked down the drive to reclaim his mount from the patient groom. As he rode back to the capital, he felt that sheer luck had given him the key to the most difficult of his problems.

But he had yet to resolve that of Colonel George Gunston.

The crisis between them arose two days later. On Roger's return from St. Pierre, Fergusson had handed in his report. It was a grim document. It stated that the hospitals were insanitary; that the food given to the sick was unsuitable and often unfit for human consumption; that the military surgeons were few and mostly drunken incompetents; that French civilian doctors refused to give their aid because they had been subjected to unbearable insults; that the nursing orderlies were callous, slothful and corrupt, and that medical supplies were almost non-existent.

Roger sent for Gunston, made him read the report, then said: 'I have decided that drastic measures must be taken. I intend to appoint Fergusson as Surgeon-in-chief. I shall give him absolute powers to take all measures he sees fit to cleanse these pest houses and ensure proper nursing for the sick. More, I will have arrested and tried by court-martial any of the army surgeons who ignore his instructions or fail to keep the orderlies under them up to the mark and so lose a patient through neglect.'

Gunston gave a low whistle. 'The devil you will! Then you will be bringing a hornets' nest about your ears. Were you an Army man you would realise that the medicos are a law unto themselves.'

'A fig for that!' Roger gave a grim little laugh. 'You have yet to learn that does the occasion warrant it I can be far more ruthless than yourself. It is true that I have never held an officer's commission; but I was sent as *Représentant en Mission* to General Dumouriez during his first Flanders campaign. His army was then largely a rabble of murderous *sans-culottes,* and as it was necessary for me to win the General's confidence, several mornings each week, I had a dozen or two of them shot behind the nearest barn, so that from fear of me the others might more readily obey the orders given them.'

A strange look came into Gunston's eyes, and he muttered: 'I had no idea you were that sort of man, Brook. I'll say no more then. These croakers need a lesson and it seems you are the fellow to give it to them.'

Roger nodded, and went on: 'That is but part of my plan. 'Tis my belief that fresh air and, particularly, sea breezes are what the garrison needs to restore it to health. In consequence it is my intention to commandeer all the merchant shipping lying both in the harbour here and in that of St. Pierre. Such sick as can be moved are to be put aboard, together with two-thirds of the men still considered fit for duty; and the whole are to be taken for a fortnight's cruise.'

'God Almighty!' exclaimed Gunston. 'You cannot mean this!'

'I certainly do.'

'You can't! You must be crazy! Your scheme for setting the doctors by the ears is a mere bagatelle to this. It is utterly preposterous!'

'Why so?'

'Surely you have the sense to realise that death and sickness have already reduced our strength below the safety limit. Did you send two-thirds of our remaining effectives to sea it would be as good as handing the island back to the French on a platter. They would rise and seize it overnight.'

'In that I think you wrong,' Roger replied quietly. 'I have good hopes that if due precautions are taken they will not rise at all. In the worse case they might, perhaps, capture the fortress; but. . . .'

'Capture the fortress!' Gunston's eyes seemed about to pop out of his head. 'How can you sit there and contemplate such a disaster. It is nothing short of treachery. Yes, treachery!'

'I was about to add that I intend to keep two of the outlying batteries fully manned. In the event of trouble their guns could be trained on the town, and, much as I would regret to do so, I should not hesitate to give the order for its bombardment as a means of bringing to reason any part of the population which had taken up arms against us.'

'No! No!' Violently Gunston shook his head. 'No, no, no! The risk involved of losing the island altogether is too great. Send the sick to sea if you will. Although, in their weak state, I'd have thought the tossing they must receive would have been more like to kill them than cure them. But not the men still fit for duty. That would be madness.'

'I do not agree. They may be counted fit on your duty roster, but that many are not so in fact was plain to me when I made my inspection. Few had the ruddy faces that one associates with vigorous health, and quite a number were lean-cheeked and too bright-eyed: a sure indication that the fever was already working in them. Two-thirds of them, that Fergusson shall pick out for me, must be sent for a sea voyage, Gunston; so make up your mind to that.'

The Colonel had already come to his feet. Now he thumped Roger's desk with his fist, and cried: 'I'll be damned if I will! I am the Garrison Commander, and I'll not see our hold on the island jeopardised for some cranky notion about bettering the health of my men.'

'I am its Governor,' retorted Roger. 'And, if God so wills, I would rather see it lost to the British Crown through the action that I propose to take, than stand by while His Majesty's troops are so reduced by death from fever that there are no longer enough of them to man its batteries.'

'You fool!' stormed Gunston. 'Have you never heard of such a thing as reinforcements? I have already written home urging their despatch. It is true that Whitehall always leaves such requests in abeyance until the last moment. But our people there are not quite such numbskills as to risk losing Martinique for the lack of another few Companies. If you are determined upon this mad scheme of yours, you must wait to enter upon it until reinforcements have reached us.'

Roger too now stood up. His long lashes almost veiled the anger that was in his blue eyes, but his jaw stuck out, as he said harshly: 'I'll not wait a day to start upon it. You have heard the orders that I intend to give. Should you attempt to thwart them you shall face a court-martial.'

'I'll not be bullied into criminal complaisance!' bellowed Gunston. 'Your infatuation with the lousy French has induced you to plan a means of selling us out to them. This is treason! Nothing less! 'Tis my duty to resist the measures you contemplate to the limit of my powers. To-morrow I'll despatch an officer to General Williamson. I'll warn him of what's afoot, and urge him to use his powers as Commander-in-Chief to suspend you.'

Roger's eyes opened wide with a disconcerting suddenness. He had now got Gunston where he wanted him, and his voice held a new sinister silkiness, as he said: 'Oh no, you won't. Instead you will leave tomorrow yourself, carrying a despatch from me to General Williamson setting forth the reasons for our difference of opinion. You see, I am fair enough to recognise that yours is an honest one, and by making you my messenger I give you a better opportunity than myself to convince him that you are right.'

Gunston's plump cheeks turned almost purple. 'You swine!' he cried. 'You're gambling on the General being too chicken-hearted to interfere with a political appointment, and mean to rob me of my command by refusing to have me back.'

Roger nodded. 'That is so. For once you are proving quite intelligent.'

'Damn it, I won't go!' Gunston roared. 'I refuse to walk into this dirty trap that you have laid for me.'

'Should you do so,' Roger shrugged, 'I shall be compelled to regard such flagrant disobedience in time of war as open mutiny. For that I could have you shot.' His eyes seemed to become entirely soulless as he added: 'A while back I deliberately took occasion to inform you that I have often watched firing squads carry out my orders; and, believe me, the sight of your dead body would not give me a single qualm.'

Gunston had no doubt that Roger meant what he said. He almost felt the icy hand of death closing round his heart. Slowly his mouth fell open in sheer horror; then, turning, his sabre-tache no longer banging on a gallantly swung thigh, he walked from the room.

Sitting down, Roger calmly began to write the despatch that his defeated enemy was to carry to General Williamson.

With Gunston's departure, Roger's affairs soon took a turn for the better. He appointed a sound-minded middle-aged Colonel of Artillery, named Thurgood, as the new Garrison Commander. Then, he wrote to Colonel Penruddock informing him of his plans to send the greater part of the troops in Fort Royal for a fortnight's cruise. He added that should the experiment prove successful he meant to do the same with those at St. Pierre; but that for the time being they were to be held in a state of readiness; so that should the French in the capital attempt a rising they could swiftly be marched upon it.

Two days later he took Amanda and Clarissa out to meet Madame de Kay. She welcomed Amanda with delight and, after exclaiming at Clarissa's beauty, declared that she would find a rich husband for her from among the nobility of Martinique.

As they again sat over the tea-cups, she told Roger of a plan she had formed for bettering his relations with the colonists. She meant to give a garden party where he could meet all her influential friends, and the invitations to it had already gone out. But they said nothing of his being the Governor, stating only that her young kinsman had recently arrived in the island and she wished to present him to them. It was decided that Amanda and Clarissa should not attend the party, as should they do so they would either have to prevaricate when asked about themselves or give away Roger's official position, and the intention was for him to avoid doing that for as long as possible.

The party was held a week later and as none of the guests had previously seen Roger, apart from a few who had caught a distant sight of him while driving through the town, it was over an hour before a rumour began to run round that he was the new Governor. Up till then he had met all enquiries by a casual statement that he was in the Government service; but upon being openly challenged on his identity by an elderly Marquis, he laughed and admitted it.

Meanwhile, by his frank smile, perfect French, and polished manners, he had charmed half a hundred people. When they learned that he was the Governor a few of the most bitter Anglophobes showed some resentment at the trick that had been played upon them, and left soon afterwards. But the majority were people of sense, who realised that they owed the preservation of their lives and properties from the terrorists Victor Hugues had sent there to the intervention of the British. It was Gunston's insults and his needlessly repressive measures that had antagonised them, and now that they had met Roger they were quite prepared to give him a fair chance to redress matters.

Among them were a number of deputies who congratulated him upon the skilful way in which he had passed off as a joke their non-appearance when summoned to the Assembly. From them he learned that he had been right in his surmise that Gunston knew what would happen. On the last occasion when they had met he had brought drummer boys into the chamber with him, and each time the deputies had begun a protest on any point he had had their voices drowned by ordering a roll of drums; so they had publicly announced their intention of ignoring any further summonses to attend. But now they said they would talk to their fellow deputies, and that Roger could be sure of a good attendance whenever he chose to summon them again.

He did so a week later with most satisfactory results. Having delivered the King's message, and announced the repeal of numerous edicts which gave offence, he spoke to them of conditions in Guadalupe, which had been retaken from the British, before they had had time to fully establish themselves there, and how Victor Hugues had since butchered every priest and person of property in that island. Then he told them of his own experiences in Saint-Domingue, and how that colony had been brought to utter ruin by the dissensions of its inhabitants. Finally he pointed out that in Martinique they had been spared from the fate which had overtaken the colonists in other French territories only because the British had arrived there before the Terror in France had reached its height. But, he added, the danger was not yet past. If the French inhabitants continued to bear ill-will to the British Authorities, evil men would take advantage of their differences and, perhaps, stir up a new and greater slave rebellion which, owing to his garrison having been so weakened by sickness, it might prove beyond his powers to put down. Therefore, the two nationalities must stand shoulder to shoulder, and the colonists must give loyal obedience to such new decrees as he might issue in the name of His Majesty King George III who had sent them this message of goodwill.

He had hardly ceased speaking before he knew that he

had succeeded beyond his most sanguine hopes. The difficulty they had had in putting down the first slave revolts was still fresh in their minds, and they lived in constant fear of fresh outbreaks. His frank confession about the weakness of his garrison, and his plea for unity among the white population, had gone straight to their hearts. For ten minutes on end they gave him a tremendous ovation.

The following day, with full confidence that he need fear no trouble, as Fergusson's arrangements were already completed, Roger ordered to sea the ships on which the sick and seedy had been embarked. Then, with Amanda's help, he entered on arrangements for a great reception, at which Madame de Kay—or Cousin Margaret as she now asked them to call her—was to present the ladies of the island. It was held on March the 4th, and proved another triumph. From then onward Roger knew that he had both the official and social leaders of French opinion in the island solidly behind him.

Had Georgina's father, the shrewd Colonel Thursby, been there to witness these events he would have had good cause to smile. For it was he who had said on the night that Roger had received his appointment that, in making it, Mr. Pitt had shown not only generosity but sound good sense, as there were few men better fitted to rule a colony recently taken from the French than Roger Brook.

By early March further news had come in from Europe. That extraordinarily astute diplomat, Catherine of Russia, had outwitted the Prussians by entering into a pact with the Emperor of Austria for the partitioning of Poland. It was true that Prussian troops were in occupation of a considerable part of Poland, but in the face of such an alliance the Prussians would now have no alternative but to accept the Empress's decisions on how the remnant of that unfortunate country was to be permanently split up among the three powers concerned.

The transfer of a great part of the Prussian army to the east was now having disastrous effects upon the Allies in the west. The French Army of the Rhine, under General Jourdan, was carrying all before it on a front stretching from Cleves to Coblenz, and another under Pichegru had penetrated to Amsterdam, where the French had been welcomed as liberators by the Dutch republicans. Still worse, from the British point of view, General Moreau had with great daring performed an amazing feat of war. In January, followed by a few squadrons of cavalry and a battery of horse artillery, he had galloped across the ice at the estuary of the Helder to the island of Texel, where the Dutch fleet was frozen in at its moorings, and captured the whole of it intact, so that its ships had now been added to those of the French.

Bad as this news was, three days after giving his big reception Roger received news of a much more distressing nature from nearer at hand. A sloop arrived in the port with an express from the Attorney General of Grenada. It stated that without warning on the night of March the 2nd an insurrection had broken out there, the town of Grenville had been surrounded, and the whole of its British inhabitants—men, women and children—massacred. The Governor had chanced to be in another part of the island with a party of friends, and on hearing the news they had taken a sloop round to the small port of Gouyave, only to be immediately captured on landing by another band of insurgents. The revolt had been led by a coloured planter named Julien Fédon and it was now known that he had received his directions for the plot to seize Grenada from the indefatigable Victor Hugues. After sacking Grenville, Fédon had established his headquarters on an almost inaccessible hill-top outside the town and from there was now doing his utmost to set the whole island ablaze. Any help that could be sent was most urgently needed.

Grenada being the southernmost of the Windward Islands, its nearest neighbours were, to the south Trinidad, but that was held by the Spaniards, and to the north St. Vincent, St. Lucia and Martinique, in that order, with Barbados slightly nearer than the latter but further out into the Atlantic. Hugues had already started trouble in St. Lucia and engineered a rising of Black Caribs in St. Vincent; so, apart from anything the Governor of Barbados might be able to do, Roger felt that the responsibility for the prevention of further slaughter lay mainly with him.

He was in no position to send a considerable force but was determined to do his best, and rode over to consult with Colonel Penruddock. The major part of the Fort Royal garrison was due back from its cruise in two days' time; so it was decided that as soon as it had landed three hundred and fifty men of the St. Pierre garrison should be despatched to Grenada under a promising young Major named Marsden.

When the commandeered ships returned to port it transpired that nineteen of the sick had died while at sea but the remainder were convalescent, and that the health of the seedy men had greatly improved. As those who had succumbed would almost certainly have done so anyway, Roger was highly pleased, and thought with gratitude of his old friend Droopy Ned who had suggested to him this method of combating the scourge. He could hope now that the three hundred and fifty men of the 57th who were soon to leave for Grenada would not only turn the tide in favour of its small garrison, but return equally improved in health.

Having seen the expedition off he now allowed himself a greater degree of relaxation. Since the reception, invitations had been pouring in from all the leading families in the island. To accept as many of them as possible was obviously good policy, so Amanda, Clarissa and himself were fêted and dined and shown the beauties of the island in the pleasantest possible circumstances.

The news received from Europe in April continued to be bad. In February the Prussians had actually opened peace negotiations with the French at Basle; the Dutch Army which had been fighting to maintain the Prince of Orange had received such a mauling that it had been forced to surrender; and Tuscany had seceded from the Grand Alliance, which now seemed to be falling to pieces.

From France there were indications that the Moderates were at last getting the upper hand. The sale of the property of the relations of *émigrés* had been stopped and the priests and nobles sentenced to deportation had been released. More indicative still, the Government had offered liberal terms, including liberty of worship, to the Royalist

Army in la Vendée, and its Chief, the brave Charette, had signed a peace at La Jaunaie by which he acknowledged the Republic. But that meant that still more French troops were freed to fight against the remaining Allies.

The news from Grenada was also bad. Fédon still remained secure in his natural fortress and the British troops were dying like flies in the fever swamps below it. Marsden had himself gone down with Yellow Jack, and, in a fit of despair, committed suicide.

Roger was distressed, and much angered by this wastage of his men, but there was nothing he could do about it; so, very sensibly, he continued with his pleasant round of entertaining and being entertained.

Clarissa had, justifiably, become one of the most popular 'toasts' in the island, and was having the best of both worlds. As comparatively few of the young British Officers could speak French she was their unrivalled darling, and as she went frequently into French society with Amanda, there was a score of young Frenchmen always seeking her company. Roger watched her with interest, wondering for which of her many beaux she would soon show a definite preference; but, although she was obviously having the time of her young life, the weeks went by without any sign that she had entered upon a serious romance.

At the beginning of May, as the hot season was approaching, they moved to a smaller but very pleasant Residence high up among the hills in the interior of the island; but they continued their social life, except for modifying it to the extent that from the 1st of June no engagements were ever entered into between eleven in the morning and five in the afternoon, as for the greater part of those hours the heat was too intense for them to do anything but doze nearly naked on their beds under mosquito curtains.

In June a slave revolt broke out in the extreme south of the island, but by prompt and firm handling it was stamped out within a week; and Roger, who had gone down there to superintend operations, afterwards held a special court of justice at which he showed no mercy to the ringleaders. He also occasionally signed a death warrant for a hanging, as he gave short shrift to any of Hugues's agitators whom his own spies caught at their nefarious work. In consequence, Martinique remained tranquil.

It was in June, too, that news arrived of the Prussians having finally agreed peace terms with the French, and that there had been an insurrection in Paris. On April the 1st—or 12th Germinal, Year III, according to the Revolutionary calendar—the *sans-culottes* had risen in protest against the relaxation of the persecution of the *bourgeois*; but they had been put down with a firm hand by the victorious and popular General Pichegru, on his being given command of the troops in the capital.

Within a few weeks of Roger's arrival in Martinique, he had appointed a retired merchant named Beckwith to act in the rather nebulous capacity of his Commercial Adviser and Comptroller of his Household. Mr. Beckwith's mother had been French and he had long been resident in the island, but he had never wavered in his personal allegiance to Britain, was still in the vigour of robust middle-age, and rich enough not to be corruptible; so he was an admirable choice to act as the guardian of Roger's financial interests. Without being extortionate, he saw to it that as each administrative post fell vacant a successor for it was appointed who was both politically sound and could afford to contribute a suitable sum to the Governor's 'expenses'. He also kept a sharp eye upon the payments of dues, and for licences, that were the Governor's official perquisites.

In consequence, by midsummer Roger had been for some months in receipt of a steady and quite considerable income. Having no worry neither about money nor the carrying out of such decrees as he issued, and with the troops in far better health from shifts of some ten per cent of them being sent to sea each week in a few coasting vessels acquired for that purpose, he was now able to enjoy to the full the gracious social life of the island, which still retained a distinct flavour of the *ancien régime*.

Amanda too was in excellent spirits and enjoyed abundant health. Vague and forgetful as she was by nature, now that her household was run for her by Cousin Margaret, who had accepted an invitation to move up to the summer Residence with them, she made a charming and most decorative hostess. Now, too, that she and Roger had been together again for some months without strain, he fell in love with her anew, and during this halcyon summer they enjoyed what amounted to a second honeymoon.

During August, news of further troubles in France reached them. In many parts, particularly in the cities of the south, a White Terror had set in, and bands of revengeful citizens were hunting out and murdering many of the Red Terrorists at whose hands they had suffered such miseries. Paris was said to be near starvation, and general discontent with the Government had gained wide support for another rising, in which the Jacobins and remaining extremists of the Mountain had endeavoured to use the mobs in an attempt to reimpose the old terrorist dictatorship. On May the 20th—or 1st Prairial—the storm had broken; once more the Chamber had been invaded by a howling mob and blood had been spilled in it. But the Thermidorians still controlled the army. Twenty thousand troops had been rushed into Paris overnight, this time with General Menou in command. By the 23rd the insurrection had been suppressed, and a number of its instigators sentenced to transportation to the fever ridden island of Cayenne—a punishment which had recently been meted out to the majority of those found guilty at treason trials, instead of death; but which had become popularly known as the 'dry guillotine'.

It was early on the morning of August the 18th that Roger rode down to St. Pierre, to confer on various matters with Colonel Penruddock, and spend the night there. That evening the Colonel suggested that it might amuse him to visit a new house of entertainment that had recently been opened on the outskirts of the city. It was, he said, a brothel and a gaming-hell of the more exclusive kind; but there was no obligation to patronise either its pretty mulatto wenches or probably crookedly-run tables. It had other attractions, in that an excellent dinner was served in its garden, and afterwards one could sit and listen to strangely fascinating negro music.

At first, Roger demurred on the score that although regarded by the Catholic clergy of the island as an heretic, several of them had held him up to their congregations as a man who by his happily married life gave a fine example; and as he set some store by their opinion of him he did not want it noised abroad that he had been seen in such a place.

To that Penruddock replied that His Excellency was far from being alone in his desire to protect his reputation; and it was for that reason that many of the French nobility made a practice of hiding their identity under masks on such occasions; so why should they not do the same. To that Roger willingly agreed, and as dusk was falling, accompanied by young Cowdray and three other officers also masked, they set off in a coach driven by a coachman in plain livery for 'Belinda's Parlour', as the place was called.

They had not been there long before Roger decided that the Colonel's recommendation had been fully justified. The establishment was clean and well run; they were not pestered by the girls and the twenty odd tables in the garden were set far enough from each other to ensure the parties at each of them a pleasant privacy. The Creole dishes served proved excellent and the wines were of the first quality; so few ways of passing an evening could have been more enjoyable than to dine there in the cool, after a day of torrid heat, under a tropical sky bright with a myriad of stars.

It was not until they had finished their meal that they saw Madame Belinda, the proprietress. She came to their table then to enquire if they had everything they wanted and had been pleased by the efforts of her cook.

She had come up quite silently, and as Roger was saying something to Cowdray he did not glance at her as she first spoke. But a familiar note in her voice caused him sharply to turn his head, and he got one of the shocks of his life. Madame Belinda was none other than Lucette.

As he sat there staring at her through the slits of his mask, he marvelled at her audacity in coming to Martinique and opening a public establishment there. She must have learnt that he had survived and taken up the Governorship of the island; and there were other people such as his Cousin Margaret and the de Taschers who, even after a lapse of years, might recognise her.

He could only suppose that, after he had wrought havoc among de Senlac's lieutenants and left his crew without a suitable leader, she had decided to sever her connections with the rabble that remained and make off with her share of the spoils; and that then the island in which she had spent her youth had exercised such a pull upon her that she had made up her mind to face the risk entailed in running this expensive whore-shop there.

Yet, on further thought, he realised that the risk she had taken, under a changed name, was not really very great. That he, the Governor, would ever visit her establishment must have seemed to her most unlikely. That Cousin Margaret or Madame de Tascher would do so could be entirely ruled out. And even if some men she had known as a young girl came there, and recognised her, she would be in no danger from them because they would not know that for thirteen years or more she had lived by participating in innumerable abominable crimes.

True to his principle of always looking before he leapt, Roger kept control of himself and made no move which draw her attention particularly to him. There was no risk of her running away and he did not wish to spoil the evening, which had begun so pleasantly, for the others.

For the best part of another two hours they sat on there drinking good French cognac and listening to the strange, haunting melodies of the negro singers. Then, when Penruddock suggested that perhaps the time had come to make a move, Roger said:

'Yes, Colonel; and all my thanks are due to you for a delightful evening. However, I trust that you will forgive me for marring a social occasion by attending to one small piece of business before we leave. Strictly speaking we should have here for it a corporal and two men; but I have little doubt that we can manage it between us, and find a room for one extra passenger in our coach. Would you be good enough to send for Madame Belinda.'

A few minutes later Lucette, handsome as ever, and all smiles, arrived at their table and said: 'You sent for me, Messieurs; but I have guessed already what you want. I have six lovely girls reserved for you and they await your pleasure upstairs.'

By way of answer Roger turned to his A.D.C. and, gesturing towards her, said: 'Captain Cowdray, oblige me by arresting this woman. Tomorrow morning I intend to charge her with piracy and murder.'

But the following morning Roger was no longer in St. Pierre; and he never charged Lucette. Less than twenty hours later he was at sea, on his way back to England.

17

In the Toils Once More

Roger had undressed and was just about to get into bed when Colonel Penruddock, wearing a tasselled night-cap and chamber-robe, came into his room with a despatch. It had arrived in a sloop-of-war that had docked at Fort Royal that evening and been brought on by galloper. Having broken the seals Roger saw that it contained only a few lines; but they were in Mr. Pitt's own hand and read:

> *My need of you is immediate, I have no wish to deprive you of your governorship; but desire that you should appoint someone to act for you in your absence, and return to England at the earliest possible moment.*

There was no alternative to regarding the message as a command; so Roger at once set about making preparations for his voyage. Sitting down at a writing table he scribbled an order empowering the Captain of the sloop to have his vessel reprovisioned as a matter of urgency; then he asked Penruddock to send the galloper to Fort Royal with it and to have horses saddled, including one for himself.

By four o'clock in the morning they reached the summer Residence. Poor Amanda was roused by Roger's kiss, only to learn of this bolt from the blue which meant for them another separation of uncertain duration; then she got up to see that Dan included everything that Roger might need in his baggage. He had already decided to make Penruddock acting-governor, so took the Colonel to his study and spent two hours advising him on the civil administration of the island. When they had breakfasted Roger had a talk with Mr. Beckwith about his financial affairs; then they all drove in to Fort Royal, arriving there in time to snatch a siesta during the hottest hours of the day.

On rousing from it Roger learned that a Lieutenant Tasker, R.N., who commanded the sloop, was waiting to report to him. The Lieutenant proved to be a squat young man with a pugnacious face, but a merry twinkle in his eye. He said that acting on the Prime Minister's instructions he had spared no effort to make a swift passage, and that by cutting out a call at Madeira he had achieved a near record, having made the crossing in twenty-six days. He added that in another three hours his ship should be ready to put to sea again.

Roger invited him to dinner; then, after the meal, accompanied by Amanda, Clarissa, Cousin Margaret and several members of his staff, they drove down to the harbour. Dan already had the luggage aboard, the last sad farewells were said, and as the brief twilight fell the sloop started on her homeward voyage.

Over dinner Roger had learned from Lieutenant Tasker the latest news about the state of things in Europe. The war generally was still going badly for the Allies, but there had been a new development upon which high hopes were now pinned. On June the 17th a considerable expedition had set sail from Portsmouth with the object of invading Lower Brittany. On the 22nd a French fleet under Villaret-Joyeuse had been defeated, and on the 27th the invading force had been safely landed on the promontory of Quiberon.

To use British sea-power as a means of striking right at the heart of the Republic in this way was a policy which Roger had been advocating ever since the spring of '93. It was then that the first Royalist risings had taken place in the Vendée, and he had argued with good sense that if the fanatically religious peasant bands could be supported by disciplined British troops, it might well be possible to launch a drive on Paris which would bring about the downfall of the Terrorist government.

That such a campaign might still pay a good dividend seemed to Roger probable; although he felt that postponing it for so long had robbed it of much of its original promise, as many thousands of the Vendéeans had since given their lives to no purpose and, recently, on being offered freedom of worship, the survivors had made peace with the Republicans.

The expedition's prospects of success were suddenly reduced from fair to highly dubious in Roger's mind that night, when in a later talk with tasker he learnt that it was not composed of British troops. It consisted only of several regiments of French volunteers, raised in England from the Royalist refugees, supported by a force of regulars which had been detached for this purpose from the Prince de Condé's army of *émigrés* on the Rhine.

Knowing the habits and mentality of the French nobility, Roger could well imagine how such an army would be conducted. Pedigree would have been given preference over ability in selecting the commanders of its units; and, as every Frenchman of gentle birth would insist on his right to a commission, officers would far outnumber other ranks. This topsy-turviness would be further aggravated by endless time-wasting due to the strict observance of forms and ceremonies inherited from the *ancien régime*. At every Council-of-war held by its leaders some out of stupidity, and others from jealousy, would oppose the proposals of the professional soldiers; with the result that before their support for any plan had been won by a series of dubious intrigues, the best opportunities would be lost. There was little doubt that when it came to actual engagements these Royalists would fight with great gallantry; but that alone could give them little prospect of defeating any of the young Republican generals who had recently been gaining so many successes owing to their new and vigorous methods of waging war.

That, at least, was how Roger saw it; and the news that the expedition was entirely French greatly increased his concern for his own immediate future; as on learning of the landing at Quiberon he had at once jumped to the conclusion that it was on account of it that Mr. Pitt had sent for him. The assumption was a very reasonable one, for his wide knowledge of everything to do with the Revolution would make him invaluable if attached as a sort of *Représentant en Mission* to the General commanding the invading army; not, of course, with the almost unlimited powers he had wielded when with Dumouriez, but to interrogate important prisoners, assess the abilities of enemy generals and advise on a score of different problems. Much as he resented being recalled from Martinique he would have found such a post at a British Headquarters congenial, but the thought of the frustrations to which he would be subject in endeavouring to persuade a crowd of arrogant, selfish, pig-headed French nobles to do the sensible thing, and do it swiftly, filled him with dismay.

The sloop, for her homeward run, took a course which carried her many hundreds of miles away from the track of her outward passage. Starting at ninety degrees to it she headed due north, and after ten days' sailing reached the cooler latitudes off Bermuda. There, she picked up the South West Trades which would take her north of the Azores and direct to England.

Among the personal possessions that Roger had been compelled to leave behind in the *Circe* were his artist's materials; but he had since bought others in Fort Royal, and in the past few months had occasionally found time to do a little painting. Now, as Amanda had made sure that his paints and brushes were packed, he was able during these long days of leisure to indulge freely in his hobby as an alternative to reading.

Apart from two days of squalls as they were approaching the entrance to the Channel, the weather proved favourable; and although Lieutenant Tasker was unable to repeat his fine performance on the outward run, his fast little vessel accomplished the passage in thirty-one days. Late in the evening of September the 19th she docked at Southampton, and Roger and Dan at once went ashore. By ten o'clock they were leaving the town in a post-chaise hired to drive them through the night to London.

At a little before six in the morning the post-chaise set Roger down outside No. 10 Downing Street. Having sent Dan on with the luggage to the Marquis of Amesbury's great mansion in Arlington Street, where, as a son of the house, Droopy Ned lived when in London and a room was always at Roger's disposal, he rang the bell.

It was answered by a night porter who informed him that the Prime Minister was in residence there, but was not normally called until seven. Roger then said he would wait, and shortly afterwards the ground floor became a bustle of servants preparing the rooms for the day. The steward came on the scene and, recognising Roger, ordered a footman to bring him a tray. The hot chocolate, crisp new rolls, cold York ham, and fruit upon it were most welcome after his night on the road, and he had not long finished eating when he was summoned to the presence.

The Prime Minister was in his dressing-room, lying back in a tilted chair being shaved by his valet; so he did not see Roger enter, but, as the footman announced him, called out:

'Come in, Mr. Brook. You are most welcome; and the more so as I had counted your arrival unlikely for another fortnight at the least.'

'Thank you, Sir. That I am here so soon you owe to Lieutenant Tasker's having spared no effort to carry out your instructions. He had his sloop ready to leave Martinique within twenty-four hours of her arrival, and made two near-record trips.' As Roger spoke he walked over to the window so that he could face his master.

'I'll note the name and see that he is commended for his diligence,' Mr. Pitt murmured. Then, when the valet had wiped the remains of the soap from his face, he sat up. As his glance fell on Roger he exclaimed:

'Devil take me! Had I met you in the street I doubt if I would have known you.'

Roger smiled. 'Shaving in a choppy sea can be a plaguey tricky business; so as there were no ladies aboard I decided to let my beard grow. After five weeks it needs the skilled hand of a barber to remove it; but seeing the urgency of your summons I felt it my duty to wait upon you immediately I reached London, rather than to hang about waiting for the shops to open.'

'And you did rightly. I'll tell you what I have in mind while we breakfast.'

'Your steward has already stilled my cravings in that

direction, Sir; but I shall be happy to attend you while you eat yours.'

A few minutes later Mr. Pitt moved over to a small table where breakfast had been laid for him. As he sat down and the valet left the room, Roger said:

'I take it that you sent for me because you wish me to act as political adviser to the General commanding the Royalist army that landed on the Western coast of France?'

The Prime Minister gave a bitter laugh. 'The Royalist army! Did you not know, man, that it no longer exists. The expedition was a complete and utter failure.'

'That is indeed bad news. I knew nothing of it apart from what Tasker told me of our having in June defeated the French fleet and a few days later landed the expedition successfully. I'll confess, though, that I had some doubts about its making a swift penetration of the country, as the stroke must have lost much through having been delayed until after the Vendéeans had entered into an accommodation with the enemy.'

' 'Twas not that which caused its failure. The terms of the pact entitled the Vendéeans to retain their arms, and a large part of them had even remained embodied as militia. The Republicans infringed the terms of the treaty by arresting certain Vendéean officers; so they had ample pretext for denouncing it. The *Chouan* leaders Stofflet and Cadoudal both did so, and thousands of peasants flocked to their banners, only a few weeks later to be killed or captured.'

Roger sadly shook his head. 'Alas for these poor gallant country people! They had already suffered so much in the Royalist cause, and appealed so long for help in vain. To have their hopes raised at last then meet such an end must have been doubly bitter. Was it then divided councils, and petty jealousies among the French nobility who went upon the expedition, that led to this sad fiasco?'

'You have said it, Mr. Brook.' The Prime Minister dealt with the piece of beefsteak on his fork, then went on: 'His Majesty has always distrusted the French aristocracy, so opposed the project and showed his acumen by predicting the manner in which it was brought to ruin; where as I was fool enough to allow myself to be persuaded to it by

Mr. Windham and the Comte de Puisaye. The former has long made himself the champion of those who hope for a restoration in France, and since his appointment as Secretary of State for War had never ceased to press the Cabinet to sponsor a landing in Brittany. Then de Puisaye arrived here last winter and encouraged us to believe that he could raise the whole of Brittany again, would we but give him arms, money and a token force to form a rallying point.'

Between mouthfuls of his steak, Mr. Pitt continued gloomily to relate a tale of incompetence and disaster.

'We set about raising eight French regiments. Gentlemen by the hundred offered themselves for commissions, but there was a sad dearth of volunteers willing to join as privates. De Puisaye then urged us to offer French prisoners-of-war their freedom if they would serve in the ranks of the monarchist army. We did so and recruited satisfactory numbers, though I fear that many of these turncoats had experienced no true change of heart, and seized upon the offer only as a means of getting back to France.

'Soon after the expedition had sailed my Lord Bridport dealt a sharp blow at the enemy fleet by capturing three sail-of-the-line and bottling the remainder of the squadron up in L'Orient. Commodore Sir John Warren then had a free hand to disembark the Royalist troops from their transports. Throughout he stood by them, showing great initiative in using the guns of his ships to support their operations as far as that was possible, and later he took off some eighteen hundred of the survivors; but it was entirely beyond his powers to prevent the débâcle which engulfed the majority.

'As you can imagine, my enemies seized upon the disaster as good ammunition for a new attempt to blacken the Government, and particularly myself, with the people. They said we could not have failed to realise that an expedition entirely composed of volunteers must end in failure, and that our not having sent with it a force of British regulars was proof of our criminal intention—namely that we had planned to rid ourselves in this manner of the *émigrés* who had plagued us for so long.

'Charles Fox surpassed himself in unscrupulous vindictiveness and, for once, abandoned his championship of the Republicans to accuse Ministers of "having deliberately sent noble gentlemen to be massacred"; and Sheridan with eager spite declared that "though British blood had not flowed at Quiberon, yet British honour had bled at every pore"—a phrase that ran round England.'

'That members should use the privilege of the House to utter such diabolical slanders in it fills me with disgust,' said Roger angrily. 'But may I ask, Sir, why you did not stiffen these inexperienced French with some regiments of well-disciplined British troops?'

'You well may,' the Prime Minister replied bitterly. 'That was my original intention, but those stiff-necked French aristocrats would have none of it. They were ready enough to accept British money, British arms and a British fleet to put them safely ashore; but they insisted that, in the initial operation at least, only Frenchmen should be allowed to set foot on the sacred soil of France. For a year or more General the Earl of Moïra's force had been standing by in the Channel Islands held ready for just such an employment; but I was brought to agree that it should be used only as a follow-up when the invasion was well under way. In consequence, apart from a few score of our Marines, the landings were entirely French.

'Their reception by the Breton people could not have been more enthusiastic. De Puisaye's optimism in that respect was amply justified, except in one important respect. M. de Charette, who has proved himself the most able and resourceful of the Vendéean leaders, refused to join in the revolt from personal jealousy. Nevertheless, on the day following the landings, the Bishop of Dol, who had accompanied the expedition, celebrated a Mass in the open which was attended by many thousands of persons, all of whom declared their willingness to lay down their lives for the church and monarchy.

'Thus, apart from de Charette's churlish aloofness, the campaign could not have had a more favourable beginning. It was with the opening of military operations that serious dissensions first threatened its success. It had been the Cabinet's intention that de Puisaye should assume the over-all command; but, most unfortunately, their Lordships of the Admiralty had issued a document which could be read by the Comte d'Hervilly as giving him the command of the French forces raised in England. Had de Puisaye accepted that it would have left him with authority only over the *Chouan* bands which had risen at his call. In consequence, the two nobles were soon at loggerheads; and not solely over the question of command either. De Puisaye was all for taking the utmost advantage accruing from the surprise landings by an immediate advance inland, whereas d'Hervilly favoured first consolidating their position and taking a fortress that dominated the Quiberon peninsula.

'The fortress soon surrendered and, with almost unbelievable folly, d'Hervilly allowed some of the men in it who protested their monarchist sympathies to remain there as part of its new garrison. In the meantime the energetic General Hoche had rallied the Republican forces, driven in de Puisaye's *Chouan* outposts and bottled up the Royalists by entrenching his men across the peninsula's neck.

'With Sir John Warren's willing collaboration, de Puisaye then despatched a force under his most trusted lieutenant, de Tinténiac, by sea, to land further up the coast and attack the Republicans in the rear. At the time I was, of course, unaware of it, but later it transpired that, in approving the arrangements for the campaign, the Bourbon Princes were using de Puisaye only as a cat's paw, because he favoured a Constitutional Monarchy. Being set for absolutism they intended to cast him aside as soon as he had served their purpose by raising his followers in Brittany. But the treacherous fools acted prematurely. In order to discredit de Puisaye as a General, the Princes' agents in Paris sent instructions to his Lieutenant on landing that there had been a change of plan and he should now make for St. Malo. Tinténiac, believing that he was acting in accordance with de Puisaye's wishes, obeyed. In consequence, when the Royalists made their attempt to break out of the peninsula, the attack on the Republicans' rear, on which they had counted to aid them, never matured.'

Roger groaned. 'What a shocking tale of mismanagement and perfidy.'

'It is not yet done.' Mr. Pitt pushed aside his plate with an angry gesture. 'The attack in the isthmus was made on July the 16th. That morning the transports bringing fifteen hundred veteran *émigrés* from Germany, under the young Comte de Sombreuil, arrived in Quiberon Bay. From fear that de Sombreuil might deprive him of sole credit for a victory d'Hervilly insisted on attacking before there had been time to disembark these reinforcements. His volunteers were routed, and the pursuit of them by Hoche's cavalry was checked only by the heavy fire brought to bear by Sir John Warren's gunboats.

'On being informed of the Royalist dispositions de Sombreuil pressed to be allowed to take over the fortress, which was the key to the whole position, and substitute for its garrison some of his seasoned troops; but d'Hervilly would not hear of it. His refusal led to his own defeat and that of everyone else concerned.

'Some of the men of the original garrison who had pretended to have monarchist sympathies went secretly to General Hoche, and suggested to him a plan by which the fortress could be retaken. On the night of July the 20th, under cover of a storm, that by ill-fortune had forced Sir John Warren's ships to withdraw from the rocky coast to the safety of the open sea, these traitors led Hoche's men along the beach past sentries, who were also in the plot, to the fortress. There, aided by other traitors within, they were hauled up over the battlements, and in the dawn took by surprise those of the garrison who had remained loyal.

'Simultaneously Hoche, no longer having to fear a bombardment from the British fleet, launched a resolute attack upon the Royalist positions. The fortress fell, and its guns were turned upon d'Hervilly's men. He and his regiments of volunteers, the *Chouans,* and with them hundreds of women and children, were driven back into the sea. De Sombreuil and his veterans threw themselves into a smaller fort, but instead of having the sense to hang on there until our ships could rescue them, they surrendered. As a result of this débâcle the Republicans took over six thousand prisoners, near seven hundred of them being *émigrés,* to whom they later gave a mockery of a court-martial and then shot.'

Roger nodded. 'This ghastly business puts then a final end to any hope of embodying the Vendéeans in a future army of liberation.'

The Prime Minister selected a peach and began to peel it. 'Not quite; but as nearly as in my opinion makes little difference. It had been agreed that the British troops under my Lord Moira should follow de Puisaye to Quiberon, and that with them should go the Comte d'Artois. At the news that His Royal Highness meant to assume command of the expedition in person, Charette suddenly emerged from his fit of sulks and declared that the presence of a Prince of Blood was all that was needed to ensure a victorious campaign by his partisans. Accordingly, we had d'Artois and his feckless, venal household conveyed to the Isle of Yeu, which lies some distance off the coast of Brittany. But there he sits, and I am convinced has not the courage to join Charette in the new revolt that temperamental but gallant man is now leading.'

'I trust, Sir,' said Roger with an uneasy glance, 'that you have no thought of despatching me to His Highness, with the idea that I might induce him to put himself at the head of the Royalist forces, then act as adviser to him?'

'Good gracious, no!' Mr. Pitt gave a pale smile. 'I set a better value on your talents than to ask you to waste them in an employment like to prove so unprofitable. Yet it was, in part, this Quiberon disaster which caused me to send for you.'

'How so, Sir?'

'For once I acted on an impulse. It was on July the 22nd, which may be accounted the blackest day that Britain has known for many a year. That morning the Spanish Ambassador had informed my Lord Grenville that his country found herself so hard pressed that she was compelled to withdraw from the Alliance. Then in the evening there arrived the news that the Quiberon expedition, the spearhead of the invasion on which we had pinned such hopes, had been completely annihilated. That night I wrote the order for your recall.'

Roger's forehead creased in a puzzled frown, and he murmured: 'I still do not see . . .'

'It is quite simple, Mr. Brook. The appreciation which you gave me when we last met of future political trends in France has, God be thanked, proved wrong. But your pessimistic views about the war showed an uncanny foresight and have proved terribly correct. I make no promise to follow your advice; but I desire you to tell me what, were you in my place, you would do now?'

'Really, Sir!' Roger's face showed his astonishment. 'You rate my abilities far higher than they merit. Besides, how can I even venture an opinion, when I have been out of touch with events in Europe for so long?'

'You know the broad picture, and that is sufficient for our purpose. During the past eight months the Grand Alliance has fallen in pieces about our ears. In February Tuscany caved in and the Netherlands' army collapsed. In April we lost Prussia, till then our most potent ally, together with Westphalia and Saxony. In May the Dutch went over to our enemies. In July the Spaniards too betrayed us, and since then Hesse-Cassel, Switzerland and Denmark have all sued for peace. It is true that Catherine of Russia has now made a pact with the Emperor and promised to send him some support; but she is old, ill and has little to gain, so I doubt if she will despatch more than a token force; and in the meantime our Austrian allies are near played out. Everywhere the armies of the French Republic are victorious, and with the destruction of the Quiberon expedition there disappeared our last hope of striking a blow at its heart.'

Roger considered for a moment, then he said slowly: 'There seems nought for it, then, but to initiate measures which, while safeguarding the interests of such allies as are left to us, might bring us an honourable peace.'

Mr. Pitt raised an eyebrow. 'Knowing your hatred of the Revolutionaries, Mr. Brook, I had never thought to hear you advocate such a policy.'

With a shrug, Roger replied: 'As long as I live, Sir, I shall feel a loathing for the men who must still make up the bulk of the Convention. But it would be wrong to allow one's sentiments to influence one's judgment on such an issue. If there is no longer any hope of our emerging victorious from the war, its continuance can result only in a profitless draining away of our country's resources. Therefore, the sooner we can negotiate a reasonably satisfactory peace, the better—and it would be better still if some formula could be found to bring about at the same time a general pacification of Europe.'

'Well said, Mr. Brook; well said!' The Prime Minister smiled. 'Although I challenged you, I am entirely at one with you in this. As you must know, I have always regarded war as senseless, barbarous, and the worst scourge that can afflict the people of any nation. Although under great pressure, I succeeded in restraining our country from entering the present conflict until the French declared war upon us; and, just as our cause is, I would give much to put an end to it, providing that can be done with honour. The problem is, how can we set the stage for an accommodation which I believe would now be as welcome to the war-weary French nation as to our own?'

'You tell me, Sir, that I proved wrong in my prediction that the terrorists in Paris would continue to cut one another's throats, and that the survivors would preserve in their policies of greed, ruthless repression and determination to spread their nefarious doctrines by force of arms. I still find it hard to believe that they have acted otherwise. May I ask your grounds for believing that these leopards have changed their spots?'

'They are numerous, and I think sound. During the months following Robespierre's fall many laws restricting the liberty of the subject were repealed, and the public journals were again given a substantial degree of freedom. Last November that hotbed of iniquity, the Jacobin Club, was closed. In December the seventy-three deputies whom the Terrorists had expelled from the Chamber were welcomed back to it, thus greatly strengthening the hands of the Moderates. In March their return was followed by that of such of the Girondins as survived the Terror, either in prison or as hunted outlaws. This spring, too, the *sans-culottes,* furious at the turn things were taking, twice endeavoured to overthrow the Government, but on each occasion both the National Guard and regular troops sided with it; so these revolts were swiftly crushed. By summer a degree of religious toleration had been granted, and in almost every village the Mass was again being celebrated. Lastly, since June, the French journals have carried many reports of minor Terrorists being lynched by the people they once persecuted. Is that enough for you?'

Roger smiled. 'All of it is most excellent news; but I pray you tell me this. Do the names of Billand-Varennes, Collot d'Herbois, Fouché, Tallien, Fréron, David, Amer, Rewbell, Merlin of Douai, Bourdon of the Oise, Cambon and the Abbé Sieyès, still appear as those of active deputies in the reports furnished you of proceedings in the Chamber; and does the real power still lie in the hands of the Committee of Public Safety?'

'The first two you mention are among a group of Jacobins sentenced to transportation after the revolt last May; but, as far as my memory serves me, most of the others are still leading figures; and although the powers of the Committee have been much curtailed, it remains the executive body through which the nation is governed.'

'Then, Sir, I must confess that I am a man who "convinced against his will is of the same opinion still." Yet it seems that pressure of public opinion has forced these monsters to disguise their true feelings for the time being; so advantage might be taken of that while it lasts. What is to prevent you from putting out peace feelers to them through diplomatic channels in some neutral country?'

'Should we do so and they met with a rebuff, we would have only encouraged our enemies by disclosing signs of weakness; and my agents in Paris inform me that there is little hope of such overtures being received favourably.'

'That, Sir, as you may recall, was my own opinion; but you maintain that during the past year matters have changed. It can hardly be doubted that after all the French people have suffered during the last six years they must crave beyond all things a cessation of strife. Indeed, it is computed that not less than a million of them have died in massacres, purges, revolts and the Vendéean wars; universal conscription has brought ruin to their industries and agriculture; they have lived on the verge of starvation since '93 and the war continues to put an appalling strain upon their man-power. Therefore, admitting your contention that since the fall of Robespierre sheer weight of public opinion has forced his successors to give the people a much greater degree of freedom, surely that same weight of opinion might result in compelling them to give favourable consideration to overtures for peace?'

Mr. Pitt shook his head. 'It is not as simple as that. Peace would inevitably lead to a further relaxation of the strangle-hold that they still exercise on the nation. Such has been the change of sentiment in France recently that fresh elections would result in the return of a Chamber overwhelmingly in favour of the restoration of the Monarchy.'

'The reaction of which you speak was sooner or later inevitable; but I am a little surprised to learn that you think such a volte-face already assured of the support of the masses.'

'I am certain of it. They have come to look back on the *ancien régime* as an era of peace and prosperity. Of course, they would not agree to the re-establishment of an aristocracy; but nine-tenths of them would favour a Limited Monarchy based on the Constitution granted by Louis XVI in '91. The Girondins, and other excluded deputies who have returned to the Convention, still exercise caution in their pronouncements, but I have reliable information that the majority of them are only waiting their chance to bring about a Restoration.'

'The old gang would never agree to that.'

'Exactly. And as long as the war continues they have a reasonable excuse for keeping the Rump Parliament, that they still dominate, in being. With peace they would be forced to go to the country. They would lose their seats and a Restoration would follow. Near all of them voted for the late King's death; so, apart from all else, on the count of regicide they would be liable to lose their heads.'

'Then, as I have always maintained, there can be little

hope of peace until the hard core of the old Convention is, in some way, deprived of its power.'

'That is the situation; but could it be done I believe our chances of bringing the conflict to an end are excellent.'

Roger remained thoughtful for a moment, then he said: 'It seems then, what we need is another General Monk, who will turn his army about, march it on Paris, and declare for the King.'

A slow smile lit the Prime Minister's lined face. 'I am glad to find, Mr. Brook, that your sojourn in the Indies has not deprived you of your resource. It makes me all the more happy to be able to tell you that we have already anticipated you in this admirable solution to our difficulties. We have bought General Pichegru.'

'The devil you have!'

'Yes, I am given to understand that he is not only a fine soldier but a patriot and honest man, who feels great distress at the sad state into which his country has fallen. As the reward for marching his army on Paris, he has been promised the baton of a Marshal of France, the Government of Alsace, a million francs in cash, an income of 200,000 *louis*, an *hôtel* in Paris and the Chateau of Chambord.'

'Honest he may be!' Roger laughed. 'But for a half of that I'd march an army to Cathay.'

Mr. Pitt waved the remark aside. 'In an issue of such importance what matter the size of the reward—providing he does what is required of him? The trouble at the moment is that he makes no move to earn it.'

'He might do so, yet to actually secure all these fine things he would still have nought to rely on save the word of the Bourbon Princes. It may be that he hesitates to trust them.'

'That has not occurred to me, although it may in part explain why he is holding back. The reason, according to the agent handling these negotiations, is that he feels misgivings about the reception he will meet with when he reaches Paris. Apparently he is loath to set out on the venture until fully convinced that by overthrowing the present French government he will be carrying out the wishes of a majority of the French people.'

'His information on the state of things in France should be as good as your own. Are not the sort of things you have been telling me enough for him?'

'One would have thought they should be. But, remember, until quite recently, he has been a staunch Republican. For such the "will of the people" is no more than a catch phrase. I think what he really requires before committing himself is a definite assurance that a majority of the more moderate deputies, intellectuals and others out of the common rut, like himself, have also experienced a change of heart, and now favour a Restoration. In short, he will act only if we can provide him with reliable evidence that the type of people he respects will not regard him as a traitor.'

Roger's expression did not change by the flicker of an eyelid but as though a thick curtain had suddenly been reft aside he saw how the Prime Minister had ensnared him. With a skill which, now Roger realised it, he could not help but admire, Mr. Pitt had led the conversation by gradual stages up to its present point. He assumed, and probably rightly, that Roger was the only man in the world who could get for him evidence that such men as Barras, Carnot and Dubois-Crancé were willing to commit themselves. To have asked Roger straight out to return to Paris would have been to risk a flat refusal. Instead his advice had been asked, with the foregone conclusion that he would advocate the only sensible course. Then he had been shown how the course he advocated could not be pursued unless certain undertakings were secured in order to set General Pichegru's mind at rest. Into his racing speculations there broke the quiet voice of the tall, grey-faced man on the opposite side of the little table.

'A penny for your thoughts, Mr. Brook?'

'They were, Sir, that, unless I am much mistaken, you have played me a scurvy trick by presenting matters in such a way that I could be taken for a coward did I ignore their implication.'

'Nay; do not say that. No man who knows you would ever impugn your courage. But in view of your attitude when last we met I felt justified in acquainting you very fully with the great issues at stake before once more asking you to undertake a mission to Paris.'

'Ah, there's the rub!' Roger made a grimace. 'Were it to any other capital I would willingly accept your instructions. But these new developments in the political scene of Paris have made it no less dangerous for me. On the contrary, it is now probably even more so. Fourteen months ago I had already enough to dread from Fouché, knowing me to be English and your agent, and probably having had me listed for immediate arrest should I show my face there again. That risk I still run. Now, added to it, since many Royalists have been liberated from the prisons, I might at any time run into some gentleman who would recognise me as the Chevalier de Breuc, once honoured with the friendship of Queen Marie Antoinette; and, believing that I had betrayed her cause, seek to bring about my ruin.'

Mr. Pitt nodded. 'It may be true that during the past year conditions in Paris have not changed to your advantage. But you have changed. When you refused to serve me further you were sick in mind and body. Today I rejoice to find that is no longer so. Surely, now that you are fully restored, you will not refuse my plea once more to encounter danger, when by doing so you may be able to render a great service to your country?'

For a moment Roger did not reply, then he said: 'I wonder whether what you ask is really necessary. It may not be. I mean, of course, for me to go to Paris. The kernel of this problem seems to be General Pichegru's attitude. Ought we not, as a first step, to obtain more definite information on the cause of his hesitation? Distrust of the Bourbon Princes may well be at the bottom of it. In any case, I feel we should get from him the exact conditions on which he is prepared to act, before proceeding further. To do otherwise would be to put the cart before the horse.'

'There is good sense in that. Will you then undertake a mission to the General's headquarters?'

As Roger nodded, the Prime Minister stretched out a long bony hand and patted him lightly on the knee. For such a shy and undemonstrative man it was a most unusual gesture. With a smile, he said;

'I felt sure that I could count upon you, Mr. Brook; but I am none the less grateful.' Then he went on in a brisker tone. 'Now with regard to your journey. These secret negotiations with Pichegru have, of course, been handled through the Prince de Condé, who commands the *émigré* army on the Rhine. It would be best if you went to his headquarters first, in order to ascertain if there have been any further developments in the matter of which I have not yet heard. Have you still the Letter of Marque I gave you some years ago, stating that on the affairs of our country you speak in my name?'

'Yes, Sir. It is safely locked away in the vaults of Hoare's Bank.'

'Then that will be sufficient introduction for you to His Highness. I will, however, give you another letter to a gentleman you will find at his headquarters, named the Comte de Montgalliard.'

Roger suddenly sat bolt upright. 'I pray you, Sir, do nothing of the kind—at least if it is of the same man we are thinking, for I believe there are two brothers both of whom bear the title and the name.'

'This is Count Maurice. He is a man of medium height with jet-black eyebrows, an over-long chin and slightly hump-backed.'

'That is the rogue I have in mind. While I was involved with the Baron de Batz in an attempt to rescue Queen Marie Antoinette from prison, the Baron once pointed Montgalliard out to me. He bid me beware of him as the most plausible and unscrupulous villain unhung; then gave me chapter and verse for many of his treacheries.'

'What you say perturbs me greatly, Mr. Brook. He is certainly most plausible and possesses both brains and charm, but it is he who initiated this affair and, having acted as go-between for the Prince de Condé and myself, holds all the threads of it.'

'Then, Sir, you may be certain that he intends to betray you both, and General Pichegru into the bargain, for what he can get out of it. This makes it all the more imperative that negotiations with the General should be opened through a new channel. It is quite on the cards that Montgalliard has lied to him, and kept for himself any sum that he was supposed to have handed over as earnest money. In any case, I have always sought to minimise my own risk by working alone; so I would much prefer that my mission should not be disclosed to any Royalist agent.'

'In that, no doubt, you are wise; and it seems now that Montgalliard would prove a special source of danger to you. To relieve you of it, I will give you a letter to him, asking him to come immediately to London for further consultation. Then when he arrives I will find some pretext for keeping him here.'

'For that I should be grateful, Sir. I take it you wish me to set out as soon as possible?'

'Yes. I will have a word with my cousin Grenville. Be good enough to wait upon him tomorrow at the Foreign Office. He will provide you with ample funds and make such arrangements for your journey as you may think best.'

During a further half hour Mr. Pitt gave Roger much useful information on the general situation, then Roger took his leave. As he came out from Number 10 a chill autumn wind was blowing gustily up Downing Street. His blood having become thinned by the heat of the tropics, he shivered slightly.

He was hoping that Montgalliard, for his own evil purposes, had lied about General Pichegru's attitude. If so, with the Count out of the way, a firm and frank understanding with the General might prove all that was necessary. If not, Roger knew that he would then have no option but to proceed to Paris. Grimly he faced the fact that he was once more in the toils of a great conspiracy; and he wondered a little unhappily when, and if, he would ever see Martinique again.

18

Enter Robert MacElfic

In Whitehall Roger picked up a sedan-chair and had himself carried to Amesbury House. The great mansion showed few signs of life; as, with the exception of Droopy Ned, the family was still in Wiltshire, and he had returned only the day before after his annual surfeit of mulberries. But the skeleton staff had been apprised by Dan of Roger's coming, and a footman in undress livery took him straight up to his friend's suite.

Droopy, in his favourite morning déshabillé of a turban and oriental robe, had only just risen. He welcomed Roger with delight, then laughed at the sight of his beard; on which Roger promptly declared his intention of having it off before the morning was out. A table was wheeled in with Droopy's breakfast, and as it was now getting on for ten o'clock, Roger felt quite ready for a second, more substantial, meal; so the two old cronies sat down to a brown trout brought in ice from the Avon, a big venison pasty and a couple of bottles of claret.

Roger had no secrets from Droopy; so as soon as they were alone he described how Mr. Pitt had recalled him from Martinique and, that morning, inveigled him into a new mission. When he had given particulars of it, Droopy nodded his bird-like head, and said:

'Seeing that this may prove the key to the pacification of all Europe, you could not possibly have refused. I'll vow, too, that despite the long face you are pulling about it you are by no means altogether displeased to find yourself back in your old harness. A nature such as yours could not remain content with the humdrum life of the Indies.'

'Humdrum!' Roger laughed. 'I have yet to tell you how near the women all came to being raped and myself murdered, first by pirates then by revolted negro slaves. Still, I'll not deny there's something in what you say. I had been privy to half the intrigues in Europe far too long not to miss the spice that compensates for the danger of dabbling in them. In fact, if the truth be told, most of my misgivings evaporated on the way here from Downing Street, and one half of me is already agog to get to grips with this new problem.'

Droopy smiled. 'I'd have wagered a monkey on that proving so. As to your harrowing experiences on the voyage out, I greatly look forward to hearing your account of them; although the beautiful Georgina gave me the main particulars soon after she got back here late in March.'

'Of course! How fares she now? Poor Charles's death was a sad blow to her.'

'Aye, she took it mighty hard; and on her arrival went directly into retirement. She bade me to Stillwaters for a night, but only to give me news of you. Dowered with such vitality as she is, I'd not have thought her capable of grieving so long for any man; except perhaps yourself. In the circumstances it was a great blessing that she had the carrying of her child to occupy her mind.'

'Child!' exclaimed Roger.

'Yes. Did you not know? She told me she had written you that she was expecting one. You should have had her letter sometime in May.'

Roger shook his head. 'It never reached me; so I suppose the ship carrying it must have been lost or taken by a privateer. As Georgina was ever an erratic correspondent I did not wonder greatly at not hearing from her; though I wrote to her myself three times from Martinique.'

'Then it will also be news to you that you are now a godfather. But that, of course, you could not know; as her son was not born until the 17th of August. I acted as proxy for you at the christening; so can vouch for it that the little Earl is a right lusty fellow, and Georgina herself looking even more lovely now that she has become a mother.'

'Well, strap me! I am more delighted than I can say. I

must write to her in my first free hour; and will drive down to Stillwaters with gifts for my godson should time permit.'

'You are then already under orders to set out?'

'Yes. I wait upon my Lord Grenville tomorrow, and leave as soon after as a ship is available to carry me.' Roger took a swig of wine, then added with a worried frown, 'I would, though, that I had been called on to pit my wits against some people other than the French. So many of their leading men already have preconceived beliefs about me: the aristocrats that I am one of themselves but turned traitor, the ex-terrorists that I was a *sans-culotte* before becoming a member of that den of iniquity, the Paris Commune, and one at least of the latter knows me for what I am, an English spy. These tabs from the past that I must carry with me immeasurably increase the difficulties of my mission.'

'Then why carry them?' Droopy rubbed a finger along the side of his beaky nose. 'That brown beard you grew upon your voyage may now prove a Godsend. With it you should have little difficulty in assuming a new identity.'

'Egad; what an excellent thought!' Roger's blue eyes suddenly lit up. 'Mr. Pitt scarce recognised me, and with a few other changes I could, sure enough, pass as a different person.'

When they had finished breakfast, Droopy summoned his valet, who also served him as his barber, and after an hour in the man's capable hands Roger's metamorphosis was completed. His eyebrows had been plucked to half their former thickness, his long eyelashes had been shortened by an eighth of an inch, and the ball of his chin shaven clean. The last operation did away with a suggestion of scruffiness that the new-grown beard had given him, and now put him in a new fashion for growing a moustache and pointed side-whiskers, which was beginning to be effected by a number of young cavalry officers.

It remained only to invent a personality; and for that, lest anyone should still think he was himself disguised, he decided to use the additional cover of a family resemblance by passing himself off as a non-existent cousin, and taking the name of Robert MacElfic.

As he was now anxious not to provoke gossip about his changed appearance, this debarred him from going to his club or looking up such old friends of his who might have been in London at this comparatively dead season; so he called only at Hoare's Bank, not to collect the Letter of Marque, as that would be useless now he had decided to take the name of MacElfic, but for some other papers identifying him as Citizen Commissioner Breuc, which, although out of date, might still serve him when he had to make his way through the lines of the Republican Army to General Pichegru.

In the afternoon he drove out to Richmond to assure himself that Thatched House Lodge was being properly taken care of, and it was decided that Dan, who had accompanied him, should remain there. That night he dined quietly at Amesbury House with Droopy, and gave him a full account of the perils through which he had passed on his way to Martinique and the happy months he had since spent there.

Next morning he went to the Foreign Office. That stiff, unbending man, Lord Grenville, received him most courteously, and with the little affability of which he was capable, then handed him the letter from Mr. Pitt to Montgalliard. Having approved Roger's design to assume a new identity, he furnished him with a British Diplomatic passport on special thin paper, in the name of MacElfic, credentials to the Prince de Condé, a bag of gold in various currencies and open drafts for the much greater sums he might need for bribery on both a banker named Mayer Anselm Bauer in Frankfurt and a holder of British secret funds in Paris. He then announced that, subject to Roger's approval, he had already made arrangements for a naval cutter to put him ashore, weather permitting, between Dunkirke and Ostend in the early hours of the following morning.

If the vessel was to catch the tide this meant for Roger an almost immediate departure; but, having no reason to suggest a postponement, he agreed, and hastened back across St. James's Park to Amesbury House, There he wrote letters to Amanda, Georgina and his father, then, accompanied by Droopy Ned, he drove down to Greenwich, where the cutter was lying in readiness to take him across the Channel.

No sooner was he aboard than she cast off from her buoy and began to drop down river. Once more Roger waved good-bye to Droopy, who stood, a tall stooping figure, peering short-sightedly after him from the wharf. Then, as it was still not yet two o'clock, he settled himself comfortably to watch through the long afternoon the multifarious activities of the shipping in the lower reaches of the Thames.

When dusk fell the cutter was still in the estuary of the river; but soon afterwards she picked up a good southwesterly breeze, and at half-past four in the morning, Mr. 'Robert MacElfic', now wearing a heavy multi-collared coat, was landed without incident on a deserted beach only a few miles from Ostend.

As a result of the long occupation of the Belgian Netherlands by Austria, much German was spoken in those parts as well as the local Flemish; but, owing to the proximity of the French frontier, most of the better-class people also spoke some French. The French Republicans were, too, now the masters there; so Roger decided to use their language, and from the beginning pose as a French official, since to do so offered the best prospect of getting his wants promptly attended to.

By six o'clock he was breakfasting at a good, but not pretentious, hotel in the town; and soon afterwards set out in a post-chaise he had hired from its landlord to take him to Brussels. He reached the city by two o'clock in the afternoon and there proceeded to make more elaborate arrangements for the continuance of his journey. As he was going into the war area he had to put down a considerable deposit to secure a light travelling coach, but that means of transport had the advantage over taking to horse that he could sleep in it, and so arrive at his destination more speedily and less fatigued. He then purchased a small valise, toilet gear, a change of linen, and a supply of food and wine; so that he need stop for a meal on the way only if he felt inclined. Having tucked away a good hot dinner, he had his things packed into the coach and at six o'clock, with two coachmen on its box to drive turn and turn about, took the road south-east to Namur.

Mr. Pitt had given him roughly the dispositions of the armies, and he had, as far as possible, confirmed them while in Brussels. There were still considerable British forces in Hanover, and as the Prussians in their peace treaty with the French had guaranteed the neutrality of the North German States, it was a sore point with Ministers that they remained tied up there to no purpose. But, out of pride, King George had refused to allow his German dominion to be denuded of troops; so to the French Army of the North, commanded by General Moreau, there was now no opposition, and it was employed only in garrisoning the fortresses of Belgium and Holland.

Further south the Army of the Sambre and Meuse, under General Jourdan, and the Army of the Rhine and Moselle, under General Pichegru, had been co-operating, with the evident intent of endeavouring to drive the two Austrian armies back on to the Danube. Jourdan had laid siege to Luxemburg and, with the assistance of Pichegru's left wing, to Mainz, but, but the sieges had gone slowly, owing to Carnot's no longer being at the Ministry of War, and the incompetence of his successors in furnishing the armies with adequate supplies. In June Luxemburg had at last surrendered; so Jourdan had then been able to push on. Throwing the bulk of his army across the Rhine at Dusseldorf, he had swung south down the right bank of the river, driving the Austrian General, Clerfayt, before him until he reached the Main.

General Wurmser, with the other Austrian army, aided by the Prince de Condé's corps of *émigrés,* which was still further south, and based on Baden, had in the meantime been holding Pichegru. But in Brussels, Roger had learned that on the day he had reached London, September the 20th, Pichegru had captured Mannheim; so he too was across the Rhine and it now looked as if the two French armies were about to form a junction which might prove disastrous for the Austrians.

It was this new move of Pichegru's, indicating so clearly

that the last thing he had in mind at the moment was to march his army on Paris, that had determined Roger now to regard his mission as of the utmost urgency. Had this not been so he would have proceeded north, into Holland, then made a great detour through the still peaceful states well to the east of the Rhine, and so reached Baden without having to enter any area so far affected by the war; but that would have taken him the best part of a week. The alternative was to go via Namur, Luxemburg and Saarbrucken direct to the Upper Rhine opposite Baden and find some means to cross the river there. As the whole of the territory through which he must pass was in the hands of the French, that meant his having to chance some unfortunate encounter and, in the last phase, possibly being shot at as he attempted to cross the river; but as the journey could be accomplished by driving all out in two days, he felt that these risks were worth taking.

He found it easy to slip back into the role of a Republican Commissioner; and, by a combination of a confident, authoritative manner coupled with lavish tips to his two Belgian coachmen and the ostlers who changed the horses at the posting houses, he kept the coach moving at a very satisfactory pace. On the second afternoon, as he neared the Rhine, he was several times challenged by patrols of French troops; but fortunately none of them knew that the Citizen Commissioner Breuc had fled from Paris fourteen months before, and after a cursory glance at his old papers, they accepted his statement that he was on his way to General Pichegru's headquarters.

Wissembourg, which lay on the west bank of the Rhine, almost opposite Baden, had been used by Pichegru as his headquarters throughout the summer; so, although he had recently moved north, the town was still cluttered up with a large part of his baggage train and many officers of the administrative services. Seeing this as his coach entered the narrow streets, Roger decided to try to pick up as much information as he could about the progress of the new offensive before planning his attempt to cross the river that night.

It was as well that he did so, for events had been moving

fast during the past few days. Thanks to his impeccable French, some officers at an hotel at which he pulled up readily accepted his invitation to join him in a glass of wine, and proved eager to acquaint him with the latest news. Gaily they described how the capture of Mannheim had thrown the whole of south-west Germany into a panic, and how both the Landgrave of Darmstadt and the Margrave of Baden were reported to have fled from their capitals.

If the last report were true, and Roger had to regard it as at least probable, it meant that the Prince de Condé would also have hurriedly evacuated Baden; so to attempt a clandestine crossing of the river there would now be to run a pointless risk. In these altered circumstances, with the Prince's whereabouts no longer known to him, Roger felt that his best plan would be to take the road north into the area where both banks of the Rhine were held by the French; as, with luck, he might then be able to cross it openly in his coach, the retention of which would prove invaluable to him while searching for the Prince's new headquarters.

Accordingly, he bade the officers a cheerful farewell, and collecting his two Belgian coachmen from the tap-room took them outside.

They were employees of the owner of the coach and responsible to him for its safe return, but had contracted only to take Roger to the left bank of the Rhine, opposite Baden. He now put it to them that he wished to keep the coach on for two or three days, and that if they would continue with him, obeying his orders without questions, and keeping their mouths shut whatever they might see or hear, he would reward them by giving them a letter which would enable them to claim the considerable deposit he had paid on the coach when they got back with it to Brussels.

At first the men showed some hesitation, but on Roger's producing a purse full of gold coins and giving them ten *thalers* apiece as a bonus in hand, they agreed. So as dusk was falling the coach took the road that ran parallel with the river towards Mannheim.

A three-hour drive brought it opposite to the city. There

Roger learned that during the assault the stone bridge had been too severely damaged by cannon fire to be safe for vehicles; but the French Engineers had since succeeded in throwing a pontoon bridge across for military traffic. Again he told his story, that he had urgent business with General Pichegru, and once more, their suspicions lulled by this bold assertion, a guard who had halted the coach allowed it to proceed.

Roger had been told by the guard that the General had installed himself in the *Rathaus* but, after crossing the bridge, instead of following the directions the guard had given him to find it, Roger told his coachmen to take the first turning they came to on the right, and to keep on going until they were clear of the city.

All went well until they reached its outskirts. There a man in the middle of the road swinging a lantern called on them to halt, and from a barrier a few yards behind him a sergeant approached the coach.

Before the N.C.O. had a chance to open his mouth, Roger thrust his head out of the window of the coach, and shouted: 'I am a surgeon! General Pichegru's nephew has been wounded out in front there, and the General has despatched me to do my best for him. Open the barrier! Lose not a moment; the young man's life may depend upon it.'

The ruse got them through, and the coach had hardly halted before it was on the move again.

Having reason to believe that the battle was still fluid, in which case no continuous line would yet have been formed in front of Mannheim, Roger now hoped that under cover of darkness he might make his way between the various French units, most of whom at this hour would be sleeping in their bivouacs, without further challenge; but in that he was disappointed.

Some three miles from the city they were again called on to halt, and this time the N.C.O. in charge of the patrol did not swallow Roger's story so readily. He said that he knew of no units further advanced than his own, and demanded to see the traveller's papers.

Having committed himself, Roger's only possible course

was to maintain his bluff and intensify it. Sharply he told the man that when a valued life hung in the balance one did not wait for special papers before setting out to save it, and that if he could not tell a good Frenchman from a foreigner he did not deserve to serve under so great a soldier as General Pichegru; then he let forth a spate of filth and obscenity couched in the *argot* of the Paris gutters that he had picked up during the months when he had himself lived as one of the *sans-culottes*.

Reeling under the impact, and with all his suspicions dissipated, the N.C.O. waved the coach on. Yet he did so shaking his head and muttering uneasily: 'Have your own way then, Citizen; but I know of no units forward of us, and if you go on for more than a mile or two you'll like as not find yourself in the hands of the enemy.'

That was precisely what Roger hoped, and his hopes were fulfilled. Next time a call came for the coach to halt it was in a strange tongue, and a moment later it was surrounded by a vedette of Moravian Hussars. Finding it impossible to make himself fully understood, Roger fished out from under the thick turn-up of his cuff, the envelope containing his British passport, waved it beneath the sergeant's nose and pointed vigorously towards the rear of the Austrian position.

The coach was then sent on under escort for a mile or more to a farmhouse, from which there emerged a haggard-looking officer who spoke a little German. Using such stilted phrases of that tongue as he could put together Roger asked to be taken to the nearest headquarters, and with its escort the coach moved on through the darkness.

An hour later it drew up in front of a country house, in one of the ground floor rooms of which a light was burning. Roger was led inside and found the night-duty officer there to be a young exquisite dressed in a uniform of blue and silver with a sable-trimmed half cloak, and whiskers in the new fashion, very similar to his own.

To him Roger presented his passport, which carried the name of MacElfic, and told him that he was *en mission* from his Prime Minister to the Prince de Condé. The young man immediately became all politeness and offered to put him up for the night; but on Roger's replying that his mission was urgent, the Austrian promised to provide him with a guide, a change of horses and a new escort; and, in the meantime, sent an orderly for food and wine.

Three-quarters of an hour later, pleasantly fortified, Roger was on his way again; but the guide did not know the exact whereabouts of the Prince's new headquarters, only that they were somewhere in the neighbourhood of Heilbronn; so on reaching that area numerous enquiries had to be made, until they were at last located some five miles from the town in a castle to which a modern wing had been added.

Roger arrived there at eight o'clock in the morning, on the fourth day after he had landed on the Belgian coast. In seventy-six hours he had traversed some four hundred and fifty miles of roads which, as the time included all waits while changing horses, gave the highly satisfactory average of just under six miles an hour. But he had even more reason to be pleased that after his quarry's flight from Baden he had had the good luck to get safely through the battle zone and locate him again with so little delay.

Rubbing the sleep from his eyes, he climbed stiffly out of the coach, walked past a sentry up to the main entrance to the *Schloss* and asked the servant who was on duty in its porch to ask his master to receive a messenger who had arrived with urgent despatches for him from England. The footman gave his dirty, travel-stained figure one supercilious glance, and replied haughtily:

'His Royal Highness does not receive couriers. At the east door you will find someone who will accept delivery of your despatch, and doubtless it will be placed before His Royal Highness by the proper person when His Royal Highness returns from the hunt.'

Roger's blue eyes suddenly blazed with anger. It was bad enough that at this crisis in the war the Commander of the Royalist army should have gone out hunting, but to be subjected to insolence from his servants was intolerable. Lifting his jack-booted right foot, Roger brought its heel down with all his force on the footman's toes, and snarled:

'Go, fellow, this instant; and find someone of rank to attend me!'

The men let out a howl of pain, staggered back and, whimpering loudly, limped swiftly towards the doorway of the castle.

He was met in it by another footman and a senior servant in black clothes, who had come running at his shout. As he sobbed out the cause of his woe the others cast angry, frightened glances at Roger, then they helped their weeping companion through into the hall, slamming the door behind them.

Some three minutes later a very fat priest, with the voluminous skirts of his cassock swirling about his short legs, came puffing out into the porch. Roger made him a polite bow, and, now taking pains to use indifferent French, in keeping with his new rôle, introduced himself as Mr. Robert MacElfic, adding that he was the personal emissary of His Britannic Majesty's Prime Minister.

At that the priest's chubby face instantly lost its look of apprehension. Raising his plump hands, he exclaimed: 'Then you come from our second Father on Earth! I will have that oaf caned for his lack of respect to you. I am the Abbé Chenier, His Royal Highness's secretary. Welcome; thrice welcome. Be pleased to come in.'

This was much more the style in which Roger had expected to be greeted, and he was by no means surprised to hear Mr. Pitt referred to as the second Father on Earth of the *émigrés,* as that gentleman had furnished him with particulars of their misfortunes. During the early years of the Revolution numerous German Princes had in turn received them most hospitably, but as their own resources had dwindled and their numbers had increased to several thousand they had proved too great a burden on their not very wealthy hosts. The Austrians had then accepted responsibility for them, but only to the extent of furnishing twelve cents and one loaf of munition bread per man per day, which was what they gave their own troops.

In consequence, by the previous winter they had been reduced to positive destitution. Even the Prince's household had had to live on coarse soldier's fare, and to keep them from freezing his mistress, the Princess of Monaco, had sold her last jewels to buy firewood. From this desperate situation they had been rescued by Mr. Pitt, who at the instigation of Montgalliard had arranged for them a British loan of three and a half million francs. How much of the money had stuck to the villainous Count's fingers could only be guessed but it was no wonder that, after the Pope, they regarded Mr. Pitt as their 'Father on Earth.'

Murmuring that the footman had already been punished enough for his stupidity, Roger followed the Abbé across a lofty banqueting hall and through some corridors in the new wing of the castle to a small room that had a pleasant view across distant forest-covered slopes. After fussily seating Roger in an easy chair, the Abbé sat down behind a table covered with papers and enquired about his journey.

Roger confined himself to saying that it had been tiring but uneventful until he had entered the battle zone the previous night, and that he had been lucky enough to get through without serious trouble. Then he asked when the Prince could he expected back.

'Soon after midday, Monsieur,' replied the Abbé. 'We have been through terrible times—terrible times; and it was too bad that having established ourselves in reasonably comfortable quarters we should again have been driven from them by the advance of these Godless revolutionaries. But we have been fortunate in the Graf von Hildersheim's, who owns this *Schloss,* placing it at his Royal Highness's disposal. The *Herr Graf*'s forests are well stocked with game and he keeps a pack of boar-hounds; so His Royal Highness can hardly be expected to deny himself the pleasures of the chase while he is here. But he will be back in good time for dinner. By the by, pray forgive the enquiry, but are you of gentle birth?'

'My Mother was titled and the daughter of an Earl,' Roger told him, suppressing a cynical little smile at the question.

'Good! Good! That is most fortunate; as otherwise we should not be able to have you with us at dinner in His Royal Highness's salon. The preservation of a proper etiquette has become all the more important since the world began to tumble about our ears. Now, perhaps you will be good enough to inform me of the business that has brought you here.'

'It is a matter for His Royal Highness's personal consideration; so I fear that I must defer speaking of it until his return.'

'Your discretion is admirable, Monsieur,' wheezed the Abbé. 'But I give you my word that I am privy to all His Royal Highness's secrets.'

'Then,' replied Roger smoothly, 'no doubt he will invite you to be present when I submit Mr. Pitt's proposals to him. However, there is another matter of some urgency which I should like to deal with. I bear a letter for M. le Comte de Montgalliard.'

The Abbé nodded. 'The Count is not addicted to the chase; so he should be in the castle somewhere. I will have him sought for.'

When, in response to the ringing of a handbell, a footman had appeared and been given the order, Roger asked that his two coachmen should be looked after and his coach and horses stabled. He had not intended it as a hint, but apparently the Abbé took it as such; for he quickly added that a meal and a room were to be prepared for the Chevalier MacElfic.

As soon as the man had gone Roger slit open the lining of his coat and took from their hiding place the papers with which Lord Grenville had furnished him. Having put his credentials and the letters of credit in his pocket, he retained the missive for Montgalliard in his hand. A few minutes later the Count entered the room.

With his heavy black eyebrows, thick nose and sallow skin, he looked like a Portuguese Jew; but his manner was brisk and on being introduced his face lit up with a deceptively frank smile that anyone would have thought charming.

When Roger handed him the letter he asked permission to open it, skimmed quickly through its single paragraph, and said: 'I see Mr. Pitt desires me to pay another visit to England, and at once. Have you any idea about what it is that he wishes to see me?'

'I gathered the impression,' lied Roger glibly, 'that he is anxious lest His Royal Highness should become embarrassed for funds with which to maintain his army throughout the winter; so has it in mind to arrange well in advance another loan through you.'

'Our second Father on Earth,' murmured the Abbé, his fat face creasing into an unctuous smile, 'our second Father on Earth. What a good man he is! Our Father in Heaven will surely reward him.' But Roger was watching the Count, and saw at once that he had swallowed the bait.

Taking a fat bejewelled watch from his fob, he glanced at it and said to the Abbé: 'It would ill become me to delay in obeying the summons of our Preserver. I can be packed by ten o'clock; and if I leave soon after shall reach Wurzburg in time to lie there tonight on my way up to Hanover. Should I then be lucky in catching a ship about to sail from one of the ports, I'll be in England in little more than a week. Seeing the nature of the business I am going upon, I feel confident that His Royal Highness will pardon me for not having lingered to kiss his hand. Be kind enough, Abbé, to explain and make my *devoirs* for me.'

'Gladly, my son.' The Abbé raised a hand in blessing. 'May God be with you in this worthy undertaking.'

As Roger watched Montgalliard bow, flash a swift smile at them, then stride from the room, he thought how fortunate it was that the Count, like himself, was no man to let the grass grow under his feet. True, his making for Hamburg or Bremen showed that, despite his long experience as a secret agent, he preferred to lose three or four days rather than take the risk of travelling through enemy-held territory. But Roger was concerned only to get rid of him, and for that, clearly, nothing could have served better than leading him to believe that he had sniffed British gold.

For some ten minutes the Abbé and Roger talked about the war, then the black-clad groom-of-the-chambers appeared to announce that a tray had been set for Roger in the small library. The Abbé said that after his meal he would no doubt like to rest, and that he would have him called as soon as His Royal Highness got back from the chase; so with the usual expressions of politeness they took temporary leave of one another.

As Roger sat down to a belated breakfast of cold roebuck and a half bottle of Moselle, he said to the servant: 'When I have eaten I shall go to my room. Have ready for me there a hip-bath and plenty of hot water; also a valet to take and brush my clothes. Be diligent in this, for as I think you saw a while back I am not accustomed to being kept waiting.'

He would never normally have used such a tone in a house where he was a guest, but having been given only cold meat and a half bottle of wine riled him; and as Britain was paying the bills for the household he was in no mind to be treated as a person of no consequence by its servants.

In due course the man took him up to a small, chill room in the old part of the castle, but apologised for that, remarking that it was the best of the few remaining unoccupied; and as all Roger's other wishes had been attended to he accepted this new concern for his welfare graciously.

After bathing and shaving the ball of his chin, he lay down on the bed. It was the first time for four days that he had been able to do more than doze while subjected to a rocking or jolting motion; so almost instantly he fell asleep.

Some three hours later the valet woke him, helped him to dress, then led him down to a pair of double doors giving on to the first of a suite of large lofty rooms, and there handed him over to the Abbé Chenier. The first room was an antechamber, the second a big salon in which a score or more ladies and gentlemen were conversing. Nodding his way ingratiatingly through them, the grossly fat priest piloted Roger to the big doors at the end of the room, and opening one just widely enough to squeeze through, drew him into a spacious bedroom.

The Prince had evidently been changing in it after the hunt, and was now holding his *petit levee*. He was still only in silk stockings, breeches and shirt, while his buckled shoes, flowered waistcoat, and coat were being held by three of a small semi-circle of noblemen who stood deferentially by.

Roger remembered seeing him several times at Versailles,

and thought that six years had not changed him much, except to emphasise still further his protuberant blue eyes, sloping forehead and fleshy, hooked nose, which were such marked features in all the Bourbon Princes.

On catching sight of him the Prince at once beckoned him forward and, with a toothy smile, extended his right hand. Roger duly kissed it and presented the letter from Lord Grenville. Throwing it unopened on the bed de Condé exclaimed:

' 'Twill be time enough for us to attend to business when we have dined! The Abbé Chenier tells me that you have brought us excellent news. That dear Mr. Pitt is already thinking of our winter comfort. Such tidings are introduction enough. You have no idea, Chevalier, how we suffered last winter. The river frozen, the horses dying in the stables, and ourselves with not enough cheese in the larder to tempt a hungry mouse. You are welcome, most welcome. After France your generous nation will ever be nearest to my heart.'

As Roger murmured his thanks and bowed himself away, he wondered a little uneasily if Mr. Pitt would, in due course, furnish the funds he had invented to get rid of Montgalliard. He was inclined to hope so, as one could not but pity these people, all of whom had been born to riches and since been robbed of everything; yet their evident petty jealousy, as they each endeavoured to draw the Prince's attention to themselves, and preoccupation with the necessities of an outmoded etiquette made him secretly despise them.

Of the latter he was to have further evidence when they went down to dinner. Had he arrived at the Court of Russia, the old Empress Catherine, for all her vast dominions, would have had him sit next to her; so that she might the sooner hear the latest news out of England. So, too, in his day would have the late Gustavus of Sweden, the Stadtholder of Holland and even Queen Caroline of Naples; but the Bourbon Princes in exile still considered that it would be demeaning themselves to have any but the bearers of ancient names near them at table. Roger found himself placed near its bottom, between another Abbé and a nephew of the Marquis de Bouillé. Both were pleasant men and the Abbé talked interestingly on the ways in which the Revolution had affected the numerous independent Prince-Bishoprics that peppered the Rhineland, but Roger was glad when the meal was over.

Soon afterwards the Abbé Chenier drew Roger aside and introduced him into the Prince's cabinet. De Condé was already there and had just opened Grenville's letter. It would have been contrary to etiquette for him to invite them to sit down; so looking up at Roger, he said:

'This expresses only his lordship's willingness to serve us, and states that you will convey Mr. Pitt's views to us on certain matters. Fire away then, and let us hear everything with which that most excellent of Ministers has charged you.'

Roger at once launched into the subject of Pichegru, but after a moment the Prince cut him short by exclaiming to the Abbé: 'Ah, how unfortunate that de Montgalliard has already left! He knew far more of the ins and outs of this business than anyone else; and I am at a loss to see how we are to reopen negotiations with this traitor General without him.'

'My instructions are,' said Roger quietly, 'that, subject to your Royal Highness's permission, I should now take over the negotiations with General Pichegru myself.'

De Condé gave a slight shrug. 'Since that is your Prime Minister's wish, by all means do so. Are you acquainted with the fellow?'

'No, *Monseigneur*. But that is of little importance, provided that you will make quite clear to me your intentions towards him. May I hear from your own lips the price you are prepared to pay him for marching his army on Paris and restoring the monarchy?'

The lavish list of rewards that Roger had had from Mr. Pitt was promptly reeled off by the Prince, who added with an ugly chuckle: 'In the Chateau of Chambord there is an excellent *oubliette*. I hope he falls down it when drunk one night, and breaks his dirty neck.'

To Roger the wish seemed a miserably mean one, seeing that only as a result of Pichegru's staking his own life and honour could the thousands of people who had fled from France hope to return home, and have some prospect of regaining at least a part of their former possessions. Ignoring the remark, he asked:

'Has your Royal Highness sent these promises to the General in writing?'

'*Mort deiu,* no!' The Bourbon's pale blue eyes popped. 'The word of a Condé is enough.'

'Permit me to observe, *Monseigneur,* that in this instance you are not dealing with a gentleman.'

'Oh! Ah! Well! Yes! I see your point Chevalier. If you wish, then, I will give you written particulars of the proffered bribe.'

'I thank your Royal Highness. And now,' went on Roger —for this most delicate of questions sliding behind the shadow of Mr. Pitt—'as a matter of form my master charged me to enquire if you, *Monseigneur,* had authority from His Royal Highness the Comte de Provence to offer these terms?'

'You refer to His Most Christian Majesty King Louis XVIII,' the Prince replied with sudden sharpness.

For a moment Roger was taken aback. He knew that young King Louis XVII was dead, and he had told Amanda how the boy had died; but he had the most excellent reasons for supposing that they were the only people in the world who possessed that knowledge. De Condés sharp rebuke must mean that, although Mr. Pitt had omitted to tell him of it, the child in the Temple, whom only Barras, Fouché, and perhaps now a few others, knew to have been substituted for the little King, had also died. Recovering himself, he said hastily:

'Your pardon, *Monseigneur*. In England we have been used for so long to refer to His Majesty by his former title.'

The Prince shrugged. 'No matter. Your slip was understandable and you may set your master's mind at rest about my powers. For reasons of health His Majesty is now at Mitau on the Baltic, and '*Monsieur*' his brother at present has only a small force under him in the island of Yeu off the coast of Brittany. Therefore, as Commander-in-Chief of the Royal and Catholic Army, I have been invested by

His Majesty with full authority to act in his name, and use any and every means seemingly good to me which may assist in restoring his dominions to him.'

Roger bowed. 'Then it remains, *Monseigneur,* only for me to ask when the Comte de Montgalliard had his last interview with General Pichegru, and the outcome of it?'

De Condé guffawed and the Abbé gave a wheezy titter. Then the former said: 'The Count was far too wily a bird to go poking his own head into such a hornet's nest as a Republican headquarters. He employed a Swiss named Fauche-Borel to do his dirty work for him. You know the Count's cat's-paw better than I, Abbé. Tell the Chevalier about him.'

His great paunch wobbling with laughter, the Abbé proceeded. 'Fauche-Borel is a common little man who has made a modest fortune as a bookseller in Neuchâtel. He is the veriest snob that ever was born, and his one ambition is to hob-nob with the aristocracy. The Revolution gave him his opportunity. Many persons of quality took refuge over the Swiss border, and by trading on their urgent need of money Fauche-Borel ingratiated himself with a number of them. How de Montgalliard came across him I do not know; but the Count brought him here and, after making His Royal Highness privy to the use to which he was to be put, asked that he should be received. On being permitted to kiss the hand of a Prince of the Blood, he nearly fainted with emotion; but it made him our willing slave, and it is he who on several occasions has gone through the enemy lines to discuss matters personally with General Pichegru.'

Roger would have given a lot to have said: 'You dirty cowards; how dare you, on account of his simplicity, despise this brave little man,' but disciplined tact of years restrained him; and, keeping the cold contempt from his voice with an effort, he asked: 'Where is this person now?'

'As far as I know, he is in Paris,' replied the Abbé. 'I gathered that General Pichegru asked him to go there and endeavour to find out what support might be expected for a counter revolutionary movement by the Army.'

That was bad news for Roger, as it confirmed the reason Mr. Pitt had given for Pichegru's hesitation in declaring his adherence to the Royalist cause; and meant that he, Roger, would probably have to follow Fauche-Borel to the capital on a similar mission, as the only means of bringing about the conditions which would induce the General to act. Still thinking about the Swiss bookseller, he muttered:

'As well send a sheep into a den of lions.' Then he added more briskly: 'However, that is none of my business. If your Royal Highness will be good enough to append your own signature to a document stating the terms of the offer to Pichegru, I will set out this evening on an attempt to carry it to him.'

The Prince yawned, belched mildly, stood up and said: 'Draw up the document now, Abbé, append my seal to it and bring it up to my bedroom. I am weary after the chase and must have my rest, but will sign it before I sleep.' Turning his protuberant blue eyes on Roger, he went on: 'I regret that you should have to leave us so soon, Chevalier; but it is in a good cause, and I trust your absence will be only temporary. I shall pray for your safety and success; and can assure you that we shall all be a dither with anxiety until we can make you doubly welcome on your return.'

Roger let the glib lies flow over him, and again kissed the beringed hand that the Prince extended. Whatever his luck with Pichegru, he had no intention of returning to anyone except, God willing, Mr. Pitt and in due course, Amanda. Two hours later he drove away from the *Schloss* in his coach, soberly aware that the really dangerous part of his mission had now begun.

19

The Treachery of General Pichegru

Although Roger had given the Abbé Chenier the impression that he meant to penetrate the enemy lines that night, he did not mean to do so. For one thing he was badly in need of a good night's sleep, and felt that, urgent as coming to an understanding with General Pichegru might be, the delay of a few hours would be more than compensated for by renewed freshness when he entered Mannheim and would need all his wits about him.

Had the atmosphere at de Condé's headquarters been more congenial to him he would have slept there; but the sight of the servile nobles and unctuous priests had so sickened him that solitude at a wayside inn seemed definitely preferable.

He had also to rid himself of his coach and the two coachmen. Although most Belgians had now become antagonistic towards the French owing to the extortions inflicted on them by the Republican Commissioners, when first the so-called 'Army of Liberation' had invaded the country, the masses in the towns had received them with open arms; and Roger had no means of knowing for certain whether his two men were ardent revolutionaries or reactionaries. True, they had not betrayed him when he had pretended to be a doctor in order to get through the French outposts, but if left either at the *Schloss* or in Mannheim they might have endangered his future operations by gossiping, in the one case about his use of fluent French while posing as Citizen Breuc on the journey from Brussels, and in the other by letting out that he had been at the headquarters of the *émigrés*; so the best means of insuring against both these eventualities was to pay them off at some lonely place on the road, where he could also sleep.

The Abbé had provided him with a *laissez-passer*; so he had no difficulty with the occasional patrols of Austrians in the back areas who challenged the coach, and four hours of good driving brought them to the little town of Sinsheim. As it was by then ten o'clock, he began to look out for a likely place in which to spend the night, and a few miles beyond the town, on the crest of a long slope up which the horses had had to be walked, they came to a fair sized inn.

It was in darkness; but getting out, he knocked up the landlord: a fat German who came down and opened the door. Roger asked him if he had a bedroom free, and a riding horse he could sell in the morning.

The man said that he was welcome to a room, but a horse was another matter. For the past week the Austrians had been commandeering every horse to be had in those parts, and three days before had taken all four of the horses he had had in his stable.

Realising that enquiries elsewhere were unlikely to have better results, Roger decided to use the off-lead from the team drawing the coach; but he said nothing about that for the moment, simply telling the Belgians that he meant to lie at the inn for the night and that after they had drunk as much beer as they wanted they could for once enjoy a long sleep. As they had slept most of the day they were now less tired than he was, but ample beer and a snug corner in a hay-loft over their animals was to them a pleasant enough prospect, so they thanked him and drove the coach into the yard of the inn.

At six o'clock Roger woke after an excellent night, dressed and went downstairs to find the landlord already about; so he asked him for pen and paper, and if he could sell him a saddle. The man produced the writing materials from a cupboard and said that he had several saddles so would be willing to part with one for a fair price.

While breakfast was being prepared Roger wrote out an instruction to the owner of the coach to pay to the two coachmen the big deposit he had left on it; then, after making a good meal, accompanied by the landlord, he went out to the stable. Some gold pieces soon induced the Belgians to surrender the off-lead horse, and he added a handsome *pourboire* to the chit entitling them to the deposit; so the parting was effected with goodwill on both sides.

By seven-thirty he was on his way to Mannheim, with the small valise strapped to the back of his saddle. In addition to the few things he had bought in Brussels, it now contained the uniform of a private in the *émigré* army, which he had asked the Abbé Chenier to provide for him after their talk with de Condé the previous afternoon.

His return through the war zone was almost devoid of risk, as the units of both armies were scattered over a wide area, and even when he got to within a few miles of Mannheim he heard only the occasional shots of snipers in the distance. The sight of his *laissez-passer* was enough for the Austrian pickets to wave him on, then when he came to the French he told the simple truth—that he was on his way to General Pichegru—and taking him for a Frenchman they directed him towards the city.

He entered it at one o'clock in the afternoon, stabled his horse at the *Drei Könige* and took an attic there, which, owing to the crowded state of the town, was the best the hotel could do for him. In it he changed into the *émigré* uniform, put on his long, dark multi-caped coat over it, then went downstairs, wrote a brief note, slipped it into his pocket and walked along to the *Rathaus*.

There were sentries on its entrances, but evidently only as a formality, for among the officers constantly going in and out there was an occasional civilian, and none of them was being challenged. All the same Roger knew that once inside he might very well come out of it as a prisoner on his way to be shot; so he had to make a conscious effort to appear entirely carefree as he ran up the steps and walked through its main door.

In the stone-flagged hall beyond, a sergeant stopped him, and asked his business. With an indignant air he declared that he, a citizen of the glorious French Republic, had been cheated and insulted the night before in a brothel, and had come to demand that the dirty Germans who ran the place should be taught a lesson.

This was a complaint with which the sergeant could sympathise, and he directed Roger up a staircase to the right, saying that he would find the Provost-Marshal's office on the second floor. Roger had felt confident that it would be somewhere in the building, but he had no intention of going to it. On reaching the first floor he turned right along the principal corridor, hoping that now he was free to roam the place he would be able to locate the General without having actually to ask for him.

Pichegru's headquarters bore not the slightest resemblance to de Condé's. Here there were no lackeys, no priests, no respectful hush at the approach of prominent personalities. The place was as busy as a bee-hive, and it was the constant bustle of officers, clerks and orderlies hurrying to and fro which enabled Roger to move about quite freely without risk of being questioned further.

After a time he came upon a minstrels' gallery which overlooked the great hall in the centre of the building. It was obviously there that in times of peace the wealthier merchants of Mannheim periodically gorged themselves at civic banquets; but it had now been turned into a huge mess. Here again, in striking contrast to His Royal Highness's dinners, duly announced by a gentleman who rapped sharply with a rod on the parquet floor of a salon, and served to the minute each day, there was no trace whatever of formality. The service appeared to be in perpetual session; officers, some clean and others filthy, marched in and plumped themselves down where they would, the waiters put plates piled high with food in front of them, they ate voraciously, often not even exchanging a word with their neighbours, then marched out again.

Here and there among them was a civilian official, and it was their presence which caused Roger his greatest anxiety. At the *Schloss* he had stood within a few feet of three noblemen with whom he had been acquainted in the past, and a fourth whom he had been instrumental in saving from the guillotine; but a combination of his false name, changed appearance and the execrable French he had then been using deliberately, had protected him from recognition. Whereas now, should he come face to face with one of his ex-colleagues of the Revolution, he would have to rely solely on his moustache and whiskers.

Worse still, many of them had seen him about Paris for far longer than he had been known to any of the Prince de Condé's gentlemen, and he had reason to believe that there were at least two men at this headquarters whom he had special reason to dread. They were the Citizens Rewbell and Merlin of Thionville, two out of the three *Représentants en Mission,* sent by the Convention to keep an eye on Pichegru, and with both of whom Roger had sat on Committees.

For a long time he sat up in a corner of the deserted gallery watching the scene in the banqueting hall below, and feeling certain that sooner or later the General would come in to have a meal there. At length, at close on five o'clock, his patience was rewarded. A tall, handsome man in his early thirties came swaggering in with Citizen Merlin beside him and followed by half a dozen other officers. From the circumstances of his arrival and the description Roger had received, he knew at once that the tall officer must be Pichegru.

It was now that the greatest risk had to be run, as Roger might just as well not have come there unless he could obtain a private interview with the General, and he could see no way to succeed in that without disclosing that he was acting as the Prince de Condé's agent. If, as seemed quite possible from Pichegru's sudden advance on Mannheim, he had come to the conclusion that Montgalliard and Fauche-Borel were untrustworthy, or if one of the *Représentants en Mission* was given the least cause for suspicion, the game would be up as far as Roger was concerned, and, ten to one, for good. But it would have been contrary to his nature to back out now; so, drawing a deep breath, he stood up, then made his way downstairs.

Owing to the constant coming and going in the big hall, he attracted no attention when he came into it by one of its side entrances and took up a position near to a service door that gave on to the kitchen. In his hand he had, folded into a small thick triangle, the note he had written at the

Drei Könige, and a twenty *mark* piece. As the waiter who had been serving the General came by he plucked the man by the sleeve, gave him a quick glimpse of the coin and the note, and said in a low voice:

'I am a tradesman anxious to secure a share of the General's patronage. Do me the favour to give him this.'

The man hesitated only a moment, then with a sudden grin he stuck the note in his cuff and pocketed the gold.

When he next emerged from the kitchen, carrying another load of platters, Roger followed his movements with a heavily pounding heart. He saw him place the note beside the General's plate, but for what seemed an eternity, Pichegru did not appear to have even noticed it. At last he picked it up, opened it, and read the few lines that Roger had written, which ran:

Citizen General,

I am a partner in the firm of Fauche-Borel, booksellers and printers. I crave the distinction of being permitted to print such proclamations as Your Excellency may desire to issue to the people of Mannheim and its adjacent territories.

The die was cast. The name Fauche-Borel could not fail to register in the General's mind. In another minute he might order the arrest of the sender of the note or make an assignation with him.

As Roger watched he saw Citizen Representative Merlin lean towards Pichegru. There could be little doubt that he was enquiring the contents of the note, which, in his capacity as one of the Convention's watch-dogs, he was fully empowered to do.

It was at that moment that Roger saw Rewbell join the group. His heart seemed to jump into his throat, for Jean-François Rewbell was one of the old gang who had survived the fall of Robespierre. An Alsatian by birth, he had started life as a lawyer, had soon become a fanatical revolutionary, and had advocated many of the most ruthless measures of the Terror. He had already sent two Army Commanders back to Paris to be guillotined, and his shrewd, suspicious mind made him an expert at smelling out treachery.

To Roger's momentary relief the three men laughed at something one of them had said. Then Pichegru beckoned to the waiter who had brought the note. They both looked in Roger's direction, and the waiter began to walk towards him. His mouth went dry and again he was seized with near panic. Rewbell or Merlin might have found out that Fauche-Borel was a Royalist agent. If so Pichegru would have had no option but to save his own skin by sacrificing the bookseller's colleague. Perhaps they had laughed at the idea of his presenting himself there to be led out and shot. There was still time to turn, slip through the nearest entrance and make a bolt for it. Even with so short a lead, among the maze of staircases and corridors he might succeed in eluding pursuit, and perhaps in the attics find a hiding place until darkness increased his chance of getting away from the building unrecognised. His palms were moist and his feet itched to be on the move; bu twith a great effort of will he stood his ground until the waiter came up to him, and said:

'The General says that if you'll wait in the outer hall he'll try to find time to see you later.'

Suppressing a gasp of relief, and still too internally wrought up to trust himself to speak, Roger nodded; then made his way out of the great noisy chamber.

When he reached a low archway that gave on to the hall, he looked anxiously through it; and was much relieved to see that the sergeant to whom he had told his story about the brothel had been relieved by another. Stationing himself in an out-of-the-way corner and taking out his handkerchief, he mopped his face with it. Gradually the beating of his heart eased and he tried to persuade himself that his worst danger was over. But he could not be certain of that, as now that the offensive was going so well Pichegru might have decided against declaring for the Royalists, and, if he wished to strengthen his position with Rewbell, the turning over of an *émigré* agent to a firing squad would be a cheap way of earning himself a good mark.

The time of waiting seemed to Roger interminable, and

actually it was over two hours before a club-footed private came down the wide staircase opposite the main door, limped up to him, and asked:

'Are you the Citizen printer?'

On Roger replying that he was, the soldier took him upstairs to a suite of rooms on the second floor. The first was an ante-chamber and had the General's military equipment scattered about it. Pointing to a chair there, the soldier told him to sit down, and taking up a jack-boot set to work polishing it.

Through an open doorway Roger could see the bedroom, which he guessed to be normally used by the Mayors of Mannheim when in residence at the *Rathaus*. It was furnished with a vast bed and other heavy, ugly pieces, and Roger could well imagine that many a fat German City Father had fallen into a drunken slumber there after doing the honours in the banqueting hall below.

Still racked with anxiety about what might follow his coming interview with Pichegru, Roger endured a further twenty minutes' wait; then, at last, the General strode into the room.

Charles Pichegru was the son of a labourer, but had been educated by the Church and sent to the military school at Brienne, after which he had become an artillery officer. The Revolution had given him his chance and he was one of the most brilliant Generals it had produced. After successful campaigns in '93 and '94 his conquest of Holland the preceding winter had made him the most outstanding of them all. He was a tall, fine looking man, possessed of enormous physical strength, and was now thirty-four.

Giving Roger a penetrating glance, he motioned him into the bedroom, followed him in, told his man that on no account was he to be disturbed, and swung the door shut.

'Now!' he said without preamble. 'Had your approach to me been only a little less subtle I would have had you taken straight out to a firing squad; and I may yet do so. Fauche-Borel has already endangered me more than enough by forcing himself upon me with wild-cat schemes that lack any concrete backing, and when last I saw him I told him if he pestered me again I would have him shot.'

It was far from being a propitious opening, but Roger was on his mettle now and replied with a calmness that he was far from feeling: 'Citizen General, 'tis because it has been realised in the highest quarters that Fauche-Borel was incompetent to handle such business that I have been selected to replace him. I bring you a firm undertaking from His Royal Highness the Prince de Condé.'

The General's eyes narrowed slightly, and he asked: 'Do you mean that the Prince has actually put his hand to the terms that I supposed Fauche-Borel to have invented in the hope of gulling me into declaring for the Royalists?'

'That I cannot say, but if these are they I scarcely think you can regard them as ungenerous.' As Roger spoke he handed over the list of bribes that the Abbé Chenier had had signed by de Condé.

After reading slowly through them, Pichegru looked up and said: 'These differ from those offered by Fauche-Borel only in that the sum to be paid in cash has been doubled.'

Roger smiled. 'Fauche-Borel acted only as the cat's-paw of a rogue named Montgalliard. It was he who inspired these negotiations, and as he handles many of de Condé's transactions, no doubt he counted on being nominated to make the payment, which would have enabled him to keep half the money for himself.'

Sitting down in a huge arm-chair, Pichegru murmured, 'The Prince's having sent me this document puts a very different complexion on matters.'

'Then may I take it that you agree the terms?'

'I know not. I must think. Upon my decision depends the whole future of my country.'

'Do you accept and act with vigour, it will make you, after the King, the most powerful man in France.'

'I am already near that; and need no help from the Royalists to elevate myself still further. By marching on Paris I could have myself proclaimed Dictator.'

'Perhaps; but what of the war in the meantime? Did you turn your army about, the Austrians would be back over the Rhine and hot upon your heels. Only by entering into this pact could you prevent them doing so.'

The General shook his head. 'Nay, you are in error there. As I hold your life in my hands, I see no reason why I should not speak frankly to you. General Jourdan's army has reached the north bank of the Necker. I have only to make the dash on Heidelberg, which I have been preparing for these past few days, to join up with him. With our combined forces we shall far outnumber either of the Austrian armies. 'Twill be child's-play for us first to defeat Wurmser, then Clerfayt. That done, Austria must sue for peace; then I should be free to march on Paris.'

That was the very thing Roger feared, and he saw that he must play every card he had in an attempt to prevent it. Knowing the French hatred of the English, he had intended to pose as a French *émigré*, but he realised that Pichegru must know that de Condé was penniless, and that the huge money bribe he was offered could come only from England; so now he felt that it might serve him better to disclose his true nationality. After a moment, he said:

'Even if the Austrians came in you will not be able to secure peace for France. Britain will fight on. The English are a dogged people, and the Scots and Irish no less so. Only twelve years ago, alone in arms, Britain fought all Europe to a standstill. To them surrender is unthinkable.'

Pichegru nodded. 'I fear you are right in that. The English, too, are so vastly rich that with their gold they will suborn other nations to take up arms against us. Moreover, they love fighting for its own sake and are most ferocious enemies. I am told that such is their lust for blood that when at peace they spend all their time hunting, and devour raw the beasts they kill, tearing at them with their big teeth.'

Roger could not help laughing. 'Nay, they are not quite as uncivilised as that. It is true that they make good fighters, but by far the greater part of them would much prefer to remain at home tilling their rich fields, to enduring a hard soldier's life abroad and as often as not dying on some distant battle-field.'

'You speak as though you knew and liked them.'

'I do; for although I have lived for many years in France, I am an Englishman myself.'

'The Devil you are! Then I am inclined more than ever to have you shot.'

'No, General, I do not think you will do that.' Roger made the statement with quiet confidence, and, opening his coat, displayed the *émigré* uniform beneath it. 'You see, I have come to you as one soldier to another; and, apart from the laws of war, I cannot believe that you would act like a Rewbell. So brave a man as yourself would not descend to soil his hands in the manner of these terrorists.'

'You have me there;' Pichegru's handsome face broke into a smile. 'I may, though, have to imprison you for my own protection. But you are a brave fellow yourself, and a clever one. Why in thunder did not that fool of a Prince send you to me before, instead of a woolly-minded fumbler like Fauche-Borel?'

'Because I had not then been brought into this matter. However, we were speaking of the English. Britain holds the seas, and even were you master of all Europe you could not drive her from them; therefore you can never bring her to her knees. While she, if need be for a generation to come, can deny the oceans to your commerce, blockade your ports, starve and harass you. That she will never make peace with a Revolutionary Government I am convinced. On the other hand she is ready to do so with a Constitutional Monarchy. I give you my solemn word that, whatever you may have been led to believe, Mr. Pitt is at heart a man of peace, and greatly desires it. If you will but bring about a Restoration, I am confident that he will agree to any honourable terms. He would, I believe, even go so far as to support France at a conference of the Powers in her claim to what she asserts to be her natural boundaries; and thus enable her to retain much of the territory that you and her other Generals have won for her in the present war.'

Pichegru stared at him, and asked slowly: 'Who are you, that though dressed as a private in an army of outlaws, you should speak as though you knew the mind of Mr. Pitt?'

'I am the personal envoy of His Britannic Majesty's Prime

Minister,' Roger replied with suitable dignity. 'I visited de Condé's headquarters only to secure for you the document you are holding.'

As he fired his big gun, he watched anxiously for the General's reactions. They came at once. Jumping to his feet, he exclaimed: 'Then it is not de Condé alone who is behind this proposition! His name written in his own hand should be good enough; but there have been times when Princes of the House of Bourbon have gone back upon a bargain. If the British Government is prepared to guarantee the terms, I can count the fortune I am offered as good as already placed to my credit in the Bank of England.'

Roger bowed at the implied compliment. 'That certainly is true as far as the money clauses are concerned. As to the honours, I can only say that, without casting doubt upon the Prince's word, should Mr. Pitt's influence be needed to secure them for you, I feel sure he would exert it in your favour.'

With a vigorous nod, Pichegru murmured: 'We have got a long way. A very long way. In a quarter of an hour with you I have got further than in all my weeks of dickering with Fauche-Borel.'

'You agree, then?' Roger asked, his hopes rising with a bound.

'Nay; I do not say that. There are matters of far more weighty import than my own future to be considered. You spoke just now of the British Government's being willing to agree a peace if France were a Constitutional Monarchy. Can you give me an assurance that the Bourbon Princes are prepared to make her one?'

'No; that I cannot do. I had no converse with de Condé on that subject.'

'It is, though, the vital question upon which the whole future hangs. It is my belief that nine-tenths of the French people would now welcome a Restoration, were it based on the Constitution of '91. Last June, when the poor child in the Temple died and that fat dolt the Comte de Provence became technically Louis XVIII, he already had the game in his hands, had he only exercised a modicum of tact. He had but to announce that he accepted the principles of '91 and would grant an amnesty to all who had taken part in the Revolution, for half France to have risen and spontaneously demanded his recall. Yet dull-witted bigot that he is, he had the folly to declare in public that the Constitutionalists were more detestable to him than Robespierre himself. How can we hope to restrain the *émigrés* from taking their revenge for past ills, and the pursuance of liberal policies, should I put such a man upon the Throne?'

It was a hard question to answer, but Roger did his best. 'I think,' he said, 'you overrate that danger. Whatever the personal views of the King and a handful of ultra-Royalists may be, theirs will be voices crying in the wilderness. The Governments of Britain and Austria no longer care a rap for the pretensions of the *ancien régime,* and should they make peace at all they will use their utmost endeavours to ensure that it has the basis for a lasting one. Such pretensions to autocracy could lead only to another revolution, with the prospect of further war; so you may be certain that the Allies would insist on the new King opening his reign as a monarch with strictly limited powers. After that, matters will be in the hands of yourself and men like you. Free elections would produce a Chamber almost entirely composed of Moderates, and the King's only alternative to accepting its views would be to go once more into exile.'

'Perhaps you are right,' Pichegru muttered. 'Yes, I suppose with virtually the whole nation behind us we could exert a reasonable control over him. There, is, though, another matter. Although I am satisfied that the majority of the people would welcome a Restoration, there are many prominent men who would not, and among them are several holding key posts in the Administration. When I was last in Paris, Carnot told me that did he have the King's pardon in his pocket he would still not consider his life worth ten *sous* were a Bourbon monarch once more installed at the Tuileries; and, though for long a member of the Committee of Public Safety, he has harmed no man without just cause. Barras, Cambacérès, Larevelliére-Lépeaux, Cambon and Sieyès are of the same mind. As for villains like Rewbell, Tallien and others whose hands have dripped with innocent blood, they would rather die fighting in a ditch than trust to the mercy of a descendant of St. Louis. And rightly, for they would receive none.'

Roger's blue eyes glinted. 'What is to prevent you from having Rewbell hanged to the nearest flagstaff. As for the other ex-terrorists, make a list of them; then when you reach Paris put a price upon their heads, and have them shot at sight.'

'With Rewbell and Merlin I can deal at my pleasure. But the situation of the others is very different. As I advance on Paris they will do their utmost to rouse the mobs. They will denounce me in the Chamber as a traitor, and give tongue to their old rallying cry that the Revolution is in danger. When I reach the city scores of agitators paid or inspired by them will mingle with my troops, and will inevitably undermine the loyalty of a great part of them to myself. Overnight the forces upon which I must rely may melt away, or turn against me. That is the great danger.'

Agitatedly the General began to walk up and down.

'I spoke of this to Fauche-Borel, and he at least had the sense to admit that I was right. He said that he would go to Paris and endeavour to arrange with certain Royalists there that the most dangerous of our potential enemies should be either bribed into silence or forcibly muzzled. That is what must be done. To be certain of success it is essential that a *coup d'état* should be organised to synchronise with my arrival before the gates of Paris. But to bring a few hundred monarchists shouting into the streets is not enough. And how could a nonentity like Fouche-Borel succeed in doing more. What we need is someone who could win over to our designs a few such men as Barras and Dubois-Crancé. They have the power to arrest the ex-Terrorists who would otherwise sabotage our project. That is what we must have. And I'll make no move till something of the kind has been arranged. But where in the world are we to find a man capable of such an undertaking?'

Roger sighed. 'I fear, *mon General,* that he stands before you. Or at least one who might succeed in it if fortune favoured him.'

'What! You! An Englishman! How could you possibly hope to gain the ear of the most powerful men in France, and persuade them to participate in a monarchist plot?'

'I told you a while back that I have lived long in France. Throughout the greater part of the Terror I was in Paris. I know well all the men you have named. There was a time when they trusted me completely. But I have been absent from Paris for above a year. Everything hangs on whether I can re-establish myself in their confidence. Either I shall be in prison within twenty-four hours of my return to the capital, or I will stand a fair chance of bringing about the conditions you require.'

Pichegru suddenly took a step forward and, grasping Roger by the hand, exclaimed: 'You are a brave man! And from the open expression of your countenance, I believe an honest one. I am prepared to trust you. If, on your return, you can give me your word that measures to stifle opposition will be taken at the right moment, I promise you that I will march my army on Paris. Not for my own ends, or for the King, but as the only hope I see of restoring peace and prosperity to my country.'

Pressing the General's hand firmly, Roger replied: 'I thank you for the confidence you place in me. That I will do my utmost you may rest assured, for the future happiness of my countrymen is concerned in this as much as the happiness of yours.'

For a moment they stood in silence with hands clasped, then Roger asked: 'But what of the immediate future? Even should I succeed in keeping my freedom and manage to organise a plot designed to smother opposition by the fanatics of the old Jacobin Club, two or three weeks at least must elapse before I can return and report to you. What, in the meantime, are your intentions towards the Austrians?'

With a shrug, the General replied: 'The war must go on. My plans are laid and must be put into operation. The Austrians will be defeated, but that is their misfortune, and can have no bearing on this other matter.'

'Ah, but it may!' Roger protested. 'Should you inflict crushing defeats upon both their armies, this might cause them to sue for peace prematurely. If Britain becomes the only Great Power left with the right to make terms, any influence she might exert upon Louis XVIII to grant a

Liberal Constitution is bound to be weakened. And in this, as in all other things, it is a good maxim to keep ever in the forefront of one's mind the ultimate object of the operation.'

Again Pichegru stared at him, then muttered: 'I would I had you for my Chief-of-Staff. Yet in this matter I have little choice. General Jourdan is expecting me to launch a thrust against Heidelberg, and I'll confess that I am all impatience for this new stroke to bring additional glory to my army and myself.'

Roger shrugged, but a diabolically subtle note had crept into his voice as he said: 'Upon glory foolish people have become drunk, *mon General*. Personally, as a *bon viveur,* I am inclined to feel sorry for those who wake up with bad heads and empty pockets in the morning. But I have no admiration for them.'

'There is no question of bad heads, or of pockets being full or empty.'

'I differ from you there. Should I fail to bring about the conditions you require in Paris, and in the meantime you have launched this new offensive, all hope will be gone, not only of your doing what is best for France, but also of your securing any part of the great fortune that has been promised you. My master would, I know, approve my language in putting it to you that a bird in the hand is worth two in the bush.'

With a frown the General replied: 'I fear that I am at a loss to comprehend your meaning.'

'I pray you pardon me if my words have seemed obscure.' Roger's blue eyes bored into the General's brown ones. 'But I have told you that I am the emissary of Mr. Pitt, and you have yourself remarked on the great wealth of Britain. Do you agree to leave the Austrians more or less unmolested until the greater issue has been decided, here and now, as an earnest of our good intentions, I will make you a payment of a million francs.'

'A million francs!' Pichegru gasped; 'but how could you?'

Smiling, Roger fished a paper from his inner pocket and said: 'Here is a blank order on Mayer Anselm Bauer, banker of Frankfurt-on-Main, I am prepared to fill it in for a million francs, payable to you, if you can see your way to deal gently with the Austrians.'

'A million,' the General repeated with awe in his voice. 'Is it true then that the streets of London are paved with gold?'

'Not quite. But many of our hunting nobility, whom you had supposed to devour game raw, are served with it cooked, and in considerable state, off gold plate, in their mansions. What say you to my proposition?'

'The money bags of these German Jews are said to be bursting: but a million in gold is an enormous sum to pay out on demand. I greatly doubt if this man Bauer could meet the order.'

'Since he is an agent of the British Treasury, he should be able to do so at comparatively short notice.'

For a moment Pichegru remained thoughtful, then he said: 'Time is of importance if I am to enter into this transaction. Should I delay my offensive for more than a few days, and it afterwards transpires that the Jew is unable to pay, I shall have lost my chance of joining forces with General Jourdan yet be no better off.'

'How long can you give me?' Roger asked.

'For what?'

'Why, to go to Frankfurt and get the gold for you; or at least a written promise that in the course of a week or so it will be paid over to anyone you choose to nominate.'

The General nodded. 'That would certainly settle the question definitely. Frankfurt is near a hundred miles from here, but a light coach would get you there by tomorrow morning. The collection of the gold would require special arrangements; so for that I am willing to wait. But the day after tomorrow, at latest, I must have an assurance that it will be forthcoming.'

'Barring accidents, I should be able easily to get back by then.'

'That is unnecessary. One of my A.D.C's, a Captain Gusiot, is fully in my confidence. I will send him with you. He can bring me back the answer. If it is satisfactory I will send only two divisions against Heidelberg. That will be sufficient to prevent General Jourdan from suspecting that

I have departed from our agreed plan, but insufficient to take the place. Unless the Austrians are bigger fools than I take them for, they will then be able to prevent our joining up, and a stalemate result which must last at least a month.'

Roger knew then that, providing the money was forthcoming, he would have achieved the equivalent of a great allied victory; but he knew too that the final act yet remained to be played and that to play it he must now once more risk his head in Paris.

20

The Aftermath of the Revolution

Pichegru had spoken gloomily and it was evident that he was much troubled by this contemplated betrayal of his army's prospects of achieving another great victory; so Roger was careful to conceal the elation he felt at having won him over. Refraining from comment, he said quietly:

'As time is of importance, the sooner Captain Gusiot and I set off, the better.'

'I agree; but it would be preferable that you should not be seen together in this headquarters.'

'There is no reason why we should be seen together at all until we are well out of the city. I have taken a room at the *Drei Könige* under the name of Bertrand, and Captain Gusiot can pick me up there. It is already dark and there will be no necessity for him to leave the coach; he can simply send in for me.'

The General smiled. 'I see you are well practised in discretion.' Then, after glancing at his watch, he added: 'It is now a quarter to eight. Two hours should be enough for me to give Gusiot his instructions and for him to make his preparations. Be ready to join him in a coach at ten o'clock.'

For a short time they discussed various political leaders in Paris, and the chances of getting them to combine in a *coup d'état*; then they shook hands on their bargain, and Pichegru told his club-footed soldier servant to see Roger safely out of the *Rathaus*.

In his attic at the *Drei Könige,* he changed from the *émigré* uniform back into his own clothes, repacked his valise and went down stairs for a meal. He had not long finished it when the coach arrived for him. Darkness prevented him seeing the man in it except as a vague figure, and as soon as he had taken his place with a muttered greeting, the vehicle drove out of the inn yard.

A reluctant but instinctive caution kept both men from speaking until they were clear of the town, and even then they made no mention of the business they were bent upon. For a while they discussed the war, then they settled down in their corners to doze as well as they could while the coach jolted its way through the night, averaging some eight miles an hour.

For well over half the journey they travelled by the road along the right bank of the Rhine, which was in the hands of the French; and as they had an escort of hussars they were nowhere challenged. But at about five in the morning they reached the fork road, the right arm of which ran north-east through Darmstadt to Frankfurt; and, as the territory they were about to enter was in a state of dubious neutrality, they decided that it would be best to dispense with their escort.

In the grey pre-dawn light Roger now saw his companion properly for the first time. He was a well set up man of about thirty with flashing black eyes and a fine upturned moustache; and Roger was relieved to see he had taken the precaution, against falling in with the Austrians, of obtaining for himself a suit of ill-fitting but adequate civilian clothes. However, they encountered no Austrian troops, breakfasted heartily in Darmstadt and, soon after ten o'clock, crossed the bridge over the Main into Frankfurt.

Without difficulty they found the Judengasse, and the dwelling in it of the banker Bauer. It proved to be sizeable mansion and above its door, as a sign, there hung a red shield. Roger and Gusiot went inside. The ground floor was in use as a counting house, and when Roger told one of the young men there that he wished to see the banker in person, they were obsequiously bowed through to a private section partitioned off from the main office.

A Jew of about fifty, clad in the traditional cap and gown rose to meet them. Keeping his hands tucked inside the sleeves of his robe, he begged them to be seated and enquired their business. Roger produced the order and enquired if, when filled in for a million francs, it could be met.

Bauer asked a moment's grace, went to a cabinet and compared the signature on the order with one he had there, then he said: 'Nobleborn, no one could doubt that the British Treasury is good for a mere fifty thousand pounds; but in these troublesome times one does not keep such a sum in one's cellar. How soon do you require it?'

'How soon can you produce it?' Roger asked.

'Permit me, nobleborn, to consult my son,' Bauer replied; and, on Roger's nodding, he rang a handbell four times. In response three young Jews, the eldest of whom appeared to be only in his early twenties, came in. For a few minutes their father talked with them in the tongue of their race, then he turned to Roger and said:

'Nobleman; if you will accept mainly *marks* and *thaler*, in four days' time we shall be prepared to meet your order with the equivalent of one million francs in gold.'

Roger glanced at Guisot and the Frenchman nodded. The formalities were soon completed, then the banker and his three sons accompanied them to the front door. The youngest, a stripling of eighteen, went out to the coach with them and said to Roger:

'Pardon me, nobleborn; but it is evident that you are a trusted agent of the English. Do you think there might be a future in England for a young man like myself?'

With the habitual kindness that was second nature to Roger, providing due respect was paid to him, he smiled, and replied: 'Why not? We have Lloyds' House where more shipping is insured than anywhere else in the world, the India Company and the Hudson Bay. With the coming of the mechanical age Britain's own industries are booming, and loans for their expansion are always in good demand. On London's 'Change in these days many a fortune is being made by shrewd men within a few years.'

'I thank you, nobleborn.' The young Jew bowed low. 'I have hopes of coming there to settle one day.' Pointing to the red shield above their heads he added: 'There are so many of us in the German States named Bauer that my branch of the family has decided to be known in future as the Rothschilds. Would you be gracious enough to remember that, and should I come to England put in a good word for me where you can, because our house, although not a very rich one yet, has done its utmost to meet your heavy demand upon it promptly.'

'Indeed I will. Only my return to England I will tell Mr. Rose, who decides all things at the Treasury, of the great assistance your family has been to us.' Roger gave the promise willingly; the future being a closed book to him, he could not know that he was pledging his support to a man whose financial genius and unshakable faith in Britain would make him second only to Wellington in bringing about the final downfall of Napoleon.

Gusiot and Roger then adjourned to a good inn for a meal. After it, with Bauer's written promise to pay, the Captain set out on his return journey, Roger, now aching in every limb from his many hours in jolting coaches, took a room and went straight to bed.

Next morning, September the 28th, he caught the diligence into Mainz, which was in the hands of a French garrison. There, he hired another travelling coach, and after some trouble, two French speaking coachmen to drive it. Late in the afternoon he crossed the Rhine, now heading west. On the night of the 30th, the cumulative effect of the jolting forced him to sleep in a bed for the night at Verdun. But without any further break of more than a couple of hours in his journey, he reached the outskirts of Paris soon after midday on October the 2nd.

As the coach drew level with a big rambling building in the Faubourg St. Martin, Roger halted it. Before the Revolution the place had been a convent, but a board attached to its tall wall announced that it was now a depot for army clothing. Having settled up with his two coachmen, Roger picked up his little valise and walked through one of the tall gates, thus giving the men the impression that the depot was his destination. Of its janitor he enquired for an imaginary Citizen Rollo, and the man obligingly sent his son to ask the heads of various departments if they had anyone of that name working under them; with, of course, negative results. Twenty minutes having been occupied in this way Roger walked out to find, as he expected, that he had again freed himself from the possibility of hired drivers gossiping about where he had come from at the inn at which he meant to stay.

Half a mile down the road stood the Porte St. Martin. During the Terror, this gate, and all the others of Paris, had been manned as barriers at which passes had to be shown; but he found that it was now open again to both inward and outward traffic between dawn and sunset. Another mile's walk brought him to *La Belle Étoile* in the Rue de l'Arbe Sec, not far from the Louvre. Going in he found the landlord in his little office, and asked for a room.

To Roger's amusement and satisfaction Mâitre Blanchard did not recognise him, and if anyone in Paris was likely to have done so it should have been he; for he had known Roger first as the impecunious secretary of the Marquis de Rochambeau, seen him mysteriously blossom into a young nobleman who had the *entrée* at Versailles, and later proved a most stalwart friend to him, with the knowledge that he was a secret agent, during the dark days of the Terror.

As they were alone together, and it was during the quiet of the afternoon, Roger laughingly declared himself. The good Norman was overjoyed at seeing him again, and ran to fetch his wife from the kitchen. Both of them fussed over him, Mère Blanchard declared that she would cook him his favourite dish of duck casseroled in red wine for dinner, and her husband promised to produce his best Burgundy and oldest Calvados.

When they escorted him upstairs, most poignant memories flooded back to him, as when last he had lived there he had loved and lost his beautiful Athénaïs; but, knowing that, they tactfully refrained from giving him his old room.

Two hours later he dined with them in their private parlour, and, during the meal, they gave him the latest news. Paris was once more in a ferment—this time on account of the final decisions taken by the old Convention on the form of the new Constitution. The clauses had been argued with great violence ever since June, when Boissy d'Anglas, a

Liberal Deputy who had recently come much to the fore, had put forward the recommendations of a Committee which had been debating the question all through the spring.

The salient points of the Committee's findings were that the executive power must once more be divorced from the legislative, that there should be two chambers instead of one, that the members of both must be owners of property, that universal suffrage should be abolished and that only those who paid taxes should be entitled to a vote.

While these proposals did not deprive the people of any of the real liberties they had won by the Revolution, they were clearly aimed at destroying once and for all the dictatorship of the proletariat and concentrating power in the hands of the middle-classes. In consequence, all the old catch phrases of the Revolution had been revived by the mob orators, and the surviving Jacobins, who still formed a formidable bloc in the Chamber, had fought them tooth and nail.

The re-establishment of an executive independent of the law-makers was denounced as a move to restore the monarchy; so it had been decided that it should consist of a Directory having five members, one of whom was to retire annually.

The measure for the two Chambers had been agreed: the lower, called the *Cinq-Cents,* was to have 500 members and to initiate legislation; the upper, called the *Conseil des Anciens,* was to have 25 members and the power to veto any measures passed by the lower for one year. But the property qualification for election was ruled out by one motion of the Jacobins, and by another they secured a vote to anyone willing to tax themselves to the value of three days' work.

These brakes upon further reaction had not aroused much opposition amongst the general public, but the arrangements for the election of members to the two new Chambers had provoked a universal outcry.

As Mr. Pitt had rightly appreciated during his talk with Roger, a free General Election in France must sweep away at one stroke every ex-Terrorist from the new governing body. Barras, Tallien, Fréron and the other Thermidorians who had conspired to bring about Robespierre's fall, and still held the reins of power, had been equally quick to appreciate this; so they had allied themselves with the remaining Jacobins to prevent it. To the indignation of the electors, they had forced through a decree by which two thirds of the members of the two new Chambers must be selected from the deputies of the old Convention; leaving the electors only the choice of which individual members they should return.

To the vast majority of the people the Convention stood for murder, arbitrary arrest, the seizure of property, forced loans, and every other form of injustice and tyranny. It had, too, brought France to a state of poverty and general misery undreamed of in the old days of the monarchy. In consequence the idea that it was to be perpetuated under the thin disguise of a new name, by a majority of its members continuing as the rulers of the country, was already causing riots which threatened to develop into a mass movement aimed at overthrowing the government.

Roger was delighted to hear all this, as it showed that the state of popular opinion could not have been more favourable to the Allies' designs, and that if Pichegru could be persuaded to march upon the city there really was every reason to believe that it would fall into his hands like a ripe plum. He then asked about conditions in general, to which Maître Blanchard replied with a bitter laugh:

'If anything, Monsieur, they are worse than when you left us. Food is scarce, prices high. For an honest silver *écu* one can get a purse full of the republican paper money, yet we are forced to accept it; and the streets become ever fuller of poor fellows disabled in the wars begging for a crust to keep the life in their bodies. It has become a popular jest to say: "Under Robespierre we starved and dared not complain; now we may complain but that will not prevent us from dying of hunger".'

'At least people who have made themselves unpopular with the mobs are no longer liable to be set upon and strung up to a lamp-post,' Roger remarked; but Mère Blanchard quickly put in:

'Monsieur is mistaken about that; only it is a different type of people who are now the victims of a different kind of mob. The young *bourgeois* have invented a new form of sport. By night packs of them hunt out and kill one or more of the many thousands of so-called 'patriots' who held posts as jailers, police-spies and minor officials of all sorts during the Terror. Few people would now object to them throwing the busts of Marat in the sewers, or booing when the Marseillaise is played in the theatres, and some whom they knife or strangle may deserve their fate, but others do not; and it is wrong that any man should be done to death without a trial.'

Blanchard nodded. 'On account of these *jeunes gens*, Monsieur will be wise to keep a sharp look out should he go into the streets at night. They call themselves by such names as the Companions of the Sun, and the Companions of Jesus, but many of them are little better than bands of licensed robbers.'

'Licensed?' Roger picked him up. 'Do you mean that they are actually protected by the Government?'

'Not officially; but the authorities make no attempt to put them down.'

'It surprises me greatly that while there are so many declared atheists still in the Chamber it should tolerate any body calling itself the Companions of Jesus.'

With a shrug, Blanchard replied: "In matters of religion, as in all else, everything is at sixes and sevens. Not long since, Boissy d'Anglas denounced it in the most violent terms as pandering to childish and absurd superstition; but he went on in the same speech to say that there must be no further religious persecution. His views, I think, express the opinion of even the moderates in the Chamber. They are hoping that if held up long enough to contempt and ridicule it will die out; but, of course, it will not. Now that they no longer need fear arrest, hundreds of priests have secretly returned to France; and all over the country people are attending Masses with all the greater fervour from the right to do so openly having been so long denied them.'

'You should add, though,' remarked his wife, 'that side

by side with this evidence of piety, never before has there been so much open sinning.'

'That is true,' he agreed. 'In the main hunger is responsible, for from the age of twelve upwards there is now hardly a female among the working population who will not readily sell the use of her body for the price of a meal. But vice of every kind is also rampant among the better off. For that Barras, and others of his kidney, are much to blame; as they set the fashion by publicly flaunting a new mistress every week. Yet it is not entirely that. When you were last here many thousands of men and women were in prison. Believing themselves to have no chance of escaping the guillotine, to keep up their courage they adopted a philosophy of "eat, drink and be merry, for tomorrow we die". On their release they emerged imbued with this cynicism, and with life once more in their grasp the younger ones gave themselves up to the wildest profligacy. Last winter the *jeunesse dorée,* as they are called, organised "Victim Balls" in which no one was allowed to participate who had not lost a near relative by the guillotine. For these, both the men and women dressed their hair high, leaving the neck bare, as it had been the custom to arrange it immediately before execution; and at the beginning of each dance they cried in chorus "Come, let us dance on the tombs!" It is said, too, that the costumes worn at these parties are becoming ever more shameless, and that many young girls of good birth now openly rival the *demi-mondaines,* by according their favours to any man willing to give them a jewel or provide them with elegant clothes.'

For some three hours longer Roger absorbed the atmosphere of this post-Robespierrean Paris through the reasonably unprejudiced accounts of his honest host and hostess; then, as he was about to leave them for the night, he asked Maître Blanchard:

'Do you know what has become of Joseph Fouché, the Deputy for the Lower Loire?'

The Norman shook his head. 'No; that one keeps very quiet these days. Last autumn, by denouncing others whose deeds were no less black than his own, he managed to coat himself in a layer of whitewash. But he must realise that it is no more than skin deep, and that a false step might yet bring about his ruin. I imagine, though, that being a Deputy, he is still living in Paris.'

'Could you find out for me tomorrow; and, if he is, his present address?'

'Certainly, Monsieur. The officials of the Chamber must know his whereabouts; so there should be no difficulty about that.'

Next day, in accordance with his principle of never taking any unnecessary risks, Roger went out only to call on Harris, the banker in the Rue du Bac upon whom his orders for British secret service funds had been made, and drew a considerable sum in gold. But from the Blanchards and the inn servants he learned of the rising tide of unrest that was now agitating the city. The decree of Fructidor—as were termed those concerning the packing of two thirds of the seats in the new Chambers with members of the old Convention, and others similarly unpopular passed in that month of the revolutionary calendar—had been rejected by all but one of the Primary Assemblies in the forty Sections of Paris, and deputations by the score carrying petitions demanding that they should be rescinded were besieging the Convention.

In the afternoon, Blanchard told Roger that Fouché had left his old apartment in Rue Saint Honoré and was said to be living in a small house in the Passage Pappilote, on the Left Bank near the old Club of the Cordeliers. From the big trunk that for several years had been stored for him up in the attic of *La Belle Étoile,* Roger collected a sword cane, and a small double-barrelled pistol which would go into the pocket of his greatcoat. Then, after he had supped, he started out with the intention of getting to grips with his enemy.

Having crossed the Seine by the Pont Neuf he made his way to the Café Coraeza, which had been virtually an annex of the Cordeliers, and there enquired for the Passage Pappilote. It proved to be little more than a short cul-de-sac, as at its far end it narrowed to a dark archway through which nothing wider than a barrow could have passed. Lit only by a single bracket lamp affixed to a corner building that abutted on the main street, the greater part of it was in deep shadow; but Roger succeeded in identifying Fouché's house, noted that there were lights behind the drawn blinds of its two upper windows, and rapped sharply on the front door.

There were sounds of someone coming downstairs, then the door was opened by a red-headed young woman carrying a candle. She was an ugly anaemic-looking creature, and Roger recognised her at once as the middle-class heiress who had brought Fouché a modest fortune on his marriage to her three years before.

When asked if her husband was in she replied that he was not, and might not be back for some time; so without stating his business, Roger thanked her and said that he would call again in the morning. As she closed the door his retreating footsteps rang loudly on the cobbles. But he did not go far. After waiting in the main street for five minutes, he tiptoed back and took up a position within a few feet of Fouché's front door, but hidden in the deep shadow cast by a nearby projecting wall.

Madame Fouché had not recognised him, and he now felt confident that none of the people he had known in Paris was likely to do so. That would be a big advantage if a warrant was issued for his arrest, and he had to leave the city in a hurry. But if he were compelled to do that it would mean the failure of his mission.

The trouble was that to do any good, he must disclose his return to, and re-establish himself in his old identity with, the very people who were most likely to get him thrown into prison. Of these, by far the most dangerous was Joseph Fouché.

Fouché was doubly dangerous because he knew Roger's real name and nationality. It was very probable that he had passed that information on to other people after Roger had last left Paris; but he, at all events, was fully aware that Roger was an English spy. Therefore, as a first step, before anything else could be attempted, Roger had to find out if he had passed on that information, and to whom; then either buy his silence or kill him.

Over an hour elapsed before Roger saw a tall, thin figure

turn the corner under the lamp and come with long strides, yet quiet footfalls, towards him. He knew then that within a few minutes he must enter on the deadly contest he had set himself, and again pit his wits against a man who was as cunning as a serpent and as remorseless as a pack of jackals.

21

Into the Lion's Den

As Fouché approached, Roger slipped his hand into the pocket of his coat, cocked the small pistol, and drew it out. Once before, he had had an opportunity to kill Fouché without endangering himself. To have done so could well have been considered as an act of justice, executed on a man who had sent many hundreds of innocent people to their deaths; but from personal scruples Roger had refrained. Now, a second chance had arisen. He had only to fire both barrels at point-blank range, then take to his heels, for Fouché to be gasping out his life in the gutter and himself be swallowed up in the pitch dark night.

His hatred of Fouché was such that his fingers itched upon the triggers. Had he pressed them he would have saved himself many future dangers and difficulties; but he could not be certain that killing Fouché would make Paris again safe for himself. Only Fouché could be tricked or persuaded into telling him the degree of risk he would run should he disclose himself to their old associates.

Without suspecting his presence, Fouché walked past him to the door, took out a key, unlocked and opened it. Stepping up behind him Roger pressed the pistol into the small of his back, and said quietly:

'Go inside. Make no noise. Take six paces then turn and face me. Lift a finger or raise your voice and I shall put two bullets into your liver.'

The lights in the room above had gone out soon after Roger had begun his vigil; so Madame Fouché could be assumed to have gone to bed and was, he hoped, asleep. But the narrow hall-way was still lit by a single candle in a cheap china holder on a small deal table. Without a word Fouché walked past it, then turned round. Meanwhile Roger had closed the door and stood with his back to it, watching his old enemy narrowly.

Fouché was then thirty-two, and a more unattractive looking man it would have been difficult to imagine. His cadaverous face had a corpse-like hue, his hair was thin and reddish, his eyes pale, fish-like and lacking all expression; his nose was long and, in spite of his frequent snufflings, it sometimes had a drip on its end, as he suffered from a perpetual cold. His tall, bony frame suggested that of a skeleton, and he looked too weak and ill to be capable of any effort; but no appearance could possibly have been more deceptive. Actually he possessed considerable physical strength, and his mind was such a dynamo of energy that he often worked for twenty-four hours on end without relaxation.

As a means of preventing people from guessing his thoughts he had formed the habit of never meeting anyone's eyes with his own; but his shifty glance had swiftly taken in Roger, from his bewhiskered face to his shiny boots, and after a moment his bloodless lips moved to utter the words:

'So, Englishman; you have come back.'

'How did you recognise me?' Roger asked with quick interest.

'By your voice, your hands, and your principal features. Any one of the three would have given me the clue to your identity. I have trained myself to be observant in such matters. There was too, the manner of your arrival. I took it for granted that when you did appear you would take the precaution of catching me unprepared.'

'You were, then, expecting me to return to Paris?'

'Certainly. I have been wondering for some months past why you had not done so.'

'You surprise me somewhat; as many men in my peculiar circumstances might well have decided against ever again risking their necks in this pit of vipers.'

Fouché shrugged. 'Ah, but not a man of your resource and courage. How otherwise could you hope to reap the benefit of your last great *coup*?'

'I thank you for the compliment; but I might have sent someone else on my behalf.'

'That would not have been in keeping with your character. You are too vain to believe that anyone other than yourself could have played the Royal Flush you hold to the best possible advantage. You had to return to Paris yourself, and you had to come to me.'

Matters were developing in a manner entirely unlike anything that Roger had visualised, and after a second's thought, he said: 'You are, then, prepared to talk business?'

'Of course. Surely you did not suppose that I should refuse, and do my best to get you arrested the moment your back was turned? I am not such a fool as to cut off my nose to spite my own face. Put your pistol away and come into the living-room. We will discuss our mutual interests over a glass of wine.'

Roger needed no telling that not one single word Fouché uttered could be relied upon, but it now seemed possible that his formidable enemy believed that there was more to be gained from a temporary alliance than by an immediate betrayal; so he lowered his pistol and nodded.

Picking up the candlestick, Fouché led the way through a doorway opposite the foot of the stairs, and set it down on a table where some cold food had been left for him. Glancing round, Roger saw that the inside of this obscure dwelling was no better than its outside. It was clean and neat, but sparsely furnished, and in places the plaster was peeling from the walls. He wondered what Fouché had done with the ill-gotten gains he had accumulated during the Revolution, and assumed that this apparent poverty was no more than a mask assumed to protect himself, now that the tide had turned and he might be accused of peculation.

Fouché picked up a bottle of red wine that was already a quarter empty, fetched an extra glass from a cupboard and poured out. Both men sat down and Fouché made no comment when Roger, knowing that he must continue to observe every possible precaution against sudden treachery, laid the still cocked pistol on the table beside him. Lifting his glass, Fouché said with a pale smile:

'Well! Here's to the little Capet. May he make the fortunes of us both.'

Roger knew that young Louis XVII would now never make anyone's fortune; but he echoed the toast and drank of the cheap red wine: then he asked:

'How, think you, can we handle the matter to the best advantage?'

With his bony hands Fouché made a little gesture to which no significance could be attached. 'There appeared to me two ways to play this game. Had you arrived earlier in the year, we might have blackmailed a great sum out of the Government to refrain from exposing the fact that the child in the Temple was not Marie Antoinette's son. That would have entailed handing him over to them. Alternatively, we could have sold him for an equally large sum to the *émigrés*. But since then an event has occurred which greatly alters the situation.'

Pausing, he took a mouthful of wine, then went on: 'The death in June of the boy whom everyone but a few of us believed to be the young King will make the Government much less inclined to submit to blackmail. With one of the children in a grave no physical comparison of them can now be made, and as Citizen Simon so debased the real little Capet, turning him into a witless caricature of his former self, should they take the line that we have produced a fake most people would believe them. That factor, too, now seriously prejudices our chances of selling him to the *émigrés*. The Comte de Provence, having had himself proclaimed King, can hardly be expected to welcome the resurrection of his nephew, and might decide also to declare the boy a fake; whether he really believed that to be so or not.'

'What, then, do you suggest?' Roger enquired.

'Whether your arrival in Paris at this time is the result of excellent intelligence or simply chance, I do not know. But the fact remains that it could not be more opportune. Within a few days it is certain that a *coup d'état* will be attempted. Unless fate introduces some unforeseen factor, there is every reason to believe that it will prove a succesful one. Barras and his crew will be swept away and the so-called

Moderates will emerge triumphant. In fact, they are not Moderates but Reactionaries, as nearly all of them have now secretly become Monarchists at heart; and in that a great part of the nation is like them.'

Again Fouché paused to take a sip of wine. 'There are plenty of people in Paris who saw the real little Capet when he was still a prisoner in the Temple and, the spirit of the nation now being what it is, after a *coup d'état* would be prepared to swear that the child you could produce is he. Therefore, as I see it, all we have to do is to take into our confidence a few men of influence, and at the right moment present the boy to the new Government. Having secured his person they would be in no danger of losing their posts to a crowd of *émigrés,* and by forming a Council of Regency they could reign in his name. The Bourbon Princes would at first declare the whole thing a fraud, but later they would have to come to heel, and probably be permitted to return. Whatever line they took would not affect us in the least; for you and I would be the men who had restored the young King to his throne, and from him receive our reward. We should, too, have good prospects of becoming the most powerful men in the State. What say you to that?'

Roger had always known Fouché to have a brilliant mind, but even so he was filled with admiration for the simplicity yet subtleness of the proposed plot. By making the new Government a present of the boy all the difficulties and dangers entailed in an endeavour to blackmail it were automatically eliminated; and the prospects of obtaining great rewards would be infinitely better than through long negotiations with the Bourbon Princes, which might end in failure or betrayal. The men who should be in power within a week could not conceivably fail to see how greatly it would be to their advantage to proclaim a Restoration, for, as members of a Council of Regency, their own positions would be secured; and, by bringing about a Restoration in this way, instead of having to fight the *émigrés* over every clause in a new Constitution, they could dictate one embodying all the liberal doctrines they believed in themselves.

Even with the certain knowledge that, at some point in the

conspiracy, Fouché woud have done his utmost to trick him out of his share in the triumph, Roger would have been greatly tempted to enter into such a partnership. But there could be no question of that; for the golden link in the chain which alone could have made the plot possible was no longer in existence. Despite that, Roger's strongest card lay in Fouché's belief that he still held it; so, having no option but to play the game out, he said:

''Tis a truly masterly conception. Only one thing in it surprises me. I had never thought to hear you plan a Restoration.'

Fouché shrugged. 'Times change. The era when a politician could earn a tolerable remuneration by occasionally allowing the *sans-culottes* to have their heads is over. I have a wife and child to think of, and I must provide for them somehow. Already I am in dire straits and an object of persecution by the Moderates. This is my chance to re-establish myself once and for all, and secure my future. Did not the Protestant King, *Henri Quatre,* declare that to win over Paris it was worth going to Mass? Well, for the portfolio of a Minister and the Order of St. Louis, I should not find it too great a price to kiss that repugnant youngster's hand.'

Knowing the way in which Fouché had already more than once repudiated his sworn political convinctions and betrayed his backers, Roger could well believe him; so with a nod he said tactfully: 'It is not the first time that a man has felt himself compelled to sacrifice his opinions for the sake of his dependants. But tell me; why do you suggest taking others into our confidence? It seems to me neither necessary nor wise.'

'It is a wise man who knows his own weakness,' Fouché retorted with a bitter laugh. 'And politically, at this moment, I am as weak as a new-born babe. From last spring, when the Girondin Deputies were allowed to return to the Chamber, my position has become ever more precarious. They refuse to believe that it was Collet and not I who was mainly responsible for the massacres as Lyons, although it can be proved that I put an end to them as soon as I dared, and then at some risk to myself. The agitation against me reached a peak eight weeks ago. With several others I was denounced in the Chamber by Boissy d'Anglas and our arrest was decreed.'

With a snuffle, he broke off to blow his nose, refilled Roger's glass and went on. 'Fortunately, having been privy to so many matters, I was able to persuade certain still influential people that it was not in their best interests to send me to prison; so the warrant was not put into execution. Then, ten days ago, with the promulgation of the new Constitution, an amnesty was granted to all imprisoned on charges like that against myself; so the warrant is no longer valid. Nevertheless, my enemies have succeeded in undoing me; for jointly with the amnesty it was decreed that no one named in it should be eligible for election to the new Assembly. So, you see, I no longer have even the status of a Deputy; and, having been stripped of all credit, must for this *coup* seek the co-operation of others in whom the men of tomorrow will place a greater trust.'

In view of Fouché's record, it was remarkable that he should have saved himself from the fate that had overtaken Carrier and other leading Robespierrists; yet, somehow, Roger had not expected to find him reduced to such complete impotence. That, with his remarkable brain, should he retain his freedom, he would not remain in obscurity for very long, seemed a foregone conclusion; and Roger asked with considerable interest whom he thought the most promising men to approach on the present business.

'Fréron for one,' he replied promptly.

Roger raised an eyebrow in surprise. 'Recalling the treatment he meted out to the anti-Revolutionaries in Toulon after its evacuation by the Allies, I should have thought him to be in no better case than yourself."

'He is well on the way to living that down; for he has acted with great shrewdness. Soon after liberty was restored to the Press he again began to edit and publish a journal called *L'Oranteur du Peuple*. It has now been running for over a year, and every month it has become more reactionary. In fact, he has now become the idol of the *jeunesse dorée*, and wields great influence with all in the Chamber who incline to the Right.'

'That was certainly a clever way of whitewashing himself. Who else?'

'Tallien.'

'What! Has that old wolf also procured himself a suit of sheep's clothing?'

Fouché gave a sickly grin. 'He has, but he has since spilt much blood upon it. Therefore he will be only too eager to cleanse it in the Royal washing tub to which we can give him access.'

'I am at a loss to understand you.'

'Did you not hear of the part he played after the Quiberon affair?'

'No. I have conversed with hardly anyone since my return to France.'

'Well then. You will recall that in '94, for all their burning of villages and ferocity, General Turreau's *colonnes infernales* failed to suppress the revolts in La Vendée. After Robespierre's fall General Hoche was sent there to replace him. Hoche is not only a good soldier but an able young diplomat. Instead of shooting all the prisoners he took, he treated them humanely, then recommended a general amnesty. That is why after the landing at Quiberon had been defeated, the *émigrés* who had come from England surrendered to him, instead of fighting on and selling their lives dearly. They expected to be treated as prisoners of war. But Tallien was sent as *Représentant en Mission* from Paris to take charge of matters, and, despite Hoche's pleading, he had all the *émigrés* of good family—six hundred and twelve of them—shot.'

Roger endeavoured to keep the horror out of his voice, as he asked: 'What in the world impelled him to such an act, when for over a year the guillotine had been used on no one but a few Robespierrists, and thousands of monarchists have been liberated from the prisons?'

'Ah; thereby hangs a tale,' snuffled Fouché. 'I knew, and others knew, that before the Quiberon landing took place he had already been in secret negotiation with the Royalists. But he was betrayed. His wife, learning of it, sent him an express to Brittany, warning him of his danger. That he might be able to rend his accusers on his return to Paris, and stigmatise them as calumniators, he needed to produce fresh evidence of his incorruptible patriotism. That is why he had those six hundred poor devils butchered.'

'Surely, then, he must now be shaking in his shoes from fear of the fate that will overtake him should the coming *coup d'état* by the Moderates prove successful?'

'Of course. And only we can save him. Therefore, he will stop at nothing to aid us; and by gaining him we gain that clever aristocrat bitch, his wife, who in the past year has become the most powerful woman in Paris.'

'Who else do you intend to sound with a view to joining us?'

'That requires most careful consideration. We should need only two or three more at the most. Providing all are men of prominence and resolution a camarilla of six, including ourselves, should be sufficient. But what of yourself? Have you thought of a means by which to explain away your long absence from Paris; so that you may shave the hair from your face and go about openly as your old self to aid in this secret *coup* which we intend?'

Much relieved that at last the matter that had really brought him there had been raised, and by Fouché himself, Roger replied:

'That depends on what account you gave of my disappearance. If you told Paul Barras, and perhaps others, the truth, then I see nought for it but to remain under cover.'

Fouché made, what was for him, an impatient gesture. 'Every secret has its value. Only a fool gives another information which may later prove to his own advantage; and this was a secret worth a fortune. I thought it possible that you might hand the boy over to Mr. Pitt. Although that would have been a stupid thing to do; as, at best, you might have got from him a few thousand guineas and the right to call yourself Sir Brook. I counted it much more likely that you would keep him in hiding until you judged the time ripe to offer him to the French Government at his true value. With myself knowing you to be an English agent I felt certain you would not dare to reappear here and approach anyone of importance without first buying my silence. That meant you must share whatever you got for the boy with me; so, naturally, I kept my mouth shut.'

'You must have had to give some explanation of what occurred between us in the Temple.'

'Naturally. But you, myself and Barras were the only people who at that time had become aware that the child in the Temple was not the little Capet; so I needed only to invent a story which would satisfy Barras. I said that while there together we had stumbled on a clue to the whereabouts of the right child. That we had then quarrelled violently over which of us should remain to prevent the jailers getting a sight of the substitute, and which should reap the distinction of bringing back the real one from his hiding place. I said that you had won and locked me in; and that as soon as I was freed in the morning I had set off post haste on your heels in the hope of out-distancing you. I said that you had reached the farmhouse in the Jura, where the boy was, before me, but that his protectors had outwitted you and got away with him. That they had fled with him towards the Swiss border, and that you had gone after them. That on reaching Lake Geneva I had lost track of both them and you; and that I assumed you had followed them, in the hope that you might yet secure the boy, although he was on foreign soil, and bring him back with you.'

Roger smiled. 'That was certainly an ingenious explanation. But what story did you tell the guards at the Temple when, the morning after my flight, they broke the door in, and found you on the floor trussed like a turkey cock?'

'Simply that over a past disagreement which had arisen again while we were talking together, we had come to blows; and that to revenge yourself on me you had left me tied up there.' With a slightly acid note in his voice, Fouché added: 'I passed a far from comfortable night; but at least during it I had ample time to think out what I should say to the guards when they found me, and, with a view to future possibilities, a suitable tale to tell Barras should you succeed in getting away with the boy. Incidentally, what did you do with him?'

'He had, as you know, been brutalised into almost a

moron, and been persuaded that his idea that he had been born the son of Louis XVI was no more than a delusion. But he was still capable of working with his hands; and since he had been trained as a cobbler's apprentice under Citizen Simon, when I got him back to London, I apprenticed him to another cobbler, in a quiet suburb called Camden Town.'

Fouché accepted Roger's lie without comment, and asked: 'Have you brought him with you?'

'Nay. I wished first to reconnoitre the lie of the land.'

'That was wise. But I take it you could produce him at fairly short notice?'

'Yes. I think, though, that every move in our game should be settled before I do so.'

'I agree; and I have no intention of even whispering anything of this, to any man, until the *coup d'état* which is now in the making becomes an accomplished fact.'

Roger nodded. 'I was about to suggest just such a policy of caution.'

'Of course,' Fouché remarked after a moment, 'there is always the possibility that, owing to some unforeseen factor, the *coup d'état* may not succeed. But, even should it fail, another opportunity to use the boy as we have planned should present itself before very long.'

'Seeing the temper of the nation, that is as good as certain,' Roger agreed, 'and as I have already waited for so many months before attempting this big *coup,* I can quite well afford to wait a while longer.'

Fouché made a wry grimace. 'No doubt you can; but I am already at my wit's end for money.'

'You surprise me. What have you done with all the jewelled crosses, chalices and copes of which you deprived the churches while you were acting as Proconsul for the Convention in Nevers? Surely you have not spent all the proceeds from them? But perhaps you have them buried and feel that it is now too great a risk to dig up and sell some of them.'

Snuffling again, Fouché shook his head. 'Like many others, you misjudge me concerning that. I swear to you I sent every single thing that I seized, both from the churches and private individuals, back to the Convention; so that they might turn it into money wherewith to help pay the armies. The plantation my family had in the West Indies has been burnt and ravaged by revolted slaves; so I no longer receive an income from that, and my wife's little fortune was swallowed up by two bankruptcies. Now that I have been deprived of my salary as a Deputy I cannot think how I am to keep my family and myself from starvation. I wonder though, now we are becoming partners, if . . . if you could see your way to making me a loan?'

Roger had no means of knowing if the corpse-like man opposite him was really in desperate straits, or simply playing a part in the hope that he might get something for nothing. He had, however, come prepared to offer Fouché a heavy bribe, if that had seemed the most likely way to achieve his end; so he had several purses of gold distributed about him. Now, he decided that it would be worth while to part with one; so that if Fouché was in fact near destitute, he would be the more likely to remain at least temporarily trustworthy, in the hope of receiving others. Standing up, Roger put a silk net purse on the table, and said:

'There is a hundred *louis*. That should keep you from want for the time being.' And, knowing that he who appears to give willingly gives twice, he added: 'You are welcome to it.'

Fouché too stood up. Even now, his dull eyes showed no flicker of delight; but his voice did hold a warmer note that sounded like gratitude, as he picked up the purse and chinked the coins in it. 'I shall not forget this. It means a lot to me. Perhaps a time will come when I may be able to repay you with some service that you could not buy for ten times this sum.'

Having diplomatically smiled an acknowledgment. Roger said: 'One more thing. After my disappearance, many other people besides Barras must have wondered what had become of me. What form did their speculation take?'

'That was attended to. Both Barras and I were anxious that no rumour should get around that the boy in the Temple was not the King; so the last thing we wished to do was to give people grounds for supposing that you had gone off in pursuit of the real one. The two of us put it about that you had been sent on a secret mission.'

That was all Roger wished to know; so he pocketed his pistol and prepared to take his departure. At the door Fouché asked him casually: 'Where can I get in touch with you?' But with a guile that matched Fouché's own, he replied:

'For the time being I think it wisest to spend no two nights in one place, and to disappear from each without leaving an address; so I cannot give you one. But as soon as events develop in a manner satisfactory to our plan, I will communicate with you.'

As Roger walked back through the dimly-lit streets he knew that Fouché might be already running to the nearest police office to betray him, give a description of his new appearance, and have him hunted down. The ex-terrorist was entirely capable of having played a part from the start to the finish of their long interview. On the other hand he had been led to believe that by holding his tongue a wonderful prize was to be gained; so if he really had kept what he knew of Roger to himself so far, he now had the best possible reason for continuing to do so.

That he had, in the main, been telling the truth seemed to Roger more than likely and, if so, no set of circumstances could have been more favourable to himself; for, if the explanations given about his disappearance were to be believed, it meant that he had very nearly a clean bill for reappearing in Paris as *Citizen Commissioner Breuc*.

One fence, and a stiff one, still had to be got over. He had to explain his long disappearance to Barras, and give him some plausible account of what had happened to the little Capet. If he could succeed in that he would be free to set about forming a secret camarilla pledged to collaborate with Pichegru in bringing about a Restoration.

But Barras was one of the men who would have no truck with that, and to even hint at it to him would mean immediate arrest. Yet, unless he could lie his way back into Barras's confidence, his apparent success with Fouché would be completely worthless. Barras, too, was too rich to bribe and too courageous to bully. Moreover, unlike Fouché, he was still one of the most powerful men in France; so to set about tackling him was an undertaking bristling with even greater dangers.

After recrossing the Seine, in spite of the lateness of the hour, Roger found the central Sections of the city still restless. By dropping into conversation with a group on a street corner he learned that the electors of the Section Lepelletier, which was in the forefront of the agitation, had held a meeting in the Théâtre Français, and that all the evening the Place de l'Odeon outside it had been packed with sympathisers from other Sections. In alarm, the Convention had passed an emergency decree declaring the meeting to be illegal, then despatched police and dragoons to disperse it; but the mob in the Place had driven them off, and the meeting had passed a resolution declaring that the Convention no longer represented the Sovereign People.

Next morning Roger had a horse saddled for him in the stable of *La Belle Étoile* and rode out from the city to the pleasant village of Passy. He was technically the owner of a charming little house there, as his friend M. de Talleyrand-Périgord, the wily Bishop of Autun, had made it and its contents over to him when he had had to fly from Paris in order to protect his property from being sold by the revolutionaries as that of an *émigré*. Roger had used it on numerous occasions since as a safe hide-out, and when last there had left with a couple named Velot, who had been de Talleyrand's butler and cook, a considerable sum for their support until either he or their real master could come to the house again.

He found old Antoine Velot working in the garden, and was both relieved and delighted because he was genuinely fond of the dear old man. Marie Velot returned soon afterwards from shopping in the village, and the couple could not have done more to make Roger welcome. All through the months, knowing that he never announced his coming, they had kept the best bedroom ready for him, and they both expressed the hope that he had come for a long stay.

He told them that he might return late that night, or the next, and lie low there for a while, but as yet could not be certain; so, in case his return should be prevented, he made them a further liberal payment which would keep them in comfort for at least another year. They gave him an excellent early dinner, then he rode back to Paris, approaching the centre of the city late in the afternoon.

As he did so he could hear the roll of drums from several directions, which could be taken as an indication that the National Guards were being summoned to their respective Section headquarters. All work had ceased, and processions were marching through the streets carrying banners and shouting such slogans as 'Down with the Two-Thirds' and 'End the Tyranny of the Convention.' Among the marchers there was a high proportion of respectably dressed men. Many of them wore grey great-coats with black collars and green cravats, thus openly displaying the colours which had been adopted by the Royalists, while others in woollen caps with bobbles were obviously Breton *Chouans*, who had been brought into Paris to aid in a rising.

On arriving at the *Belle Étoile,* Roger got hold of Maître Blanchard, who was always a good source of news owing to his many customers, and from him learned the latest rumours.

The Convention had declared itself in perpetual session and, it was said, had sent for General Menou, who commanded the Army of the Interior, to bring troops from his camp at Sablons. In the meantime it had only the fifteen-hundred men of its own special guard at its disposal; so, for its further protection, an emergency measure had been passed permitting the re-arming of the 'patriots', as the *sans-culottes* were termed; and the weapons which had been taken from them after the quelling of the riots in the previous May had been reissued to many hundreds of them that morning.

On the other hand this official arming of the mob had been seized upon by the Sections as an excuse to call out the National Guard, which was mainly composed of middle-class citizens and was overwhelmingly anti-Convention in sentiment. Nine Sections had already declared themselves in open rebellion, and called upon the others to join them in maintaining the public safety which, they alleged, was now menaced by the Terrorists.

Late in the evening General Menou arrived in the capital, but with only a limited number of troops; and that, together with the fact that had he obeyed the Convention's order promptly he could have reached it by midday, seemed to Roger a clear indication of his luke-warmness.

Menou was the General who had put down the rising of the *sans-culottes* in May, and he had done so with considerable vigour; but he was now called on to do the very opposite. It was whispered that he had monarchist sympathies, and it was certain that he had many friends among the leaders of the Sections; so he could not be expected to use force, except in the last extremity, and his tardy arrival now made it seem possible that he was even in league with the Sections, and might go over to them.

The rapid development of the crisis gave Roger furiously to think how it might affect his own affairs. He had hoped that it would be delayed for a few days, in order that he might first have an opportunity of seeing Barras privately in his own house. Now it seemed very unlikely that he would be able to do so for, the Convention being in perpetual session, and also the Committee of Public Safety, it was as good as certain that Barras would be at one or other of them.

Yet, that he should see Barras before the clash occurred was imperative. During the last rising the mob had broken into the Chamber, slain a Deputy named Féraud, cut off his head, stuck it on a pole, and held it up face to face with Boissy d'Anglas, who had been occupying the rostrum. A similar fate to Féraud's might overtake Barras that very night. If it did Roger would be debarred from proceeding with his plans owing to the extreme danger of resuming his old identity while still uncertain how many people knew the real reason for his flight from France. Only through Barras could he learn if Fouché had told the truth, or deceived him so that he should disclose himself and be promptly arrested.

At nine o'clock he decided to take the plunge involved by going to the Convention. The risk was a high one as, should

Barras prove an enemy, from his own house it might have been possible to escape, but there would be little chance of doing so from a crowded hall, or a Committee room, with soldiers within easy call. All Roger could do was to take the precautions he had already planned, by going in the *émigré* uniform under his long coat, and on horse-back; so that if he had to make a bolt for it and could reach his mount, he would stand some chance of outdistancing his pursuers.

Soon after ten o'clock he dismounted outside the Tuileries, tied his horse to a hitching post and went inside. In the lobby leading to the Assembly Hall there was more than the usual crush of people, and they were now exchanging agitated rumours. It was known that General Menou's troops had surrounded the Convent of the Filles de St. Thomas, which was the headquarters of the Lepelletier Section; but he was said to be parleying with the enemy.

On enquiring for Barras, Roger learned, with almost stupefying thankfulness, that, having spent all day in the Convention, he had gone home to supper. Securing the address of his house, Roger ran outside, jumped on his horse and rode away, praying frantically that he might catch Barras there before he returned to resume his duties.

The house was a large one in the Rue de Grenelle. When Roger reached it he saw that a coach was waiting outside; and as he tied his horse to the railings the front door opened. A man and a woman stood for a moment in the lighted doorway. The broad shouldered, soldierly figure Roger instantly recognised as that of Barras; the woman was fashionably dressed, and had a willowy figure.

As Barras led her down the steps Roger saw that she was about thirty, olive complexioned, brown-haired and beautiful. He waited until Barras had seen her into the coach, then as his quarry turned to re-enter the house he nerved himself to move forward. If a visit to Fouché's dwelling could be likened to entering a snake-pit, one to Barras's house was certainly equivalent to walking into a lion's den. Ready to spring back and run on the instant, he stepped forward and said in a loud, cheerful voice:

'Good evening Citizen Commissioner. I am happy to see

that you have not lost your good taste where the fair sex is concerned.'

'Who the devil are *you*?' growled Barras.

Roger laughed. 'It's not to be wondered at that you don't recognise me; but I am your old adherent, Citizen Breuc.'

The die was cast. In an agony of apprehension Roger waited for Barras's reply. It seemed an age in coming, yet actually it was only a few seconds. Having stared at him for a moment in the uncertain light, Barras exclaimed:

Ventre du Pape! So it is! Where on earth have you been all this time?'

Roger breathed again. There was no trace of the hostility he had feared in Barras's voice, but a warm note of pleasure.

''Tis a long story,' he replied. 'But if I may accompany you inside I'll tell it to you as briefly as I can.'

'Come in, my dear fellow. Come in and welcome.' Barras threw a friendly arm about his shoulders and side by side they went up the steps.

In the lighted hall Roger was able to get a better look at him. He was, in his southern, Provençal way, as flamboyantly handsome as ever. His big nose and pugnacious chin proclaimed the forcefulness of his character: his full, sensual mouth and bright eyes his boundless zest for good living. As a *ci-devant* Comte and an officer of the old Royal Army he had the easy manners and striking bearing of the born aristocrat who has long been a soldier.

'You have not changed much,' Roger remarked with a smile, 'either in appearance or, it seems, in your devotion to the ladies. That was a rare charmer that you saw to her coach just now.'

Barras grinned back. 'Oh, she is a little protégée of mine, and a friend of Madame Tallien. Her name is Josephine de Beauharnais. No doubt you will remember her husband the General, whose head some of our old friends had cut off. She is still a widow, and a deucedly attractive one.'

Roger almost exclaimed, 'Why! I met several of her relatives in Martinique', but just stopped himself in time. His heart lurched within him at his narrow escape, and when he recovered, he said instead:

'From what I see of the condition of the streets, it surprises me somewhat to find you philandering at such a time.'

Barras shrugged his broad shoulders. 'I had made an appointment some days ago for her to sup with me tonight *à deux*; and she is too excellent a morsel for me to put off. As for the riots that are in progress, it would need more than noise to divert me from my pleasures, and if I am fated to die before morning I'd as lief do so here in my own house after a good meal shared with a beauty as on the dirty floor of the Convention. But tell me about yourself, and the little Capet?'

'Fouché must have told you of our stupid quarrel in the Temple,' Roger opened boldly, 'and how I set off to secure the boy after we had stumbled on a clue to his whereabouts. Some Royalists had him hidden in a farmhouse in the Jura, but they proved too many for me and got away with him. I followed across the Swiss border but once out of France I no longer had the power to seize him openly; so could only keep track of them in secret, hoping that some chance might arise to abduct him. After a short stay in Geneva they took him to England. Still imbued with the thought of how necessary it was for us to get hold of him, I followed them, and traced him to a country house in Hampshire. There he fell ill with diphtheria, and before I could make further plans died of it.'

'Did he indeed! Well, that has saved us one worry. Although he could have caused us no great trouble after the death of the other boy enabled us to proclaim him officially dead. But why did you not then return?'

Now well launched on the story he had prepared, Roger replied promptly. 'I stowed away in a smuggler's yawl, but had the misfortune to be caught. Since my name is known in England as a so-called terrorist, and I could give no proper account of myself, judging that I would receive better treatment as a soldier than as a civilian, I gave a false name and said that I was an escaped prisoner-of-war; so they sent me to a prison on the Isle of Wight. Three times I attempted to escape, and each time failed. But last summer I saw a chance to get back to France. They asked for volunteers willing to renounce the Republic and serve as privates in the Royalist Army.

'I took that course and for some weeks had to submit to training under strict supervision. I was, though, buoyed up by the rumour that the Quiberon expedition was preparing and hoped to be sent upon it; for once in Brittany it would have been easy for me to desert. But my battalion was not sent with the first invading force, and when the news came that the landings had been a failure, our embarkation orders were cancelled. I had then to remain on there with such patience as I could until six weeks ago, when we were despatched via Hanover to join de Condé's army on the Rhine. As you can imagine, once there I lost not a night, but stole a horse and rode for Paris. I entered the city no more than two hours ago, and without even taking time to get a meal came straight to you.'

As Roger ended this dramatic account of his fictitious adventures, he flung open his coat and cried: 'Look. Have you ever before seen the uniform of an *émigré*? The poor devils have only the cast-offs of the Austrians, upon which are sewn special facings. But I possessed no other clothes to come in.'

'Well, I'll be damned.' Barras's hearty laugh rang out. 'What a time you have had, my poor friend, through your zeal to serve the Republic. But you must be starving. Come into the dining-room, and my people shall bring you food and wine upon the instant.'

At last, Roger could breathe freely. Fouché had not lied, and the jovial Barras had swallowed his story hook, line and sinker. But as they turned away from the door a violent banging sounded upon it.

With the courage that was one of Barras's greatest assets, although it might have been a mob coming to kill him, he did not call for a servant to open it, or even pull the pistol from his sash. Without a second's hesitation, he opened it himself. On the door-step stood two officers of the Convention Guard. One of them gasped out:

'Citizen Commissioner! General Menou has betrayed us! He has jammed his men into a few streets adjacent to the Filles de St. Thomas. The houses in them are packed with National Guards, who man all the upstairs windows. Our troops have been led into a trap, for should they now raise a finger they will be butchered.'

Thrusting a despatch into Barras's hand, he hurried on: 'This is from the Convention. They beg you to take charge in this terrible emergency and save them. By it they appoint you Commandant General of Paris.'

The other officer nodded and burst out: 'You are our only hope! We are five battalions at the most, with only a rabble of undisciplined patriots to stand by us. Thirty-nine out of the forty Sections of Paris have declared for the insurgents. They can now muster near forty thousand National Guards; so we are hopelessly outnumbered. As Commandant General on 9th Thermidor you saved the Republic. You are the only man whom we can hope may save it again.'

With a laugh Barras thrust the commission into his sash, and cried: 'So be it then! I'll teach these miserable plotters a lesson, or die for it.'

Then he turned and slapped Roger on the shoulder. 'Old friend, you could not have arrived at a more opportune moment. You were as good as another right hand to me on 9th Thermidor, and you shall be so again. Get yourself a sword! There are a dozen in the rack. And follow me!'

It was the sort of courageous cry that went straight to Roger's heart. Turning swiftly he stretched out a hand to take a weapon from the hall sword rack. He had barely grasped it when he was seized with sudden dismay. Like a bolt from the blue a paralysing thought struck him. He had landed himself on the wrong side of the barricades.

22

The Unforeseen Factor

There was no way in which Roger could get out of his most unhappy predicament. Barras had already acclaimed him in front of the two officers as a long lost comrade returned to the fold. Nothing could possibly have suited him better had it occurred a few days earlier. Then, he would have had the opportunity he had taken such risks to gain of re-establishing on a safe footing his connection with a score of other political leaders. That would have committed him to nothing. When the insurrection developed he could have pretended illness, so as not to have become involved on either side, awaited its outcome, then entered into secret negotiation with the most promising men of the party that emerged triumphant.

But now he was committed, and committed irrevocably, to serve the party whose downfall it was his object to bring about. If he refused to accept the rôle that Barras had thrust upon him he would instantly lose his regained status as a good Republican. Should the Convention succeed in suppressing the insurrection, that would deprive him of all credit with many of his old associates and, at worst, possibly lead to his arrest as a traitor.

On the other hand, to be seen by scores of people at Barras's side, fighting the forces of reaction, might land him in still graver difficulties. For, should the insurrection succeed, its leaders, amongst whom must obviously be the men most likely to lend a favourable ear to the proposals he wished to make, would put no trust in him. Worse still, unless he could escape, he would probably be arrested with Barras, and share his fate. Either way it now looked as if he stood a good chance of being sentenced to the 'dry guillotine' and transported to Cayenne.

Faced with this most distressing dilemma he decided, after only a moment's hesitation, that to sacrifice Barras's confidence immediately after having so fully regained it would be both rash and foolish. He must at least pretend to stand by his old colleague for the moment, and trust that as the situation developed some means would offer by which he might safeguard his future. Grasping the sword more firmly, he hurried after Barras down the steps into the street.

The two officers had come in a coach. Barras entered it with them, while Roger mounted his horse in readiness to accompany the vehicle. The evening had been dark and blustery, but now the wind had dropped and rain was sheeting down. That was all to the good, as it had already driven numerous bands of malcontents off the streets who might have held up the coach and on finding Barras in it attempted to lynch him. Even as it was the coach was three times challenged by pickets of National Guards, but on shouting that they were 'Sectionists on their way to a meeting' it was allowed to pass. Soon after midnight, much relieved, they arrived at the Ministry of War in the Boulevard des Capucines.

Barras showed his commission as Commander-in-Chief to a duty officer down the hall; then they all went up to a big room on the first floor. In it a dozen officers with gloomy faces were sitting and standing about. Only one of them appeared to be doing any work; a thin, dark-haired young man in the stained and worn uniform of a Brigadier General. He was seated at a table, poring over a big map, a pair of dividers in his hand, with which he was measuring distances upon it.

General Carteaux, the senior officer present, came forward to greet Barras, and at once expressed his willingness to serve under him. Then Barras said: 'Be good enough, Citizen General, to show me the dispositions of your troops and those of the insurgents.'

Carteaux led him over to the table. The officer seated at it glanced up and nodded. Roger recognised him, then as a little Corsican Captain of Artillery who had got the better of him in a heated argument during the siege of Toulon. At the siege, partly because he was an enthusiastic follower of Robespierre and partly because he was one of the very few officers there who understood anything about the positioning of batteries, he had been given brevet rank as a Lieutenant Colonel, and the command of all the Republican artillery. Having witnessed both his competence and pushfulness, Roger was not surprised to see that, in these days of rapid promotion, he had so soon risen to Brigadier, and decided that he might be worth keeping an eye on.

Meanwhile, Barras had asked: 'What are you measuring there, Citizen Brigadier Buonaparte?'

Ranges,' came the prompt reply. 'So as to decide where I would position our forces were it my responsibility to put a swift end to this insurrection.'

'Let us suppose it is then,' said Barras. 'How would you set about it?'

The young Corsican stood up. He was below middle height and so thin that, although only nineteen months younger than Roger, he appeared a stripling beside him. His complexion was sallow, the yellowish skin being drawn taut across gaunt cheeks but becoming whiter towards the top of his fine forehead, the width of which was concealed by lank black hair, parted in the middle and falling over his ears nearly down to his shoulders. In profile his sharply defined features would have made an admirable cameo: full face he might, for a moment, had been taken for an ascetic; until one noticed the unusually powerful development of the muscles at the base of his lower jaw, and the expression—determined, contemptuous and ruthless by turns—that animated the direct glance of his dark eyes.

Turning towards Barras, he showed not trace of the diffidence usual in a junior officer submitting his views to his senior; but, speaking the chronically ungrammatical French of one brought up to use Italian, he gave in short staccato sentences an appreciation of the situation as if he were an instructor teaching a cadet a lesson.

'At our disposal we have some five thousand troops of the line, a battalion of approximately fifteen hundred patriots armed yesterday, and the armed police. Total: eight thousand. Opposed to us we have over thirty-five thousand trained National Guards; the "golden youth", numbering perhaps two thousand; the returned *émigrés,* at least another thousand; and a considerable number of *Chouans* known to have been secretly drafted by the Royalists from Brittany to Paris. Total: approximately forty thousand. Were we in open country, vigorous and skilful direction, coupled with the better training and discipline of our troops, might serve to outweigh the heavy odds against us. But street fighting entails scores of localised conflicts over which simultaneous control by one General is impossible; and for storming a barricade courage is a greater asset than training. Therefore to take the offensive against the insurgents must inevitably result in our defeat.'

'What, then, do you suggest?' Barras asked.

Buonaparte's hands, which were of unusual beauty, began to move swiftly about the map. 'We must regard the Convention as the keep of a fortress that is besieged. There, in the Tuileries, it could not be better situated. From the south it can be approached only across the river by three bridges, Pont Neuf, Pont Royal, and Pont Louis XVI. They are easily held. To the west lie the gardens, giving us excellent fields of fire. To the east is the Palais du Louvre, by manning the windows of which we can deny the streets to columns advancing from that direction. One thousand of our men should be sufficient to hold each of those three sides. That leaves us five thousand for the north, and no greater number can be brought against us through the streets there opening on to the Rue St. Honoré. Naturally, I should give additional protection to our most vulnerable side by establishing strong advance positions in the Place Vendôme, the Cul-de-sac Dauphin, and other places north of the St. Honoré; and I should hold a reserve against emergencies, including all our cavalry, in the Place du Carousel. With such dispositions I consider we could render the area that should be held, impregnable.'

'All that is well enough,' Barras commented. 'But what if it develops into a regular siege? Within forty-eight hours our men would be out of ammunition, and starving.'

'Citizen General! do you take me for a fool?' the little Corsican snapped. 'Were I in command here a strong detachment would already be on its way to secure the heights of Meudon and the Arsenal there. By morning sufficient munitions could be brought in to keep us supplied for a month. The same applies to food. Troops should be sent at once to commandeer the main stocks in the depots, and bring them to the Tuileries. I would, too, send arms to the Section *Quinze-Vingts,* which alone has supported the Convention. A rising of the patriots there could draw off considerable numbers of the insurgents, and make our break-out the easier.'

'You visualise a break-out then?'

'*Sacre nom!* Yes. What sort of General would contemplate sitting down to be shot at indefinitely? To entrench ourselves is only a temporary expedient forced on us by the superior numbers of the enemy. Our object is not to protect the Convention: it is to crush the insurrection. But for that we need cannon. Our one piece of good fortune is that the Sections were made to give up their cannon after the risings in the spring. They have none; and if we can bring in the batteries from the camp at Sablons we shall have the enemy at our mercy.'

'No, no!' General Carteaux shook his head. 'We could not use cannon on the people. God knows, during the past three years there has been enough fighting in the streets of Paris, but cannon has never been used by either side.'

'Where lies the difference between killing your fellow citizens with a pike or grape-shot?' asked Buonaparte acidly. 'Personally I am against spilling any blood at all, if it can be avoided. In any case, whatever provocation may be given to the Convention's troops, they should be ordered to hold their fire until they have been fired upon. But if fight we must, let us be sensible about it. The more potent the weapons we use, the sooner it will be over and the fewer people will be killed. Without cannon I would wash my hands of this. But if given leave to make such dispositions as I wish, and to call in the batteries of artillery from the camp, I'd pledge my head to crush all opposition against the Convention before the week is out.'

With a laugh, Barras brought a heavy hand down on the little man's shoulder. 'That is the kind of language it pleases me to hear. Go to it, then, Citizen Brigadier! Under me you shall handle this thing; for I am convinced you will do it well. Give any orders you wish with my authority. I ask only that you should acquaint me with them.'

Instantly the young Brigadier's face lit up. His threadbare jacket, ill-cleaned boots and slovenly appearance, which had earned him the nickname of the 'little ragamuffin', were forgotten at the sight of his flashing eyes, and the ringing tones of his heavily accented voice.

Seizing Barras's hand, he wrung it; then, without a moment's hesitation, he began to allocate duties to the officers round him. His first order was to a Major Murat: a tall, dark, grossly handsome cavalryman who, with the liberty about uniform usual in those days, had a large ostrich feather fixed in his busby. He was despatched with his squadron to fetch the forty cannon post haste from the camp at Sablons. A Captain Marmont was sent with another squadron to sieze the Arsenal at Meudon, and a Colonel Brune to follow him with a battalion of infantry and wagons to bring in ammunition.

The three future Marshals of France had scarcely hurried from the room before other officers were dashing after them to secure supplies of food and to establish strong points round the perimeter of the area that Buonaparte had decided to hold.

The command of the fifteen hundred *sans-culottes* had been given to a brave old General named Berruyer. To him Buonaparte gave the task of having barricades thrown up in the streets to the north of the Rue St. Honoré; then he turned to the senior of them all, General Carteaux, who was looking far from happy at seeing himself supplanted by a junior who till then had been reckoned of little importance, and said tactfully:

'For you, *mon père,* I have reserved the place of the greatest danger and the greatest glory. It is certain that the insurgents will endeavour to reach the Tuileries by the shortest route, across the Pont Neuf. Take four hundred men and hold the bridge for us, if need be to the death.'

The older man's expression changed instantly. Raising his hand in salute, he cried: 'Rely upon me! They shall not pass!' And, snatching up his hat, he ran from the room.

It was now empty except for Barras, Roger, Buonaparte and his two young A.D.C.'s, Junot and Muiron. Barras waved a hand towards Roger and said:

'Do you know Citizen Breuc? He was with me on the night of 9th Thermidor, but was later made a prisoner by the English, and has only tonight got back to Paris after making his escape.'

Buonaparte's sudden smile flashed out and he shook hands warmly with Roger. 'Of course. I thought I knew your face, but could not for the moment place you, owing to the whiskers and moustache that you have grown. You were the *Citizen Représentant* who led the charge against the Spanish redoubt at Toulon. Its early capture greatly facilitated our assualt on Fort Mulgrave later that night; so yours was a valuable as well as gallant act.'

Roger bowed. 'I thank you, *Citizen General*. I see that since last we met your rapid promotion has continued. Allow me to congratulate you.'

Making a wry face, Buonaparte replied: 'All is not gold that glitters. I was given my present rank shortly after Toulon, and as Commander of the Artillery in General Masséna's campaign into Italy proved that I knew my business; but for all the use it has been to me these past thirteen months I might as well have remained a Captain.'

'You surprise me. I should have thought that many employments could be found for a man of your obvious abilities.'

'They could have been; but after Thermidor my friendship with the younger Robespierre was held against me. On my return from a diplomatic mission to the Republic of Genoa my countryman, the deputy Salicetti, from having been my patron turned against me, and as one means of whitewashing himself had me arrested.'

'You were not confined for long,' Barras put in with a shrug. 'And whereas, after 1st Prairial, Salicetti was forced to fly the country, you are still here; so it is foolish to continue to chew upon this year-old grievance.'

'Ah, but I was deprived of my command, and have been given no other since,' the young Corsican retorted bitterly. 'For months, so that they might the more easily spy upon my comings and goings, they kept me here at a desk in the Topographical Office. What sort of work is that, for a soldier?'

'You were offered a command in La Vendée.'

'Yes, as a means of testing my patriotism! But I prefer to kill Austrians, Sardinians and Englishmen to Frenchmen, whatever their political convictions. In any case, at the time, I was too ill to accept it.'

'You have had the appearance of being ill ever since I first met you,' Barras remarked shrewdly; 'so it is not to be wondered at that certain people suspected the validity of your excuse.'

'Excuse or no excuse, after my services at Toulon, Ventimiglia, Oneglia and at the Col di Tenda, they have treated me shamefully. Because of my refusal to go to Brittany, I was struck off the list of Generals. I have no post, no pay, and am allowed a table in this office only on sufference, because I have a gift for writing despatches, which others find a tiresome busines.'

'No matter,' Barras said with a laugh. 'Do you but handle this present crisis aright, and the Convention will let bygones be bygones. In a few hours the dawn of 13th Vendémiaire will break and the day may even prove the making of your fortune.'

Those few hours seemed to go very swiftly, as staff officers and orderlies hurried in and out bringing Buonaparte confirmation that his orders had been executed, or asking for further instructions where hitches had occurred. The *Poisonnière* Section stopped the consignment of arms that had been despatched to the 'patriots' of *Quinze-Vingts*, and that of *Mont Blanc* seized a convoy of provisions destined for the Tuileries; but otherwise everything went smoothly.

Roger had been in Paris during many of the major outbreaks of the Revolution, so knew well the pattern that they followed. First, for a few days, there were deputations to the Chamber, while street-corner agitators harangued anyone who would listen to them. Then processions paraded the streets demanding bread, and declaring that the Revolution had been betrayed. Finally several ill-co-ordinated mobs clashed with the equally ill-directed forces of a hesitant and jittery Authority. As brains and resolution played little part in the eventual clashes the side with the greater numbers emerged victorious. Therefore, according to precedent, the Convention was about to be overthrown.

But, as a witness of the night's skilful, systematic planning and its results, long before dawn Roger made up his mind that precedent could no longer be taken as a guide for this occasion. That 'unknown factor' of which Fouché had made passing mention had been produced by Barras in this seedy-looking little Corsican soldier who for the past year had remained unemployed and discredited.

By six o'clock his chances of succeeding in suppressing the insurrection were enormously strengthened. Murat, drenched to the skin and leaving pools of water behind him with every footstep, came stamping into the room. His thick lips parting in a grin, he told them that he had reached Les Sablons simultaneously with a battalion of National Guards from the Section *Lepelletier,* also sent to fetch the cannon. In the open plain the infantry had not dared to face a charge by his dragoons; so, after furious but useless protests, they had given way to him, and he now had forty cannon, with gunners and a good supply of ammunition, drawn up in the gardens of the Tuileries.

Buonaparte put on a shabby grey overcoat, stuck a round crowned black hat, which had an upturned brim in front, on the extreme back of his head, and declared his intention of making a round of the troops.

Barras, Roger was secretly amused to see, though happy to make use of the Corsican's abilities, had no intention of letting him get the lion's share of the credit for the arrangements he had made. Clapping his three-plumed hat on his hair that, to conceal its premature greyish, he had, in contemptuous defiance of the *sans-culottes,* kept powdered all through the Revolution, he said:

'As Commander-in-Chief, I will inspect our forces. Be

good enough, Citizen Brigadier and the rest of you, to attend me.'

During the next two hours, in the teeming rain, they rode from post to post. At each Barras spoke a few words of encouragement to the soldiers; and, depressed as they were from having stood about all night in the cold and wet, his resolute mode of address never failed to raise a cheer for the Convention.

The weather, apparently, had had an even more damping effect on the spirits of the insurgents; for, although their pickets continued to occupy buildings within musket shot of the Convention's troops, no major force of National Guards had as yet made its appearance. This delay gave Buonaparte still further time to strengthen his dispositions, and as the morning wore on without event it looked as if the day might pass without any major clash occurring.

By midday, the weather eased and strong columns of the insurgents began to surround the whole of the defended area. General Danican, who had been given the principal command of them, feeling certain of victory owing to his greatly superior numbers, but anxious to avoid bloodshed if possible, then sent an A.D.C. under a flag of truce to offer terms to the Convention. The officer was blindfolded and taken by Barras and Buonaparte into the Assembly Hall, where, after threatening the Deputies, he offered them peace if they would disarm the 'patriots' and rescind the decrees of Fructidor.

The deliberations took some time but it was finally decided not to answer. Instead twenty-four *Représentants* were nominated to go out and fraternise with the Sections and attempt to pacify them individually. By this time it was half-past four and, having received no reply, General Danican gave the order to attack. Thereupon Buonaparte sent eight hundred musket and cartridge boxes to the Convention Hall with the suggestion that the Deputies should cease talking and come out to help defend themselves.

For some hours past the Convention troops had been under severe provocation and General Carteaux had, with Buonaparte's approval, even withdrawn his men from the Pont Neuf to the Quai des Tuileries rather than have them shed first blood. But now a company of insurgents that had taken up its position on the steps of the Church of St. Roch began to fire down on Buonaparte's gunners.

Reluctant as he was to have his name associated with killing Frenchmen, now that he was left no option he acted swiftly and ruthlessly. In a few minutes, blasts of grapeshot from his cannon rendered the steps of the church a tangled mass of dead and dying. Ordering the guns to be swung about in sections back to back he then had them sweep both ends of the Rue St. Honoré for its whole length with their devastating fire. His horse was shot under him, but the faithful Junot, ever at his side, got him another, and leaping on to it, he personally led a company of 'patriots' into the nearest fray.

In the hour that followed, his extraordinary instinct for directing a battle sent him from point to point so that he appeared as though miraculously at every place where danger threatened. At each he rallied the troops, ordered a charge or himself directed the fire of the nearest cannon, so that they mowed down the heads of the packed columns of the insurgents.

The most determined attack was made from the east, where some eight thousand men endeavoured to force their way past the Louvre. Their object was to join up with the troops of the Comte de Maulevrier in the Rue Dauphine, and the column on the Pont Neuf led by a young Royalist named Lafond, who showed great gallantry. But Buonaparte deployed several batteries on the Quai des Tuileries and, by blasting both the exits of the streets and the bridge, drove the insurgents back everywhere in hopeless confusion.

By six o'clock the conflict was over, and the final dispersion of the great mobs that had gathered was brought about by a continued firing of the cannon, but with blank ammunition. There remained only three strong points—the Place Vendôme, the church of St. Roch and the Palais Royal—in each of which bodies of the insurgents had fortified themselves. These Buonaparte promptly surrounded, and a few musket shots the following morning proved sufficient to bring about their surrender.

Barras and Buonaparte both received a tremendous ovation from the Convention, which they had undoubtedly saved. The former was appointed Commander-in-Chief of the Army of the Interior. The latter, whose name for the first time became one of national significance, was given the post of Second in Command; which transformed him overnight from an obscure Brigadier, suspended and penniless, to a highly paid and influential man in the second rank of France's Generals.

Roger, by an apparent eagerness to help, and a great display of activity, had succeeded in retaining Barras's esteem without having had actually to participate in the fighting. There had been no means by which he could influence the battle in favour of the monarchists; so he had had to watch their defeat while riding to and fro with Barras and cheering lustily on every suitable occasion.

Consequently, with a dozen others, he came in for a minor share of the triumph; and, when the story of his escape from the Army of Condé got about, scores of his old acquaintances welcomed him back to Paris. As he had no post Barras promptly gave him one, with the rank of Colonel, in his new office; and nothing could have suited Roger better, as the job was a sinecure having no hours and few duties, yet gave him access to all the papers concerning the Army of the Interior.

Thus, by having inadvertently backed the right horse at what had appeared to be the wrong moment, he now found himself more safely entrenched in the favour of the men who governed France than he ever dreamed could again be possible. Yet he was quick to realise that it was only at a price—it had now become impossible to carry out his intentions.

Within twenty-four hours it became clear that, having triumphed, the Convention intended to pursue a policy of conciliation rather than revenge. A few of the most belligerent Sections were disarmed and the National Guards of the others placed under Buonaparte; but, except for Lafond, who had been captured and stubbornly refused a pardon, the leaders of the insurgents were permitted to escape. Against the *jeunesse dorée* no move was made at all. They were allowed to continue going freely about Paris wearing the reactionist colours of black and green, and to boast unchecked in the *salons* of the bravery they had displayed in facing the 'little ragamuffin's' cannon; so in a very short time, apart from those who mourned four hundred dead, all trace that there had been of an insurrection disappeared from the capital and it resumed its feverish post-Terror gaiety.

Nevertheless, the fact remained that the Monarchists and the Moderates had shot their bolt. They had never had an acknowledged leader or formed a coherent party, but were a score of groups with different aims knit loosely together only by a mutual hatred of the Convention. Their numbers and readiness to rise, had they continued to simmer for a few weeks longer, would have made an excellent lever for Roger to persuade two or three of his old colleagues who still had real power to collaborate with Pichegru. But now that the discontented had blown off their steam, months must elapse before they were ripe for another outbreak; and men like Fréron, Dubois-Crancé, Tallien or Boissy d'Anglas were not going to risk their necks by arresting the die-hard members of the Committee of Public Safety unless they could be assured of immediate popular support.

An even greater obstacle to the fulfilment of Roger's plans had emerged in the person of Buonaparte. This swift-thinking, resolute young man would neither have panicked nor sat still when he learned that the conqueror of Holland had left the Rhine and was marching his army on Paris. His readiness to defend the Convention, although it had treated him ill, showed where his sentiments lay; at all events for the present. With every man he could muster he would have marched out of Paris and given battle to Pichegru; and who could say which of them would have proved the victor?

These considerations decided Roger that there was nothing really worthwhile that he could do by remaining in Paris; yet he felt that it would be a mistake to leave the city precipitately. Should he do so without giving any adequate excuse, his disappearance was now certain to arouse considerable comment, and after another prolonged absence it would be more than doubly difficult to lie his way back a second time into the sort of position he held; in fact he could not possibly hope to do so. The limitation of his commitment to Mr. Pitt made it unlikely that he would wish to return; but, all the same, it seemed like repudiating the good fortune with which he had been favoured by fate, not to consolidate his gains before, in due course, retiring smoothly from the scene with an aura of goodwill about him.

In consequence, as his duties with Barras entailed little more than appearing on public occasions in a fine uniform as a member of that ostentatious potentate's staff, he shaved off his whiskers and moustache, and spent most of his time cultivating the society of the day. Many doors were already open to him, and through them he passed to others; so that within ten days he had become an accepted frequenter of the leading *salons* in Paris.

Tallien had been known to Roger ever since the desperate night upon which the legally elected members of the Municipality of Paris had been violently deposed to make way for the Commune, and during the even more desperate days of Thermidor they had risked their lives together to bring about the fall of Robespierre. As an opener of doors no one could now have served better; for, not only had he just been made the head of a Committee charged with governing until the new Constitution came into force, but, as Fouché had informed Roger, his wife had become the most influential woman in Paris.

Theresa Tallien was the daughter of the Spanish banker François Cabarrus, and the divorced wife of the Comte de Fontenay. Tallien, while deluging Bordeaux in blood as a *Représentant en Mission*, had seen her, fallen in love with her on sight, saved her from the guillotine and, after the fall of Robespierre, married her. In the meantime, by her influence over him she had saved many other people; and such was her beauty, compassion and grace that she had become known as 'Our Lady Thermidor'.

Recently, she had taken a large house called the Chaumière right out in the market garden area between the Rond-point and the Seine, and had had it done up to look like a stage farm. In spite of its being so far from central Paris all the smart world now flocked to it; so in her *salon* there Roger met numerous old friends and made several new ones. Among the latter was a *ci-devant* Marquise of great intelligence and charm named Madame de Chateau-Renault, and it was in her *salon* a few nights later that he was first presented to Madame de Beauharnais, the ravishing brunette whom he had seen leave Barras's house on the night of the 12th-13th Vendémiaire. She was known as *La belle Créole* and was certainly a very handsome woman, although her nose was slightly retroussé and her ready smile was robbed of much of its attraction by her bad teeth.

Another *salon,* which now rivalled and was soon to surpass Madame Tallien's, was that of Madame de Staël. She was the daughter of M. Necker, the Swiss banker whose pompous ineptitude and popularity-seeking at the expense of his sovereign, while acting as Louis XVI's last Minister at Versailles, had done much to precipitate the Revolution. In '86 she had married the Swedish Ambassador to France and after Thermidor had returned with him to their Embassy, an imposing mansion fronted with pillars in the Rue du Bac. No one would have called her a beauty, and she was of a most restless disposition; but she had good eyes, a fine brow and a great gift for intelligent conversation.

In allowing Garat, the handsome singer who was at that time the idol of Paris, to take him to Madame de Staël's, Roger knew that he was running a certain risk. He had been slightly acquainted with her in the old days, and might at her house run into someone who had known him well before he had transformed himself from the Chevalier de Breuc into a Revolutionary Commissar. In that event an unpleasant incident might occur and land him with a duel. On the other hand there was a much brighter possibility, for Madame de Staël had been the devoted friend of Louis de Narbonne, Charles Maurice de Talleyrand, Mathieu de Montmorency and many other Liberal nobles who had sided with the Third Estate in the early days of the Revolution. It was therefore possible that her *salon* might prove the very bridge he needed unostentatiously to link up his two identities; and it was that which decided him to risk a visit to her.

When Garat had presented him, she gave him a searching look and said: 'Both the name Breuc and your features are vaguely familiar to me, *Citizen Colonel*. Can we have met before?'

Roger took the plunge. 'Yes, *Madame la Baronne*. It was at the house of M. le Talleyrand-Périgord, out at Passy.' Then with a twinkle, he added: 'And about that I will tell you a secret, if you will promise to keep it.'

'Certainly I promise,' she smiled. 'I adore secrets.'

She waved away the people nearest to them, and, stepping up to her, Roger whispered in her ear. 'I have looked after the house for him all through the Revolution, and when he returns he will find it just as he left it.'

'You intriguing man.' She tapped his arm lightly with her fan. 'You are then another of those whom we now discover to have disguised themselves as destroyers in order that they might act as preservers. It is quite a revelation these days to learn how many of our friends succeeded in making fools of that horrid little Robespierre and his brutal associates. How delighted our dear Bishop will be. I am so glad for him.'

Turning, she beckoned over a good-looking young man whose fair curly hair fell in ringlets to his shoulders, and introduced him. 'This is Mr. Benjamin Constant. He has recently arrived from America, and can give you news of our mutual friend.'

From Constant, Roger learned that de Talleyrand, while living in very straitened circumstances in Boston, had been employing his fine brain in evolving numerous vast commercial ventures; but none of these attempts to repair his fallen fortunes had yet come to anything. Moreover, the amorous *ci-devant* Bishop had given great offence to the ladies of Boston society by appearing openly in the street with a lovely young mulatto girl on his arm; but the less strait-laced among the men continued to seek his company on account of his charm and wit.

Garat then introduced Roger to his mistress, a beautiful

blonde cendrée named Madame de Krüdner. She was a Courlander and at the age of fourteen had been married to a Russian ambassador. It was said that she possessed mediumistic powers; and occasionally she fell into trances, which were probably mild epileptic fits, in the middle of parties.

She was certainly an angelic-looking creature, but Roger found her vapid and distrait. He was much more intrigued by an equally lovely and much more vivacious chestnut-haired beauty of eighteen. Her name was Madame Récamier, and she had already been married for two years to a man twenty-six years older than herself. He was an immensely rich hat manufacturer of Lyons, and during the Terror had not missed watching the guillotine at work for a single day; the excuse for this macabre pastime that he gave his friends being that, as he must sooner or later die by that instrument, he wished to familiarise himself with it.

Yet he had not parted with his head under its blade, and Roger now found remarkable the number of titled and wealthy people who had succeeded in escaping a similar fate although they had remained in Paris all through the Revolution. Nearly all of them had been in prison for a few months during the height of the Terror, and had resigned themselves to death; but Robespierre's fall had saved them, and by bribing the venal revolutionary officials most of them had managed to retain a good part of their fortunes.

Previously to 1789, although the Government had become bankrupt through mismanagement, and the poor in the cities were forced to toil for little more than a starvation wage. France had been by far the richest country in the world. This wealth lay not so much in the hands of the nobility as—apart from a few hundred extremely rich families, their refusal to demean themselves by engaging in any form of commerce had kept them poor—but in the coffers of enormous numbers of prosperous bourgeoisie. It was mainly the nobility that had emigrated and sent its sons to fight in the army of de Condé: while the bulk of the professional and merchant classes had remained, simply lying low.

Now, although the Government was still bankrupt and the masses starving, thousands of property-owners were digging up large and small hoards of coin from their gardens, or recovering them from under floor boards and other hiding places. The revolutionary paper money was at a huge discount, but purses full of *louis d'or* and cart-wheel silver *écus* were once more changing hands in Paris with the utmost freedom.

With the disappearance of the fear that ostentation would result in imprisonment and perhaps death, a new era of luxury had set in. It was apparent not only in the exclusive *salons,* but everywhere. No sooner had the actors and actresses of the *Comédie Française* been released from prison than the theatre had nightly become packed with well-dressed people applauding anti-revolutionary quips. The boxes at the *Feydeau* were now always occupied by bevies of lovely women and elegantly attired men. In the streets handsome equipages with coachmen in livery were again to be seen by the score. Shops long closed were once more open for the sale of jewellery, lace, furs, brocades, perfumes, wines, delicacies of all sorts and clothes in the new fashion.

Previously to the Revolution, apart from the aristocratic oligarchies of Venice and Genoa there had been no Republics in Europe; so the new France had modelled herself largely on the ancient ones of Greece and Rome. The smart women were termed *merveilleuses.* They had adopted the high waisted tunic of Corinth and wore their hair piled high in a cone bound with ribbon, leaving the neck bare. Arms and legs were also left bare and the dresses were made of the thinnest obtainable materials; while beneath them so little was worn as to be barely decent. In fact they vied with one another quite shamelessly in exposing their limbs, and often wore tunics slit down the sides which were caught together only by cameos at the shoulder, waist and knee.

The fashion for men had also changed out of all recognition. The *incroyables,* as the exquisites among the *jeunesse dorée* were called, wore their hair turned up behind but with long tresses nicknamed 'dog's-ears' in front. Their high-collared, square-cut frock coats were buttoned tightly over the stomach and had tails coming down to the calf of the legs, which were encased in silk stockings striped with red, yellow or blue. For evening wear waistcoats were of white dimity with broad facings, and small-clothes of pearl-grey or apple-green satin, over which hung double gold watch chains. But the most outstanding feature of this costume was a huge muslin cravat worn so high that it dipped from ear to ear concealing the chin and almost hiding the mouth.

As a final mark of their antithesis from the *sans-culottes* both *me'veilleuses* and *inc'oyables,* as they called themselves, spoke in drawling affected voices and dropped their 'r's', which reminded Roger somewhat of the Creole French used in the West Indies. From mixing with them he derived only one satisfaction; it showed him that he no longer had the least reason to fear being charged by some noble that he had known in the past as a renegade.

Madame de Staël's implication, that few people knew what their friends had been up to, or the true motives behind their actions during the past few years, was unquestionably correct. And, apparently, they could not have cared less. Scores of men who had, in part at least, been responsible for wholesale murder and plunder, but could point to a few acts of mercy, now dressed as *incroyables* and were freely admitted to the *salons*. Many of them were even accepted as friends by the *émigré* nobles, considerable numbers of whom, although still technically liable to the death penalty, had returned to Paris in the hope of getting their names removed from the lists of outlaws; and there were actually cases in which ex-terrorists had been taken as lovers by young demoiselles of the nobility whose fathers they had sent to the guillotine.

Such was the cynical, worthless and abnormal society, bred by a mating of upheaval and terror, in which Roger moved during October 1795. Yet he knew that side by side with it there existed plenty of families which, without being in the least puritanical, lived respectable lives; and Buonaparte, whom he saw almost daily at his office, one evening spontaneously suggested taking him to meet some old friends of his, who proved to be such a family.

They consisted of a widow named Permon, her son Albert, who was about twenty-five, and a high-spirited little daughter of eleven called Laurette, who promised soon to become a most attractive young woman. Madame Permon was a Corsican, a great friend of Buonaparte's mother, and, as she had known him from his birth, she addressed him as Napolione.

In this setting the young General seemed to Roger a different person. The contemptuous twist he could give to his mouth, and the acid rebukes, which could make much older men break out in a sweat of apprehension, were evidently reserved for his hours of duty. Here he laughed freely, treated Madame Permon with an affectionate gallantry and allowed the quick-witted little Laura to tease him to her heart's content.

Moreover, he made no secret of the fact that during the past few months, had it not been for Madame Permon and Junot, who was also present, he would positively have starved. The one had provided him with many a supper, which had been his only meal of the day, and the other had forced him to accept the major part of the remittances occasionally received from his family.

Junot, a fair, curly-haired young man of twenty-four, with a pleasing and open countenance, was a native of the Côte d'Or and the son of an official. He had been destined for the law, but the Revolution had sent him into the army. His fellow privates had elected him sergeant for his gallantry on the field of battle, and later, at the siege of Toulon, further acts of bravery had led Buonaparte to single him out for a commission and make him his first A.D.C. His devotion to his General was religious in its intensity; and he had hitched his wagon to no small star, for in course of time it was to make him the husband of the delightful little Laura Permon, the Military Governor of Paris, a Duke, and the only man who had the right to walk in on his future Emperor at any hour of the day or night.

They laughed now over the way in which Junot, who as lucky as a gambler, had more than once ventured his last twenty francs at *vingt-et-un* in order that he might pay the bills of his Brigadier and himself at the modest Hotel of the Rights of Man, where they shared a room; and how Madame Permon had often reprimanded Buonaparte for coming in with muddy boots and making a horrid smell by drying them at the fire.

But those days were past. The cantankerous, out-at-elbows young officer who had been contemptuously nick-named by one of Barras's beautiul mistresses 'the little ragamuffin' had disappeared never to return. Buonaparte had bought himself a handsome carriage and a fine house in the Rue des Capucines. His uniform was new and heavy with gold lace, and he had not forgotten those who had befriended him in the dark days of adversity. Junot had been promoted from Lieutenant to Colonel; Madame Permon, who had recently lost her husband and, although it had been kept from her, been left very badly off, was being secretly assisted through her son; and in addition the young General was supporting a hundred other families in the neighbourhood, who had fallen on evil times.

On the 26th of October the Convention, which for so long had tyrannised over the French people, was at last dissolved; but the majority of its members together with the newly elected third met the following day under the warrant of the new Constitution. As was to be expected, the nominees of the old majority were chosen to fill the offices of State in both the Council of the Five Hundred and the Council of the Ancients.

They then proceeded to the election of the five Directors who were in future to wield the executive power. At the head of the list submitted by the Five Hundred to the Ancients stood the names of Barras, Rewbell, Sieyès, Larevellière-Lépeaux and Letourneur; below them were those of forty-four nonentities none of whom was in the least suitable to hold high office. By this barefaced piece of political jobbery, and the complaisance of their old colleague among the Ancients, the Thermidorians and Jacobins succeeded in ensuring the continuance of a government wholly anti-monarchist in character.

Sieyès, out of spleen that his own draft for a new Constitution had been rejected, refused to take office; so Carnot's name was put up and he was promptly elected. After Thermidor, as a member of the dread Committee of Public Safety, this truly great military genius had been indicted with the rest of the Committee for its crimes. But he, Prieur of the Côte d'Or, and Robert Lindet had all been exonerated, as they had concerned themselves entirely with feeding the nation and maintaining its armed forces. Lindet, an honest man and a tireless worker, had gone so far as to insist on having a separate office, and Carnot had shut his eyes to all else while performing the remarkable feat of increasing the armies of France in less than a year from one hundred and twenty, to seven hundred and fifty, thousand men. Yet they had been deprived of their offices, and the loss of their competent direction had resulted in a chronic shortage of supplies of all kinds in all the French armies for many months past. So the appointment as a Director of the 'Organiser of Victories', as Carnot had been called, was hailed with enthusiasm by all classes.

Larevellière-Lépeaux had been elected because, on the one hand, he was a typical Girondinist lawyer, and, on the other, had an intense hatred of Christianity, which strongly appealed to the old *énragés* of the Mountain; so he received backing from both parties and polled more votes than any of the others.

Why Letourneur's name had been put forward was a mystery, as he was a man of no distinction: simply an ex-Captain of Engineers who had worked under Carnot at the War Office. But he was an honest man and had no enemies; so overnight he found himself a celebrity.

Barras, in spite of his vices, at least had to recommend him his courage and initiative at times of crisis, but he was incurably lazy where routine matters were concerned.

Rewbell was a much stronger character than any of the others and a dyed-in-the-wool revolutionary. As *Représentant en Mission* he had for long bullied and terrorised the officers of the Army of the Rhine. He was a fanatical believer in the type of Dictatorship practised by the old Committee of Public Safety and regarded all forms of personal liberty as harmful to the State. He was dishonest himself and had a cynical disbelief in the honesty of others. His manner was rough, he had a harsh voice and expressed his opinions with brutal frankness. Nevertheless, he had an enormous capacity for business, great ability, and a will of iron; so anybody who knew the five men could have little doubt that he would be the one to dominate their councils.

On November the 3rd, dressed in magnificent uniforms specially designed for them, the five new 'Kings of France' were installed in the Luxembourg Palace, and set about appointing their Ministers. In the meantime Roger had already made the first moves towards going home, and meant to leave shortly after witnessing this epoch-making event.

Under the new Constitution, Barras, by becoming a Director, had automatically had to relinquish his military command; so Roger's appointment as a Colonel on his staff had also lapsed. Buonaparte, who had stepped into Barras's shoes as C.-in-C. Army of the Interior, had taken a liking to Roger and told him that although he was not a professional soldier he would be happy to find him employment. Barras, too, offered to secure him a good post in the civil administration. But to both he made the same excuse for declining.

He said that the indifferent food and harsh conditions under which he had lived while for so long a prisoner in England, had undermined his health; and to restore it fully he felt the only course was to get away from Paris during the winter months to the sunshine of the South of France, where he intended to rent or buy a small property. Both expressed their sympathy, approved his decision and said that he could count on their good offices when he returned to Paris in the spring. During the round of visits to the ladies of the *salons,* and other people with whom he had recently spent much of his time, he received some expressions of sympathy and more of envy that he should be leaving cold, rainy Paris for warmer climes, but everyone said they would be glad to see him back; so the stage was set for his departure under the most pleasant auspices.

On his last night he supped with Barras in his palatial new quarters at the Luxembourg. It was a gay party of a dozen men, and as many ladies all clad in transparent draperies and hoping to play the role of Aspasia to King Paul I, as they laughingly christened their host; or failing that to ensnare one of the guests who had influence with him. The party promised to go on into the small hours, but Roger was making an early start in the morning; so soon after midnight he excused himself.

As he waited on the steps of the Palace for the porter to beckon up a coach to take him home, a tall, thin figure emerged from the shadows of the courtyard, stepped up to him and said:

'May I have a word with you, Citizen?'

By the flickering light of the torches Roger recognised Fouché; and, as the coach halted opposite them at the moment, he replied:

'Certainly, if you wish. Jump in. I will drive you home.'

When they were settled in the coach, Fouché said: 'So you are leaving Paris?'

'Yes; how did you know?'

'Things get about, and I hear most of them; just as I did that you would be among Barras's guests tonight.'

'It seems that you must have been very anxious to see me, to wait about in the rain. You've been lucky too in that I did not remain till the end of the party, as it will go on for some hours yet.'

'I have never lacked patience where my own interests are concerned,' Fouché replied acidly. 'But you might have spared me the necessity of seeking you out in so uncomfortable a manner. Why did you not get in touch with me again, as you promised?'

Roger shrugged. 'I saw no point in doing so. Thirteenth Vendémiaire rendered the plan we had evolved quite impossible of execution; so there was nothing for us to discuss.'

'I disagree. The fact that Buonaparte ruined our prospects does not affect the fact that you still hold the little Capet.'

For a moment Roger thought of telling Fouché that he could rid his mind of the hope that he might gain anything from that belief, because the boy was dead. He would either reach that conclusion or have to be told so sometime, and the fiction that the child was still alive had served its purpose. By keeping what he knew to himself, Fouché had given him a free run on his return to Paris. Luck and his own wits had enabled him to make excellent use of it. He was now as safe as the Bank of England, whereas Fouché was still friendless and discredited. The ex-Terrorist might swear until he was black in that face that Roger was an English spy; but he had not one atom of proof and no one would believe him.

But, on second thoughts, Roger decided that now was not the time to reveal to Fouché how he had been tricked. He might have a pistol or a dagger on him and, in a fit of ungovernable rage, attempt to use it. The close darkness of the coach was no place to invite a fight, and it would be folly to risk death or serious injury to no purpose. So, after a moment, he said:

'I waited in Paris to learn the results of the elections to the Directory, although I had little hope that they would provide us with a possible opening; and so it has proved. Letourneur is a man of straw. Larevellière-Lépeaux is so intense an atheist that he would die rather than assist in the re-establishment of the Church, without which a Restoration is unthinkable. Carnot, Rewbell and Barras are all regicides. Their past deeds pledge them to fight to the last ditch for the continuance of a Republic. And behind all five now stands Buonaparte with his cannon. Surely you can see that the executive power having been given into the hands of such men renders any attempt by us to use our Royal pawn more hopeless than ever.'

'To that I agree; but you could open negotiations about him with the Bourbon Princes.'

'No. When last we talked of this, you said yourself that the Comte de Provence having had himself proclaimed Louis XVIII blocked our prospects in that direction. It is certain that he would repudiate the child, and declare him to be an imposter.'

'That is possible, but not certain,' Fouché argued. 'And I am in desperate straits. Nearly all our old associates have been more fortunate than myself. They have succeeded in burying their pasts, and are now accepted as honest men who did only what they were compelled to do for the safety of the Republic in the days of its danger. I, too, could have whitewashed myself had I remained a member of the Convention. But having been expelled from it makes me a marked man, and no one will give me employment. Will you not please consider approaching the Comte de Provence?'

The drive from the Luxembourg to the Passage Pappilote, where Fouché had his little house, was a short one, and as the coach pulled up at its entrance, Roger said firmly:

'To do as you ask would be to show our hand prematurely, and with little chance of gaining anything from it. I think you should consider yourself lucky not to have been sent to the guillotine with Carrier, or despatched to Cayenne with Billaud and Collot. In any case, no man with a brain as good as yours is likely to starve. Meanwhile, I can only suggest you should be patient until some new turn of events here decides me that the time has come to return to Paris with a good prospect of our being able to use the little Capet to the best advantage.'

Reluctantly Fouché got out, and, not very cordially, they wished one another good night.

Early in the morning Roger bid good-bye to the faithful Blanchards, and mounted a good bay mare that had his valise strapped to the back of her saddle. He had decided to travel by horseback so that no coachman could later give away the direction he had taken. He also took the precaution of leaving Paris by its southern gate and riding some distance along the road to Melun before making a great detour via Rambouillet to Mantes, where he spent the night. Thence he followed the road north-west to Elbeuf, but then left the Seine and branched off to Pont Audemer. There he spent the second night, and soon after noon on the third day arrived at Harfleur.

Dan Izzard had many friends among the smugglers on both sides of the Channel, and through him Roger knew how to set about finding one who would run him across. The war had caused a huge boom in smuggling, as the demand in England for French wines and brandies was as great as ever, and, now that luxury goods could again be sold in

France, there were eager buyers there for Yorkshire cloth, Lancashire muslins and Nottingham lace. A few tactful enquiries soon produced the Captain of a lugger who was waiting only for better weather to run a cargo.

The lugger was lying in Trouville, a little fishing village a few miles down the coast; so Roger moved to the inn there. Next day the weather eased a little, so the skipper decided to sail on the night tide. It proved a horrible crossing, and Roger hated every moment of it, but the smugglers set him safely ashore twenty-four hours later not far from Deal. On the evening of November the 12th he reached London.

There, one of the surprises of his life was waiting for him. At Amesbury House he found two letters from Amanda. Opening the one of the earlier date he saw from its first few lines that she was going to have a baby.

She wrote that she had already been five months' pregnant when he had left Martinique; but had wished to keep her secret as long as possible. Then in the desperate rush of his departure there had been no suitable opportunity to tell him. Her health was excellent and she expected her child to be born about Christmas. He need have no fears for her, as Cousin Margaret was being more than a mother to her and had already engaged a French doctor of the highest reputation in such matters to attend the accouchment. She was plagued with no longings, except the natural one to have him near her when his child was born, but with the ocean between them she had resigned herself not to hope for that; though she did hope that his duty to Mr. Pitt would not detain him so long in Europe as to deprive her of the joy of presenting his first-born to him while still an infant.

The second letter contained assurances of her continued good health and general news about social life in Martinique, including several paragraphs about Clarissa, who continued to be the toast of the island, but would give preference to none of her beaux for more than a few weeks apiece, and had now refused at least a dozen offers of marriage.

Roger had hardly digested Amanda's great news when

Droopy came in from a meeting of the Royal Society of Arts; and over supper together the two old friends drank far more than was good for them in healths to Amanda and her precious burden.

Next morning Roger went round to Downing Street and sent up his name to Mr. Pitt. His master kept him waiting for the best part of two hours, but then received him with a smile and said: 'I feel sure you have much to tell me, Mr. Brook; so I have despatched my most urgent business and am now freed to listen to you with an easy mind. You will, I trust, join me in a glass of port?'

With a word of thanks, Roger accepted the wine the Prime Minister poured for him and sat down on the far side of the document-strewn table, then proceeded to give a lucid account of his doings for the past seven weeks. He ended by saying:

'So you will appreciate, Sir, that for several months at least our plans must lie dormant. Without assurances of support in Paris, Pichegru will not move; and I am convinced that there is no hope of such support being forthcoming until some fresh turn of fortune's wheel displaces the rogues who have recently secured to themselves the supreme power in France. That I should have failed you in this I deeply regret, but. . . .'

The Prime Minister held up his hand. 'Say no more, Mr. Brook. I was always confident that once you set your mind to it you would manage to re-establish yourself in Paris, and that you should have succeeded so completely makes it all the harder that the events of 13th Vendémiaire should have robbed you of the chance to achieve a *coup* of the first magnitude. Yet you have returned to me far from empty handed. Your handling of General Pichegru was positively masterly, and is already having most excellent results.'

Roger smiled. 'I thank you, Sir, I felt much apprehension in gambling so great sum on Pichegru's good faith; but before I left Paris reports were coming in which seemed to indicate that he intends to earn the money. His failure to take Heidelberg can hardly have been anything but deliberate; and the possession of that city appeared to me to be the crux of the whole campaign, owing to the several communicating valleys that all converge upon it.'

'Our military pundits confirm you in that; and for once the Austrians have not been slow to take advantage of an opportunity offered to them. General Jourdan's army is now dammed up behind the River Neckar and as he is dependent on supplies from the distant Low Countries, he must now either retreat or suffer defeat from his troops being weakened by starvation. Meanwhile the Austrians should be able to contain Pichegru in Mannheim; and even, perhaps, drive him out of it back across the Rhine. I would, though, that we were nearer to peace.'

'I fear that as things are there is little hope of that, Sir.'

'I know it,' Mr. Pitt agreed unhappily. 'Yet the nation needs, and is near demanding it. On the 29th of last month His Majesty's coach was stoned when he was on his way to open Parliament, by a mob yelling at him to make an end of the war. Such an occurrence, when he has for so long enjoyed great popularity with the masses, is indication enough of the state of public feeling.'

Roger sadly shook his head. 'That is indeed bad news. I only wish that I could have done better for you.'

'Nay, Mr. Brook. You have done all that any man could. Were it not for you we should be in far worse case. The Austrians might have been compelled to sue for peace this winter. At least you have gained for them a breathing space until the spring; and that is much. Meanwhile it seems there is little we can do but continue to use our forces to the best advantage and hope for better times.'

'You are then, Sir, agreeable to release me; so that I may return to Martinique?'

'Yes, if you wish. Though I would much prefer to have you nearer to me.'

'That is hardly possible if I am to do justice to my Governorship.'

'Harry Dundas tells me that you have done remarkably well there; so presumably you find such work congenial. But are you still of the opinion that a post so far from the centre of things will long content you?'

'Not indefinitely, perhaps,' Roger admitted. 'Yet it has

great attractions for me, and for a few years I am sure I could be very happy in it.'

Mr. Pitt frowned. 'I wish that I could persuade you otherwise. However, should you tire of it you have only to let me know. Dundas will have no difficulty in finding a suitable man to replace you and pay you ten thousand pounds for the privilege. In the meantime I will instruct Mr. Rose to place five thousand to your credit, in recognition of the signal service you have rendered to the Allied cause.'

'That is most generous, and I am deeply grateful, Sir.'

'Twould not go far in hiring foreign levies to much less purpose,' smiled the Prime Minister, standing up. 'Do you plan to return to Martinique at once, or first enjoy some leave in London?'

Roger, too, came to his feet. 'I mean to sail by the first ship available. I have received news that my wife is due to bear a child within a week or so of Christmas. As it is our first I would fain be with her at the time. Given an early start and a good passage that should be possible.'

'In that case I can aid you. A fleet with considerable reinforcements for the West Indies, under General Sir Ralph Abercromby, who is to be our new Commander-in-Chief there, is due to sail next week. I will instruct the Admiralty to find you accommodation in one of the war-ships. Please convey my compliments and congratulations to Mrs. Brook.'

Having expressed his thanks again Roger took his leave well satisfied with the results of the interview. Five thousand pounds made a handsome addition to the little fortune he had succeeded in accumulating during the past three years, and he was clearly more strongly established than ever in the good graces of his master.

On his return to England he had hoped to go down to stay for some nights at Stillwaters with Georgina, but the previous evening Droopy Ned had told him that she was taking the waters at Bath; so, unless the ship that was to carry him to Martinique sailed from Bristol, it now looked as if there was little chance of his seeing her. As a salve of sorts to his disappointment, he bought a number of expensive toys with which his godson was as yet far too young to play, then wrote a long letter to Georgina to be despatched with them.

In the evening he received a chit from the Admiralty. The Fleet was to sail from Spithead for Barbados on November the 18th, and accommodation had been found for him in the frigate *Swiftsure*. To go in her promised a safe and swift passage across the ocean, and there was plenty of local shipping plying between Barbados and Martinique which, given a good wind, lay only a day's sailing apart; so little knowing what he was being let in for, he felt that nothing could have suited him better.

The next three days he spent looking up old friends, and buying to take out with him innumerable presents for Amanda, together with a supply of beribboned baby clothes large enough to have clothed the inmates of a crèche. Early on the morning of the 17th he bade farewell to Droopy Ned, drove down to Portsmouth with Dan, and that evening they went aboard H.M.S. *Swiftsure*.

On the Fleet's very first night at sea it was caught by a terrible tempest in the Channel and entirely dispersed. When Roger had recovered from the miseries of seasickness sufficiently to drag himself on deck he found that *Swiftsure* was well out into the Atlantic, but had lost her foremast. The jury mast rigged in its place meant a great curtailment of her normal sail so an addition of many days to her voyage.

As she limped south-westward, he could hardly contain his impatience, but fret and fume as he did that added nothing to the speed of the frigate. It was Christmas Eve when, without having sighted a single one of her late companions, she docked in Bridgetown, Barbados, and a good merchantman could have made the crossing in considerably less than the time she had taken. Within an hour of landing Roger had hired a schooner to take him on to Martinique, and it brought him into the harbour of Fort Royal soon after dawn on Boxing Day.

Leaving Dan to superintend the landing of his baggage, he went ashore at once and jumped into an ancient carriage that a sleepy negro had just driven on to the quay in the hope of picking up an early fare. He was driven up the hill to the Chateau, where, as it was now winter again, he felt sure that Amanda would be reinstalled. When he reached it the servants were just setting about their morning duties. As he ran into the spacious hall, they stopped work and, taken by surprise by his unexpected appearance, stared at him for a moment as if he were a ghost.

Then a woolly-haired young footman, the whites of his eyes rolling, ran off down a passage. A dusky housemaid gave a squeak and flung her apron over her head; another negress fled upstairs, taking the steps three at a time.

Smiling at the commotion he had caused, Roger strode up the stairs after the flying housemaid, who shot round a corner of the second floor before he was half way up the first flight. At the time he did not realise it, but she had gone to tell Madame de Kay of his arrival. As he reached the second landing a door slammed and that lady appeared in a corridor to the left. Her hair was still in curlers and about her she clutched a hastily donned dressing-gown.

With a laugh, he called to her. 'Am I in time? A cursed frigate should have got me here days ago, but we suffered every sort of delay imaginable.'

As she walked towards him she replied: 'You have come too late, Roger dear. It was on Christmas Eve.'

'Ah well!' he shrugged. 'Never mind. But Amanda and the boy—I've felt certain all along that she'd bear me a son. How are they?'

Tears welled into Cousin Margaret's eyes, and she stammered huskily: 'You . . . you have a daughter, Roger. But poor Amanda . . . In giving birth . . . She . . . she is dead. We buried her yesterday.'

23

Midnight Interview

About those words 'we buried her yesterday' there seemed an even more terrible finality than the thought of death itself. Roger stood there aghast, rigid and motionless; shaken to the roots of his being.

Amanda was such a strong, well-built young woman, and she had had hardly a day's illness in her life. He had accepted it as not uncommon for women to die in child-birth, but it had never even crossed his mind that such a fate would overtake her.

Their marriage had been no idyll. Before it both of them had been the victims of passionate love affairs that had gone awry; so neither had had the illusion that the other was the only person in the world for them. But during their long honeymoon in Italy, and the year that followed, they had come to delight more and more in one another. After a further six months, debts and restlessness had driven Roger to resume his old work for Mr. Pitt in France; so for the next two years they had been together very little and had gradually drifted apart. Then after Robespierre's fall and Roger's return they had had a genuine reconciliation. He had believed himself done for good with the hazardous life he had led and ready to settle down. The peril in which they had both stood for many weeks after the taking of the *Circe* had drawn them still closer together, and during their seven months in Martinique they had been happier than ever before.

Unlike other women, Amanda had never made demands upon him. Her only faults had been an irritating vagueness about practical matters, and an irresponsibility about money which could at times prove embarrassing. She had been the easiest person in the world to live with; gentle, kind, generous in thought and deed, every ready for laughter. And now she was gone—gone for ever.

'Roger!' Madame de Kay's gentle voice impinged only faintly on his bemused brain. 'I know this must be a terrible blow to you. I would have tried to break the news more gently had I had warning of your coming. I wish you could have seen her. She looked so sweet, and utterly at peace. But in this hot climate the funeral. . . .'

'Please! Please!' He held up his hand. 'I beg you say no more. I wish to be alone to think.' Then he turned away and strode off to the bedroom he had shared with Amanda.

It was neat and orderly, just as he had last seen it. Amanda's toilet things were laid out on the dressing table, and pulling open a wardrobe, he stared at the dresses which still hung there. On hearing a faint movement at the door his heart almost stopped beating. For a moment he was seized with the thought that he had just woken from an awful nightmare and that on turning he would see Amanda walk into the room; but it was Cousin Margaret, who had followed him.

She had wiped away her tears and spoke in a carefully controlled voice. 'You cannot have breakfasted. You must eat to keep up your strength, my dear. Please come downstairs in a quarter of an hour. By then I will have had a meal made ready for you.'

'Nay, food would choke me,' he replied harshly. 'I want nothing. Except, yes—please have the best spare room prepared for me at once.'

'It is always kept ready for guests,' she murmured. Then, feeling that at the moment any attempt to console him would be useless, she quietly withdrew.

For some ten minutes he remained fiddling dazedly with Amanda's things. Then he walked along to the big guest room and threw himself down in an arm-chair.

An hour later Dan knocked on the door, and, receiving no reply, went in. He said nothing, but his silence as he stood with bowed shoulders, just inside the door, was more eloquent of sympathy than any words could have been.

'After a moment, Roger said: 'Bring me some wine. Madeira. Half a dozen bottles.'

Without a word Dan executed the order, uncorked one of the bottles, filled a glass, and left him.

Late in the afternoon Dan came in again, carrying a tray of food. Three of the bottles were empty and Roger was slightly glassy-eyed, but not drunk. For some inexplicable reason alcohol has little effect on some people when in a state of either great joy or great grief. He had consumed the other three bottles and was still sober when Dan came in that night, but he allowed Dan to help him off with his jack boots, undressed himself and went to bed.

Next morning his cousin came to see him, but he bid her leave him in peace; then Doctor Fergusson, but he drove that pleasant young man from the room, by snapping at him: 'I am in no need of physics; go mind your own affairs!'

That day and the next he ate little, continued to drink but with more moderation, and sat for hours on end moodily staring into vacancy. On the fourth morning his door opened and Clarissa stood framed in it. She was dressed in full black, which showed off her gold hair and milk and roses complexion to great advantage. In her arms she carried a bundle of muslin and lace. Behind her stood Cousin Margaret, looking distinctly apprehensive.

'Roger.' Clarissa addressed him with a slightly hesitant smile. 'I have brought your little daughter to see you.'

'Take her away,' he replied coldly. 'I do not wish to see her.'

'But Roger!' she protested. 'She is such a sweet little thing, and your own child. How can you possibly reject her when dear Amanda gave her life to give her to you?'

'You have said it!' he roared, his blue eyes suddenly blazing. 'How can you think that I would wish to look upon the thing that killed her? Be gone from here! Be gone this instant!'

After that they left him for three days to mope, and the New Year of 1796 came and went unnoticed by him. Then on January the 2nd Colonel Penruddock entered his room unannounced and said:

'Mr. Brook! Or, if as an older man and your friend you

will permit me to call you so, Roger. All of us here who hold you in affection are most concerned for you. No one who knew your lady could fail to sympathise with you in your tragic loss; but however deeply you may grieve within, the outward manifestation of the sentiment does not become you when carried to such excess. You have a duty to yourself and others. I am told you refuse to see anyone; but your post requires that you should listen to my report as Deputy Governor upon events which have occurred here during your absence. There are, too, enquiries from the Assembly, the Garrison and the Town Council, all asking when it will be convenient for you to receive deputations from them, so that they can make their duty to you on your return; and you cannot keep them waiting indefinitely. Above all, you are behaving with monstrous unkindness to Madame de Kay and Miss Marsham, in repulsing their sympathy and shutting yourself away. I pray you, for all our sakes, to play the man, and now face the world again.'

Eyeing him gloomily, Roger replied: 'Colonel, I appreciate the motive of your visit, but must ask that you do not repeat it. I no longer have a use for the world, and give not a damn what it thinks or does. Should I emerge I would do you little credit with these deputations. Worse, I would, mayhap, strangle with my own hands the French physician who allowed my wife to die. Then on your hands you would have a hanging. Had the Prime Minister required a continuance of my services in Europe I might not have returned here for a year or more; and for however long I was away it would have been for you to carry out my duties. This shock has rendered me incapable of attending to business, and I have not yet taken over from you; so I desire you to leave me to my misery, and carry on as though I had not returned.'

Under his icy glance Penruddock saw nothing for it but to retire; so, with a bow, he said: 'Your Excellency's servant,' and left the room.

During the six days that followed Roger made not the slightest alteration in his regime. Alternately he slept or sat in moody contemplation with a vacant look on his face. He would see no one but Dan, and, from his reports,

Madame de Kay and Doctor Fergusson feared that he was going out of his mind; but Dan would not agree to that. He insisted that his master's brain was sound as ever, but had become dormant and needed some special impulse to re-arouse it. Fergusson agreed that he was probably right, but added that unless some such impulse could be given it fairly soon, a general deterioration might set in which would rob him of his wits for good. Clarissa was present at this conversation and after it went to her room, where she sat for some time in deep thought.

That night Roger went to bed about ten o'clock, which was his usual hour. By eleven he was sound asleep. Soon after midnight he was roused by a faint noise. Opening his eyes he saw a glow of light. Then he turned over to find that the curtains of his bed had been drawn aside and that Clarissa stood there, a candlestick in her hand, gazing down upon him.

She was wearing a dark coloured chamber robe caught together at the neck by a big silk bow which stuck out on either side of her chin. Above it her oval face, framed in golden ringlets, was lit up by the candle light. For a moment he thought he was dreaming; but she caught his thought and said softly: 'I am no dream. I'm real.'

'What . . . what the devil has brought you here?' he asked sleepily.

'Don't be so rude, Roger,' she smiled. 'I am perhaps a little late, but I came to wish you a Happy Birthday.'

'Birthday!' he muttered, propping himself up on an elbow. 'Is it my birthday? I'd no idea of the date. Recently the days seem to have merged into one another. Since Amanda's death . . . Oh God!'

'I know. You have been half out of your mind with grief. But she would not have wished you to continue so. And with her last breath she charged me to take care of both her child and you.'

'Why you, and not Cousin Margaret?'

'Because she believed that I could make you happy.'

For a moment Roger remained silent, then he said roughly: 'You told her, then, that you were in love with me?'

'No. I would never have done that. She guessed it. Women instinctively know such things about one another.'

'And she did not resent it?'

'Nay. Although I did not deserve her generosity, she trusted me completely. She had no idea that I had confessed my love to you; but as she lay dying she sent your Cousin Margaret away and told me that she knew it, then expressed the hope that you would marry me.'

'I've not the least intention of marrying anyone.'

She shook her head. 'I did not suppose you had. So as it is your birthday I brought you a present.'

He gave a puzzled frown. 'A present? What have presents to do with this? I do not understand.'

As he was speaking she had set the candlestick on the bedside table and stepped back. With one hand she gave a swift pull to an end of the bow at her neck and with the other ripped open the fastenings of her chamber robe. Beneath it she had nothing on at all. Pulling off the robe she threw it over the back of a chair, then stood before him with downcast eyes, revealed in all her beauty.

'I have brought you myself,' she said in a breathless whisper.

'Clarissa!' he gasped. 'What are you thinking of? You must be mad! Put on your robe and go back to your room.'

'I am not mad!' Her blue eyes suddenly looked straight into his and she spoke firmly. 'I am nineteen, and I know what I am doing.'

'Ah, you are a grown woman,' he admitted, 'but you have bewitched yourself, or you would never behave in such a fashion.'

'It is you who are bewitched!' she retorted swiftly. 'I am no more so than any woman who has loved a man to near distraction for above a year. 'Tis you who are under a spell! A spell cast by death, which is slowly destroying your mind. And I am here to break it.'

Suddenly she shivered, took a pace forward, grasped the bedclothes and pulled them back, exclaiming: 'Roger, I am cold! For pity's sake let me come into your bed.'

'No!' he cried hoarsely. 'No, no! I'll not let you do this!'

But she was already half kneeling above him in the bed.

As he sat up to push her out her shoulder brushed against his, and the warmth of it ran through him like an electric shock. Next moment she had flung her soft arms round his neck and pressed her half open mouth on his in a passionate kiss.

Carried out of himself he clasped her to him, and his lips responded with equal vigour. As they broke the kiss she gave a cry of triumph.

'There! I have made you come alive again; and I knew that you could love me if you would.'

Silently he put up his hands, clasped her wrists, pulled them from behind his neck, and pushed her away from him. Then he said coldly:

'You are wrong in that. I have never ceased to be alive, and I have no intention of making love to you.' After a second, deciding that it was the only way to chill her, he added what had now become a lie. 'Please understand that this has nought to do with the memory of Amanda. It is simply that I have never had the least desire to have you for a bedfellow.'

His words had an instantaneous effect. Suddenly, still half sprawled upon him, she went absolutely limp; then she slid down beside him, a sob burst from her throat, and she moaned: 'Oh God! That I should have to suffer this!'

'I pray you be sensible,' he urged with swift contrition. 'I implied as much long since, that night in the forest.'

'No, you did not.' Her words came in a shaky voice. 'You led me only to suppose that out of consideration for Amanda you would not allow your thoughts to dwell on me; and, for the same reason I told you that even did you want me I would refuse you. Yet I have always hoped that some twist of fate might bring us together in different circumstances. Not her death! God forbid! I had no thought of that; but that the two of you might separate again, as you did once before. In that hope, since arriving here, I have refused offers of marriage from a dozen men of good fortune and repulsed half a hundred who have done their best to seduce me. There is scarce a man here on the island who would not give a half of all he possesses to sleep with me. Yet you—the only one to whom I would give myself with gladness—have nought but harsh words for me. Though I lie here in bed with you, you treat me as thought I were a leper. Oh Roger! How can you be so brutal?'

'I am truly sorry,' he said huskily. 'I did not mean to hurt you.'

'Hurt me!' she exclaimed. 'You could not have done so more effectually had you thrust a white-hot iron right through my body.'

On the last word she choked, and burst into tears. For a moment Roger let her cry, then he pushed an arm under her shoulders and drew her golden head down on to his chest. She made no movement either to resist or cling to him but went on crying.

'There, there!' he murmured, as to a child. 'Do not take on so, my dear. At least you may be assured that I have a great affection for you.'

At the word 'affection' a shudder ran through her, and her sobs increased in violence until they shook her whole body. In vain Roger strove to comfort her, but whether she even took in his words he could not tell. She cried and cried and cried until, after a long time, gradually her weeping eased. There followed a period of silence, during which he had not the heart to tell her to get up and go to her room. Then, from her gentle, even breathing, he realised that, utterly worn out by her emotions, she had fallen asleep.

One by one the hours of the night crept on, but he remained wide awake while she lay snuggled against his side sleeping peacefully. The arm he had about her grew stiff and cramped, yet he would not move it until he saw the light of dawn creeping beneath the curtains of the windows. Stooping his head, then, he roused her by kissing her lightly on the cheek.

She turned over and her blue eyes opened, still dewy with sleep. Suddenly they widened, and she breathed his name. Recalling her words when she had woken him at midnight, he said:

'I am no dream. I'm real.'

'Then I must have fallen asleep,' she murmured.

'Yes.' A faint smile twitched the corners of his mouth.

'This dropping asleep in one another's arms threatens to become a habit. Still, you wanted to sleep with me, and you've had your wish.'

'But nothing happened?'

'No, nothing.'

Her lovely face clouded over. 'Then I failed after all to arouse in you the sort of impulse that Doctor Fergusson said you needed.'

For the first time in over a fortnight Roger laughed. 'Oh come! I cannot believe that young Fergusson sent you to me; or that he had that sort of impulse in mind.'

'Indeed no! He implied only that some means of taking your thoughts off your grief must be found if your brain was to be restored to normal.'

'Then in that you have succeeded. I know not how; but I think it must have been your wish to heal me coupled with your nearness as you lay beside me all through the night. Something flowed out of you and into me that was balm to my troubled soul.'

'Oh Roger, I am overjoyed!'

He made a little grimace. 'I fear you may be less so when you hear the sequel. During the night I have had ample time to think. I must have work—real work—to occupy my mind; and the routine of a Governor in an island at peace will not provide it. Moreover, should I remain in Martinique I shall be constantly reminded of Amanda. I am going home by the first ship I can find to take me, and I do not intend to return.'

'What of your little daughter? Surely you do not intend to abandon her completely?'

'No. Later I will endeavour to be all that a father should be to her. But for the present she is too young to travel. When I have surrendered my Governorship, Cousin Margaret will, I am sure, give her a home.'

'What then of myself? It was I whom Amanda charged with the care of her child; and I accepted the charge gladly.'

'I know it, and am truly grateful; but I do not wish her to become a tie upon you. It is my most earnest wish that either here or in England you should find a husband.'

'Do you then force me to the choice of marrying someone for whom I do not care, or returning to live with my Aunt Jane in near poverty?'

'Perish the thought, Clarissa! What can you think of me? I had intended, whatever you decided, to regard you in future as my ward and make you a suitable allowance.'

'Bless you for that,' she smiled. 'I had not really thought you meant to abandon me. Your Cousin Margaret would no doubt give me a home, for some months at least, out of kindness; but it would make me happier if I could offer to become her paying guest. Have you thought yet what you mean to do about the babe when she is old enough for me to bring her to England?'

'As you must by now have heard, Georgina had a boy in August. The children will be much of an age so they can share a nursery. And now, my dear, it is time for you to go back to your room.'

Clarissa, still naked, had been lying on her back with the bedclothes drawn up to her chin. Now, she slipped out of bed with her back to him and stretched out a hand to pick up her robe.

'One moment!' he said, jumping out beside her, and taking her hand in his. 'Come to the window. I want to see the dawn, and you in it.'

'But Roger!' she protested, trying to pull away from him.

'Nay!' he laughed. 'After last night you have no case to plead modesty with me, and nought to be ashamed of. Never again in all my life may I have a chance to look upon such rare and splendid beauty.'

Obediently then, she allowed him to lead her to one of the tall windows. As he pulled back the heavy curtains the light came flooding in upon them. The sun had just over-topped the mountains to the east and beyond a deep belt of shadow lit the blue waters of the outer bay.

'Look!' he exclaimed. At last I can again welcome a new day—a new life. And you have made that possible.'

As he turned and stood away from her, tears welled up into her eyes, and she said miserably: 'Oh Roger! I know not what to think. You say now that I am beautiful, yet last night you put me from you. To understand you is beyond me.'

'Is it so difficult?' his voice was gentle. 'I am not made of stone; but memories of Amanda will for long make any thought of taking another wife out of the question for me. To have made you my mistress, then left you, would have been a cruel thing to do. Moreover, I would not have it on my conscience that when you do find some good fellow that you wish to marry, you should be deprived of the joy of knowing physical love for the first time with him.'

'Then you did desire me?'

He smiled. 'So much so that when you have been married a while, I'll do my utmost to seduce you.'

'Must I wait for that?'

'Yes. And should your marriage prove a happy one, you'll wait in vain. But I wanted you to know that for you I shall always have the tenderest feelings.'

She held out her arms. He took her into his and gave her a long sweet kiss. Then he said: 'When I come downstairs in a few hours' time, remember to show as much surprise as the others. Now my pretty, you must go, or one of our fuzzy-haired housemaids will see you leave my room.'

He then helped her on with her robe, and from the door watched her tiptoe away down the corridor.

When in due course he came downstairs everyone was amazed to see him brisk, smiling and entirely restored to his old good humour. Apart from apologising to his Cousin, Clarissa, Penruddock and Fergusson for his boorish behaviour he made no reference to the past; except to say that he felt sure it would have been Amanda's wish that Clarissa should have all her things, and to distribute the many presents he had brought for her between Clarissa and his Cousin. Then he duly admired and caressed his little daughter, who he decided should be christened Susan Amanda.

Having disclosed his intention of returning to England, as he had already charged Penruddock with carrying on for him, he had only to spend an hour with the Colonel informally, discussing the affairs of the island. Another hour, with Mr. Beckwith, revealed that during the year he had held the appointment of Governor he had netted well over four thousand pounds, in addition to his salary, and, as the post was unlikely to be taken over for several months to come, he could expect at least another fifteen hundred; which was most satisfactory.

No ship was expected to leave for England under a fortnight, but a schooner was due to sail from St. Pierre for Jamaica next day; so he decided to take passage in her. Penruddock turned out the regiment there to do him the honours as he went aboard, and, after farewells as cheerful as they could be in the circumstances, the schooner put out from the harbour to the thundering of cannon up in the fortress firing a Governor's salute.

On the second day crossing the Caribbean he had great cause to wish that he had waited for a larger ship, as that afternoon the schooner was chased by a Dutch privateersman. In view of his dire experience the previous year he was for some hours filled with the most nerve-racking apprehensions. But nightfall saved the schooner from capture and on the 15th brought him safely to Kingston, where he found at anchor a large British Fleet.

The Williamsons were pleased to put him up again, but the General was in poor shape and had a gloomy story to tell. He had spent most of the past year directing operations in Saint-Domingue, but owing to the unreliability of the troops under the French Royalists, lack of stores and the ravages of Yellow Jack among his own men, he had made no headway whatever against Toussaint and the Revolutionaries inspired by Victor Hugues. Ill and worn out by his endeavour to make bricks without straw, he had in the autumn been granted long furlough; but his successor, Sir Ralph Abercromby, had arrived only the previous day.

The Fleet with which Roger had sailed had, owing to the tempest, had seven transports wrecked on the coast of Dorset with a terrible loss of life. It had then made another false start, during which thirty ships had been driven back into the Solent; so he was, after all, lucky not to have suffered an even greater delay in reaching Barbados.

That night he met the new C. in C. at dinner. Sir Ralph looked like a Highland terrier. He was purblind and was already sixty-two; but he still possessed tremendous energy and had earned a great military reputation by covering the retreat and evacuation of the British expeditionary force from Holland in the preceding winter.

Before him there lay a task which would have daunted a lesser man. Apart from the war in Saint-Domingue, there were major slave rebellions to be put down in St. Lucia, Grenada, Dominica and St. Vincent. Demerara had to be taken from the Dutch as it was now being used to fit out French privateers; the Spaniards too, although still technically neutral, were allowing Trinidad to be used for the same purpose; and, last but not least, Victor Hugues, the cause of all the trouble, remained the solidly entrenched master of Guadaloup.

Sir Ralph heartily blessed Roger for having kept his island in good order and begged him to change his decision about going home. Roger firmly declined, but added that any man should be capable of doing the same provided he observed three maxims. Namely: to win the goodwill of the French inhabitants; to hang half a dozen people at the first sign of trouble, even if some of them should later be proved innocent, rather than allow matters to develop to a point where hundreds might lose their lives in a general conflict; and to place the health of the troops before any other consideration.

The General heartily agreed with him, and showed the greatest keenness with regard to the last recommendation. Apparently some imbecile in Whitehall had deprived the Scottish regiments of their bonnets and kilts and instead equipped them with broad-brimmed felt hats and duck trousers. The idea of this well-meaning theorist had been to protect their faces from the sun, and their legs from mosquitoes; but in the tropical rains this new uniform became sodden, and could not be dried for hours, with the result that pneumonia had now become a scourge second only to Yellow Jack. Roger readily acceded to Sir Ralph's request that on reaching London he should press Mr. Windham as a matter of urgency to have the Scots' bonnets and kilts restored to them; then he put in a good word for Colonel Penruddock as a capable and reliable man, and wished Sir Ralph success in the numerous campaigns he was about to undertake.

Two days later he set sail in a fast mail packet for England. She made an excellent crossing and landed him at Liverpool on February the 14th. Next day he took a coach to London, and the following evening was once more installed in Amesbury House; although to his regret he had learned on his arrival that Droopy had temporarily removed himself to Brighton in order to enjoy some winter sunshine. On the morning of the 17th, after a wait of an hour, he secured an interview with Mr. Pitt, and told him the reason for his return.

Having commiserated with him on his bereavement, the Prime Minister said: 'From you, Mr. Brook, I need be at no pains to conceal that the Allied cause is now in a more parlous state than ever before; and my anxieties on that account, at times, near as much as I can bear. All that can be done with ships, men and money is being done already; so our best hope of better fortune lies in original ideas carried out by men who have the courage to apply them. You may be able to help us in this way. If so your return is doubly welcome.'

Roger shook his head. 'I fear I have nothing to suggest, Sir. I can only say that I have decided to accept your offer to have Mr. Dundas dispose of my Governorship for me, and am now ready to serve you wherever you feel I might prove useful to you.'

'How well informed are you of the present situation?'

'But poorly, Sir. I left here in mid-November and got back to London only yesterday; so I know practically nothing of fresh developments which may have taken place during the past three and a half months.'

'Then I will briefly review them for you.' Mr. Pitt took a swig of port and went on: 'The Austro-Sardinian army in Italy managed to hold its own against General Kellerman until the late autumn. But since the French Commander was replaced by General Schérer, things there have gone far from well. At about the same time we relieved Admiral Hotham of the command of the Mediterranean Fleet and appointed in his stead Sir John Jervis. His major task has been to continue the blockade of Toulon; so he could afford to detach only a small squadron, under a promising young senior Captain named Nelson, to do the best they could to interrupt French communications with the Italian coast. In consequence, and probably also because Carnot is once again directing the French war effort, considerable quantities of supplies got through. The French, from being short of everything, were enabled to launch a new offensive.

'I am advised that General Schérer is no great master of war; but he appears to have several daring and capable corps commanders under him. Their names are Augerau, Serurier, Joubert and Masséna. The latter, with some help from the others, inflicted a severe defeat on our allies at Loano towards the end of November. Fortunately for them, instead of taking advantage of this victory, General Schérer then decided to go into winter quarters. But now that spring approaches the outlook of the Allied cause in Italy is far from good.

'With regard to the Rhine, you saved us there. On Pichegru's deliberate failure to take Heidelberg, General Jourdan's army was compelled to fall back. He recrossed the Rhine and retreated down the Moselle to Traabach. The Austrians followed but the winter has been so severe that by December neither army was in a state to fight further. On about the 19th they agreed an armistice, and Jourdan has established himself in a fortified camp on the heights above the town. Pichegru, meanwhile, had allowed himself to be thrown out of Mannheim. He then retired across the Rhine to his old lines at Weissenburg. There, on December the 31st, he too signed a winter armistice. But there has been a leak, or at least a suspicion, that he is no longer to be trusted. As far as I know he has not yet been arrested; but he has been suspended from his command.'

'Then we cannot hope to buy further help from him.'

'No; and when we attempted to bribe Jourdan we failed in it. He hung our agent from the nearest tree.'

'What of Russia?' Roger enquired. 'Has the old Empress Catherine furnished the Austrians with the help she promised?'

'No. We now have little hope of her doing so, and I greatly doubt the capacity of the Austrians to get the better of General Jourdan in the spring; for now that General Hoche has again pacified La Vendée the bulk of the great army which has been tied up there for so long will probably be transferred to support that on the Rhine.'

'May I ask, Sir, if you have further considered letting the French know through diplomatic channels that you would be willing to enter into negotiations for a peace?'

'We have gone so far as to consult with Vienna on possible terms which would be acceptable to the Emperor and to ourselves; but he is adamant on the question of the Austrian Netherlands. As you will recall, last October Belgium was divided into nine Departments and incorporated into France. This measure being so recent, it is highly improbable that the French could be persuaded to give these territories up; yet the Emperor insists that their return should be a fundamental article of any settlement, and Britain could not desert her ally. Therefore no indication of our willingness to treat has yet been transmitted to Paris.'

Roger nodded gloomily. 'I asked only to ascertain if any move of the kind had been made. Even if it could be, and the terms were favourable, I'd place little hope on their acceptance. That is, unless there have been radical changes in the composition of the French government.'

'There have not. The five Directors are the same as when you left Paris; and they appear to be more firmly seated in the saddle than ever. I gather, though, that they are a venal crew; and since they are now virtually all-powerful, I have been wondering if we could not succeed in bribing one or more of them to sway the rest. France needs peace every whit as badly as ourselves. If the bribe were big enough, and they were guaranteed against reprisals for their pasts, they might be tempted to call on the people to support them against their old colleagues in the two Chambers.'

After refilling his glass from the decanter that Mr. Pitt pushed towards him, Roger shook his head. 'What could you possibly offer them more than they have? Dukedoms, Governorships and Orders would be regarded as poor bait by men who are each one fifth of a King already. As for money, their situation enables them to collect it by the bushelful. Besides, peace in due course must bring a Restoration, and they would place no faith in any guarantee that could be given them. As I pointed out when last we talked of this, in upholding the revolutionary system of government lies their one and only hope of safety.'

'What think you, then, of reverting to our old plan of attempting to find among the Revolutionary Generals another Monk, who would seize Paris for us. As I have said, our attempt to suborn Jourdan failed; but there are Moreau, Hoche, Kellerman, all men of great reputation, and this new man, Buonaparte, who commands the Army of the Interior.'

For a moment Roger considered the matter, then he said, 'Buonaparte would suit our purpose best, as he is already in Paris; so could secure it, if he would, without having to march upon it. Moreover, unless he was also privy to the plan, any of the others would find him a hard nut to crack. Unfortunately he is a convinced revolutionary, so his political convictions would prove a nasty hurdle to get over. However, he struck me as a young man of inordinate ambition; so there is just a chance that a Marshal's baton, the Château of Chambord, and all the other things Pichegru was to get, might tempt him to pull our chestnuts out of the fire for us.'

'Then, Mr. Brook, the best service you can render me would be to return to Paris and endeavour to come to an arrangement with General Buonaparte.'

Roger now had reason to be thankful that, instead of simply disappearing from Paris without explanation, he had evolved and put into execution a plan to cover his withdrawal. It meant that although there were always unforeseen possibilities in his dangerous work, on this occasion he could readily agree to Mr. Pitt's request, and reappear in the French capital without any evident risk.

However, the Prime Minister, giving as his reason that all too soon spring would be upon them and fresh campaigns be opening which might prove disastrous for the Allies, did press him to start upon his new mission with the least possible delay. In consequence, he again had to forgo the chance to see Georgina; and, with new blank drafts on secret funds in Paris concealed upon him, he left Rochester in a specially employed Revenue Cutter the following afternoon.

She landed him near Calais soon after dawn next morning. For the next two days he suffered cold, misery and boredom, as the diligence conveyed him, or he helped to push it, over rutted muddy roads to Paris; but he arrived there without incident a little before midday on February the 21st.

At *La Belle Étoile* the Blanchards once more welcomed him and asked no questions. Upstairs he had a most welcome bath, changed into one of the Paris-made suits that he had left in the secret wardrobe he kept there, then came down and enjoyed a meal with his host and hostess.

This time they had little to tell him. The poorer half of the population of Paris was literally starving, but entirely cowed by the Government's troops and the reconstituted National Guard, which was now loyal to it. Another third, which had either goods, or services superior to manual labour, to sell, was now benefiting from the long-hidden gold that was once more in circulation. The upper sixth crowded the *salons*, theatres, public ballrooms and cafés, flaunting a luxury unseen since the monarchy and a licentiousness which would never have been tolerated in the days of that most immoral of Kings, Louis XV.

At six o'clock Roger had himself driven in a coach to the Luxembourg, and enquired for Barras. He was told that at eight the Director would be holding an evening *soirée*; so he spent the intervening time in a café and returned at that hour. As in the old days at the Royal Palaces, anyone who was respectably dressed was allowed to enter, and the long gallery was soon crowded with *merveilleuses, incroyables*, officers, deputies, and prominent citizens. A number of them were already known to Roger; so he spent an hour exchanging bows, kissing women's hands, gossiping and repeating over and over again his story that he had that morning returned from a stay of nearly four months in the South of France.

In due course ushers formed a lane through the throng, then Barras, resplendent in satins and with powdered hair, appeared. Walking slowly down it he paused here and there to chat with friends, had a smile for every pretty woman who caught his eye, passed to M. Bottot, his secretary, who followed him, every petition presented with a promise to read it personally, and listened graciously to a score of requests for a variety of favours.

When he noticed Roger, who, owing to his height, could afford to stand a little way back in the crowd, he waved a hand and called gaily to him: 'It is good to see you again! You must join us later in the *salon,* and tell me what you have been doing with yourself.'

The *salon* was reserved for the élite and into it, after Barras had walked back up the human lane, some hundred and fifty people followed him, to drink pink Champagne and eat foie-gras sandwiches or pineapple ices. At about half past ten, when the party had thinned a little, Roger saw his chance and got a ten minute *tête-à-tête* with the Director over a glass of wine.

After reporting that his health was much improved, Roger said that he had bought a pleasant property on the coast near the old Roman town of Fréjus where he intended to spend a good part of each year in future, as it included a number of vineyards, which he felt it would be interesting to have cultivated by the most modern methods.

'Ah!' exclaimed Barras, simulating envy. 'How wise you are, my dear fellow! Nowhere in the world does one find such passionate girls as among the dark-eyed beauties of my native Provençe; and in its first season I would sooner drink the *rosé* which will come from your presses than a good Bordeaux. With wine and women, sunny days and warm nights to make love in, what more could a man want. I am a fool to stay here, wearing myself out among this riff-raff.'

Roger smiled. 'Even so, your prospects of continuing to derive a certain enjoyment from life appear to be considerably better than they were on the night when I last arrived in Paris. Do you remember—the 12th Vendémiaire?'

'Do I not!' laughed Barras. 'But, with the help of the little Corsican, we soon put things to rights.'

'How fares your one-time ragamuffin?'

'You'll do well not to remind him of his old nickname

when you see him. Nowadays he struts about like any turkey-cock, jingling his spurs and ogling the women. But don't let me lead you to suppose that he is idle. He is positively bursting with ideas. And since we gave him the task to prepare plans for the invasion of England, I am really coming to believe that we shall have conquered that damned island before the year is out.'

24

The Brigand in Uniform

Not a muscle in Roger's face moved but his ears felt as though they were standing out from the sides of his head. With Hoche's army in Brittany now freed, and that dynamic young Corsican charged with the invasion of England, a turn might be given to the war which had hitherto been unthinkable. In a matter of seconds his mission had been changed from a matter of investigation which might produce valuable results, to one demanding that he should stop at nothing to save his country.

That night, after leaving Barras's reception, he put in some very deep thought. The last invasion of England had been that by William of Orange, just over a hundred years before, but others had been threatened many times since; and, having spent his boyhood on the south coast, he well remembered the drills of the local fencibles, the beacons kept always ready and the occasional false alarms, which had formed a part of every-day life there until the Peace of Paris, in '83.

Since then the deterioration of the French fleet, owing to revolution and a long series of defeats, had in the present war so far made any chance of invasion seem most unlikely. But the British Fleet was now dispersed between the Gulf of Genoa and the West Indies in many squadrons; a break-out from the French Ports was always a possibility; the enemy might succeed in landing a considerable army before their communications could be interrupted; and, as Britain had been almost denuded of troops for foreign service, that might prove positively calamitous—especially if the invading force were led by a man like Buonaparte.

Unlike Jourdan, Moreau, Hoche and several others, the

young General had little military prestige to support his sudden elevation. He had rendered good service as an Artillery Commander at Toulon and afterwards for a few months on the Italian Riviera, but in the field he had not yet commanded even a Division. His present appointment was a political one, and solely due to his having saved the Convention on 13th Vendémiaire. If he was to maintain his status in the High Command, he must direct a victorious campaign, or before very long he would find himself supplanted by officers of greater experience.

For the laurels he needed what could offer better prospects than a descent on England? But it would be all or nothing. There could be no question of joining up with other French armies, going into winter quarters with hopes of better fortune the following spring, or strategic withdrawals. Cut off by the British Navy, he would have to conquer or fail utterly; and, if defeated, even if he got away himself, having lost an army he would never be given another. Therefore, he would fight with utter ruthlessness, burning, slaying and laying waste the fair English countryside in a desperate attempt to reach London before he could be stopped.

Roger recalled hearing a revealing episode concerning his mentality. In '93, when the structure of the old French army was falling to pieces owing to the Revolution, he had virtually deserted, retiring to his native Corsica because he believed he could get himself made a Colonel in the National Guard of Ajaccio. There he had become one of the most violent members of the local Jacobin Club. Several of his friends among the lesser nobility, from which his own family came, endeavoured to dissuade him from inciting the roughs of the port to make trouble. Instead of agreeing he at once made another inflammatory speech, in which he declared that in such times there could be only friends and enemies, that all moderates must be classed by true patriots as enemies, and that, like Solon in ancient Greece, he advocated punishing with death every man who remained neutral during civil discord.

If he had really meant that, it suggested that he would show no mercy to man, woman or child should he command an army that succeeded in landing in England. In any case he promised to prove a most formidable opponent, and Roger decided that any approach to him must be made with the utmost wariness; so that before even hinting at his purpose to the Corsican, he would do well to get to know much more about him than he had learned during their short acquaintance.

The following day, as a first step, he called on the Permons; because their apartment in the Chaussée d'Antin was the only place in which he had seen Buonaparte relaxed and natural. Madame Permon, with her son and little daughter, was at home, and received him kindly; but he soon learned that his hope of meeting Buonaparte there again, through cultivating the family, was doomed to disappointment, for not long since he and Madame Permon had had a serious quarrel.

Apparently she had asked him to secure for her cousin a commission in the Guards, and he had promised to do so; but, although reminded several times, had failed to bring it to her. In consequence, when next he had called she had upbraided him as though he were still a schoolboy, and snatched her hand from him as he was about to kiss it. As this had occurred in front of several of the young General's staff officers, he had been deeply mortified, and had ceased to visit her. However, as the ex-protégé of the unpretentious family had now become such a luminary, they were willing enough, when encouraged by Roger, to talk about him.

Monsieur Permon had been a French official of some standing, and while the family were living in Toulouse it had transpired that one of three Corsicans lying ill and in money difficulties at a local inn was the husband of Letitia Buonaparte, Madame Permon's girlhood friend. They had at once taken him into their house where, after a long illness through which Madame Permon had nursed him, he had died. This had naturally strengthened the ties between the two families and when the Permons had moved to Paris they had taken a special interest in the orphaned Napoleon.

His father, being without fortune but able to prove that

his family had been noble for four generations, had secured his admission as a King's charity pupil to the Military School at Brienne, at the age of nine. It was his poverty in contrast with the wealth of his noble school-fellows there which had formed a bitter streak in his character and, later, led to his becoming such a fervid revolutionary.

Of this bitterness the Permons had had plenty of evidence after he had graduated to the Military School in Paris in '84. He was too proud to accept money, until M. Permon forced upon him a small sum on the pretext that it had been left by his father to be given to him in an emergency; and at times his outbursts against his rich brother cadets had been quite terrifying. He had, too, in his early years been fanatically devoted to the cause of Corsican independence, and had never forgiven his father for deserting Paoli, the Corsican patriot leader. On this score too he had been given to launching the most violent diatribes, and while at Brienne had been severely punished for shaking his fist and screaming imprecations at a portrait of the Duc de Choiseul, Louis XV's minister, who had urged on the conquest of Corsica by France.

His nickname there had been 'the Spartan' but, on the rare occasions when he could afford it, he loved personal display. Little Laura related how, when he had at last obtained his commission, he had come in his new uniform to see them. Having been made by an inexpensive tailor it was of poor material and ill-cut, and his legs were so lean that, in his big high boots, they looked like broom sticks; but he had strutted up and down as though he were already a Field Marshal. Laurette had been so amused that she had christened him Puss-in-Boots; but he had taken her childish raillery well, and, although he could ill afford to buy expensive toys, had, next day, brought her a walking Puss-in-Boots carved from wood.

The violence of his temper was equalled only by his colossal assurance about his own abilities, and by the vividness of his imagination; as he was always producing grandiose schemes for his own advancement. During the period of his disgrace he had conceived the idea of going off to reorganise the army of the Grand Turk and, without even writing to ask if the Sultan would like to employ him, had applied to the War office for permission to do so. It had been granted, and he had only been prevented from leaving for Turkey because somebody else at the War Office had suddenly discovered that he had ignored an order to report for duty with the Army of La Vendée; so cancelled his permit to go abroad and had his name erased from the list of Generals.

The possibility of improving his fortune by a good marriage had also occupied his imagination. First he had proposed to Désirée Clery, the sister of his elder brother, Joseph's wife; but she had refused him. Then he had produced an extraordinary project for a triple union between the Permon and Buonaparte families. Albert was to marry his pretty young sister Paulette, Laura was to be given to his boy brother Lucien, and he, although the recently widowed Madame Permon was more than twice his age, was to espouse her. They laughed a lot over this crazy notion, but Madame Permon assured them that he had made the proposal to her in all seriousness.

From the evening's talk with the Permons Roger formed the impression that Buonaparte had inherited from his half-peasant mother the temper, pride and toughness of a Corsican brigand, and that his mind was subject to erratic twists sufficiently marked for him to be regarded as a little mad.

Next day, however, to get another intimate opinion he invited Andoche Junot to dine with him, and afterwards he felt that he ought to modify his opinion, at least to the extent that the Corsican's madness generally had method. Making liberal allowances for the young A.D.C.'s passionate devotion, it could not be contested that his idol had frequently displayed a cool head, sound judgment and shrewd foresight.

There had been, for example, the occasion of Buonaparte's arrest and imprisonment after 9th Thermidor. Had he been sent to Paris, as the protégé of the elder Robespierre and the bosom friend of the younger, his risk of following them to the guillotine would have been a high one. Knowing that, Junot had offered to collect a few friends, break into the prison and rescue him. But Buonaparte had refused the offer, and the reason he afterwards gave for his refusal was that if—as he did succeed in doing—he could get his case dealt with locally, he would stand a good chance of being acquitted, whereas if he allowed himself to be forcibly rescued he would become an outlaw and have lost his Commission for good.

Again, his having ignored the order to proceed to La Vendée had not been a temperamental act, but a calculated risk. For one thing he had not wanted to have it on his record that he had been engaged in fighting French peasants; for another he felt that, although he was then employed only in the Topographical Section of the War Office, if he remained in Paris, where all appointments of importance were made, luck or intrigue might lead to his securing a far better one.

The handsome Junot, now resplendent in the uniform of a Colonel of Hussars, spoke with glowing admiration of Buonaparte's qualities as a soldier: his eagle eye for a battery position, his instantaneous decisions, and his complete fearlessness in battle; then with a shade of awe in his voice he touched on his General's other qualities: his intenseness, his extraordinary personal magnetism, and his ability, by no more than the direct glance of his eyes, to reduce men who were much older than himself, and in authority over him, to stammering inanity.

After dining well at the Café Rampollion they parted, and Roger went on to Madame Tallien's. Tall, graceful, her dark hair cut *au Titus,* in an aureole of short curls round her shapely head, Theresa Tallien looked as lovely as ever. As Roger edged his way through the court she was holding, to kiss her hand, he thought it by no means surprising that her uncle, whose ward for a time she had been, had gone so mad about her when she was still only fourteen that he had done his utmost to persuade her to marry him. On the other hand, Roger was quite shocked by Tallien's appearance, as he now looked much more than his age, grey-faced and ill. Later in the evening he heard from a fellow guest that his old colleague of the Commune had recently been subjected to a most unpleasant shock, which, no doubt, partially accounted for his lack-lustre eyes and woebegone appearance.

In order to marry Theresa he had divorced his first wife, but as she was still a young and attractive woman, and remained in love with him, he had continued to feel a tenderness for her, and kept her in their old home. However, his treatment of her had been capricious and so much so in recent months that, on his ignoring an invitation to breakfast with her one morning not long since, she had decided that he had at last made up his mind to abandon her for good. Actually that was far from being the case and he had all the time intended to go as a little surprise for her. On arriving at the house he found her being carried downstairs covered with blood. She had just committed suicide from despair.

The affair had shaken him terribly, but Roger could not help feeling that it was only a very small instalment of what was due to him for his many crimes during the Revolution.

After a while Roger got Madame Tallien to himself for a few moments, and, when they had conversed for a little, he remarked: 'I have not so far seen General Buonaparte. I had expected to find him here, as he was always a regular attendant at your evenings.'

'He comes no more,' she replied, then added with a laugh: 'He is angry with me. A few weeks ago he suggested that I should divorce poor Tallien, in order to be able to marry him; and when I refused he took great offence. But he consoled himself quickly enough. For the past month he has been dancing attendance on my sweet friend Josephine de Beauharnais.'

'She has, then, received him more kindly?' Roger hazarded.

'Poor dear, she hardly knows what to do. He is pressing her to marry him with the same fierceness as if she were an enemy fortress upon the taking of which the fate of France depended. And his letters to her! You should but see them. The passion he displays for her is quite frightening, and in parts they would make a grandmother blush. Fortunately, she has a pretty sense of humour; so is able to alleviate her fear of him by keeping her mind on the comic spectacle he presents when he declares his passion for her.'

After two more days given mainly to apparently idle chatter with numerous other people many of whom had known Buonaparte for a considerable time, Roger decided that he was now as well briefed as he could hope to be for a meeting with the Corsican. Wishing it to appear a chance one, on the 26th he spent some hours hanging about the Jardin des Plantes as Junot had happened to mention that, either in the morning or afternoon, the General usually took his exercise there; and soon after two o'clock Roger's patience was rewarded. At a brisk walk, coming down one of the paths towards him, was a short, spare figure wearing a grey overcoat and an enormous hat, the brim of which was turned up in the front and at one side, and had a three-inch wide border of gold *galon* round it.

On their greeting one another it transpired that Buonaparte had heard of Roger's return from Barras; so when they had spoken of the South of France and touched on their mutual memories of 13th Vendémiaire, it was quite natural that they should fall into step and continue their walk side by side. Roger had then only to mention the war to set Buonaparte off on a non-stop monologue.

He had an ugly Italian accent and his speech was frequently ungrammatical, but everything he said was lucid, and the trenchant expressions he used were always to the point. As he reviewed each battle area in turn he criticised without mercy the Army and Corps commanders, although he had never handled a Brigade himself, and they were the men who in the past three years had gained France a score of victories. He declared that the failure of the campaigns of '95 on both the Italian and Rhine fronts had been due to scandalous incompetence, and proceeded to lay down the law about what each of the generals should have done and when he should have done it.

When he had talked himself hoarse Roger managed to get a word in, and remarked: 'No doubt you are right about the Italian campaign; but are you quite convinced that it was not something other than incompetence which led to our armies having to fall back across the Rhine?'

After giving him a sharp glance, Buonaparte rapped out: 'You have, then, heard these rumours about Pichegru? Do you believe them?'

'I hardly know what to think,' replied Roger cautiously. 'His failure to take Heidelberg was in such striking contrast to the abilities he previously displayed that either the rumours are true, or he has become the victim of a sudden softening of the brain.'

'The latter must have been the case, or something like it. Even conceding that he may not at heart have been quite such a pure patriot as he pretended, and making allowance for the weakness to which all men are subject, I cannot believe that he sold his country. What could he possibly have stood to gain?'

Roger had now brought the conversation to the point he wanted, and he said casually: 'I'm told that he was offered the baton of a Marshal of France, a Dukedom, the Governorship of Alsace, the Chateau of Chambord, an income of . . .'

With an impatient gesture Buonaparte cut him short. 'What do such baubles and fripperies amount to in these days? Since we now have no Marshals, as the most successful General in the Army of the Republic he was already the equivalent of one. And who but a madman would wish to be called Duke or Excellency at the price of having to dance attendance on that fat fool of a Bourbon Prince? As for Chateaux and incomes, they will fall like ripe plums into the hand of any man who has the ability to carve with his sword a writ for them in the broken armies of our enemies. No, I cannot believe that any sane General who had victory in his hands, as Pichegru had, or even a remote prospect of it, would barter glory for such a mess of pottage.'

So it was that Roger received the answer to his mission. As Buonaparte clearly believed that it was now only a matter of time before he got an opportunity to cut an enemy army into pieces, there could be no doubt whatever that he was unbribable. To wage war and win glory was his lodestar, and had he been offered the Crown Jewels, a Viceroyalty and the Bank of England, he still would not have given such a proposition a second thought.

There was only one thing upon which Roger felt that he could congratulate himself. It was that his approach had been made so skilfully that the young General could not possibly suspect that he had started the conversation with any ulterior motive. He was, therefore, shaken to the roots of his being when, a moment later Buonaparte said:

'Am I right in believing you to have been born an Englishman?'

25

Desperate Intrigue

The question was a really alarming one. It might mean only that Buonaparte had heard a garbled version of one of the several accounts Roger had given of himself in the past; but it might mean that recently there had been some leak connecting him with London, and that Buonaparte, who now combined the functions of Chief of the Police with his Command, had come upon it in a report; so did in fact suspect him.

'No,' he said, after only a second's hesitation. 'What gave you that idea?'

'Your name cropped up at Madame de Staël's one night a few weeks ago. Someone was asking what had become of you, and an argument developed between the Deputy Fréron and a *ci-devant* Marquis, whose name I do not recall. The one maintained that you began your career as an English journalist, and having been sent over here, like the Deputy Tom Paine, you abandoned your country out of enthusiasm for the Revolution; the other, that you were an Alsatian who had once been secretary to a nobleman, and later appeated at Versailles, a young exquisite, calling yourself the Chevalier de Breuc.'

Greatly relieved, Roger was able to reply: 'There is something of truth in both their accounts of me; but I was born a Frenchman and my political convictions have ever been those of a Republican.' Then, feeling that this was an admirable opportunity once and for all to dovetail the varying beliefs held about him by different stratas of society in Paris, he went on:

'I was born in Strassburg. My father was a Frenchman

of moderate fortune, my mother the daughter of a Scottish Earl who had run away with him. Both died when I was quite young; so my mother's sister, who had married an English naval officer, took charge of me and I went to live with her in southern England. She gave me a good education, but I always longed to get back to France. At the age of fifteen, I ran away and succeeded in doing so. For some years I devilled in a lawyer's office in Rennes; then I became secretary to the Marquis de Rochambeau. In '87, owing to a duel, I was compelled to fly from France; so naturally returned to England. There I took up journalism, and through it became acquainted with many of the Whig nobility who were eagerly following the agitation for reform in France. Their influence with the French Ambassador secured me a pardon which enabled me to return, and their introductions gained me the *entrée* at Versailles. But, after a while, the news-letters I sent to my paper proved too revolutionary for the liking of my paymasters, and when I became a member of the Jacobin Club they cut off my remittance. Having no other source of income I was again compelled to return to England, but my Aunt was also out of sympathy with my revolutionary principles; so refused me help, and for the best part of two years I had a hard time of it making enough by my pen to support myself. By then the Revolution had progressed to a point where I felt that I must play a further part in it; so once more I came back to France. Shortly after my return I was elected a member of the Commune. Later I was given several missions as *Citizen Représentant* by both Robespierre and Carnot. It was in that capacity, you will remember, that I first met you at the siege of Toulon. My more recent history you already know.'

He had taken certain liberties with his earlier cover stories, such as stating that his mother had been Scottish, and that it was not a godmother but an aunt who had had him educated in England, because he felt that the nearer the truth he could go the safer he would be against future eventualities. But no one would, after all this time, be able to recall with certainty the exact degree of relationships he had given them; and he felt great satisfaction at having at last blended into a concrete whole the two roles he had played.

As he ceased speaking, Buonaparte, seizing upon the one essential that interested him, exclaimed: 'Then you have lived long in England, and must know that country well! There are matters in which you can be of great use to me. Please return with me to my office.'

'With pleasure,' Roger replied. 'I take it you refer to your projected invasion of the island?'

The young General halted in his tracks, swung round and snapped: 'Who told you aught of that?'

Roger shrugged. 'Why, Barras, of course. Since it was I who first brought him, Tallien and Dubois-Crancé together for the planning of 9th Thermidor, he naturally takes me into his confidence about many matters.'

'I am relieved to hear that it was not through idle gossip which might get to one of Mr. Pitt's agents. This concept is of the highest secrecy, but seeing that you are to be trusted, it is as well that you should know the whole truth. It will enable me to use your knowledge of the country to much better advantage.'

As they walked towards the entrance of the gardens Buonaparte asked: 'Have you seen Tallien since your return?'

'Yes. I was at his house three nights ago. I thought him looking very ill.'

The General grunted. 'Tallien is finished. His first wife's suicide has disturbed his mind. In any case he played a double game once too often when he ordered the execution of those poor devils of *émigrés* after Quiberon. The reactionaries will never forgive him, yet we now have proof that he was coquetting with the Royalists, so he will never again be regarded with confidence by the Government. I told his wife as much. But she is a fool, and I have no patience with her.'

Roger, knowing the reason for this outburst, had a quiet laugh to himself, and was even more amused when Buonaparte went on:

'Now her friend, Madame de Beauharnais, is very different. She is a most sensible as well as charming creature; and the way she has brought up her two children does her the greatest credit. The Revolution hit her hard, but instead of whining about the shifts to which it brought her, she courageously adapted herself to changed circumstances. Her little girl, Hortense, she apprenticed to a milliner, and the boy, Eugène, to a carpenter; yet owing to their mother's training neither has become the least degraded by their menial occupations. On the contrary the manners of these two lovely children are most distinguished. It so happened that the father's sword came into my possession, and not long since I gave it to young Eugène. His acceptance of it brought tears to my eyes. His one ambition is to be a soldier, and he swore to me that he would die rather than dishonour it. Such a family show all the best qualities of the old aristocracy, and I greatly delight in their friendship.'

By this time they had reached the gate, where the General's coach was waiting. As they got into it and drove off Roger began to run over in his mind all that had transpired in the past half hour. His original mission had gone up in smoke, as it was clear that he might as well have tried to bribe a brick wall as the fiery little Corsican; but luck and the skilful handling of the conversation had compensated him by providing a new opening. If he continued to play his cards well it looked as if he would at least be able to obtain full particulars of Buonaparte's plans for the invasion of England.

The coach set them down in the Rue des Capucines, at the fine house Buonaparte now occupied adjacent to his headquarters. Without a word he took Roger straight upstairs, unlocked a door, and led him into a room containing a huge table littered with papers, and having several large maps pinned up on the walls.

Throwing his gold-laced hat down on a chair Buonaparte motioned Roger to another, shuffled through the papers, selected a bulky folder from among some others, sat down himself and said sharply: 'Now, be good enough to give me your help by answering these questions to the best of your ability.'

The interrogation, on the results of which Buonaparte made copious notes, lasted over three hours. It concerned not only forts, beaches and the approximate strength of garrisons along the part of the south coast that Roger admitted to knowing, but also on the ability of various areas to support men and horses, and the degree of sympathy for the principles of the Revolution which an 'Army of Liberation' might hope to find among the labouring population of the towns.

In answer to the purely military questions Roger gave more or less truthful replies, as he knew they could, and would, be checked by minor spies. About the amounts of stored grain, fodder and other foodstuffs which were likely to be found by an invading army he could afford to be fairly pessimistic, and when it came to the question of support from the Methodists, Corresponding Societies, and other anti-monarchist bodies in Britain he was able, quite honestly, to pour an icy douche upon the General's hopes.

'You must not,' he said, 'judge these people by the amount of noise they make, and the fact that from time to time troops have to be called out to put down some local riot. They already enjoy a far greater degree of liberty than did our people here in France before '89. That there is a widespread agitation to bring about a more even distribution of wealth is true; but if it succeeds it will be mainly through gradually increasing pressure being brought to bear on Parliament by the many gentry, and others, who in recent years have shown a strong desire to better the lot of the masses. As for the idea that English *sans-culottes* in Southampton or Portsmouth would rise on the appearance of your troops and set about massacring their masters, pray disabuse your mind of it. They would not even lift a finger to help you. In fact all but a very few would instantly forget their grievances and, remembering only that they were Englishmen, rush to help in defending their country. I have addressed meetings of these men, and wasted much of my time endeavouring to incite them to more vigorous action; so in this you may rest assured that I know what I am talking about.'

Buonaparte looked somewhat disappointed, but shrugged his narrow shoulders. 'Ah well, that will make little difference. Victories are not gained by mobs but by superior numbers of well-disciplined troops; and we shall have that, for the British have practically denuded the island of regulars.'

'You have got to get your troops there, and a great quantity of stores, to enable you to launch your first offensive. Are you not afraid that the British Navy will come upon and destroy your transports?'

'No. We shall send a squadron of our oldest ships out from the Biscay ports to lure the Channel Fleet down towards Portugal. That will give us two or three clear days at least for our crossing. The main French Fleet will then offer battle to the British on their return.'

'It could never hope to emerge victorious from such an encounter.'

'I do not expect it to. It is to be sacrificed.'

'You mean that every ship will be ordered to fight to a finish.'

'Yes; the loss of a score or so men-o'-war is a bagatelle to pay for the success of an operation of this magnitude. By their action they should so cripple the British Fleet that it will no longer be in any state either to blockade our ports effectively or protect more than a small part of the coast of England. Thus we shall be able to make subsidiary landings in other areas at an acceptable risk; and by the time the British have summoned their squadrons from the Mediterranean and the West Indies I shall be in London.'

Roger shook his head. 'The plan sounds feasible enough but, saving your presence, I doubt the ability of any man to carry it out. I have good reason to hate the English, but I know them well. It is seven hundred years since the island was conquered; so they have freedom in their blood, and will resist far more desperately than would the people of any Continental nation.'

'I tell you it is entirely a matter of troops and their handling. We shall have more and better trained ones. Their generals, like those of the Austrians, are old and set in their ways. They will not stand a chance against me.'

'The whole country will swarm with partisans. You will find a man with a shotgun behind every hedge, and every village will become a death trap.'

Buonaparte laughed, but it was not a pleasant laugh. 'Don't worry! I shall find a means to subdue them. England is at the bottom of all our troubles, and sooner or later must be conquered. Until she is France will never enjoy her rightful place in the world; so it might as well be now. Once we get ashore there I'll be in London in a fortnight, and if need be I'll burn the capital to the ground unless these stubborn English submit to my will.'

This, coupled with what had gone before, was evidence enough that Roger had been right in his assessment that the Corsican would set about matters with complete ruthlessness, and having failed to damp his enthusiasm for the task it seemed pointless to produce further arguments against its chances of success; so he asked:

'In what month do you intend to launch this great operation?'

'That depends on several things. There is much yet to be done. Hundreds of ships and barges will have to be collected, and great quantities of stores sent to the ports for loading into them. I shall need the whole of General Hoche's army. He favours the plan, but wishes himself to create a major diversion by leading a descent on Ireland. That would mean an unsound dispersal of our forces, so must be stopped. Then although the Directors are much interested in the project, they have not yet given a definite assent to my proceeding with the preparations.'

'Should they finally decide against it, what then?'

'Then they must give me one of the other Armies. I have no intention of remaining here to act as their pet policeman.'

'You have been so successful at it that they may well insist upon your doing so.'

Buonaparte's dark eyes narrowed. 'I do not think they will. They have failed to please every section of the people, even their own party. They are the pinnacle of a pyramid that has a hollow base. A single jolt would be enough to bring them tumbling down. They cannot afford to offend a man like myself.'

'Yes, I think you are right about that,' Roger agreed. 'All the same, for your own reputation, I could wish that you were pressing them for some other employment than the conquest of England.'

'I am, but they refuse it to me. England can wait. Her turn will come. First we should smash the Austrians in Italy. That is the task I covet beyond all else. I know something of that country already, and have made a special study of the rest. Look! I will show you how it should be done.'

Jumping up, he began, with hands which Roger noted again were remarkable shapely, to point at place after place on a map of Northern Italy affixed to the wall. As he spoke his fine eyes dilated, and it was evident that every mountain chain and valley of the country stood out as sharply as an etching in his mind. From the rapidity with which he outlined his plan it was clear that he must have already endeavoured to persuade many people of its possibilities. It had boldness, vision and grandeur—involving no less than the seizure of the Lombardy Plain, a great turning movement through the Alps to join up with the Army of the Rhine and, finally, an advance direct upon Vienna.

When he had done, Roger asked: 'What had the Directors to say to this great plan of yours?'

'Carnot approves it, and in such matters the others defer to his judgment. But for some reason they are averse to entrusting me with its execution. He has sent it to General Schérer; but so timid a man as he is certain to reject it.'

'Then,' smiled Roger, 'you will have to content yourself with the conquest of Britain.'

'As spring is near upon us they must soon give me a decision on that matter. If it proved favourable I should like to take you with me. Your knowledge of these troublesome people may be of considerable use. Will you, as you did with Barras, accept the rank of Colonel on my staff?'

Roger stood up and bowed. 'I should be honoured, Citizen General. You have only to let me know when you have received consent to proceed, and I will place myself unreservedly at your disposal.'

From this long interview Roger carried away only one fresh thought for comfort. The expedition had not yet been definitely decided upon. It was now for him to find out if the Directors really favoured the plan, and if so use his utmost endeavours to change their minds, or at least try to prevent their giving so competent a man as Buonaparte the direction of it.

That evening he spent a long time thinking over all that the Corsican had said, and particularly of his references to the Directory. There could be no doubt that it was extremely unpopular. The upper strata of Paris was still a sink of glittering iniquity which offended all respectable citizens; the middle-classes groaned under every form of vexatious restriction, and the poor were nightly dying by the score from cold and hunger; yet the government appeared incapable of remedying any of these ills.

Carnot was the only Director for whom anyone had the least respect, and he, as ever, concerned himself solely with the high direction of the war. The harmless military engineer Letourneur had, quite naturally, dropped into place as his assistant. It was said that the two always voted together, but on civil questions were always outvoted by the three rogues they had for colleagues.

Barras, resting on the great prestige he had earned on 9th Thermidor and 13th Vendémiaire, apart from making an occasional brief, trenchant pronouncement, devoted himself entirely to his scandalous pleasure. Larevellière-Lépeaux was a crank of the first order. As the leading light of a sect called the Theophilanthropists, which was a hotch-potch of Nature worship and the teachings of numerous philosophers, he gave all his endeavours to fighting the open return of Christianity. Rewbell, meanwhile, did the work and dominated the other four; but on account of his coarseness, brutality, cynicism and tyranny was the most hated man in the country.

There being no hope of buying Buonaparte, Roger again considered the posssibility of trying to buy one or more of the Directors; but all the old arguments decided him that such an attempt would be hopeless. An alternative was to try to get them turned out, in the hope that among a new set there might be men elected who would be more amenable to his purpose. Buonaparte had implied that should they get up against him he would do the job, but to incite him to it would be a dangerous game to play. It did not take Roger long to decide against risking such a move; for his interview that day had convinced him that the little Corsican might easily become a greater menace than any other man in France, and that somehow or other his guns must be spiked before he got more power than he had already. On that thought he went to bed.

The following day he succeeded in securing an interview with Barras. Once they were closeted together, he wasted no time in beating about the bush, but said straight out:

'Tell me, is *Le Directoire* really giving serious consideration to this plan for allowing Buonaparte to invade England?'

'Well, more or less,' Barras admitted cautiously. 'It started by our instructing him to investigate the possibilities, simply to keep that active mind of his out of mischief. But he has produced such cogent arguments in support of its practical application that we are much tempted to let him have his way. Hoche is in favour of it, but he differs from the little Corsican in wishing to make a simultaneous landing in Ireland.'

'Of that I am aware. I spent about three hours yesterday discussing the project with Buonaparte.'

'And what is your opinion of it?'

'That it cannot possibly succeed. He knows nothing whatever about England or the British people. I, on the other hand, as you may know, was sent there as a child and spent most of my youth there; so I am in a much better position to judge what a hornets' nest the place would be become did we stick a finger into it.'

'Apart from your misadventures after 9th Thermidor I did not know that you had lived there for any length of time; although I was aware that you acted as Paris correspondent for several English papers during the early years of the Revolution. So you do not approve the plan?'

'I am convinced that it would be suicidal.'

Barras made face. 'It would open with mass suicide anyway; for Buonaparte declares it essential that we should sacrifice the whole of the Fleet. That is the major reason why Carnot hesitates to give the plan his support.'

'You may take it from me that in addition to losing the Fleet you will lose an Army. Buonaparte must have hypnotised you all, or you would not give another thought to this madness.'

'His personal magnetism is, I admit, quite extraordinary; but it is not that alone which has led us to being near giving him his head. You may perhaps have remarked that he has grown in stature since 13th Vendémiaire.'

'He certainly has. I see the situation now. You are afraid of him?'

'I am not personally. After all, he is my protégé. I made him what he is; so he will never do me any harm. But *Le Directoire* as a whole feel that he is a man who can no longer lightly be crossed.'

'In other words they fear that if he is not promoted he will promote himself?'

'Exactly.'

'They are right in that. He said as much to me yesterday. He is as avid for glory as a pirate for loot. Unless he is given the command of an Army in the field I rate him capable of overturning the Government.'

'I agree. That is why we are contemplating letting him go off to England.'

'Surely to lose the Fleet and fifty thousand men is an expensive way to placate him?'

'We might not lose them, but gain a great triumph over our enemies.'

'You might be crowned Paul I of France in Rheims Cathedral, but that is equally unlikely. Why not give him another Army? Give him the Army of Italy. It is that after which he really hankers.'

'No.' Barras shook his head. 'To do so would be too dangerous. You cannot have forgotten the lessons that the Romans taught us. In a dozen instances their victorious Generals turned their legions about and marched on Rome. If we gave Buonaparte the Army of Italy or the Rhine that is the risk we should run. At any time he might decide to oust us and make himself First Magistrate. But the Army of England would be a different matter. If he succeeded in conquering the island we would make him Proconsul of it. That would keep him busy for a long time to come, and we should have nought to worry about.'

'You will if you adopt his plan. When he has lost his Army and the Fleet, it is you and your colleagues who will be called to account for it. You'll be lucky if you get as far as the guillotine. 'Tis more likely that the people will tear you all limb from limb.'

'It is a Government's business to take such risks. All decisions which may lead to major victories or defeats are gambles.'

'One does not gamble *sous* against *louis d'or*. Ask some of the *émigrés* who have lived for several years in England if I am not right. Those stubborn islanders will fight to the last ditch. If you could land a quarter of a million men in a week the thing might be done; but that is utterly impossible. Again, Buonaparte's pet theory is that given anything near equal numbers the side which uses its artillery more skilfully will always win a battle. Within three days of landing he'll have run out of shot.'

'No. He plans to seize the arsenal and cannon foundry at Portsmouth.'

Roger gave a contemptuous laugh. 'That cannot be done overnight. He must land on beaches out of range of the forts. To reach the Hampshire coast his men must be conveyed over near a hundred miles of sea. Nine tenths of them will stagger ashore helpless as children from seasickness. They'll be hard put to it to defend themselves even from the local militia for the first twenty-four hours; so the garrison at Portsmouth will have ample time to set its house in order. Should the port appear likely to fall, you may be sure that they will blow up the arsenal and the foundry before Buonaparte can capture them. And what then? Within a week every man in Southern England will have armed himself and be on the march. Like a countless pack of wolves they will fall upon our troops, and from sheer weight of numbers drive them back into the sea.'

'It is a grim picture that you paint; but I think you over pessimistic. In any case, this *enfant terrible* must be given active employment of some kind; and what alternative have we?'

'Give him the Army of Italy, which he so much desires.'

'I have already told you that *Le Directoire* are averse to doing so, and their reason.'

During the lengthy consideration that Roger had given to the whole subject the previous evening, he had foreseen that the Directors might be afraid of entrusting Buonaparte with an Army which could be turned against them; so he had thought out a scheme which would, perhaps, overcome their objections. Having, he felt, got Barras into the right frame of mind to consider his idea seriously, he said:

'I think there is a way in which you could make reasonably sure of Buonaparte's fidelity.'

'I should be much interested to hear it.'

'You will be aware that for the past year he has been subject to a most powerful urge to get married?'

'Yes. He has now set his heart upon Josephine de Beauharnais, and is wooing her with the impetuosity that he displays in everything.'

'Exactly; and she is a *chèr amie* of yours. Everyone knows that she is greatly indebted to you, and it is even said that the house in which she lives is your property. How far would you trust her?'

'To almost any length. She is a sweet natured and honest creature. Out of gratitude for all I have done for her, I feel confident that she will ever use such influence as she may have in my interests.'

'From what I know of her myself, and all I have heard, I supposed as much. I suggest that you should bind her still more strongly to you by persuading her to make what can hardly fail to turn out a brilliant marriage. Give her as a dowry the command of the Army of Italy for Buonaparte. Then he will be bound to her, and you will have someone in the closest possible relation to him who will put a curb on his ambitions should they threaten the authority of the Directory.'

Barras considered for a moment. 'It is a most ingenious scheme; but before it could be put into operation there are several objections which would have to be overcome.

Firstly she does not love him.'

'That is what makes the plan all the sounder. If she did she could not be trusted; as things are she can. Somehow we will persuade her to accept him.'

'Perhaps that could be done. But the Army of Italy is not mine to give. Carnot was greatly impressed by Buonaparte's plan for the destruction of the Austrians, so might agree; but Rewbell is the stumbling block. He would certainly refuse, as he has several times expressed the opinion that Buonaparte is getting too big for his boots and that we shall be well rid of him if we send him to England.'

'If you can win Carnot over, Letourneur will follow his lead; and that will give you a majority.'

For a further quarter of an hour they discussed the plan in detail. At length, Barras said: 'Then I will see *La Belle Créole* tonight, and if you will call upon me at the same hour tomorrow I will let you know the result of our talk.'

The evening Roger attended Madame de Château-Renault's *salon,* as it was there he had first met Josephine, and he felt that, now she had become such an important pawn in his game, he would do well to develop her acquaintance. His hope of finding her there was realised, and having engaged her for some time in conversation he remarked that he had heard that she had two very beautiful children. She replied with becoming modesty, yet her pride in them was evident. He then said how fond he was of young people, and asked permision to call upon her so that he might see them. Her consent was readily given and she invited him to take tea with her the following day.

Next morning, eager to learn how his plan was working, he waited as arranged on Barras. The Director told him that matters had not gone too badly, then he said:

'To be the wife of the Commander of the Army of Italy is a position which any woman might envy, and Madame de Beauharnais is much tempted by the idea. But she is still troubled with grave doubts, and she did not disguise from me that she was greatly worried about some other matter. What it is she would not confide in me, but I've a shrewd suspicion that Citizen Fouché is at the bottom of it. Not once, but several times, she dragged his name into our conversation and begged me to get him made a junior Minister, or give him some other considerable post that would rescue him from the poverty and disgrace into which he has fallen. But he is a rogue and mischief-maker of the first order, and I had to tell her frankly that I'd lift not a finger to help him.'

'It is unfortunate that some private worry should be distracting her mind at this particular time,' Roger remarked. 'However, it is good news that where previously she made a mock of the little Corsican you have now persuded her to consider him seriously. What is the next move to be?'

'I shall see her again, of course, and continue to press her. It might help now, though, if she could be encouraged to it from some other angle. Do you know her well enough to call on her and, apropos of nothing in particular, sing Buonaparte's praises?'

'With that very object in mind I got her to invite me to take tea with her this evening.'

'Excellent!' Barras smiled. 'Keep in touch with me, and I will inform you of any fresh developments.'

At six o'clock Roger had himself driven to the house that Barras had lent *La Belle Créole*. It was a small two-storey villa at the end of a long passage and its entrance was flanked by two stone lions. On arriving there he recognised it as the *petite Maison* that the wife of Talma, the famous actor, had formerly been given by one of her rich lovers; so it had a somewhat dubious reputation, which matched Josephine's own. Roger had already learned that although quite a number of *ci-devant* nobles frequented her twice-monthly 'drawing-room', very few of their wives did so, and he wondered again why a woman of her age and circumstances should hesitate to make a marriage which would both restore her respectability and secure her future.

He was shown into a drawing-room at the back of the house with two french windows opening on to a little garden. There a few moments later Josephine, accompanied by her pet poodle *Fortuné*, joined him.

She received him with the unaffected grace that was one of her principal assets, and in the intimacy of her own apartment he soon began to realise more strongly than he had previously done the peculiar quality of her attraction. It lay in a melting expression, languorous grace of movement, and a mysterious suggestion that her body, if embraced, would be found to be quite exceptionally soft and yielding. After a few minutes she called in her children and presented them to him. The girl, Hortense, promised to be a beauty, as she had a good skin, a profusion of fair hair and a pair of large dark-blue eyes. The boy, Eugène, who was getting on for fifteen, was a fine manly lad, and it was obvious that both of them adored their mother.

While Roger had served on Barras's staff during the previous October, he had seen quite a lot of Buonaparte at the War Office; so, in due course, it was easy for him to bring the General's name into the conversation, and speak of his fine qualities. Josephine did no more than murmur polite agreement, and began to fiddle a little self-consciously with the tea things; but young Eugène took up the tale with unrestrained enthusiasm. The Corsican was now his hero; the episode of the sword was told in glowing phrases, and it transpired that, when old enough, he had been promised a commission.

'If you are to become one of General Buonaparte's officers you will also need pistols,' Roger remarked. 'Have you any?'

'Alas, no, Monsieur,' came the quick reply. 'After my father's death, my poor mother was compelled to part with nearly all his things in order to feed us.'

'Then Madame,' Roger bowed to Josephine, 'permit me, I pray, the pleasure of presenting your charming son with a brace of weapons to go with his sword.'

At first Josephine demurred, but she was quite used to accepting gifts from men; so she needed only a little pressing to agree on behalf of her boy.

The matter had only just been settled when the Deputy Fréron was announced. Roger had got to know him well at the siege of Toulon and had met him on many occasions since. He was now a man of thirty, and after the *coup d'état* of 9th Thermidor, in which he had played a vigorous part, he had become more strongly reactionary than any other of the ex-Terrorists. As Fouché had told Roger some months before, Fréron, with extraordinary astuteness had used his paper *L'Orateur du Peuple* to make himself the leader of the *jeunesse dorée*; but his past was far from having been forgotten by Roger.

It was Fréron who, while *Représentant en Mission* at Marseilles, had ordered a volley to be fired into a mass of Royalist prisoners; and, when they had fallen in a screaming, bloody heap, called out: 'All of you who are not dead, stand up, and you shall be spared.' Then, when the survivors took him at his word and staggered to their feet, he had ordered a second volley to be fired.

To find such a man in the house of a woman whose husband had been guillotined was no more than a symptom of the times, and Roger had no reason to believe Josephine to be particularly high principled; but he was slightly nauseated by what followed. Fréron had not come there to pay his respects to Madame de Beauharnais; almost at once he began openly to ogle pretty little Hortense. Then he produced some tickets for a public ball at the Hotel de Richelieu and asked if he might take the mother and daughter to it; upon which the young girl jumped for joy. Roger made suitable excuses and took his leave.

Having allowed a day to elapse, so that he should not appear to have an ulterior motive in his visits, on March the 2nd, somewhat later in the evening, Roger called on Josephine again. With him he brought a case containing two fine silver mounted pistols, which he had bought the day before. Eugène was delighted with them, as they were far more beautiful and expensive than anything he had expected. At the sight of them, Josephine became somewhat thoughtful; then after a while she sent her children out of the room. When they had made their adieux she said to Roger:

'Monsieur, please tell me why, since we have no claim on you other than the honour of a slight acquaintance, you have made my son this magnificent gift?'

He smiled. 'Madame, I will at least take the credit for a genuine wish to give so promising a young man pleasure; but, since you ask me, I will confess to having also had the hope that should General Buonaparte come to hear of it, he too will be pleased by this small attention to a family in which he is so deeply interested.'

'You have, then, heard of the attentions with which he has honoured me?'

'More, Madame. When I was last with him he positively raved to me about you. In fact, unless you take pity on him I really fear that from unrequited love of you he will be driven out of his mind; and that would be a great loss to France, for I am convinced that a splendid future lies before him.'

'So others also tell me; and I have formed the greatest respect for his character. But, at times, he makes me almost afraid of him.'

'You have no need to be. Look at the affection with which your children speak of him. Young people have an instinct for judging the true disposition of their elders. And for them you could not find a better step-father in the whole length and breadth of France.'

'There is much in what you say, Monsieur.'

'Indeed there is. Once married to him you would have no more anxieties. As his wife all Paris will bow before you. When little Hortense becomes of an age to marry, a score of rich and titled suitors will be contending for her hand. You will be able to make a match for her such as her beauty deserves. As for Eugène, since it is his wish to be a soldier, to rob him of the chance to attach himself to one who promises to become the first soldier of the day would be little less than cruel.'

Josephine nodded. 'I have thought much upon the same lines, and these arguments weigh greatly with me. Should I accept him it will be because the interests of my children are so near to my heart. But there are other considerations. For one, it would be childish of me to attempt to hide the fact that I am past my first youth. So volatile a man might soon turn to other distractions, and. . . .'

Josephine got no further; for at that moment Madame Tallien was announced. Her entrance deprived Roger of the chance of reassuring his hostess about the power of her charms and, to his intense annoyance, of saying numerous other things about her mooted match with Buonaparte that, having broken the ice, he had hoped to say to her that evening.

Not long afterwards Buonaparte arrived, and, knowing that he would wish to have Josephine to himself, Roger took an early opportunity of offering to see Theresa Tallien home. She too appreciated the situation and, although she had been there less than a quarter of an hour, with her usual good nature she readily consented. Just as they were leaving, she said to Josephine:

'Do not forget, my dear, that we have an appointment to visit Madame Le Normand together at three o'clock tomorrow afternoon. We will go masked, of course, and I will call for you in a hackney coach, as the appointment has been made simply for two ladies, and it will be all the greater test of her powers if we can continue to keep our identities a secret from her.'

'I had not forgotten,' Josephine laughed. 'I adore fortune tellers, and I do hope that this renowned sibyl will predict exciting futures for us both. Adieu, sweet Theresa! Adieu till tomorrow!'

On the way downstairs Roger asked the stately Theresa for Le Normand's address, saying that he must, some time, consult her himself. She gave it to him and in her coach he saw her to her front door, but politely declined an invitation to come in; whereupon she insisted on it taking him back to *La Belle Étoile*. There he went up to his room, loosened a floor board, and took from beneath it one of the purses of gold that he always kept hidden against emergencies. Then, going out again, he walked through a misty drizzle that had just begun to Le Normand's house in the Rue de Journon.

At first the woman who answered the door there refused to admit him on the plea that her mistress had to conserve her powers, so never saw clients after six o'clock. But Roger clinked his gold and slipped her a piece, which induced her to let him in and lead him to a parlour on the ground floor.

As she lit the candles in it he saw that on a table in its centre there lay scattered face up a pack of Tarot cards, and among them a large crystal on an ebony stand. There was no stuffed alligator hanging from the ceiling, no tambourines, or other charlatan's aids, left about; but Roger had not expected there would be, as he had often heard of Le Normand and she had the reputation of a mystic with genuine gifts. She had according to current belief, correctly predicted the dates upon which numerous people who had consulted her would be sent to the guillotine and, with great boldness, foretold to Robespierre his approaching fall.

When he had waited there for a few minutes a middle-aged woman came in. Her clothes were of rich material but untidily worn, and beneath the fine lace draped over her head wisps of grey hair stuck out. She had big eyes, very widely spaced, and regarded Roger from them with quiet self-composure. Having curtsied to his bow, she asked:

'What does the Citizen require of me?'

'I come,' Roger replied, 'not to ask you to tell my fortune, but on a business matter. First let me make it clear that I respect such gifts as yours; I have a dear friend who has several times foretold the future correctly for me, but through her I have also learned the limitations of such powers. They cannot always be called upon at will. Therefore, when used professionally there are times when aids having nought to do with the occult must be employed to give a client satisfaction.'

A slow smile dawned in Madame Le Normand's large eyes, and she said: 'Since the Citizen is so well informed upon such matters, I will not deny that a skilful probing of the enquirer's circumstances is often most helpful in becoming *en rapport*.'

Roger bowed. 'I can then aid you beforehand with regard to two ladies who had an appointment to consult you at three o'clock tomorrow afternoon. The taller of the two is Madame Tallien, the shorter and slighter Madame de Beauharnais.'

'Why does the Citizen bring me this information?'

'Because I wish you to exert a beneficial influence on the mind of Madame de Beauharnais. She has recently received an offer of marriage, but is hesitating about accepting it. That she should do so is greatly in her interest, because her present position is precarious; whereas this match would both secure her own future and ensure a most promising future for her two children. The proposal does not come from myself but from General Buonaparte. It would, I think, be overdoing matters to disclose his name, but I should like you to speak well of him, as a man of generous disposition and a soldier of great promise, who will bring happiness to the woman he marries.'

Producing the silk net purse through which the gold glittered dully, Roger laid it on the table and added: 'If you are willing, I should like to leave this with you; so that you may buy some article of value, by which to remember your part in promoting the fortunes of a widow and two orphans.'

The sibyl took up the purse and held it tightly clasped in both hands for a few moments, then she said quietly: 'Citizen, you have lied to me. This purse may contain *louis d'or* but it is, nevertheless, foreign gold. It was not concern for a widow and two orphans that brought you here tonight. You have some other motive for desiring this marriage to take place. And endeavour to alter a person's Fate by such means always recoils on the head of him who makes it. It will do so in your case. Yet I will do as you wish; because never before have I felt so strongly the influence that guides me, and I already know beyond any shadow of doubt that to do so will be for the glory of France.'

'Citoyenne,' Roger replied a trifle huskily, 'what you tell me is most perturbing; but in this I have no personal end to gain, and I honestly believe that this marriage will be to the advantage of Madame de Beauharnais; so I can only hope that Fate will let me off lightly.'

Her strange, widely-spaced eyes held his for a few seconds, then she said: 'I believe you. It must then, be not you who will suffer, but the cause you serve.'

As the door of the house closed behind Roger, he found himself badly shaken. For the first time it occurred to him that it might have been better to let Buonaparte break himself once and for all on the shores of England, than simply to get him out of the way for the time being by engineering his being sent to Italy, from whence he might return covered with glory to become an even greater menace But on second thoughts he decided that he was playing the right game. With England practically denuded of troops, the risk that the invasion might succeed was too great a one to take. Even now that awful possibility was far from having been ruled out, as it was by no means certain yet that Josephine would accept Buonaparte; or, even if she did, that the Directors would finally decide to give him the Army of Italy.

On the latter question Roger was given better grounds for hope when he went to see Barras the following morning. General Schérer had returned Buonaparte's plan to Carnot with a curt note to the effect that he had no use for it, and that if the Directory were set upon it they had better send the rash fool who had made it to carry it out. Thereupon Carnot had decided to support a policy of taking him at his word. But the proposal had still to get through the *Comité*.

It was Barras's vote which would now prove the deciding factor; but, in spite of all that Roger could say about the criminal lunacy of an attempt to invade England, the Director made it clear that he would not support the proposal that Buonaparte should supersede Schérer, unless the plan for exerting a secret influence over the Corsican by means of Josephine could be carried through. He added that no time must be lost in getting a definite decision from her, as once the proposal came officially before the *Comité* it would have to be settled one way or the other.

More anxious than ever now to learn what effect Josephine's afternoon visit to Le Normand had had, and feeling sure she would speak of it if he could get a word with her, Roger went that evening to Madame Tallien's, but Josephine did not appear there; so somewhat belatedly he went on to Madame de Château-Renault's. There he found her, but she was with Buonaparte, who soon afterwards escorted her home, and Roger was left to exercise as much patience as he could till next day.

As early in the afternoon as convention permitted, he went to the little villa in the Rue Chantereine. Josephine looked somewhat surprised to see him, but he took the bold line of saying that he had been sent by Barras to tell her that Carnot's opposition to Buonaparte's being given the appointment he so greatly desired had been overcome, and that it now remained only for her to say if she was willing to present it to him as her dowry.

Raising her eyebrows a little she said: 'I was not aware that Barras expected any opposition to his plan. He led me to suppose that everything depended on myself.'

'Ah!' Roger hedged. 'That was because he wished to give you time to get used to the idea, while he was working to win over two colleagues on *Le Directoire*. Now that he has done so, within forty-eight hours the matter must be settled one way or the other. As voting is by secret ballot he can still sabotage his own proposition if he wishes; and will, do you not consent. But he would be mightily put out should you now refuse to take this splendid opening that he has been at such pains to provide for you.'

She motioned Roger to a chair and said as she sat down on another: 'I would be a heartless wretch were I not sensible of the gratitude I owe him. No woman could ever have had a more generous protector. As for the future that this marriage promises, yesterday I went with Theresa Tallien to consult the sibyl Le Normand. Should only half the things that she predicts for it come true few fortunes could equal mine. I am still overwhelmed by the things she told me.'

'She has a great reputation,' Roger smiled. 'And I am truly delighted that the omens should be favourable. Will you not tell me what she said?'

'It sounds utterly fantastic. She spoke of palaces and crowns. She said that Buonaparte's star is the most brilliant in all the heavens. That Kings will bow down to him. That he will make me a Queen. That in his footsteps my Eugène will also become a great General. He will, too, be a Prince, and little Hortense like myself a Queen.'

For a moment Roger wondered uneasily if any of this might be due to true second-sight, or if it was simply that the sibyl had given him full measure in payment for his gold. Then Josephine caught his attention again as she went on:

'I'd not believe a word of it, but for one thing. When I was a young girl in Martinique an old negro woman of partly Irish descent predicted just such a future for me. More, she also foretold the troubles that would come upon France, my marriage to M. de Beauharnais, and the manner of his death.'

Roger was much impressed and no little perturbed; but true to his principle that first things must come first, he said seriously: 'Such confirmation can leave you in no doubt of your destiny. Pray, Madame, accept my congratulations. With your permission then, I will return to Barras and tell him the good news; leaving it to you to acquaint General Buonaparte that through you he is to receive the first step to his magnificent fortune.'

'Nay! Wait!' She stretched out a hand to stop him as he rose.

'What!' he exclaimed. 'Surely you cannot mean that you are still troubled by doubts?'

'Yes. Indeed I am!'

'How can you even contemplate the rejection of these great gifts that the gods are prepared to shower on you and your children?'

'I do not wish to; but it may be that I must.'

'How so? You are your own mistress! What in the world is there to prevent your marrying General Buonaparte other than your own hesitations?'

Instead of answering his question, she leaned forward and said earnestly: 'Monsieur; you are most sympathetic. Although our acquaintance is a short one, I feel that you are my friend. You are, I know, a great friend of Paul Barras. Could you persuade him to grant me a favour?'

Roger returned her glance with some surprise. 'Madame, I can hardly think that my influence with him is greater than your own. But I will willingly serve you in any way I can.'

'It concerns Citizen Fouché. Much ill has been said of him, but he is a good man at heart. His calumniators have brought about his ruin, but I would much like to see his excellent mind once more employed in the interests of his country. If you would serve me, use your utmost endeavours to persuade Barras to give him some suitable appointment.'

'Forgive me, Madame, if, before agreeing to do as you wish, I ask you one question. What has this to do with the project of your marriage?'

Josephine began to twist her fingers together in evident agitation. 'I beg you, Monsieur, do not press me on that. It concerns a matter in my past which I would prefer not to discuss. Please let it suffice that though I do not love General Buonaparte, I would do my best to make him a good wife—if . . . if only this other matter could be settled.'

'Madame, you imply that Fouché is holding you to ransom?'

'No, no! he is most well disposed towards me, and acting in this as my friend. It is for that reason I wish to oblige him. He comes of a shipping family that once owned estates in the West Indies but the Revolution robbed him of any private income, and now that he is no longer a Deputy he is in sad straits.'

Her mention of the West Indies suddenly rang a bell in Roger's brain. Coming to his feet, he exclaimed: 'I have it now! Fouché had found out about your marriage to William de Kay.'

Josephine's big eyes widened. Springing up, she gasped: 'How . . . how can you know aught of that?'

Roger had to think quickly. After a second he replied: 'When I was living in England I had the story from a Mr. Beckwith, a British merchant who had lived in Martinique for many years.'

'I knew him,' Josephine murmured, pale to the lips. 'Oh, Monsieur! You are wrong in thinking that it is Fouché who is blackmailing me, but right in thinking that I am again being victimised on account of that youthful folly. It has proved the curse of my life.'

'I happened to hear of it only by the merest chance; and would have thought it by now long since forgotten.'

'I had hoped it was, or at least that I was cleared of it. A few years after I was married to M. de Beauharnais, ill-fortune caused us to take a mulatto among our servants. He turned out to be the brother of a woman slave who had been brought up in my father's household, and from her he had had the whole story. He demanded money from me as the price of his silence. For a time I paid him; then when I could no longer afford to meet his demands, I told my husband. I swore to my innocence and he believed me. All would have been well but for an evil woman who pretended to be my friend while having designs upon him. She so worked upon his mind that he decided to go to Martinique and ferret out the truth. When he returned he brought an action with intent to repudiate me. Fortunately for myself, good friends of mine succeeded in having the case removed from Paris to a provincial court where he had no influence. There was no proof that my marriage to William de Kay was a legal one, or that it had been consummated; so a verdict was given in my favour. Later my husband and myself were reconciled, and I lulled myself into the belief that I had been punished enough for the deceit I had practised on my parents.'

'Indeed you have, Madame. But I beg you to calm yourself. That this mulatto rogue should have appeared again is naturally a grave annoyance to you, but now he should not prove difficult to deal with.'

'He has no part in this. I know it for certain that he was killed in a riot during the Revolution.'

'I see. So some other is now attempting to blackmail you. Am I to understand that Fouché is acting as your agent, and endeavouring to buy this person's silence?'

'Not that, exactly. I am not quite so simple as to fail to realise that in serving me he hopes to serve himself. But I think him right in his contention that it is far better to eliminate the blackmailer than to pay, perhaps indefinitely. His suggestion is that, if I could obtain for him some Ministerial office or high appointment in the Police, without giving any reason he could issue a warrant for the rogue, then secure an order for his deportation; and that would be the end of the matter.'

'But Madame, one moment!' Roger spread out his hands. 'Why allow the restoration of your peace of mind to be dependent on restoring Fouché's fortunes? Why not go direct to Barras? He could do all that is required with a stroke of the pen.'

'It is not so simple, Monsieur. Fouché refuses to reveal the identity of the blackmailer.'

'Even so, Barras could deal with this. He could put his police on to shadow Fouché night and day. The one rogue would soon lead them to the other, and the whole affair be settled without causing you the least embarrassment.'

'No,' she shook her head violently. 'That I will not have. Fouché may be a rogue, but he knows how to keep a secret. Barras does not. He is the biggest gossip in all Paris. Did I confide in him it would ultimately do me near as much damage as if I allowed the blackmailer to do his worst.'

For a moment Roger was silent, then he said: 'But really, I cannot see what you have to fear. Since the Court gave a verdict in your favour, you are already proved innocent. Should this old scandal be dug up you can afford to laugh at it.'

The laugh that Josephine gave was a bitter one. 'Monsieur, I have not yet acquainted you with the crux of the matter. This person has in his possession a diary that I wrote during my love affair with William. That he actually has it I know, for I have been sent some of the more harmless leaves from it. In it I referred to William as my husband, and wrote many things the memory of which now causes me to blush.'

Roger drew in a sharp breath. 'You are right, Madame. This is serious.'

'Serious!' she echoed, her voice rising hysterically. 'Should my diary be published, for me it would be the end! The end, I tell you! The ultimate degradation! For all their lives my poor children would bear the stigma of bastards. As for myself, should I marry Buonaparte and this were disclosed, for having consciously made him a party to bigamy and the laughing stock of Paris I believe he would strangle me with his own hands.'

In a swift succession of flashes, like those given off by an exploding Chinese cracker, Roger saw the sequence of situations which threatened to arise from this new development. Unless the diary could be recovered Josephine would not dare to marry Buonaparte. If she would not marry him, Barras would not risk entrusting him with the Army of Italy. Unless Buonaparte was given the Army of Italy he would insist upon being allowed to carry out his plan for the invasion of England.

Once more, Roger had a mental picture of the old High Street of Lymington, his home town, in flames; and he knew that it would be only one of many; for, although the invasion might be repulsed later, nothing short of a tempest could stop the initial landings. Somehow, if it was the last thing he ever did, he had to get hold of and destroy that diary.

26

Blackmail

That evening, after Roger had supped, he went to Fouché's little house. The ill-favoured Madame Fouché answered the door and showed him into the poorly-furnished sitting-room. Fouché was there working upon some papers. As soon as the two men had greeted one another, she discreetly withdrew and went upstairs.

Without looking at Roger, Fouché motioned him to a chair and said: 'I heard you were back in Paris; but the state of things here has altered little since you left; so I felt that it would be pointless to seek you out.'

'It would have been,' Roger agreed. 'The time has not yet come to make a move in the matter that we talked of when last we met.'

Fouché sighed. 'I feared as much; although your coming here momentarily raised my hopes that I might be wrong. To what, then, do I owe this visit?'

'I wished to inform myself if your circumstances had improved during my absence.'

'That was considerate of you. The answer, alas, is no.' Fouché made a gesture of disgust towards the papers on the table. 'Here is fine work for one whose words were once hung upon in the Chamber. These are calculations showing how much it will cost to feed young pigs until they reach a certain weight and can be sold at a few francs profit.'

'Indeed! I had no idea that you had any experience of farming or raising animals.'

'Nor have I. But the ex-Deputy Gérard offered to finance me if I would buy a few litters and fatten them swiftly by forcible feeding, then share the profits with him. So now I spend my days on a farm in the suburbs cleaning out pig-sties.'

'You would, then, be glad if I could put you in the way of earning a considerable sum?'

Fouché gave a quick snuffle. 'There are few things you could ask of me that I would not do in order to improve my present wretched situation.'

'The matter depends only on your willingness to do a deal with me. This afternoon Madame de Beauharnais confided to me the gist of some recent conversations she had with you.'

'Ah!' Fouché's bloodless lips twitched in a faint smile. 'So you know about the diary, and have come to try to buy it for her?'

'Yes. How much do you want for it?'

'I have not got it.'

'No matter. You know who has, and could get hold of it.'

'Even if I could, I would not sell it.'

'Why not? I am prepared to pay you handsomely.'

Fouché shook his head. 'It is worth more to me than money. That diary should prove the means of obtaining for me a new chance in life.'

'In that, I fear you wrong.'

'Why so? Madame de Beauharnais has great influence with Barras. He could easily procure for me an appointment in the Administration, and that would bring me in a regular income. Once back, too, I should soon find opportunities of furthering my fortunes. Such a prospect is much more valuable than a sum of money down.'

'It would be if Barras were agreeable to do as you wish; but he is not.'

'I see no reason why he should refuse. Everyone knows my capabilities, and there are plenty of men with far worse records than mine holding office. My enemies in the two Chambers might make some outcry; but they have no power in such matters now. Within twenty-four hours people would be talking of something else; Barras would have done himself no material harm, and I should have the means of supporting my unfortunate family.'

Roger shrugged. 'Your reasoning is sound enough; but the fact remains that Barras has refused Madame de Beauharnais's appeal on your behalf.'

'Then she will not get back her diary. The person who has it is no fool, and would not part with it even if I offered the half of as big a sum as I might hope to get from you. The intention is to retain it and keep her bled white through monthly payments of as much as she can afford. That, my own interests apart, is why she should give Barras no peace until he does something for me. I have always wanted a post in the Police. If she could get me one, I could deal with the blackmailer for her in such a way that she would have no more to worry about.'

'Again your reasoning is sound enough; but is made impracticable of application owing to the ill-will that Barras bears you. Therefore some other means must be employed.'

'What have you to suggest?'

'That you should sell me the blackmailer's name and leave me to handle the matter of getting back the diary.'

Fouché gave an angry snort. 'I have already told you that in this lies my only hope of re-establishing myself in the career for which I am best fitted. Is it likely that I would sacrifice such a chance for a hatful of ready money?'

'You would be well-advised to; otherwise you may get nothing.'

'There, you are quite wrong. Even if Barras proves adamant, a steady income can be made out of Madame de Beauharnais; and as the go-between I'll get my share of it.'

'Do not delude yourself. She is far from rich, and you will be lucky if you receive even a first small payment.'

'On the contrary, the prospects of *La Belle Créole* becoming a good milch cow were never better. A reliable little bird told me that General Buonaparte is pressing her hard to marry him. In her situation she would be mad to refuse such an offer. Once she is Madame Buonaparte, not only will she feel it more necessary than ever to buy our silence, but she will have ample means to do so.'

'You have yourself alluded to the factor which will prove the nigger in your woodpile,' Roger announced with a grim little smile. 'Madame de Beauharnais opened her heart to me this afternoon. She is shrewd enough to guess that you are banking on General Buonaparte's proposal to her, and knows that should she not give you satisfaction you may attempt to bring about her ruin. But she is a courageous woman, and so prepared to face up to this crisis you have forced upon her. She is also an honest one. She declared to me that nothing would induce her to marry the General with this sword of Damocles hanging over her head. And she went further. Rather than suffer a perpetual drain upon her very limited resources as the only alternative to having her children proclaimed bastards here in Paris she will take them to Martinique. There, her youthful indiscretion is known to most people and already condoned; so the most you can hope to gain is as much as you can screw out of her to buy your silence while she makes her preparations for leaving France.'

Roger had misrepresented matters with considerable ingenuity as Josephine had no idea of returning to Martinique, and the suggestion that Fouché might get a little money from her rather than nothing at all was a touch of genius. It was that, no doubt, which caused him to accept the statement as the truth. His grey, blotchy face twitching with annoyance, he muttered:

'How cursed am I with misfortune that this bridge to a steady income should have broken under me. I was counting on it to ease the burden that my poor wife has already carried far too long. Since, then, I must do a deal with you, what are you prepared to pay?'

'One hundred *louis*.'

'Such an offer is absurd, and you know it! To this woman the securing of her future must, at the very least, be worth a thousand.'

'It might be if she had a thousand; but she has not. It is I who am paying, simply to buy her future goodwill. To me that is worth one hundred, and no more. That is double what you might hope to get from her direct; as did you press her to the limit I doubt if she could raise fifty to keep you quiet. Remember, too, that having settled with you I shall still have to deal with the person who has the diary.'

'What sum do you propose to offer for it?'

'By adopting your own plan, I hope to get it for nothing. I have no doubt that if I tell Barras a suitable story he will furnish me with a deportation order. The threat to execute it should be enough to ensure the surrender of the diary. But rather than go to extremes, which might result in the story getting about, some payment may be necessary to clinch the matter; so for your part in it I'll go to no more than a hundred.'

Fouché's red-rimmed eyes narrowed slightly as he stared down at his long bony hands, which lay crossed upon the table. Suddenly he spoke again. 'You have always stood well with Barras, and the casualness with which you speak of getting a deportation order from him is evidence that you do so still. I'll make a bargain with you. Get him to give me some post and I'll forgo the hundred *louis*.'

'I have already told you that he is averse to giving you anything.'

' 'Tis true that he refused the pretty Créole; but perhaps he feels that he has already done enough for her. If you put in a good word for me he might view the matter differently.'

'I greatly doubt it.'

'I feel sure he would; particularly if the request were a modest one. I will forgo my hopes of a Prefecture, or something of that kind. Let it be only a Commissionership in the Post, or Customs, or in connection with Supplies. Anything will serve provided it enables me to get back into the service of the Government. Surely you could persuade him to do that much for me.'

Roger considered for a moment. After all, it meant nothing to him if there was one rogue more or less in the Directory's Administration; and Fouché was not asking for the moon. If he could be procured a minor post and the British Government be saved a hundred *louis* in consequence, so much the better.

'Very well, then.' With a nod, Roger stood up. 'Mark me, I promise nothing; but I'll do my best for you. Now, what is the name and address of the person who has the diary?'

Fouché too stood up, but he shook his head. 'I fear you

must wait for that until I learn what Barras is prepared to do for me.'

'No.' Roger's voice was sharp. 'This matter is of no great importance to me, and I've no mind to run back and forth to Barras about it. That he will not give me a blank deportation order is certain; so if I am to ask for one I must have the name. Give it me and when I ask him for the order I will also ask him to do something for you. If that does not content you, then you had best count me out of the matter altogether.'

As Fouché could have no means of knowing the immense importance that Roger actally did attach to the affair, and, from his point of view, the great urgency of settling it, he was taken in by the bluff, and said:

'I see that I must trust you. The woman's name . . .'

'Woman?' Roger echoed in surprise.

'Yes; woman. She is the sister of a mulatto, who before the Revolution was a footman in the Beauharnais household.'

'I see. Yes; Madame de Beauharnais mentioned him to me. Please go on.'

'Her name is Madame Rémy.'

'And her address?'

Fouché hesitated and, Roger guessed, was about to hold it back as a last card, on the pretext that to secure the deportation order it was not necessary; but now he had the name the game was in his hands, and he said quickly:

'Come! Since you have trusted me so far, there is nought to be gained by hedging. I need only ask Barras to put his police on to her to have her run to earth.'

'True. Very well then. She lives not far from the prison of La Force. You proceed past it down to a row of dwellings that back on to the short stretch of river between the bridge to the Isle St. Louis and the bridge to the Isle Louvier. Her lodging was at one time an artist's studio and lies on the immediate right of a drinking den frequented by the wharf-hands who work in those parts.'

'Good. Tomorrow morning there is this big parade of troops returned from La Vendée, at which the Directors are to take the salute; so I shall not be able to secure an interview with Barras until the afternoon at earliest. Be in all the evening, and some time during it I will call to let you know what Barras has decided regarding you.'

With a nod, Fouché followed Roger out into the passage. As he opened the front door for him, he said: 'This means a great deal to me. Please remember that and do your utmost to get me something with a salary which will enable me to keep my wife in a little comfort.'

'Everything depends upon how deeply Barras is prejudiced against you,' Roger replied, 'but I promise you I will do my best.' Then he went out into the night.

As soon as he had dined on the following day, Roger went to the Luxembourg. It was a dull, rainy afternoon and the twilight of early March was already falling as he descended from a hired coach outside the Palace. Having paid off the man, he sent up his name, but he had to kick his heels in an antechamber for over an hour before M. Bottot came out and said that Barras was free to see him.

As soon as they were seated, Barras said: 'When your name was brought in I was on the point of sending for you, to let you know that our project with regard to Madame de Beauharnais has now become one of the greatest urgency. Since you were last here I have had no opportunity to see her, and if she is still opposed to the match, this evening is our last chance to persuade her to alter her mind. The question of Buonaparte's appointment is the first item on the *Comité*'s agenda for tomorrow morning.'

'Then I am happy to be able to tell you,' smiled Roger, 'that the matter is settled; and favourably to our designs. Or all but settled.'

'All but?' repeated Barras, with a sharp lift of his eyebrows.

'Yes. As I told you two days ago, she had an appointment to consult Le Normand. Her visit to the sibyl convinced her that by accepting Buonaparte she would ensure both herself and her children a brilliant future. On their account even more than her own she is now anxious to make the match; but one thing still deters her from committing herself. She is being blackmailed.'

'On account of what?'

'An episode in her past which she refused to disclose. Naturally, once married and with funds at her disposal, she fears that the screw will be turned upon her. That would be bad enough, but should there come a point at which she could no longer pay, the blackmailer might make the matter public.'

Barras shrugged. 'Surely she is making a mountain out of a molehill. Everyone, including Buonaparte, knows well enough that the life she has led since her husband's death has been far from irreproachable.'

'I agree; and so can only suppose that the episode was of a somewhat different nature from a clandestine amour the disclosure of which might do no more than tarnish her reputation.'

'I wonder, then, what the devil it could have been.'

'As far as we are concerned the particulars of it are, surely, quite irrelevant. What does concern us is her fear that, should it be made public subsequent to her marriage, Buonaparte would suffer so greatly in his *amour propre*, that in one of his well-known furies he might do her a damage. Hence her refusal to accept him, unless this menace to her peace of mind can first be removed.'

'If she will provide us with a lead to the blackmailer, I can put a discreet man in the police on to it,' Barras said with a frown. 'But the devil of it is that we now have so little time.'

'I already have the lead,' Roger replied quietly. 'And tonight should be time enough in which to do the job, providing you will give me your assistance.'

'Thank God for that! After first raising my hopes, you had me badly worried. What help do you want from me?'

'The blackmailer is a woman named Madame Rémy. As she lives down by the docks she can be of no social consequence; so her disappearance will cause little comment. Give me an order for a squad of troops, so that I may arrest her, and another for her immediate deportation to Cayenne.'

Barras nodded. 'You are right. That is the way to deal with this. Few people survive the fevers there for more than a few months; and even if she did succeed in escaping, with the order still in force against her, she would never again dare to show her face in France.'

Drawing two sheets of paper towards him he quickly wrote out the transportation order, and another empowering Roger to collect a squad of men for duty from the palace guard. As he pushed them across the table, Roger said:

'There is another matter. Joseph Fouché is involved in this. You will recall that Madame de Beauharnais has several times begged you to give him some post?'

'And I refused her!' cut in Barras with a frown.

'So you told me. But you then knew nothing of this affair. In it he has been acting as a go-between. With his usual cleverness when fishing in troubled waters, he hoped first to land himself a post, then use it to obtain a deportation order against the blackmailer.'

The corners of Barras's mouth turned down in a sneer. 'Why not say that, with his usual treachery, he hoped first to land himself a post, then use it to betray this Madame Rémy whose employment of him had enabled him to obtain it?'

Roger shrugged. 'The one statement is as true as the other; and the last thing I would undertake is to defend Fouché's morality. I was thinking of the issue simply as Madame de Beauharnais undoubtedly did when she made her plea for him to you. The question is, what can you do for him?'

'Do for him? Nothing! Now that you have stepped into his shoes for the eliminating of the blackmailer, why should I do anything?'

'Because without his help our hands would still be tied. It was he who gave me Madame Rémy's name, and her address. In return I promised to do my best to persuade you to find him a place—preferably in the Police.'

'In the Police! God forbid! I would be out of my wits did I give such a knave the chance to spy upon us and learn all our secrets.'

'Very well then; something in the Customs, or, perhaps, Education. He was once a teacher.'

'Nay, I'll not do it!' Barras shook his head. 'The Directory is already unpopular enough, for a score of reasons.

During the Terror Fouché made himself one of the worst hated men in France. To give him a post of any importance would arouse howls of protest in both Chambers.'

'Then let it be some minor position to which no one can take any great exception: chief of one of the Supply Depots, or a Prison. At the moment he is keeping pigs for a living; so any place where he could earn a reasonable income at a desk would be counted by him a blessing.'

'No! Let him continue to keep pigs. I'll do nothing for him!'

'I think in refusing you make a great mistake,' Roger said seriously. 'The man is near desperate; so might prove a danger to us.'

'In what way? With the actual blackmailer you now have the means to deal. Fouché has acted only as a go-between.'

'Even so, that has enabled him to learn *La Belle Créole*'s secret. Admittedly he could bring no proof of her lapse, whatever it may have been; but there is nought to stop him from accusing her of it. How he gets his information these days, I've no idea; but somehow he had picked up the rumour that she is contemplating marriage with Buonaparte. Unless you provide him with something to keep his mouth shut, there is always the risk that out of spite he will go to the General. His word alone, if the story he tells is sufficiently plausible, might be enough to put Buonaparte off the match; then we'd have had all our trouble for nothing.'

'I see, I see,' Barras murmured, half closing his eyes. 'You are right. In that way he might still upset our plans at the last moment; and the one thing we cannot afford to risk is the marriage falling through after Buonaparte has been appointed to the command of the Army of Italy. Very well then.'

Taking another sheet of headed paper he wrote several lines upon it, signed it, sanded it, put it in an envelope, sealed it, then gave it to Roger with the remark:

'There! That should serve to keep his mouth shut. Take it to him with my compliments. When you have dealt with the other matter I should be glad if you would return here, however late the hour may be. I must know that everything has been settled satisfactorily before the *Comité* meets to-morrow morning.'

Roger took the jewelled watch from his fob and glanced at it. 'The time is now ten minutes past seven. I see no reason, if the woman is at home, why this business should take me more than two hours. Should it do so you will know that I am having to wait at her dwelling for her; but at latest I should be back by midnight.'

Down in the great entrance hall he presented his order for a squad of men to the Lieutenant on duty, who from the reserve guard furnished him with a Corporal and three guardsmen. A hired coach was called up and they all got into it, then Roger gave the coachman Fouché's address, as he had decided to see him first before making the much longer journey to the other side of the river.

They were hardly out of the Palace courtyard before it became apparent that the Corporal, a middle-aged man with a walrus moustache, who said his name was Peltier, was both garrulous and disgruntled. Now that free speech could again be indulged in without fear of prosecution, everyone aired their criticism of the Government, but he seemed particularly bitter about the turn things had taken.

He was, he declared, a 'patriot', and had deserved far better of his country than it had done for him. Had he not been one of those who had led the attack on the Bastille on the never to be forgotten 14th of July, and fought with the brutal Swiss Guards in the gardens of the Tuileries on the equally glorious day when the Tyrant and his Austrian Whore had been made prisoners by the People; yet here he was still a Corporal. And the country had gone from bad to worse. He and men like him had shed their blood to rid it of the aristos who for centuries had battened on its life-blood. For a while it had looked as if true liberty had dawned at last; but the Revolution was being betrayed by self-seekers and speculators. They were letting the aristos come back, and worse, imitating them. What was needed was another Marat to rouse the People to their danger, and another Santerre to lead the men of the Faubourgs against the reactionaries.

Far from being impressed, Roger listened to this tirade

with some impatience. He thought it unlikely that the man had been at the taking of the Bastille, and doubted if he had ever shot at anyone capable of returning his fire. He was a typical *ex-sans-culotte,* for whom 'liberty' meant the right to rob, rape and murder his betters without fear of reprisal, and who had almost certainly got himself into the Convention Guard in order to escape being called up and sent on active service.

As they had not far to go the drive was soon over. Pulling up the coach at the entrance to the cul-de-sac in which Fouché lived, Roger got out, walked along to his house and knocked on the door. It was opened by Fouché himself. With a word of greeting Roger handed him the missive from Barras, and said:

'I bring this with Barras's compliments. He agreed that you merit attention and should be given a new field, even if a small one, for your talents. 'Twill at least enable you to say good-bye to your pigs.' Then, having no love for Fouché, he bid him an abrupt good night, turned on his heel and walked back towards the coach.

He was only half way to it when he heard a shout. Glancing over his shoulder, he saw that Fouché was running after him; so he called out:

'What is it? What's the matter?'

'The matter!' screamed Fouché waving the document that Barras had sent him. 'Why this? This infernal order! How dare you trick me in this fashion.'

'I've played no trick upon you,' Roger exclaimed in surprise.

Stamping with rage Fouché shook the offending document in his face. 'You must have known what was in this! You must have! Your own words as you gave it me condemn you. " 'Twill enable you to say good-bye to your pigs." That is what you said. And that Barras "agreed that I should be given a new field". A new field indeed! *Oh, Mort Dieu, Mort Dieu!* May you both be damned for ever!'

Roger stared at him uncomprehendingly, and muttered: 'I have not the faintest idea what you are talking about.'

'My poor wife! My little daughter!' Fouché exclaimed with a sob. 'As though things were not bad enough with us already. And now this!' Suddenly he burst into tears.

It was at that moment that a footfall behind Roger caused him to turn. To his annoyance he saw that Corporal Peltier had left the coach and was lumbering towards them.

'Get back to the coach,' he said sharply. 'This is no business of yours.' But the garrulous Corporal came to a halt, stood his ground, and declared truculently:

'Oh yes it is! That's Citizen Fouché standin' there. I thought I recognised 'is voice when I 'eard 'im 'olla. 'E's one o' the best, an' an ole frien' o' mine. What's goin' on 'ere? What 'ave yer done to 'im?'

'I had to bring him some bad news,' snapped Roger. 'Now, begone with you.'

Fouché had meanwhile regained control of himself, and as he dabbed at his eyes with a handkerchief, the Corporal, ignoring Roger's order, addressed him.

'Remember me, Citizen Fouché? Name of Jacques Peltier. I were in Lyons with yer. What time we 'ad there eh? Remember 'ow we tied the Bible ter the donkey's tail an' fed 'im on 'oly wafers; then made them nuns dance the Carmagnol? What a night we 'ad of it too wi' some 'o them novices. Those were the days. No one couldn't push a patriot arahnd then. You must remember me, Jacques Peltier.'

'Yes,' snuffled Fouché. 'Yes, Citizen Peltier, I remember you. But we are discussing a private matter; so be pleased to leave us.'

'Oh, orlright then,' the Corporal shrugged. 'Only I don't like ter see an ole frien' pushed arahnd; an' there a limit ter wot we should stand from these dandified new bosses they give us.'

The last remark was clearly directed at Roger, who swung round on him and said in the icy tone that he knew so well how to use on occasions: 'Do you not keep a civil tongue in your head, I'll report you to Citizen Director Barras and have your uniform stripped from your back. Now; leave us this instant!'

Cowed by the voice of authority, the man shuffled off, still muttering to himself. Turning back to Fouché, Roger said: 'I have little time to waste, but if you have any complaint to make we have better go inside. I've no mind to stand here wrangling within earshot of that big oaf and the other men.'

Without a word Fouché stalked back to the house and through into its living room. Roger followed and, as they came to a halt on the other side of the table, asked:

'Now! What is it you are making such a fuss about?'

'How can you have the face to ask, when you must know,' Fouché retorted angrily.

'I tell you I do not!'

'Then read that!' As Fouché spoke he flung the document down on the table.

Picking it up, Roger scanned it quickly. It was on official paper and read:

ORDER OF BANISHMENT

To the Citizen Joseph Fouché.

On receipt of this the citizen above named will leave Paris within twelve hours. He is forthwith forbidden to take up his residence at any place within twenty leagues of the Capital, or to return to it on any pretext without a permission endorsed by the undersigned.

He is also forbidden for reasons of State to communicate in any way with the Citoyenne Josephine de Beauharnais, the Citizen General Buonaparte, or the Citoyenne Rémy.

Should he disobey either of the above injunctions he will make himself liable to transportation for life.

Paul Barras,
For the Directory.

Suddenly Roger burst out laughing. It struck him as incredibly funny that Fouché, the ace of tricksters, should have been tricked himself. Even if he had thought of spiking Fouché's guns in this way he could not decently have done so; but Barras, being committed by no promise, had awarded the rogue his just deserts.

'Well, I'll be damned,' he exclaimed, still bubbling with

mirth. 'I asked Barras to give you something that would keep you out of mischief, and he could hardly have done so better.'

'You did intend to ruin me, then!' Fouché cried, frothing at the mouth with rage.

'No, no. I kept to my word. I asked him first for a post in the Police for you; then for one in some other department. He would not hear of the first; but at length, with reluctance as I thought, gave me this.'

'If that is true, you can still save me. Return to him and get the order withdrawn.'

'Nay. Barras is not a man who goes back on his decisions.'

'He will if you plead for me. I insist that you do! You owe it to me! You promised to get me a post in the Administration, even if it had to be a minor one.'

'I did nothing of the kind!' Roger was now angry too. 'I said only that I would do my best for you. Barras decided on this step without my knowledge; and I tell you frankly that I find his way of dealing with the matter highly suitable. You had it in your power to wreck Madame de Beauharnais's life and that of her two children. You used that power without the least scruple in an endeavour to forward your own interests. Had you succeeded in your design you then meant to turn upon Madame Rémy, who had employed you as her agent, and have her transported to Cayenne. That you have been caught in your own toils is poetic justice. Aye, and had I been in Barras's place it would not be banishment that I would have meted out to you, but transportation.'

'Now you stand revealed in your true colours,' Fouché cried, again tembling with fury. 'After what you have said how could anyone believe that you had no hand in this?'

'Believe what you like! I give not a rap,' declared Roger roundly. 'I have had to use you for my own purposes and am now delighted to be shot of you; for I rate you the vilest rogue unhung.'

'That comes well from a cheat and liar like yourself,' Fouché sneered. 'You seem to have forgotten, too, that we are partners in another matter. That is why you would like to see me transported, is it not; so that when the time comes you could keep the whole of the great prize to yourself? But try to cheat me over the little Capet and I'll see to it that you meet a worse fate than being sent to Cayenne.'

'The little Capet!' Roger gave an angry laugh. 'Why, 'tis an age since I even gave the boy a thought. You need count no more on making your fortune out of him. He is dead.'

'Dead!' gasped Fouché. 'You cannot mean that! You are lying again.'

'He is dead, I tell you; and has been so well above a year. It was in that I used you; buying your silence for a worthless partnership that you proposed yourself.'

'Then . . . then I have kept your true identity secret all these months for nothing?'

'A most fitting reward for your double-dealing with your colleagues and your treachery to your country.'

Red blotches stood out on the white mask of Fouché's face. His pale eyes were starting from his skull-like head, and he looked as if he were about to have a fit. But, when he spoke again, his voice held a quieter, sinister note.

'Now you have been too clever. Yes, too clever, *Mister* Brook. For this cheap triumph over me you have thrown away your armour. Since I can no longer hope to gain anything by keeping your secret why should I continue to do so? Before morning I will have you in jail for what you are. You accursed English spy!'

Roger shrugged contemptuously. 'Time was when you might have done so, had you played your cards with that in mind. But to denounce me so belatedly could profit you nothing. You have given me the time I needed to re-establish myself and dovetail the pieces of my story in the minds of those who would judge between us. My upbringing in England, my coming to Brittany as a youth, my secretaryship to M. de Rochambeau and duel with M. de Caylus, my return to Paris as a journalist for certain English newssheets, my life as a member of the Paris Commune, and my having become a prisoner of the English after Thermidor: all these things are now strung together as a whole, and so many people could vouch for various parts of the story that all would believe the whole of it. You might as well accuse Barras or Buonaparte; for no one would believe you. Had you even a single witness to support you, matters would be different. But you have not. It would be your word against mine. Our respective situations being as they are, ask yourself whose would be taken?'

In the face of Roger's cynical assurance, Fouché wilted visibly. Striking his forehead, he gave a bitter cry. 'Oh that I had that one witness; or my old power back, even for a single hour!'

'Had you used it less evilly you might never have lost it,' Roger retorted swiftly. Then pointing at the Order of Banishment, which still lay on the table, he gave a final turn to the screw before turning to leave the room.

'Try denouncing me if you will. You'll find it will be regarded as the pathetic effort of a man half crazed, endeavouring to revenge himself upon me because I brought him that.'

As he stepped through the doorway, Fouché, goaded beyond endurance, seized an empty bottle on the side table by its neck, swung it aloft and came at him from behind.

But Roger knew his man too well not to have kept a wary eye out for a sudden resort to violence. Swinging round, he sprang back into the hall, whipped out the slender blade from a tall sword-cane that he was carrying, jerked back his elbow, and levelled the point at Fouché's heart.

'Stand back!' Roger's voice was low but menacing. 'Drop that bottle or I'll run you through with less compunction than I'd stick one of your pigs.'

With a curse, Fouché dropped the bottle. Then, almost weeping with rage, he cried: 'To hell with you! I'll get the better of you yet.'

Lowering his blade Roger turned away, but found a parting shot over his shoulder. 'You are welcome to attempt it. But you had best be gone from here by tomorrow morning. I mean to send the police to see that you have obeyed Barras's order.'

Roger's anger had now cooled. He had, all through, had the best of the encounter. No qualms of conscience troubled him about having brought Fouché an Order of Banishment instead of the expected post. Neither did he blame Barras for having in this manner deprived Fouché of the power to menace their plans concerning the marriage of Buonaparte and Josephine. On the contrary, he was thoroughly pleased with himself for the way in which he had handled the situation.

His feeling would have been very different had he had the least inkling of the evil trick that Fate was about to play him, and the desperate straits in which he would find himself within a bare half hour.

27

The Cat Gets Out of the Bag

A quarter of an hour's drive brought the coach to the far end of the Quai de la Grève where, between the two bridges, a row of decrepit-looking buildings backed on to the river. Even in daylight it was an unsavoury part of the city, as it was adjacent both to the wharfs and to the Faubourg St. Antoine, a great area of slums, from which the most sanguinary mobs had emerged to loot and kill at every crisis during the Revolution. Now, in the late evening, ill-lit and evil smelling, its dark and crooked ways seemed to conceal a menace round every corner.

But Roger was used to taking care of himself, and his only worry at the moment was that he might not find Madame Rémy at home. As the coach rumbled, now at a walk, over the cobbles he peered from its windows, till, by the light of a lantern-lit doorway from behind which there came the muffled sounds of raucous singing, he located the drinking den of which Fouché had spoken.

Halting the coach he got out, told Corporal Peltier and his men that in no circumstance were they to leave it until he called to them, then faced about to take stock of Madame Rémy's dwelling. It was quite a tall building but had only two stories. In the upper one there was a single unusually large window, presumably put in by its late tenant, the artist, to give a good north light. Curtains were drawn across it, but through them came a dull glow. Roger noted it with much satisfaction, as an indication that Madame Rémy was probably at home. Walking forward, he rapped sharply on the door of the place with the butt end of his sword-cane.

In reply to his knocking there came the clock-clack of footsteps on bare boards, then the door was opened by a woman. As the only particulars of the blackmailer Roger had received were, that she was the sister of a mulatto who had been brought up as a slave in the household of Josephine's father, he had subconsciously expected to find her middle-aged and running to fat, as is the case with nearly all ageing females having negro blood. But the light, although dim, was sufficient for him to see that the woman who had answered the door was tall, shapely and much younger than he expected; so with a shade of doubt in his voice, he asked:

'Are you the Citoyenne Rémy?'

'Yes,' she replied in a cheerful voice that implied a smile. 'You're lucky to find me alone. But come in and we'll have a glass of wine. Then you can tell me who gave you my address.'

It was clearly the invitation of a harlot to a stranger, whom she assumed had been sent to her by one of her regulars. With a grim little smile, at the thought that she had no idea of the surprise in store for her, Roger followed her inside and took quick stock of the main room of the dwelling, which had been hidden from the street door by a hanging curtain of coarse material.

Two thirds of the place had been gutted to form a lofty studio, and it now had two storeys only at its far end. There, a steep, narrow stairway, flush with the partition wall, ran up to a four-foot square landing giving access to a single door, which was presumably that of a bedroom overlooking the river. But, apparently, Madame Rémy did not usually conduct her business up there; as, at one side of the studio before a small fire of sea-coal stood a broad couch covered with rugs and cushions. Near it was a table on which two candles, stuck in the necks of empty bottles, were burning. Otherwise, apart from a wicker chair, a battered oak chest, and a cracked mirror above the fire-place, the big apartment was bare of furniture.

Swaying her hips seductively, the woman walked in front of Roger towards the couch. As she did so she must have caught a glimpse of him in the mirror, for she said in a honeyed Créole voice:

'Down in these parts it isn't often that one sees a fine gentleman like you. But I promise you won't repent your visit. A West Indian girl can show most Frenchmen a few things they don't know; and perhaps you are the very one I have been waiting for to set me up in a better place.'

As she finished speaking she turned about and dropped him a curtsy. It was when rising from it with a smile that she got her surprise; but not the one that Roger had intended. He got one too. He found himself face to face with Lucette.

Their meeting in Paris was so totally unexpected that neither had recognised the voice of the other, and it was not until they had come into the light of the candles that they had had the chance to discern one another's features. But now it was plain from the expressions on the faces of them both that neither had the least doubt about the other's identity.

'You!' Lucette breathed the word with hatred and alarm. Next second her right hand darted downward through a placket hole in her skirt. In the same movement she stooped. As she came upright her hand emerged grasping an eight-inch long stiletto that she had drawn from the top of her stocking. Her dark eye flashing, she whirled it on high and came at Roger like a tigress.

Without moving from where he stood he thrust up the thick malacca handle of his sword-cane, and parried the slash she made at his neck. Then he hit her hard beneath the chin. With a moan she went down backwards on the couch. Throwing aside his cane, he sprang upon her, seized her wrist and gave it a violent wrench. She uttered a cry of pain. Her fingers relaxed their grip upon the knife, and it fell with a tinkle on to the bare boards. Releasing her he picked it up and stuck it in the top of his jack-boot. Then he dusted his hands together, and said:

'I owed you that. Since you remember me, you may also remember having knocked me down in the cabin of the *Circe* when I had hardly enough strength in my legs to stand up without assistance.'

'Remember you!' she panted, struggling into a sitting position. 'Is it likely that I could ever forget you, after the ill you've done me. You are my jinx! Before we met I lived a carefree life. Since, everything has gone wrong. It was you who killed de Senlac. It was you who caused the break up of the fraternity over which I reigned as Queen. I decided to settle down and keep a good, respectable house in St. Pierre. You came there and had me flung into prison.'

'You would have had a hanging, had I not had to take flight the day after I had you arrested,' Roger put in quickly.

Her face became clouded with a puzzled frown. 'What mean you by "take flight"? You were the Governor there, and they told me you had been recalled to England.'

'So I told my staff, but it was not the fact.' Roger's brain had been working overtime for the last few minutes. He thought it unlikely that Lucette could do him any serious harm, but that it would nevertheless be prudent to give her some story to account for his presence in Paris. Some adaptation of his stock box and cox autobiography was obviously the most plausible line; so, with a not very pleasant little laugh, he went on:

'From the fluency with which I speak French you must have realised that I am half a Frenchman, and although I was brought up in England I am wholly French at heart. I have long served the Republic secretly, and had hoped to strike a great blow for it by enabling Victor Hugues to retake Martinique. But he sent me warning that our plot was on the verge of discovery. I got away while I could, and from England employed a smuggler to run me across to France. What happened to you after I left?'

'With you no longer there, they could bring no evidence of piracy against me,' she replied morosely, 'but your denunciation caused Colonel Penruddock to treat me most scurvily. He had me charged with keeping a disorderly house and I was sentenced to three months' imprisonment. When I came out I found myself ruined. The pretty mulatto wenches for whom I had paid high prices had vanished; the house slaves had looted my property and run away. Only the house itself was left, and that stripped from cellar to rafters.'

'So, for a change, you have learnt what it feels like to be despoiled.'

Her eyes gleamed hatred at him. 'That I owe to you! And the wretched state to which I am now reduced. By the sale of the house I raised just enough money to get me to France. I had a project here which I have always kept for an emergency; believing that were I ever in need I could count on it to secure me a regular pension. But so far it has not matured. Meanwhile, I have been forced to become a wharf-hands' whore, and either starve or submit to the brutalities of any drunken swine who has a fancy to put me through my paces.'

Roger nodded. 'Touching this project of yours. It is upon that I have come to see you.'

'What!' she cried, springing to her feet. 'I thought your visit a chance one: that you had been sent here by one of the *maquereaux* who find men for me and take a commission on my earnings. Do you mean that you are come to play the jinx again, and rob me of my last chance to enjoy an old age in some comfort. That I must have! I must; for I am no longer young!'

She had been sitting with her back to the candles, but had turned as she sprang up, and her face, now fully lit by them, confirmed her words. From the fact that Josephine was her foster sister, Roger knew that both of them must be well over thirty. The former had kept her looks remarkably well; so had Lucette up till six months ago, but since then her imprisonment and the life she was now leading had caused a swift deterioration to set in. The muscles of her cheeks had gone slack, her complexion had become slightly raddled, there were great hollows under her fine eyes, and the outer corner of the left one was still a little discoloured from a bruise where one of her transitory lovers must have blackened it for her.

Knowing her past, Roger felt no compassion for her, and replied tersely: 'Your future means nought to me. I am now an official of the French Government, and have been sent to enquire into your doings. You have been endeavouring to blackmail Madame de Beauharnais, have you not?'

Seeing her hesitate, he added: 'Come! I have no time to

waste; and I have men outside awaiting my orders. If you refuse to answer my questions I will have them take you off to prison.'

'You put a hard interpretation on it,' she muttered sullenly. 'Marie-Rose Josephine is my foster sister. She owes me much; for it was through being of service to her that I was thrown out of her father's house, and became what I am.'

Roger gave a cynical little laugh. 'You seem to have forgotten that you told me the whole story yourself, and that there is another side to it. Had it not been for your example in taking a lover she might not have been incited to go to such lengths with William de Kay. But, that apart, it was you who planned and induced her to go through this form of marriage which has since proved the curse of her life; so she can owe you nothing but the bitterest reproaches.'

'I intended it only for her happiness. She should remember that, and that in girlhood we were devoted friends. She is rich, and could well afford to give me the small pension which is all I meant to ask.'

'She might have, had that been all, and you had gone to ask it of her yourself. But it was not. You meant to bleed her white. For that, to conceal your identity in case she went to the police, you had to have an intermediary, and for the purpose have been using Citizen Fouché.'

Fear showed in Lucette's eyes, as she said in a low voice: 'So you know about that?'

'There are now only a few minor details that I do not know about this matter: such as why you choose him for your agent.'

'It was owing to a man I met soon after landing at Nantes. He told me that Citizen Fouché was a skilful *homme d'affaires*, and not above sharing any profit to be obtained from a valuable piece of information. My friend gave me a letter of introduction to him.'

'I see. Let us proceed to business, then. Be good enough to hand over Madame de Beauharnais's diary.'

'I . . . I have not got it.'

'That is a lie. You are much too clever to have passed it on to Fouché. Had you done so, you know well enough, he would have had no further truck with you.'

'I tell you I have not got it.'

'Then that is most unfortunate for you.' Roger drew from his pocket the Order of Transportation, opened it, held it to the light, and told her to read it. Then he said:

'When I came here I had no idea that you were Madame Rémy. But I was prepared to make a bargain with her, and I will do so with you. Give me the diary, and agree to leave Paris for good tomorrow morning, and I will have this order suspended. It will be marked "to be executed only in the event of the person named being found to have returned to the Capital". Should you refuse, I will call in my men to arrest you, and I shall see to it myself that you start on your journey to Cayenne tomorrow.'

'No!' she exclaimed with a violent shake of the head. 'I'll not give it up. Send me to Cayenne if you will. I am no flabby European to take a fever and die of it. For once I'd have something for which to thank my black blood. I'll be little worse off there than I am here, and I'm not yet so ill favoured that I could not seduce one of the guards into aiding my escape.'

At her outburst Roger's confidence in his prospects of success suddenly slumped to near zero. It had not occurred to him that for a mulatto prostitute transportation threatened few of the terrors it would have held for an ordinary French woman. All he could do now was to play his subsidiary card; so he said:

'I think you underrate the horrors that you will have to face. I am told that conditions in the convict ships are appalling, and that many people die upon the voyage. Be advised by me and take the easier way. Your refusal, too, may have been influenced by lack of money. If so, I will give you a hundred *louis*; and that will see you back to the West Indies in comfort.'

Again she stubbornly shook her head. 'No. I know enough of Voodoo to survive the voyage, and within a month of reaching Cayenne I will have escaped. Then I will join another fraternity of searovers. The diary is safe enough where it is. Later I will return and collect it. Having kept it so long, I'll not give it up. It is my life-line to a secure old age.'

Roger had already thought of threatening her with prison, but whatever charge was trumped up against her she could not be kept there indefinitely. Then, as he sought desperately in his mind for a way to get the better of her, the expression 'life-line' that she had used gave him a sudden inspiration. Since she was who she was, he still had a forgotten ace up his sleeve.

Refolding the transportation order, he said quietly: 'You seem to have overlooked one thing. Piracy is just as much a crime punishable by death in France as it is in England. Unless you produce that diary, I will charge you with it; then the thing you count your life-line will become the rope that works the blade of the guillotine.'

At that her jaw fell; then she screamed: 'You fiend! You devil!' and came at him with hands rigid like claws in an attempt to tear his eyes out. Thrusting her off, he gave her a swift jab in the stomach, which sent her reeling and gasping for breath back again on to the couch.

Standing over her Roger said firmly: 'Now! Do I send you to your death or will you give me the diary?'

Still whimpering, the fight at last gone out of her, she pulled herself to her feet, and slouched across to a door at the far end of the studio under the steep stairway. Roger followed her and, as she opened it, could just make out by the faint light that beyond it there lay a kitchen. Going inside she fished about for a moment in its near darkness, and emerged holding a heavy meat chopper.

Alert to the possibility that she meant to attack him with it, Roger watched her warily. But without a glance at him she went up the twenty or more narrow stairs to the small landing; then, using the blunt back of the heavy chopper, she began to hammer with it at the end of one of the many short cross beams that supported the roof of the studio. After half a dozen blows the nails that held the end of the beam to a large rafter were loosened enough for her to pull it down. It was hollow, and thrusting her hand into the cavity she drew out a small leather-bound book. Then she came down the stairs and handed it to him.

'Thank you,' he said. 'Allow me to congratulate you on having thought of such a good hiding place. We might have hunted the house for a month without coming upon it. Indeed, I doubt if we would have found it short of pulling the whole building to pieces.'

With a shrug, she walked past him, threw the chopper on to the table, and sat down again on the couch. Meanwhile, he flicked over the leaves of the little book to make quite certain that it was the thing that he had gone to so much trouble to obtain. It was a thick book and all but the last dozen of its pages were covered with a round childish scrawl. Soon he came upon the name William repeated three times on the same page, then on a passage that made his raise his eyebrows. It was, he thought, remarkable how indiscreet young girls could be during the first upsurge of physical passion, in confinding their feelings and experiences to paper. Little wonder Madame de Beauharnais could not face the thought of her diary falling into the hands of an unscrupulous publisher. There was no law to prevent the printing of such material, however personal; and there were still innumerable books on sale describing, without the least truth, obscenities of the most revolting kind said to have been practised by Marie Antoinette, which had been published while she was a Queen living in splendour at Versailles.

Slipping the book into his pocket, he walked over to Lucette, and said: 'Now, about yourself. If you will tell me where you wish to go when you leave Paris tomorrow morning, I will do my best to aid you, and will provide the money for your journey.'

'I think I had best return to the Indies,' she murmured despondently. 'With food to be had for the asking and the warmth of the sunshine, life is at least easier there.'

'Very well. I will endeavour to secure you a passage in a blockade runner.'

As he spoke, there came an urgent knocking on the front door.

Muttering a filthy oath, she pulled herself to her feet. 'I expect that is a customer. I must open to him, but will say that I am engaged.'

Roger watched her cross the room, pull aside the coarse curtain and unlatch the door. It was immediately thrust wide. With a cry of surprise, she took a pace back. Slamming the door to behind him, Fouché stepped after her into the room.

Snatching up his sword-cane Roger called out to him: 'So you followed me! What do you want here?'

Thrusting his way past Lucette, Fouché advanced to the table, and halted. Glaring across at Roger, he panted: 'I had hoped that you might still have to collect the order of transportation you spoke of from Barras, before threatening to execute it. Even had I had the luck to pick up a coach I might have managed to get here a few minutes before you.'

'Then you have had your half-hour's walk for nothing,' said Roger quietly. 'I already had the order; but it will not now be needed.'

Fouché's pale eyes switched from Roger's waist-line to Lucette's neck and he said sharply to her: 'Then you have told him where the diary is?'

She gave a sullen nod. 'He has it. We argued over it for some time, but I surrendered it to him five minutes since.'

'You fool! You black, besotted bitch!' he snarled. 'Did you not have the sense to realise that had you kept it hidden it might yet have meant big money for us both?'

'For you perhaps, but not for me!' she cried with sudden defiance. 'He has the power to send me to the guillotine, and would have done so had I held out against him. I know this man! He is my enemy; my jinx! Had I not bought my life with the book he would have delighted in bringing about my death.'

'You know him?'

Roger felt a sudden awful sinking in the pit of his stomach, but there was nothing he could do to stop Lucette shouting back:

'Know him; do I not! He says now that he is a Frenchman, but I find that hard to credit seeing how first we met. Everyone then believed him to be an English milor. He had an English wife, English friends and was upon an English ship. In Martinique, too, everyone spoke of him as *Son Excellence* Mister Brook. But I care not what he is. I know only that he would gladly see me dead.'

'So!' Fouché hardly breathed the word. Then, swinging round on Roger, his cry of triumph rang to the rafters. 'A witness! The one witness I needed to support my oath! *Mort Dieu;* you are now no better than carrion in the executioner's cart!'

Left with no time to think or plan for such an emergency, and made desperate by the terrifying turn events had taken, Roger whipped out his sword-cane. Across the table he made a furious lunge at Fouché; but his enemy sprang back, pivoted on his heels and dashed for the door. Swerving sideways Roger jumped over the couch, but Lucette threw herself in his way. Before he could get past her Fouché had wrenched the door open and was bellowing into the darkness:

'Corporal Peltier! Bring your men! Citizens! Help! Quick! Come to my aid!'

Still hoping to transfix Fouché with one well directed thrust which would silence him instantly and for ever, Roger leapt after him. Fouché was standing in the doorway. He was still yelling for help, but from fear of another attack had his head half-turned towards the room. Roger's lunge was aimed high to take him through the throat. Fouché jerked his head back so sharply that it hit the open door a resounding crack. The movement saved him. The flashing point missed his Adam's apple by the faction of an inch, then buried itself in the wooden door jamb. The thrust had been delivered with tremendous force. Under the impact the thin blade snapped. Roger was left holding only the handle and ten inches of the steel. Next moment Peltier and his three men blocked the doorway and came pushing past Fouché into the studio.

Giving way before them, Roger darted back behind the table. He was at his wit's end for a sound course to pursue, and could think of nothing but an attempt to exert his authority. If he could succeed in that it might save him for the moment. He would then at least have a chance of destroying the all-important diary, and perhaps be able to escape from Paris before on a joint information laid by Fouché and Lucette a warrant was issued for his arrest. Pulling the order for Lucette's transportation from his pocket, he waved it in the faces of the advancing soldiers and cried:

'Touch me if you dare! I am the agent of Citizen Director Barras. Here is my warrant. Your own officer charged you to obey my orders. They are that you arrest Citizen Fouché and this woman.'

Fouché's shouts had attracted several people. As they came running up behind the soldiers he slammed and bolted the door to keep them out. Turning, he hurried back into the centre of the room. His friend the Corporal gave him an anxious look, and asked eagerly:

'What's bin 'appenin', Citizen? I saw 'im attack yer! 'E'd no right ter do that, even if 'e is a police agent. What d'yer want us ter do?'

'Ignore his orders and accept mine,' replied Fouché promptly, 'What I have long believed the Citoyenne Rémy here has now confirmed. He is an English spy.'

'*Sacré bleu!*' exclaimed the Corporal. 'An English spy! An' 'e's an aristo ter boot, or my name's not Jacques Peltier. 'E 'as both the looks an' the smell o' one.'

'You have been told a lie,' Roger cut in sharply. 'I am neither. This absurd charge is based upon my having been abroad on a secret mission which occupied me for many months after 9th Thermidor. Before that I was a member of the Paris Commune. As a Citizen Commissioner from its founding there are thousands of people in Paris who can vouch for my identity and my patriotism.'

'That's true, that is,' nodded a tall guardsman with ginger hair. 'I knew 'im by sight before that too, when I were a pot-man in the Jacobin Club. I 'eard 'im speak there against our going to war over the Spanish Treaty.'

'Yes,' supplemented one of the others, a thick-set man with a swarthy face. 'I thought I recognised him, and I do now.'

'Don't be taken in by that,' snapped Fouché. 'He has acted as one of Pitt's agents from the beginning. For years past he has consistently betrayed us. He is the son of an English Admiral and his name is Brook.'

'You lie!' retorted Roger. 'This is a plot by which you are attempting to evade arrest.'

'It is the truth, as the Citoyenne Rémy can confirm.'

'I do!' shrilled Lucette, turning to the soldiers. 'He is an English milor. I was for a week with him last year in an English ship.'

'You are mistaken,' said Roger firmly. 'I have a cousin named Robert MacElfic who much resembles me. It was him you must have met.'

She gave a harsh laugh. 'That lie will not serve you. Citizen Fouché is right. You are an Englishman and a spy. I will swear to that with my dying breath.'

'You see!' added Fouché triumphantly. 'He admits to having English relatives. He admits, too, to having been abroad at the time the Citoyenne Rémy says she met him. What more do you require?'

'That's enough for me,' growled Peltier, glancing round at the three guardsmen. 'Well men; what der yer say?'

The ginger-haired one looked doubtful, but the swarthy man said: 'I'd sooner take Citizen Fouché's word than his;' and the third soldier nodded his agreement.

As Roger took in the expressions of suspicion, anger and hatred on the faces of the five people who formed a semicircle round him, he knew that his situation was desperate. If he once let them haul him off to a police office nothing could then prevent a full enquiry into his past. He had spared no pains to get accepted a history of himself as watertight as he could make it; but there were some small holes in it, such as his statement that he had been born in Strassburg, which could never be covered up.

He had had, too, as the only means of throwing discredit on Lucette's identification of him, to say that it was his cousin, Robert MacElfic, whom she had met. She knew that for a lie, and it would not be difficult for French authorities to check a statement by her that from January to August a Mr. Roger Brook had been Governor of Martinique. Should he once be caught out on even a few minor matters, under skilful interrogation the whole false edifice he had built up would gradually be torn to pieces. Yet, although he knew that his life depended on it, he could think of no way out of the impasse with which he was faced, except to shout at the soldiers again:

'This is a plot, I tell you! This man and woman are in league together. Both are under sentence, one to banishment and the other to transportation. Don't be fooled by their lies, or you will rue it. I order you to arrest them!'

'Nay!' cied Fouché. 'It is him you must arrest; or never again will you be able to call yourselves true patriots.'

'Come lads!' Peltier took a step forward. 'Let's take 'im ter the police office. They'll 'ave the truth ahrt of 'im, an' by me old mother's grave I vow Citizen Fouché 'as the rights of it.'

'Stop!' shouted Roger. 'I represent the law. 'Twill be jail for any one of you who lays a hand upon me.'

Seeing that the men still hesitated, Lucette began to scream abuse at them. 'Go on, you cowards! You're four to one! What are you afraid of? Take him to the police and see what I will say of him. I'll prove him a liar! Aye, and a thief! He came her to steal and has a book of mine in his pocket.'

Like the proverbial 'last straw' the simple charge of theft seemed to weigh down the balance against Roger in the minds of all three guardsmen. It needed only a final cry from Fouché to spur them forward.

'I take responsibility for this! Seize him! Seize him!'

Roger saw then that his last hope of stalling them off by argument or threats had gone. He was faced with the choice of surrender or action. Surrender would mean the certain loss of the diary—for it was a certainty that Fouché would have it off him and disappear with it—and the probable loss of his life. Action might still give him a chance in a thousand. As they closed in on him he seized the table by its edge and overturned it.

The two bottles rolled off and smashed upon the floor. The candles in them continued to flicker for a moment, casting weird shadows. The meat chopper that Lucette had used to smash away the beam also slid off. It fell upon her foot, and she gave an 'ouch' of pain. Roger had been standing with his back to the fire. The sea-coal gave out no flame, only a dull glow; so but for the reddish patch it made and the final guttering of the candles the lofty room was now in darkness.

Roger was sorely tempted to make a dash for the door and the street; but on that side his way was barred by Fouché, Peltier and two of the guardsmen. He knew that he would never be able to force a passage through the four of them. On his other side there were only the thick-set swarthy soldier and Lucette. As the table went over he launched himself at the two of them. The flat of his right hand landed full upon the man's chest, thrusting him violently back. But his left hand missed Lucette, as she had stopped to snatch up the meat chopper during the last flicker of candle.

As the light died Roger was already past them and racing towards the steep flight of stairs. Behind him shouts and curses came from the angry, excited group. Suddenly a cloak of blackness descended, hiding them all from one another, and the stairs from him. But he had judged his distance and direction well; his outstretched hand closed upon the rickety banister rail. Swinging himself round its newel-post, he took the stairs three at a time, until he reached the small square landing. Frantically he fumbled for the handle to the door up there, but for thirty seconds he could not find it. Those seconds nearly cost him his life.

From the pounding of his footsteps, all his enemies knew which way he had gone. In a yelling pack, bumping against each other in the darkness as they ran, they headed for the stairs. Lucette, being better acquainted with the geography of the place than the others, reached them first. Chopper in hand she sprang up them almost on Roger's heels. He heard the patter of her feet while he was striving to find the handle of the door, but knowing that if he could not get the door open he would be done, he took the risk of continuing to fumble for it. At last his hand closed upon it and, with a swift turn of the wrist, he flung the door wide; she reached the landing at that moment, coming full tilt upon him.

The door gave on to a low-ceilinged room with two square, uncurtained windows. During the past twenty minutes the moon had risen. Its pale light made the two windows silver squares, and enough cold luminance radiated from them to transform the darkness of the landing into a pale greyness. Roger and Lucette could still not make out one another's features, but the silhouette of each was plain to the other. He saw that she had the chopper already raised to cleave his skull. Ducking his head aside as the blow descended, he thrust both his hands out against her body. In the confined space of the little landing they were so close together that the push he gave her had the force of a blow. As a result of it she staggered back. Next second there came the creak of rending wood. The flimsy banister rail gave behind her. With a high-pitched scream she fell backwards, to land with a thump on the floor below.

Having saved himself from her gave Roger only a moment's respite. The swarthy soldier had been next after her up the stairs. As she went through the banisters he was only two steps below the level of the landing; but he was a short man, so the top of his head was as yet no higher than Roger's chest. He made an upward thrust with a pike he was carrying. Roger was just in time to avoid it. Bringing up his right foot he kicked his new attacker under the chin. The man's head snapped back, his eyes started from their sockets. Without a sound he collapsed, and rolled down the stairs, carrying with him the men who were behind.

Groans, curses, shouts again filled the air; but Roger had won for himself a short breathing space. Slipping through the door, he swung it to behind him. To his relief, he found that it had a good strong bolt; but the wood of which the door was made was poor stuff, and he judged that it could not be expected to resist a heavy battering for long. Having shot the bolt he gave one glance round the room and saw that it was empty.

There was not a stick of furniture in it. But that did not concern him. He knew that an arm of the Seine lay at the back of the building. From the window to the river might mean a thirty foot drop, but he had taken many a worse risk than that in his life, and he was a strong swimmer. Full of new hope that he had as good as saved himself, he ran across the bare boards to one of the windows. Through it could be seen hundreds of twinkling lights in the buildings on the Isle of St. Louis, but as he reached it his pounding heart stopped dead for a second. He could have wept with disappointment. It was barred.

He had barely made this shattering discovery when the sound of heavy blows came from the door. Panting for breath, he ran to the other window. That was barred too. Evidently the room had at one time been used as a prison, or, more probably a nursery. Pulling up the sash of the window at which he stood, he peered out. Immediately below the water gurgled faintly against the foundations of the building, and the moonlight glinted on the ripples. It was a straight drop if only he could get through the window. The bars were quite thin but strong, as he found on grasping one of them. Exerting all his strength, he endeavoured to wrench it from its sockets. It bent, but all his efforts failed to loosen its ends where they were fixed into the frame of the window. He tried the one above it. That, too, bent, but its ends were equally firmly fixed. Straining on each of them in turn, he tried to bend the centre of the upper one up and the centre of the lower one down until the oval space between them should be wide enough for him to squeeze his head and body through it. But he soon realised that the bars were set too close together for that to be possible.

Meanwhile, blow after blow resounded on the door. The bolt and hinges held, but the upper panels began to splinter. One of the men out there had found the chopper Lucette had dropped and was hacking at them with it; another was battering at them with a musket butt. Desperately Roger's eyes roved round the moonlit room seeking for something he could use to prise the end of one of the bars from its socket. Floor, walls, and rafter were bare, but at one side of the room there was a narrow chimney piece and small grate. Running to it he strove to wrench the grate out in the hope that he might smash the bars loose with it. Again he met with disappointment; it was built into the fire-place.

The upper part of the door was now smashed in. Beyond it, a suggestion of yellow light showed that when removing the man whom Roger had kicked under the chin, his comrades had found and relit the candles down in the studio. As

Roger stared apprehensively at the great jagged hole in the door the muzzle of a musket was thrust through it, and Peltier's hoarse voice ordered him to stand back. He retreated to the partly-open window. Alongside the musket appeared an arm, then the head of the ginger-haired soldier. Leaning through the opening he found the bolt and drew it back. The wrecked door, now loose on its hinges, was forced open. Peltier and his two remaining men came clumping into the room, followed by Fouché.

'Nah we got 'im!' the Corporal, still wheezing from his exertions against the door, gasped exultantly. 'An' I'm fer makin' short work of 'im. 'E's near killed one of our chaps; an' we didn't stand fer that from aristos in the good days.'

Real fear suddenly gripped Roger's heart. Peltier's harsh voice held a ring that recalled to him some of the worst scenes that he had been compelled to witness during the Terror. Its fierce, breathless note was that of the born *sans-culotte* wrought up to fever pitch by a man hunt, and lusting for blood.

'What d'yer say, Citizen?' Peltier looked eagerly across at Fouché. 'Shall I put a bullet in 'im?'

Roger's glance, too, switched to Fouché. In the lean corpse-like face, now more pallid than ever in the moonlight, there was no trace of mercy; only apparent indifference. He meant to take no responsibility for the deed, but would be glad to see it done. To the Corporal's question he returned only a faint smile and a just perceptible shrug of the shoulders.

That was enough for Peltier. With deliberate care he cocked his musket.

'Stop him!' shouted Roger. 'Stop him.' But Fouché made no move to do so, and the two guardsmen stood looking on as though hypnotised.

Roger had dropped the broken haft of his sword-cane a second before he had grasped and overturned the table, but it suddenly flashed into his mind that he still had Lucette's stiletto stuck in the top of his jack-boot. Stooping, as Peltier raised his musket to take aim, he whipped the long thin dagger out. He was no practised knife thrower, but he hurled it with all his force at the Corporal's head.

In its swift flight the weight of the stiletto's hilt caused it to turn over one and a half times. Too late Peltier attempted to duck it. He was handicapped by having his musket held up against his bristly chin. And luck aided Roger's aim. The blunt-pointed hilt of the dagger struck him full in the left eye, smashing it to a pulp.

With a screech of agony he dropped his musket. It went off with a shattering bang. Its bullet thudded harmlessly into the peeling plaster of the wall. Through the acrid smoke of the discharge, Roger saw the Corporal clap his hands to his bleeding face and stagger back. Next moment he lurched and sank, a whimpering, gibbering bundle against the smashed door.

Fouché's face fell, showing his disappointment that the blood lust of the *ex-sans-culotte* had not, once and for all, made an end of Roger for him. But he still had complete control of the situation. Turning swiftly to the nearer of the two guardsmen, he asked:

'Is your musket loaded and primed?'

'Yes, Citizen,' came the quick reply. 'I saw to it after we had carried our injured comrade out to the coach.'

'Then give it to me.' Fouché took the weapon as he spoke, and added: 'Now pick up the Corporal's musket. Both of you; get him downstairs and out to the coach with the other man. You are then to return and guard the front door. Should the Englishman get past me and endeavour to escape, you are to shoot him on sight.'

With a muttered acknowledgment of the order, the nearest man picked up the musket; then together they took the moaning Corporal by the arms, pulled him to his feet, and half-led, half-dragged him to the stairs. As they struggled down with him, Fouché, now holding the musket at the ready, said to Roger in a voice that was all the more menacing from its complete lack of emotion:

'I would have preferred to have seen you shot, rather than shoot you. It seems though that I am left with no option but to put a bullet into you myself.'

Seized anew with fear of the fate he thought he had just escaped, Roger cried: 'You'll have to answer for it if you do.'

'Oh no! You are quite wrong about that.' A mocking smile twitched at Fouché's pale lips. 'Had I killed you in my house I might have had some explaining to do; but that does not apply here. There has been a mêlée. Two of the Directory's Guard have been seriously injured. One musket has been fired already, another might easily go off in a moment of excitement. You are an English spy. After being arrested, you attempted to escape. What could be more simple. And think of the trouble it will save me.'

A cold sweat had broken out on Roger's forehead. His hands were clenched so that the nails bit into his palms. Fouché's voice came again. Raising the musket to breast level he asked with cynical politeness:

'Would you prefer that I should shoot you through the head, or through the heart?'

He was standing against the opposite wall, ten paces away from Roger. Any attempt to rush him would have been hopeless. But Roger's wits were working overtime, and he still had a dice in the box that gave him a sporting chance. Pulling Josephine's diary from his pocket, and clutching it tightly, he thrust his arm out of the open window behind him. Then he said:

'Shoot me if you will, but I can't believe that you are quite such a fool. As I drop to the floor the diary will drop into the river and be lost forever. Downstairs, a few minutes back, you were cursing Madame Rémy for having surrendered it to me. You said that had she kept it hidden it might yet have meant big money for you both; and I know what you were thinking. It was that being a mulatto she would survive transportation: and that with her and yourself both put out of the way on the order of Barras, Madame de Beauharnais would believe herself safe to marry her General. And you were right. Barras is anxious for the match to take place; so he will not undeceive her. Neither will I. That must be obvious to you from the fact that I have been working to bring the marriage about. If, then, you still have the diary, you have only to be patient. The marriage will take place. Later you can inform General Buonaparte of the diary's contents and threaten him with its publication. To prevent that he will pay you practically anything you like to ask.'

Roger felt sure that Fouché's mind must have been working more or less on those lines. But would he take the gamble? The diary was worth nothing to him unless Josephine would marry Buonaparte without first getting it back so that she could destroy it. Would he bank on her accepting Barras's assurance that she had nothing more to fear? It was at least a tempting bet, although Roger felt certain that she would not. So, should the gamble be taken, he too would have to gamble on, somehow or other, getting the diary back. If he failed in that it meant the complete wreck of his plans. But making the offer was his only chance of saving his life; and as he watched Fouché's face he knew that his life hung by a hair.

Greed was one of the most potent characteristics of Fouché's mentality—and greed won. His eyes shifted uncertainly for a moment, then he asked:

'On what terms will you give me the diary?'

Roger breathed again. 'My life and freedom.'

'Your life, yes; but your freedom, no. If you are clever enough to wriggle out of the charges that the Citoyenne Rémy and I can bring against you, well and good. That chance I will give you in exchange for a chance that I may yet make something out of the diary, but no more.'

'For that then, you offer me only what may amount to a brief respite. That is not good enough.'

'I'll go no further. Give me the book and we'll take you to the police office. Refuse and I'll kill you where you stand.'

Roger decided that Fouché meant what he said. It was a bitter pill to have to give up the diary, for so much hung upon it. But there was no other way in which he could buy his life. 'Very well,' he nodded. 'Unload your musket and throw the cartridge on the floor.'

As Fouché hesitated, he added: 'Come; I'm not such a fool as to risk your shooting me after you have obtained the book. You will still have the weapon to use as a club. I am unarmed and even if I attacked you your shouts would soon bring the two soldiers up from the front door to your help.'

'If I unload will you come quietly to the police office?'

'What faith would you put in my word if I gave it to you? That is a risk you must take. As I have just said, you have two armed men whom you can call on to escort me.'

Without further argument Fouché unloaded the musket, and threw down the cartridge. Roger drew his arm in from the open window, walked over to him and handed him the precious diary. Instead of moving towards the door, Roger said: 'You will be good enough to go first, I have no mind to be struck down with the butt end of your musket as I descend the stairs.'

With a pale smile, Fouché replied: 'In that I will oblige you. But being of an equally suspicious disposition I have no mind to have you leap on me from behind; so you will be good enough to remain up on the landing until I have the bottom step.'

Roger gave a quick nod, and halted in the doorway while Fouché walked on down the narrow staircase. At its bottom he took two paces forward, then stopped, looking down at something that was hidden from Roger's view. Roger followed, and as he rounded the corner of the newel-post his glance fell on the thing at which Fouché was staring. It was the body of Lucette.

She lay there where she had fallen, her neck grotesquely twisted, and obviously dead. There came into Roger's mind the prophecy of which she had told him some fourteen months before. That she could not be killed by bullet, by steel or by rope, but only by a fall from a high place.

After they had stared at her body for a few moments they raised their eyes. For once Fouché's shifty glance met Roger's. Both knew that the other had realised the implications of her death. Fouché had lost his all-important witness, and Roger could swear now without fear of further contradiction from her that when she had denounced him in front of the soldiers, she had mistaken him for the mythical Robert MacElfic.

For as long as it takes to draw a deep breath, Roger was seized with wild elation. It seemed that this sudden turn of Fortune's Wheel had placed him out of danger. Then, like a douche of ice cold water, the facts of the case arranged themselves in his mind in their true perspective. Fate had robbed Fouché of his Ace of Trumps; but he still held the next best cards in the pack—the diary and two armed men who, so far, had accepted his orders.

Within an instant of grasping that, Roger saw the new sequence. Lucette, by losing her life, had brought his again into immediate peril. Now, his one chance of saving himself and the situation lay in a swift attempt to exploit the set-back that his enemy had suffered. With a great effort he forced his voice to assume the ring of triumph, and cried:

'The game is mine, Fouché! Give me back that diary.'

'No!' Fouché exclaimed. 'I'll see you in hell first!'

'If you refuse I'll call in those two men to take it.'

Surprise robbed Fouché of the power of speech for a second, then he burst out: 'It is I who will call them in! I mean to have them shoot you while I have the chance.'

That was exactly the development Roger had feared. Knowing that his sole protection from the threat lay in giving the impression that he was now master of the situation, he even managed a laugh before he said:

'Do not deceive yourself. They might have shot me in cold blood while Corporal Peltier was still with them to give them a lead; but they will not risk their necks by committing murder at your order now. They'll go no further than to escort me to the police office; and, if you wish, I will go quietly with them. You know why, do you not?'

Fouché's eyes flickered from side to side. 'You think that now Madame Rémy is dead, you have nothing to fear from me. But you are mistaken.'

'I meant only that there is nothing with which the two soldiers can charge me except having injured two of their comrades who refused to obey my lawful orders. If you wish any other charge to be made you must come with us and make it yourself.'

'And I will!' Fouché snarled. 'Even without support for my word, my denunciation of you as an English spy is certain to result in a full inquiry. Many things may emerge from it. Little things that you have forgotten. I am convinced that, with a little luck, I could yet see you convicted.'

Roger's muscles tensed spasmodically. He was only too well aware of the dangers inherent in a full investigation of his past. But in the candlelight his face was still a smiling mask, and he shrugged his shoulders.

'We have argued this before. If it comes to your word against mine there can be little doubt that mine will be accepted. Besides, has it not occurred to you that if you once enter the police office with me, you will leave it under arrest and on your way to prison?'

'Your threat is an empty one. There is no crime of which you can accuse me. The night is young. I am aware that I shall be subject to arrest should I not leave the city tomorrow; but there are many hours to go yet. Ample to first settle your business.'

The edge of a folded paper protruded from Fouché's pocket. To it a few fragments of wax from a broken seal still clung. As Roger's eye lit on it he felt sure it was the order of banishment. With a sardonic laugh he pointed at it and cried:

'Can it be, then, that you have already forgotten the terms of the order I served on you less than an hour ago?'

'They can have no bearing on what I choose to do tonight,' Fouché declared harshly. 'They do not come into operation until tomorrow morning.'

'There is one that does.' Roger's voice was mocking now. 'It is to the effect that should you communicate with certain persons, including Madame Rémy, the order would be changed from banishment to transportation. You have contravened that clause. The men outside and myself are witnesses to your having done so. You have made yourself liable to be sent to Cayenne.'

Suddenly Fouché wilted. His eyes fell and he thrust out his hands as though to ward off some horror. Roger knew then that he had him at his mercy and rapped out an ultimatum.

'I am agreeable to hold my tongue. But only at a price. Unless you wish to give me the pleasure of seeing you shackled to some other felon in the hold of a convict ship outward bound, you will hand me that diary and be out of Paris before dawn.'

Epilogue

'And then, Roger?'

Georgina's lovely face was flushed with excitement. It was late at night, and she was wearing a loose chamber robe of red velvet that set off her rich dark beauty to perfection. Her feet were curled under her as she lay snuggled against Roger on the big sofa in her boudoir. Shaded candles and a bright wood fire lit the room with a soft, rosy glow. Nearby on a small table a champagne bottle stood in an ice bucket. Beside it there were the remains of supper, and still half a dish of early strawberries from the hothouses tended by some of the forty gardeners that she kept at Stillwaters. It was mid-April and Roger had returned from France only the day before. For the past two hours he had been telling her about the new Paris that had emerged from the Terror, and of his last mission.

'There is little more to tell,' he replied with a smile. 'Once Fouché had accepted my contention that the two soldiers would not obey an order from him to shoot me in cold blood, I had him at my mercy. He gave me the diary, then we went out and he told the soldiers in front of me that it had all been a terrible mistake; that he had been misled by Lucette, and was now fully satisfied that I was not an English spy after all.

'I took the diary to Josephine that night, the 5th of March; then told Barras that I had freed her from her blackmailer for good. Next day Buonaparte's commission as Commander-in-Chief of the Army of Italy was signed by the Directors. On the 9th, he and Josephine were quietly married. After a honeymoon of only two days he left for

Nice to take up his command, and with him, as one of his A.D.C's, he took young Eugène de Beauharnais.'

'Then you saved us from invasion.'

'I would not say that. Many things might have conspired to decide the Directors against risking the attempt, and even if fear of Buonaparte had forced them to let him try his luck, he might well have been defeated by the Channel and the Fleet before he landed. It can be said, though, that I nipped the project in the bud. And to be forewarned is to be forearmed. This morning, after I had made my report to Mr. Pitt, he said that he should at once make enquiries into what further safeguards could be taken; such as raising additional regiments of militia and, perhaps, having strong watchtowers which would also serve as forts built every few miles along the south coast.'

'Surely such measures are not necessary, now that the threat is past.'

'These things take time; and that, I think, is what I have bought. Though I am far from certain that I have not paid too big a price for it, by aiding Buonaparte to be given his command in Italy. There are many rich cities in the north of the peninsula, and I know that he regards it as the treasure chest of Europe. The Revolutionary Government has no scruples about property rights, or the beggaring of the territories it conquers by the imposition of taxes, fines, requisitions and indemnities. Should Buonaparte's campaign be successful, as it seems likely to be from the reports that are already coming in, he will be in a position to send enormous sums back to Paris, and by refilling France's empty exchequer enable her to prolong the war. If that proves the case, we may yet have to face an invasion here on Buonaparte's return from Italy.'

'I think you too pessimistic, Roger dear. But were you right, thanks to you, we will at least be better prepared to resist it. And of one thing I am certain. In this delimma you did the best that could at the moment be done for your own country.'

'I only hope it will prove so in the long run too,' he said, taking his arm from about her to stand up and refill their glasses with champagne. 'We'll drink to that, anyway.'

When they had settled down again, she said: 'And what of Fouché. Do you know what happened to him?'

'I have no idea. He had to leave Paris of course; but he took with him enough money to buy himself a cottage and a smallholding; so he is probably cleaning out pigsties still, but somewhere in the country.'

'I thought you said he was near destitute.'

'Well, er . . .' Roger hesitated. 'As a matter of fact, he was. But I gave him the hundred *louis* that I had brought with me in case I had to finance the so-called Madame Rémy to get her out of the way.'

'You *gave* him a hundred *louis*!' exclaimed Georgina, starting up. 'Roger, you must be out of your mind!'

He laughed, and pulled her back into the embrace of his arm. 'Perhaps I am. On the continent they regard all us English as mad; yet I think there is something to be said for our way of doing things. I've never yet given an enemy quarter as long as he had had the power to harm me; but the poor devil was down and out.'

'Perhaps. Yet you have just said of him yourself that you think him the most despicable, treacherous villain you have ever come upon. What can have possessed you to give money to such a man?'

'Well, for one thing, I would never have got the name and address of Josephine's blackmailer had he not trusted me with them on the understanding that he was to receive some reward; and, on consideration, I felt that Barras had played him a scurvy trick. For another, there is just one human spark in his otherwise distorted mind. He loves that ugly wife of his and their child with a genuine devotion. One can tell it from the way he speaks of them, and worries for her about the hard life she has had to lead during this past year. Then, and then only, there comes into his voice a note of sincerity which is unmistakable. It may be foolish of me, but I would not have them starve.'

'Oh Roger, my sweet!' There were tears in Georgina's eyes as she turned and kissed him on the cheek. 'What a dear sentimentalist you are.'

'Nay,' he laughed. 'Put it down rather to hard business sense. For all his villainies Fouché has a magnificent brain.

He'll not spend all his life tending pigs. Sooner or later he'll find a way to reclimb fortune's ladder, and maybe he and I will meet again.' Roger spoke half in jest but, even so, he was far from underestimating his enemy's capabilities; for, nineteen years later when, after Waterloo, the Emperor Napoleon left Paris for the last time, it was in obedience to an order signed by Joseph Fouché.

'Tell me,' Georgina asked after a moment, 'why did you linger in France for near six weeks after having completed this great coup?'

'I judged it sound policy further to strengthen my position there before returning home. You will recall that to account for my last departure from Paris I told people that I was going to the South of France for my health, and, on my return, that I had bought a property near Fréjus. The day Buonaparte left Paris I went south too, and now I have actually done so. Since the Revolution, good houses at any distance from large towns can be bought for a song; and this is a pleasant place, half farm, half chateau, with a fine view over a bay in which there is a hamlet called St. Raphael. Few places could be more delightful in the winter months, and it is my fond hope that when peace does come again you will be my first guest there.'

'What an enchanting prospect. How I wish we could go there now. But from what you say there seems little hope of peace for some while yet.'

'I fear not; much as both France and Britain need it and Mr. Pitt desires it. However, in the meantime I shall go down to my new property occasionally, and so have even better cover for disappearing from Paris for a while when it is necessary for me to come to England.'

'You mean then to continue your secret work for Mr. Pitt?'

He smiled. 'Yes. The first time I tried settling down, after I married Amanda, fond as I was of her, before two years were up I found such a life too dull. The second time, when we all sailed to the Indies, I found it far too strenuous. Paris has become a sink of iniquity, but at least people there now wash themselves again; and if I were caught out, I hardly think Barras would have me dangled over a pool full of hungry crocodiles. The risk I run is a fair one, and it adds a spice to life; so I've no mind to play again at becoming a respectable householder.'

Georgina sighed. 'Poor Clarissa! Despite her lack of fortune, I thought there might be some hope for her.'

Suppressing a start, Roger asked in as casual a voice as he could manage: 'Whatever put that idea into your head?'

'You dear fool!' Georgina laughed. 'Have you no eyes in yours? Why, the girl dotes on you. Anyone could see that. What a pity it is that she has no fortune; for she is the most lovely creature and would make a most excellent wife for you.'

'Yes. She is lovely enough, and has spirit too. As for money, I am, thank God, now worth near thirty thousand pounds; so I have no need to worry on that score. But, as I've told you, I have no intention of marrying again.'

'You must, Roger. You have your little girl to think of. In fairness to her you must find her a mother.'

'Oh come! What of yourself, then? According to that argument, it is equally your duty to find that jolly fat lump of a godson of mine a father.'

'I suppose I must, some day. But not yet. In his case there is ample time. It is while young that children need a woman's love and care. Your little Susan shall have mine you know, and may share Charles's nursery for as long as you wish. But it would be better for her to be brought up in a home of her own, in which her father would be more than an always welcome visitor. Please, Roger, if lack of money is no objection, think about Clarissa.'

For a moment he was silent, then he laughed. 'Do you remember what happened last time we discussed matchmaking?'

Georgina laughed too. 'Yes. We made a pact that you should marry Amanda and I should marry my Earl. Then we slept together.'

He made a comical grimace. 'I fear that if that were generally known most people would consider us very bad lots.'

'Yet we are not, Roger; for we are bound to one another by something stronger than any marriage tie. Together, too, we have the blessed power to enjoy a thing that is very rare. With our love there has always been laughter, because we are not tied by any thought of what must come after. We are like two butterflies meeting on a summer day, rejoicing in the fine form and colouring that the kind gods have given us, and playing together without a care.'

'You are right, my sweet,' he said softly. 'And our meetings so have been all too seldom since the winter of '88. I think that the months I spent with you then were the happiest in all my life. It was tragic that our happiness should have been cut short by that terrible business following Hemphrey's unexpected arrival here.'

'That was not the cause of our parting. We had already had our only quarrel; though I had begged you to stay on at Stillwaters and love me through the spring.'

'True, but we made out quarrel up; and I should have stayed on had not fate intervened.'

For a little they went silent, then she asked: 'Have you to return to Paris soon?'

He shook his head. 'No; until the political situation shows some sign of change, there is naught of use that I can do there.'

Georgina turned her face up to his. Her red lips were moist and her eyes shining. 'We are together once more at Stillwaters, Roger,' she whispered. 'And it is only April.'

His blue eyes smiled down into her black ones, and he whispered back: 'How blessed we are that the gods should give us again the chance of which they once robbed us. I can think of nothing nearer heaven than to stay on here and love you through the spring.'